THE MYSTIC IN THE MEWS

THE MYSTIC IN THE MEWS

A METAPHYSICAL ADVENTURE STORY

Allan Ishac LLC • New York

First Edition published in
the United States of America in 2024
By Allan Ishac LLC
24 Fifth Avenue
New York, NY 10011

Book Design: Diana LaGuardia

Cover Illustration: Gavin Wilson
(www.gavinwilson.art)

Author Photo: Sophie Peters-Wilson
(www.sophiepeterswilson.com)

First Edition
ISBN: 979-8-9903897-0-0

Praise for the First Spiritual Adventure Novel Inspired by *A Course In Miracles*

"A captivating adventure story filled with pearls of wisdom. Join the compelling characters in The Mystic in the Mews as they experience the delights of self-discovery, the release from limitations, and the safety of following ever-present, loving guidance."
— **Carol Howe, best-selling author of *Never Forget To Laugh* and internationally recognized teacher of *A Course In Miracles***

"Allan knows how to pull the reader right in, and you will want to stay for a visit. The message and style are intriguing and thought-provoking. If you read his work aloud, your tongue would trip along in a pleasant tone. You 'want' to read the next word and the next and go along with him on this metaphysical and mystical journey of adventure and awakening."
— **Jon Mundy, Ph.D., author of *Missouri Mystic* and publisher of *Miracles Magazine***

"Allan has not only pioneered the genre of spiritual adventure novel, he has accomplished the writing of a book that enlightens the reader. Reading this book is not just an adventure, it's a spiritual experience. It opens the reader up to a new paradigm of possibilities and keeps you engaged and entertained the whole way through. I highly recommend it."
— **Sudie Shipman, Inspirational spiritual speaker and teacher**

See more at TheMysticInTheMews.com

*To all those who have passed through
the outer rings of fear
to arrive at the heart of things.*

*And to every aspiring mystic who knows
that there has to be another way,
and has devoted his or her life to finding it.*

CHAPTER ONE

The first time I saw him, he was more mirage than man.

It was a Friday in late May. I was checking the bank app on my phone to see if my paycheck had posted and, while I can't remember exactly what my thoughts were the moment he appeared, I know at the time that I was feeling down and discouraged.

My life was going well enough by the usual standards. I had a solid job at a global software firm in Manhattan translating online communications. I recently signed a lease on my own apartment in the West Village after a mass exodus from the city brought rent prices down. It was a shoebox-sized place but located in a historic neighborhood with a classic city vibe. I had a growing social network, too, remaining close with a few of my high school friends and making some new connections at work.

By all accounts, I was doing everything right—good job, nice apartment, decent social life—but I still wasn't happy and I was growing weary of my daily routine. The French have a great expression for it—*métro, boulot, dodo*—commute, work, sleep, repeat. I was running on autopilot, and I couldn't shake the feeling that there was something missing, some vital piece of the existential puzzle that I lacked.

I hit such a low point, I climbed into bed at night and appealed out loud to unseen forces—the old gods, lesser demons, genial ghosts of relatives past, to anyone or anything I thought might be listening. I would have happily sold my soul to any fork-tailed fiend who could release me from the sense of approaching doom that seemed to follow me everywhere. But even with all that going on, I can't say that I asked to see him.

When he materialized, it was sudden and without warning. I was walking along Hudson Street a few blocks from my apartment, passing by the usual storefronts—the drycleaners, the bagel shop, the liquor store, the lingerie boutique—when right there in the middle of them there was a sudden breach in my visual field, like a seam split open in my retina. I saw a peripheral movement, or a series of movements, that were out of phase with the usual street scene.

I had experienced brief flashes of light at the corners of my eyes before, along with geometric prisming at the edge of my sight lines—a kaleidoscopic visual effect that usually forewarned a migraine. The headaches would often punctuate the end of a work week with their textbook symptoms of temple pounding pain and vexing nausea. So, immediately after it happened, I wrote it off as a vertical mirage from this prisming effect or perhaps a play of bright light on a sunny after-noon.

Still, I remember this incident as particularly odd because I was sure I saw a lone figure standing in the crease, a face peering out from between the curtains. A man's face. Serene and wise, with a playful ex-pression. As I turned towards it and tried to adjust my focus, the image disappeared, the concrete curtain closed, and that was it. Liquor store and lingerie boutique restored as if nothing had happened.

I probably would have forgotten about it—like a déjà vu that you excitedly tell a friend about, then let slip away, never to be mentioned again—if almost the exact same thing hadn't happened less than a week later.

CHAPTER TWO

The second time I saw him, I *did* get scared. Because this time, when the crease parted and I glimpsed the motion and the man, he didn't disappear when I refocused my gaze. And while he didn't seem to be threatening, his abrupt appearance was startling and dissonant.

I was moving at a leisurely pace along the south sidewalk of Washington Mews, a quiet cobblestone alleyway that jutted off of Fifth Avenue, a half block from 8th Street and within view of the Washington Square arch. I liked to walk this peaceful stretch whenever I needed to silence the city and slow my mind, which lately I was doing a few times a week. As I mentioned, restlessness had become a frequent companion and late night walks offset my nagging tension.

I was passing some purple wisteria making its spring debut, along with a profusion of early blooming pink roses creeping up the walls of a two-story, 19th century carriage house, when 50-feet in front of me on the opposite side of the mews, a startled calico cat darted from the shadows of a recessed doorway. It jumped the expanse of cobblestones in two leaps, and quickly disappeared under the brick archway at the east end of the alley. I followed the cat's path for a moment, but my eyes were drawn back to movement in a doorway. At first, I thought someone was opening the double wide doors at number 49 as a shaft of yellow light radiated from the recess. Then, squinting in the dark, I realized that the door was closed and the windows of the apartment were black. The light was emanating from outside the apartment, not in.

I stopped walking and stared hard. The seam, which ran from the door sill to a few feet above the lintel, parted a foot wider. And there was the man again, smiling benignly and gesturing to me with his right hand to come closer. It wasn't a frantic movement or urgent in any way; it was a gentle and deliberate summons, clearly intended not to frighten me. But as I said, I did get scared, and my first impulse was to turn and run. Instead my body started moving towards him before I could think what I was doing. Then I realized I wasn't doing anything at all. I was superconducting, or floating, or hydroplaning, or whatever you call it, but I wasn't walking. And while the disorienting levitation should have caused me even more alarm, I was reassured by the man's placid gaze.

As I got closer, I saw that he was wearing a kind of purplish-brown toga, loosely wrapped around his body and cinched with a braided, rope belt the color of autumn beach grass. He had on strange sandals that appeared to be dipped in bronze. His hair and beard were gray, disheveled, and a bit wild-looking. He was maybe in his late 60's or early 70's, but he was thin and compact and moved with relaxed precision; efficient gestures radiating composure and confidence.

When we were no farther than 25-feet apart, the crease opened wider and the dazzling light surrounding the man pulled at my chest with its own magnetic field. It seemed to apply pressure from behind, in the middle of my back, like a hand urging me forward. But I knew that this wasn't possible. I knew that light didn't bend or curl, and it didn't exert pressure. It wasn't the man's hands doing it anyway, because I could see both of them hanging loosely at his sides.

I was only a few feet from him when my body abruptly went still and hovered six inches above the sidewalk. His face came into greater relief, and I saw his large almond-shaped eyes clearly—a sharp golden color with small green flecks around the edges. Not fully human. A lion's eyes.

They were attentive and animated, with a penetrating intensity that made me want to look away—but I couldn't. I tried to move my head, but it was fixed in position. The force field emanating from the man seemed to hold my head and body steady. That's when he spoke or, more accurately, that's when I heard what he was saying. His lips never moved and I didn't recognize the language he was speaking, but

I understood every word. The meaning was clear, the language was foreign.

"Hello, Metis. Good to see you again."

My name is not Metis, it's Roger Steiner, and I surely had never seen this toga-clad, fire-eyed apparition before.

"Judging by your growing restlessness, heightened anxiety, and frequent late night walks, I trust that you are now ready to get on with our mission?" Again, he spoke this into my head, an easy smile on his face. I gave my body a shake hoping to release myself from his gravity-defying grip, but that just sent my hips into a hoola-hoop wobble that lasted a second or two. Then I tried to open my lips and say something, but my jaw wouldn't budge. He mind-messaged me again: "Don't try to speak, Metis, just ask your question."

So, I did, soundlessly, maybe a bit anxiously: "Who are you? What do you want?"

"My name isn't important at the moment, but what I'm going to remind you of will change the current direction of your life immediately and unalterably." Those words got my attention and I attempted to whip my hips sideways more forcefully, again to no avail. He ignored these gyrations and continued his telepathy.

"Your Worldborn brain has temporarily forgotten me, along with the purpose of you being here. This critical gap in your memory has left you with a growing sense of agitation and emptiness. You know the feelings I speak of?"

I hesitated. How did he know these things about me? I hid my discontent from almost everyone. I tried to open my mouth again, then remembered his instructions and thought my response at him instead.

"I guess you could say I've been a little blue."

"A little blue?" he repeated. "Navy blue perhaps?"

"What I'm saying is that at the moment everything in my life seems a bit meaningless."

"Now you've hit on something, Metis, a perfectly accurate assessment. Of course this dream world is meaningless. Completely and utterly. But be careful. Hit people with that 'nothing to see here' notion too soon, they won't stand for another word. Better to gradually ease into it."

He shared all this in a lighthearted way, but his silent voice was more forceful than I might have imagined with wordless communication, especially from someone with his serene demeanor. It was oddly resonant, too, vibrating slightly in my chest.

He shifted his weight towards me a few inches and went on. "The meaningless you refer to is actually a state of profound 'missingness,' Metis, and I can assure you that it is unconsciously shared with every single Worldborn who has ever stumbled through this demented maze of made-up misfortunes—everyone, no exceptions. And it was felt even more palpably and profoundly during the coronavirus contagion. That was no accident; the world was made ready. Which is why our mission is of such importance… and needed now."

Missingness? Mission? I said nothing for a moment, just stared back at him.

"Why are you talking to me? Why'd you pick *me*?"

I saw an almost imperceptible flicker in his eyes. "We picked one another, actually—kindred spirits on the same quest. It happened a long time ago, although time is irrelevant. I am delighted to report that circumstances have now conspired in such a way that we can resume our undertaking with a high probability of success."

I responded with lips sealed: "I think you have the wrong person. My name is Roger, we're in New York City, and I don't know anyone called Metis." I felt a heat building in my chest, and I thought I was going to start hyperventilating.

He smiled wider, his teeth shone, and his cat eyes beamed. "I know exactly who you *think* you are Roger Steiner. Now go home and prepare yourself. We have much to do."

"What do you mean, 'much to do'?" I shouted from inside my head, but it was an innocuous response coming from a powerless rag doll dangling in midair.

"This world is in need of a saving idea, Metis. The time has come to lead humanity beyond this insanity, to help all Worldborns snap out of it. And forces are now aligning to do just that."

Then, poof, with those last perplexing words, the shaft of light zipped shut, my soles hit cement, and the man was gone. At the same moment, a young couple with backpacks slung over their shoulders entered the mews at the point where the calico had dashed out.

How long ago was that? Two minutes? Ten?

I was standing in the shadows now, just staring at the dark door of number 49. I must have looked suspicious—a slinking burglar readying his lock picking tools—because the couple noticed me and hesitated. The young man whispered something to the woman and they turned abruptly, walking back out the east gate. I took a few tentative steps towards the opposite gate and, after one fleeting glance back, charged out of the mews. I made a hard right at the wrought iron exit and nearly ran the six blocks home, my heart thumping all the way.

CHAPTER THREE

In the days that followed, with no more communication from the lion-eyed man, I started to wonder if I had simply imagined the whole encounter. Or if my migraines were morphing into something more ominous, an exploding brain embolism, or something that could induce hallucinatory visions.

I was so unsure about the entire experience that I didn't share it with anyone, and after a few days passed, I wasn't fully trusting my recollection. Thoughts about the man in the mews made me feel increasingly disoriented and bewildered, but there was also an unmistakable feeling of anticipation and excitement. Mystical vision or elaborate hallucination, seeing him was one of the most astounding things that had ever happened to me. The encounter dominated my thoughts, with only occasional concerns about ruptured cerebral arteries.

I reviewed each second of the mews interaction trying to recall every unspoken yet audible word, recording my memory of the exchange on my iPad in a document I labeled "Mews Man." As a professional translator, with a lifelong interest in languages, I was particularly curious about our silent, but effortless communication. Brief as it was, I couldn't help but notice that our mind-to-mind transfer of information seemed not only to be more precise but also richer and more expansive than the spoken word. There was no possibility of deceit or pretense, and it carried an added dimension to it—as if not only our minds were connected, but our bodies themselves were communing.

And what did he mean by helping people "snap out of it?" Some sort of mass enlightenment, I guess. Naïve of him, but I liked the sound of it, his message infused with a kind of rapturous hope. I added this to the list of questions I planned to ask him. He told me that I would see him again and this time I intended to be ready. Wherever I walked, I paid close attention to my surroundings looking for rips in the fabric of the cityscape, an illuminated gash between buildings, streaks of other-wordly light that might signal his return.

The mews was only a ten-minute walk from my apartment, so I went back every night for a week and lingered in front of number 49. One evening the owner of the home, a wispy, cerebral-looking man with a head of thick, tousled hair, opened the front door just as I'd started my vigil.

"Excuse me, is there a reason why you've been loitering around my doorstep for the past week?"

I got nervous and stammered. "Oh, sorry, uh… it's just that I bumped into a girl here last week and didn't get her name. I thought maybe she lived at this address or passed through the mews around this time of night." I lied.

"No, no girl lives here. And if you continue to skulk near my home, I'm going to call the police. I hope I've made myself clear."

I tried to apologize again, but he quickly closed the door. It was no big deal. Like Buddha's fig tree, I was coming to understand that there was nothing special about this particular carriage house and it wasn't going to yield any more surprises. So, I stopped going back.

The anticipation of my next encounter with the Mews Man left me preoccupied and off balance for days. I became so distracted at work that most of what I did manage to get done was rushed, haphazard, or perfunctory. One afternoon I sent a tech manual translation to our Paris affiliate that was so sketchy, I received three separate calls for clarification from my French colleagues.

I decided, finally, that I must have missed the signs of an impending visit. Another week passed, almost two, before I was simply too spent to keep up the watchful waiting. I was beginning to resign myself to the idea that the Mews Man wasn't coming back, and maybe had never existed at all.

I came home from work on a Tuesday night so fatigued I skipped my usual 7:00 spin class, ate a simple meal of hard-boiled eggs, black olives, and cucumber and, shortly after, climbed into bed. I was reading an interesting article about a shamanic healer in Albuquerque who used toxic frog skin to cure certain types of cancer, but only got a few paragraphs into it before my eyelids closed and I fell asleep.

And there he was again.

CHAPTER FOUR

No bright aura framing him this time and no toga, but his riveting eyes still had that big cat golden hue. He was sitting at the base of an enormous lighthouse painted with thick black and white horizontal stripes. I looked skyward but its beacon was so far up in the clouds I couldn't make it out. I knew this was some other dimension because no lighthouse on earth could ever be built so high.

"Come up here, Metis. Take a seat." He said it without opening his mouth, the mind merge thing again.

The lighthouse was perched on a slight rise, and I had to scramble twenty feet to reach him, but despite the incline, the climb was effortless, as if I hadn't fired a muscle. He had his back leaning up against the tower's smooth, concrete sides, his legs splayed out casually and crossed at the ankles in front of him. He was dressed in a paisley-patterned green and yellow shirt with white denim jeans and had on blue, high-top athletic shoes unlike any brand I had seen before, but I remember thinking that I wanted a pair.

His beard looked different, shorter and neater than before, and this time I could see that his hair was wavy, more black than gray and cut in a tidy, contemporary style. He looked as untroubled as he did when I saw him in the mews. I took a seat next to him, positioned my back and legs as he did, and stared at him.

"Am I… dreaming you?" I asked tentatively, out loud.

This time he opened his mouth and spoke like normal people do, audibly, and in perfectly clear, unaccented English. "The place where you appear to live, Metis, is not where you belong."

I didn't see how that answered my question, so I tried again. "I was asking if you are appearing in my dream right now?"

"We are here to help people emerge from the bad dream, the collective nightmare, that haunts all Worldborns."

He clearly wasn't understanding my meaning, but before I could restate the question for a third time, he picked up his thread from two weeks earlier as if no time had passed at all.

"Let me tell you what else I know about you, Roger Steiner. I know that you believe you are thirty-two-years-old, that you work as a translator for a prestigious software company, that you would like to ask for a raise but are afraid if you do, you might be let go, which could result in you losing your pocket-sized apartment in a desirable section of Greenwich Village. Worst case, this could require a move back to your parents' home in Scotch Plains, New Jersey, with a return to your childhood bedroom and the faded, red striped sheets on your lumpy double bed. These preoccupations are deeply embedded in your current thought patterns, causing you a high degree of distress."

He was right about all of it, except for those red striped sheets. The sheets in my old bedroom, which my folks had never updated, were a midnight blue that reminded me of a night sky. Still, his summation was freakishly accurate.

"Actually, your mother replaced those dark blue sheets with your sister's candy-striped set after your visit over Easter weekend."

His eyes were shining in a twinkly new way as he said this. Had he just read my mind? Did he know my thoughts as quickly as I thought them?

"Yes, to your question about thoughts. And I also know, Metis, that lately you've been reading a lot of self-help books. You even canceled your beloved Netflix subscription in an effort to save money and read more. Although you're wondering if all the self-improvement texts and motivational podcasts are making any difference at all."

He stopped talking long enough for me to digest the level of detail in his review of my muddled life.

"Most of that is pretty accurate," I hesitated a moment, "so, is this a dream?"

He ignored my question again and carried on. "Your social life, too, has stalled of late, and you're discouraged that you haven't been in a serious relationship for more than a year. At the very least, you would like to have a sexual encounter, if not a fulfilling future with an established partner."

Ugh. Again, right about all of it, although I thought that last part was getting a little personal.

He shot back instantly. "There is nothing personal you need to hide from me, Metis, nor could you. You believe that your thoughts are local, hovering inside your head. They are not. All thoughts are shared. All minds are one. One Mind."

I didn't know what the hell he was talking about.

"What are you talking about?" I asked.

"Thoughts are merely waves of energy, Metis, vibrating at certain frequencies and fully accessible if one is able to align with those frequencies. Which I am able to do at will. In this way, I can discern what you are thinking now, in the future, and in your past. Not only in your current life as Roger Steiner, but all of your imaginary dream pasts from hundreds of serial life illusions."

Past lives? Is that what he was getting at? Because the idea of reincarnation, of life after death, were subjects I became interested in way back when I was sixteen. That was the year my Grandpa Joe died of lung cancer. GeeJay, as I always called him, owned a paper manufacturing company in Pennsylvania. He was generous, well-respected, and cared deeply about people—not just about his family, but his friends and employees, too. Because of his magnanimity and kindness, all seventy-five of his employees came to GeeJay's wake, along with close to five hundred grieving relatives and friends, as well as elected officials and municipal workers in the community.

I recognized a woman there named Rebecca who'd been my grandfather's secretary since she was out of college—more than 20 years before. I recalled that on one visit to his office, when I was about nine, she gave me a small copper replica of the Liberty Bell that I kept on the desk in my bedroom through high school. She also looked me directly in the eyes whenever she spoke and seemed to be genuinely interested in what I had to say—never gave me that token empty chatter that most adults consider to be communication with children. Rebecca left an impression on me.

She seemed relaxed and composed at the funeral and unrattled by my grandfather's death, despite their long association. I walked up to her, and we talked for a while standing near a draped window a few steps from GeeJay's open casket. She told me not to worry about Joe, that he was doing just fine, and he wasn't far away. When I asked her what she meant, she paused for a moment, looked towards my mother who was greeting people at the viewing room door, then lowered her voice and said that my grandfather visited her after his death.

"He appeared in my living room the night he passed over," she said. "Joe looked just like he did in life, maybe a little gauzier or something, but still vibrant and happy. He said he had come to reassure me that death was nothing and that I needn't fear it. He also told me that we mustn't believe what our eyes tell us, that all of what we're looking at," she gestured around the room, "is a cleverly disguised lie. One that we must work to uncover in order to find the truth."

I had been terribly afraid of death since I was a young boy and while her words did provide me with some comfort, I remained skeptical.

"Why did he come to you? Why not my grandmother, or my mother… or me?" I asked. I was close to my grandfather and felt a little annoyed that he had singled out Rebecca.

"I'm not sure, Roger, he didn't tell me that. But there is something about your grandfather you probably never knew," she said, lowering her voice even more. "He was very interested in things most people consider silly or frivolous—mysticism, psychic phenomena, past lives, things like that. I've been curious about these subjects all my life, too, and Joe and I would have long discussions about all sorts of apparent mysteries like these, right up to the time that he got sick."

"I actually like that sort of stuff," I said. "I wish he'd told me."

"Speaking about these subjects can be frightening for many people, unwelcome," she replied. "I didn't even mention these talks to my husband… too off-the-wall for Ken. But we lived for these conversations, your grandfather and I, the stranger and more 'out there,' the better."

She smiled at that point, clearly remembering her covert conversations with GeeJay and happy for it. "Even though he was quite a bit older than I, and my boss, we were equals when discussing these spiritual ideas. We were like giddy kids sharing our latest metaphysical discoveries like favorite play toys. We both felt there was little else to talk about."

I felt her excitement and, in turn, my own. Yet I still had my doubts.

"Did your husband see my grandfather's… uh, ghost, too?" I asked.

"Ken was fast asleep on the couch next to me the entire time, snoring away. He never woke up and I never told him about Joe's visit that night. I didn't think he would have believed me anyway, and I decided this was something best kept to myself. I haven't shared about your grandfather's appearance to him or anyone else, frankly… not until this moment."

Shortly after my conversation with Rebecca at the wake, I started picking up books about life after death, metaphysics, paranormal phenomena, and other related subjects. I wanted to know what GeeJay was so interested in, and it started an on-again, off-again exploration into these fringy, fantastical ideas. At one point in my twenties, I became so obsessed with the concept of synchronicity that I lived my life with one eye always watching for meaningful coincidences. I figured if they were really cosmic messages, as so many alternative thinkers maintained, then maybe I could follow these signs like breadcrumbs from the beyond to get some reliable direction in my life.

I remember that period as uplifting and hopeful—a time when my fears were briefly quelled. But I lost interest after a while when my search didn't seem to go anywhere, and I became preoccupied with "reality"—linguistics and languages mainly. Gainful employment, too, and probably an unattainable girl, although I can't remember anymore if I had a specific relationship interest in mind back then.

Loose pebbles crunched as the Mews Man pulled his legs up closer to his chest and my attention shifted back to him and the lighthouse. It occurred to me as I looked at him that this enigmatic man might have answers to some of those knotty questions that I'd been asking myself most of my life. My metaphysical explorations had been engrossing, but I hit so many dead ends, or read so much conflicting information written by so many spiritual wackadoodles, I eventually became disillusioned and resigned myself to being stuck in a hopeless koan zone forever. Could the Mews Man's presence be a balm to my uneasiness? Could he clear up some of my confusion?

"I'm a little confused," I said, as I shifted my weight against the soaring monolith. "I need to know who you are, why you're here, and why *me*?"

"Of course," he said, "I just need to…"

"And where the hell are we right now? Is this a dream? Is this an alternate universe?"

He gestured in front of him, but I wasn't finished. "And take it slow, this is all very disorienting."

He smiled kindly and sighed, like he knew this was going to take a while. "Understandable, Metis. Putting all this information into a usable framework is a daunting challenge for anyone, even advanced students like you."

"And why do you keep calling me Metis when my name is Roger."

"My apologies. I realize that name means little to you at the moment, although I don't think it will be long before you start unforgetting our history together."

Unforgetting? Odd word choice. Did he mean remembering? Because he had told me something like this in the mews, that I would remember him, but when I tried to recall him from another time or place, I drew a blank. I liked his eyes, his manner, everything that he was saying, but he was an otherworldly stranger to me. Fascinating, yes, but still an eccentric unknown.

"Look, assuming you're real and not a delusion caused by some sort of serious brain trauma, I want to remember all the stuff you're telling me that I already know, but I don't have the slightest clue. I feel like I'm a little in between worlds right now, and it's messing with my head."

"Ah, in between worlds, now you're getting it, Metis," he responded. "Maybe you'll recall our precious pact more quickly than I anticipated."

I paused a beat. "I get that you're an advanced being, an avatar, something like that, but I still need answers, a clear explanation." My voice had become strident, betraying my fear.

"I'm happy to answer all your inquiries, Metis," he turned to his right slightly so that he was facing me, his voice modulated, but his message trenchant. "Although I must warn you—for assimilation purposes, you have temporarily, but quite thoroughly, habituated yourself to Worldborn ways. As a result, what you are going to see and hear in the weeks ahead won't fit neatly into your current view of the world. In fact, true reality is one-hundred-eighty-degrees from what you now perceive, and much of what I will share may come as an ice water shock. As your accepted worldview is fundamentally challenged, you might find yourself even more disturbed, disoriented, and frightened for a period of time."

"Oh, great, just what I need, more fear."

"As I said in the mews, Metis, intense fear caused by an abrupt separation from all that you actually are, and the inner place where you truly live, is a state you share with all Worldborns. All experience the deep sense of missingness and deprivation that I mentioned. But no one will be left in that sorry state forever."

I spent a lot of time comparing myself to others, measuring my level of struggle and success against those around me. While I felt certain that I was unique in my level of agitation and torment, he was telling me that my angst and unhappiness were a shared phenomenon. And temporary. I badly wanted to believe this because little about my life was satisfying at that moment, and much of it was making me downright miserable.

"You keep saying that I'll remember what's going on. Can you help me do that now, so I don't feel so lost?"

"Lost in space, haha, good one, Metis," he replied, as if I'd hit on one of his slippery truths and we were sharing a good laugh about it.

"But, more accurately, we should say that the Worldborn condition involves being lost in both space *and* time."

He looked at me to see if this last statement had registered, and when he could see that it hadn't, he just carried on, unfazed. "In any case, getting back to your clarifying questions, I think it's best if I address them one at a time."

I studied him as he adjusted his seat again. Despite my earlier assessment of his age, the Mews Man's features were without line or wrinkle. Those startling eyes—his dominant feature—had the same potent intensity that I felt during our alley encounter, but I was still experiencing his gaze as immeasurably calming. If there was such a thing as quiet eyes, he had them. It felt like he was administering a sedative by just casting them my way.

In spite of my trepidation and confusion, sitting there with that enormous lighthouse at our backs and his resonant voice riding the air, I felt safe and protected, and I didn't want to leave him.

At least not at that moment.

CHAPTER FIVE

"First, as for who I am," he started. "In my most notable life within this space-time dimension, I was called Empedocles."

"Emp… Empeda… uh, I don't think I've ever heard of you."

"Empedocles. Father of Rhetoric, Friend of Parmenides, Originator of Cosmogenic Theory? Doesn't ring a bell?"

I thought back for a moment to a world history class, searched other long forgotten academic lessons, but was quite sure I had never heard his name before.

"Sorry. I don't think so."

"Okay, not so famous then. But let me attempt to illuminate you. In your illusion of linear time, I lived about 2600 years ago on the island of Sicily—then, a part of Greece—in a small, coastal city named Acragas."

He seemed pleased at the remembering.

"History recorded me as a philosopher but, boof, how boring. People turn you into a philosopher when your ideas are too frightening for them. My contemporaries wanted to theorize, philosophize, speculate and endlessly debate rather than actually applying what I was showing them. Disciplined application is what matters, Metis, not the eternal play of ideas, not spending lifetime after lifetime gathering practical information that you never use."

I thought about the dozens of self-improvement books I'd read over the years and, lately, listening to a lot of mind-empowerment podcasts, often the same ones over and over again. "I think I've been one of those information gatherers, actually," I said. "I always figured the more I read, the more authors and experts I listened to, the better I would be at life, and the closer I'd come to finding the answers I was looking for."

"That's fine to build a base, Metis, but eventually you've got to do something, take action with that learning. Applying what you know is the fastest way to make the jump from theory to valuable experience… and freedom. But the people of Acragas didn't understand that and ninety-nine-point-nine percent of them didn't care. They remained entranced and ensnared in this web of futility."

His eyes softened to a warmer shade of gold. "I don't mean you, Metis. You were advanced in your mind training and approaching full understanding. A fine student you were. A loyal young friend, too."

What the hell? *Fine student? Loyal friend?* I decided to ignore this last comment. "That's interesting about novel ideas being frightening to people."

"The big truths tear at the roots of your perceived reality, upset your ossified worldview, challenge your mad ideas about who you are and why you're here. That's why people become so afraid when they sniff at the truth. Then they twist your words to fit the comfortable and familiar, yet tiny and diminished images they have of themselves. Or they accuse you of blasphemy, witchcraft, pacts with demons. Followed naturally by quarterings, hangings, disembowelments, and similarly brutal punishments and retributions."

He said that last bit like he was personally acquainted with quarterings.

"I wasn't interested in philosophy's mental gymnastics," his voice became increasingly animated, more preacher than teacher. "And I wasn't some religious recluse or holy hermit either. I was an instructor of action. My specialty was exit strategies to be exact. Surmounting material obstacles and disappearing from the hallucinatory state once and for all."

"By using an escape pod, a time machine, something like that?" I was trying to keep myself in the conversation, but I really didn't know what I was talking about.

"No, *nothing* like that. I said exit from the life dream, Metis, not exit from earth. Earth is nothing but a fabrication of the mind, a dream world you made up. I was here to free people trapped in their persistent illusion of time and space, to help them awaken permanently from the consensus trance. My techniques could have led Worldborns out of their darkened dream of despair directly to an experience of boundless peace and freedom. But they didn't want to know about that. Instead, they turned into ostriches, all of them, or withering critics and inquisitors."

I didn't know where this was leading, but I was hanging on his every word. The passion and energy with which the Mews Man spoke had me rapt.

"In the end, I realized I was trying to instruct them in an escape plan that was too rigorous, one that required too much discipline and necessitated a kind of vigilance and fierce attention that they couldn't manage and, from an evolutionary standpoint, weren't ready for. Plus, it terrified them." He hesitated for just a beat. It was a pause tinged with frustration, a hint of sadness there, too.

Then he continued. "They never got to experience the rewards that were within their grasp, so they abandoned the effort. It was my fault, really. I failed to communicate the extraordinary possibilities that were waiting for us all. I won't make that mistake again."

Another pause, definitely sadness in his voice. "Still, it was hard for me to understand why they preferred to stay hopelessly locked in a prison, shunning the keys I was holding out to them."

"Sounds hard," I said, wanting to appear sympathetic.

"I should have known, of course. Free someone who's been locked up for lifetimes, he doesn't leap for joy and run for the sunshine. True freedom is too frightening for most people, the light too bright. Eyes become used to darkness and it takes time to acclimate, to feel safe enough to venture out. People tend to linger against their cell bars, gathering strength. I should have seen that."

"Right... for strength," I said, but was not really following him.

"Ahh, it's nothing," he replied, waving his hand dismissively and returning to a tone of optimism. "The script is already written. The big stir, the transcendent spark, the final jump, whatever you want to call it, is assured for all of us. And soon, too, because now Worldborns *are* ready, and the great awakening is waiting to happen."

"Sounds fascinating," I replied.

"*Fascinating?* That's your response? I offer you everything you've ever wanted in every life you've ever lived, and all you have to say is 'fascinating?'" He was only feigning irritation—he was playing with me, looking cheerful and content. I gazed back at those intelligent eyes and felt very dull and slow. This was not the first nor would it be the last time I felt that way in his presence.

"Well, yes, fascinating and reassuring, I guess, Emp... Empreda... I'm sorry, what's your name again?"

"Empedocles... long *ee* sound at the end. But why don't you just call me Clees? Easier."

"Okay," I said, and was glad to have a more accessible name for this walking oracle.

"Clees it is then," he said, reaching out to shake on it. I looked down at his extended hand and, for some reason, hesitated. "I will feel real to you, Metis. Go ahead."

I took his waiting hand, and it was as solid as any I'd held in my own world.

"When you come to know as much I do, when you can see behind the curtain, there isn't much point in slogging around in a meat body. I was an alchemist, a magician, a sorcerer, a mystic. I learned to play with the tired illusion that Worldborns are so convinced is solid and real. Manipulation of matter is a minor achievement, but one that can be quite... entertaining. Strictly for learning purposes, mind you."

I was still holding onto his hand, then dropped it abruptly. He didn't seem to notice.

"Where and when it is useful, when someone calls on me with persistence the way you have in the past few months, I can still conjure up a reliable and recognizable human form for purposes of communication and instruction."

"I have been calling on you with persistence? How do you mean? Like when I ask for help at night?"

"Not so much then. Your entreaties at night are more like deal making—telling, not asking—which has its origins in lack and fear. Fear creates blocks and barriers to clearly picking up on the useful guidance and meaningful answers you really want." He said this as a matter of fact, without a hint of derision or judgment, but I felt embarrassed that my appeals were coming off as desperate.

"No need for embarrassment," he said, thought-reading again. "As I said, there is no one in your dream world who is not consumed with profound anxiety and confusion, whether they consciously know it or not. It goes with the territory, with the entirely made-up, suffocating limits of the Worldborn universe. It is insane here, Metis… and hopeless. The sooner everyone recognizes that, the sooner they will realize that there must be a better way, and a way out."

"Hopeless and meaningless?" I responded. "That's kind of depressing."

"Understanding the truth behind that statement is the beginning of true liberation and very good news." He said this without a hint of sarcasm. "The time will come when you'll understand that the only logical response to the waking dream Worldborns have collectively conjured is to smile at it."

He turned his head suddenly and stared down the slope in front of us. "If you don't mind, Metis, I'm going to address your penultimate question straight away."

Penultimate question? I had forgotten all my questions and just looked at him quizzically.

"You wanted to know where we are right now. Take a look down there."

Clees pointed downhill about a hundred yards in front of us to where a thick fogbank obscured the view beyond.

"All I see is fog."

"Keep watching."

A moment later I saw a lone man about forty-five-years-old emerge from the mist. He seemed surprised and looked around like he was trying to get his bearings. He noticed the lighthouse and stared up in our direction. Then a woman, roughly the same age, followed him holding the hand of a stooped, white-haired man, maybe her father. As they stood there appearing dazed, wisps of amorphous light streaked into the scene from our left and settled in front of them. These feathery shapes took on human forms and immediately surrounded the trio of mist drifters.

"The three who just slipped through the fog bank down there are Worldborns," Clees said. "A middle-aged couple and her elderly father, killed instantly when a freak tornado flattened the home they were occupying in Curtis, Nebraska. They've since vacated their physical bodies, left earth behind, and arrived in this place."

"So, they're dead?"

"No, impossible. Dead is just a scary construct of your deranged mind perpetuated by your insane world. Death is a fiction, Metis, inconceivable, it does not exist. Besides, do they look dead to you?"

"No, they look very much alive." Then I took a quick glance up at the soaring lighthouse and had a revelation. "Is this heaven?"

"Not heaven, the Borderland. The in-between life. Buddhists call it the bardo. Some Worldborns call it the afterlife. I call it a pointless pitstop."

He seemed almost bored reporting this, like it was irrelevant. I was so thrilled by this apparent confirmation of the hereafter, I jumped up to get a better look. "Wait, what?"

"I said it's called the Borderland."

"I heard what you said, but why so blasé?" I was gesturing with excitement. "This is huge, Clees. The debate over what happens when you die has been going on since the beginning of mankind. Do you have any idea how much solace and comfort this is going to bring to so many?"

I felt a kind of awe and immense gratitude watching this scene play out before me, a wave of relief unlike anything I'd experienced before. I was witnessing evidence of what would surely change life on earth forever, and alleviate a lot of fear and suffering. Starting with my own.

Clees glanced up at me standing over him, shook his head in mock annoyance, and pulled me down by the arm with one hand. "You haven't fully grasped it yet, Metis. All of this is just an empty stage, a waste of time. Utter distraction."

In that moment I knew, despite all his abundant wisdom, that this man was missing a locknut. For some reason he couldn't see what was so obvious to me—that the answer to one of creation's greatest existential and theological mysteries was being revealed right in front of us… and he acted like we were watching moss grow.

"We used to talk about this frequently, Metis, because so often you'd get stuck halfway across the bridge. This may seem captivating to you on one level, but it's really just there to distract you—pull your attention away from what's truly true. That's no end game down there, it's a meaningless ruse… just another seduction to keep you stuck and asleep for another ten thousand lifetimes."

This man Clees was hard not to like and utterly fascinating to talk to, but on this point he had a definite mental block or delusion. I wasn't going to let him rob me of the joy I felt in this extraordinary moment.

"Clees, a ten-second video post of what's happening down there would change the human condition forever. It would light up the Internet, get about a billion hits overnight." I was speaking with all the incredulity I could muster. "How could you deny people incontrovertible proof that death isn't the end, that we never really die? That is pointlessly cruel."

From the first moment I saw him in the mews, Clees had been smiling good-naturedly and giving every indication of being non-violent and even-tempered. But in that second, he flashed me a look that was pure Zeus throwing lightning bolts.

"Actually, Metis, pointlessly cruel would be letting people think that what's going on down there actually matters. Pointlessly cruel would be giving people hope that arriving in the Borderland will get them anywhere, that it offers them something worthy of who they truly are."

"But what you're not seeing…"

He cut me off, his previous words just the distant thunder. The high-voltage discharge was still coming. His voice remained composed, but his words penetrated my chest cavity like a boxer's knockout punch.

"Pointlessly cruel, Metis, would be ushering people to that old swing set in your childhood backyard with its rotten seats, broken ladder, and rusty slide and telling them this was the ultimate amusement park—all the while holding a lifetime pass to Disney World behind your back. *That* would be cruel, Metis. And heartless."

He seemed to be referring to the dilapidated swing set sitting in an overgrown patch of weeds along the back fence of my parent's Scotch Plains home. But how could he know? I felt chastened and responded sheepishly.

"You've been to my parent's house?"

He said nothing, just looked at me.

"And to Disney World?"

This must have struck him as funny because I could see the corner of his lips curl as he let out a soft groan. "No, I have not been to Disney World, Metis, although I am aware of its reputation for being the happiest place on earth."

The tempest flash had left his face. He was once again calm and equable, but he wasn't finished.

"No offense to Mickey the Mouse, but the Disney spectacular that Worldborns find so enthralling would draw a crowd of exactly *none* in the real world that lies far beyond this one."

"They have Space Mountain there, too?" I asked, still feeling knocked around by his words.

"Space Mountain? You mean the three-minute thrill ride? How about infinite happiness, Metis, and unending joy? How does that sound to you, how would you like that?"

His voice changed as he said this, his gaze looking past me.

"That's a lot of happiness."

"You have no idea. There is no meter in your illusory world that could come close to measuring the unbroken bliss I am speaking of. Not close."

I wasn't sure what to say and I spoke next at a near whisper. "But this Borderland place, Clees, this would still be the greatest discovery in all of human history."

I was spellbound by the scene below, and he could see that I wasn't going to let it go, so he let me watch a moment longer. The younger couple was now smiling broadly, enveloped in gossamer arms. The old man was no longer bent over and looked radiant as he stared into the face of a wispy, feminine form pulsing before him. She must have been an intimate acquaintance, deeply missed, because he had the relieved expression of a man who'd been holding on to way too much grief for way too long.

"Those three will stay here for a while, doing a full, birth-to-death life review, assisted by people they knew and trusted back in the world of linear time and solid space," Clees said. "Then they'll return in a few days and start over again—entrance to exit, infancy to infirmity, lessons learned, lessons lost. Like that, on and on."

His tone was so matter of fact and unimpressed it only compounded the buzzkill he had touched off in me moments earlier.

"You can think of the Borderland as a bus depot, basically," he continued, "a place where you wait around to pick up another body and then drive off to commence a do-over."

"Do-over? Wait… does that mean… are you telling me that reincarnation is also a certainty?"

"For what it's worth, yes. If they choose to go back. Which most *every body* does. More seeming lessons to learn. Cycle of lifetimes. Same nonsense, different incarnation. An endless merry-go-round, until you really question what you're doing and commit to snapping out of it. That's where the awakening comes in."

He started to rise from the crushed gravel beneath us and brushed himself off like he was getting ready to leave, scanning the horizon for our transport home. "Time doesn't work here in the Borderland exactly like it does in your false, material world," he said. "It will be a short gap here, just a couple of days. But on earth it will be something like ten or fifteen years before they return as newborn Worldborns."

"Back in two days?"

"Or three, something like that." He would have yawned his response if he could have.

"So, you're saying that we appear to die, leave our physical bodies, then reincarnate and live again? Just like Buddhists claim. No permanent death… ever?"

I needed him to etch this into my brain and I didn't want to leave this place until he did. I pressed my back firmly against the lighthouse wall, sticking to it like epoxy.

"Yes, Metis, you heard me right, no death," he said, squatting down to meet me eye-to-eye. "Look, I know it's an undiscussable subject for most Worldborns, shrouded in mystery and for many, in terror. But if people understood death, they could all finally get beyond it to what really matters. Death isn't all it's cracked up to be. In fact, it isn't much of anything at all."

"I've always found that so frustrating," I replied. "We have this inevitable event that eventually creeps up on everyone, but nobody wants to talk about it. Unless it's mentioned with a lot of quasi-magical or religious thinking, death is a conversation that's off the table."

"Worldborns pride themselves in conquering the cosmos, but death remains their unexplored frontier, the great mystery, untouchable and enigmatic," he said. "Which promotes hopeless confusion and an endless cycle of profound upsets. Turns out, Metis, that the unexamined death is more problematic than the unexamined life. Are you content to settle for that?"

My mind was whirling, and I wasn't sure what I was content with at that moment. In the space of what seemed like just a few minutes, I'd gone from a tentative belief in the afterlife to seeing it firsthand. As well as discovering that reincarnation was not only plausible but assured. Yes, Clees, I could probably be content with that for a few thousand more lifetimes, thank you.

"It's all fake, Metis, a trick of the mind. The dream world you think you see has no substance, it's nothing but an intricate mirage, an elaborate hoax. Listen to me… there is no solid, concrete, objective universe.

There is no out there, out there. It's all just a persistent dream, and a frightful one for most. But it doesn't have to go on forever. That's the good news. It's possible for Worldborns to set themselves free and exit this tangled dream together."

"Exit, okay…right." I stared at him again with a dolt's befufddlement.

"Just as we had planned, Metis, we are going to show Worldborns how to break the cycle and collectively awaken from all the nightmares the world has ever had. Now, *that* would get about a billion hits overnight, would it not?"

"I really don't mean to be stubborn, Clees," I said, aware that I was being totally stubborn, "but what I'm looking at down there is a precious gift to mankind. Maybe it doesn't apply to you, but on earth when a loved one dies, the loss causes incomparable heartbreak… the gut-wrenching separation destroys people. Proof of the afterlife would be an incalculable balm for millions upon millions of… how did you call us again… Worldborns?"

"Metis, lives come and go. You're a woman, you're a man, you live a long life or a short one, you're famous or a nobody, you have six kids and sixteen grandchildren or commit to a life of asceticism and spend your years alone. It doesn't matter. Every life on earth is filled with bitter hardships and haunting troubles of one kind or another. Do you deny it? This is an utterly feeble expression of your true nature, your true identity. And then it's repeated all over again."

"So, you're saying I have lived a lot lives, too?" I asked. "Over many centuries? Died and came back?"

"Correct, yes, you have been enslaved in the world of shadows, too, imprisoned by the solidified holographic pattern you call earth."

"So, how many lives, just out of curiosity?"

What happened next was so sudden and startling, it is a marvel for me to remember. He didn't answer my question exactly, instead he just sighed, stared up at the lighthouse for a moment, then started to walk around me in a tight circle. He was watching his feet and brushing his fingers alongside the lighthouse each time he passed. Then, as his revolutions accelerated, my physical form turned into a living, breathing flip book, morphing and re-morphing into a parade of personas, men and women of every race and ethnicity from every time period throughout history and every geographic location on earth—even a few lifeforms from places far beyond earth by the alien looks of them. Incredibly, I could also feel each body and see each face with eyes that seemed to be mine but were somehow outside of me.

I was a grim-faced dowager from the Victorian age sipping tea in silence and alone; a hunter from the Neolithic period with an open gash across my chest; a small, well-muscled black man with loincloth and spear; an Australian sheepherder with ruddy skin the texture of tree bark; and a cave woman dressed in wolfskins with long matted hair and one eye.

Then I became a giant of a medieval man, possibly a stone mason judging from the hulking hammers in my hands, and next a warrior Viking wearing a Norseman's leather helmet and carrying a heavy seax. The Viking changed into a genderless humanoid with translucent green skin and a dozen pair of deep set eyes, with hands and feet the size of anvils, before morphing into a South American shaman, covered in tattoos, wearing a jaguar mask, and carrying a flute-like instrument in one hand.

"Clees, what is happening to me, what are you doing?"

I sunk my body even more deeply into the ground underfoot and stared down at myself as I changed into a Civil War nurse covered in blood and clutching crudely made gauze bandages; then, a regal-looking man with a formal top hat and fur-lined coat whacking raggedly dressed children with a silver-topped cane along a cobblestoned street. A cripple came next with no legs and soiled clothing crushed into a wooden wheelchair in what appeared to be Prohibition-era Times Square; followed by a colorfully dressed Cossack with a weathered, determined face on a powerful charger horse—and dozens more, too many to count, all in the span of a minute or less.

Then, just as abruptly as it started, the flashcard procession of alternate faces and forms came to an end. Clees was standing still beside me again.

"Recognize anyone?" he asked, looking at me pleased, maybe even a little impressed with himself.

I said nothing.

"Metis, I asked if you recognized any of those people? They were all you, in other places, other times, other lives. They were mirage existences, of course, just costume bodies, no more real than this tower behind us." He glanced up, tapped the lighthouse's painted concrete skin with a knuckle and shot me an impish smile.

In retrospect, he must have thought that carouseling through a couple hundred of my previous incarnations would jog something in my memory and put a temporary end to my incessant questions about reincarnation and death. But with no preamble and little explanation, these sudden mutations left me shaken. Until that moment, everything that had happened with Clees was far out and fantastic, technicolor scenes in an increasingly remarkable adventure, a wild escapade that stretched the limits of possibility.

But shapeshifting through the ages was different somehow, and it unnerved me more than all the other wonders he had pulled off before that—more than his parted curtain visitations, the levitation tricks in the mews, or even his effortless mind reading.

In that instant, I understood that I had no useful reference for what he was showing and telling me, that it would now be impossible to return to my job, my friends, my city, and my life unchanged. The moment when Clees appeared in the seam between the bagel shop and the liquor store was the beginning of the end of my world. The cord to my ballast had been broken and a new kind of fear was settling in.

He was still standing there, waiting for me to answer his question about the flash card incarnations, but before I could, there was a sudden whoosh inside my head, and I felt a wave of vertigo. I closed my eyes, tilted my head back against the lighthouse wall to steady myself, and then the Borderland was gone.

CHAPTER SIX

I came to or woke up in my own bed, with my quilt thrown off to one side and a fire truck passing below my apartment window, sirens wailing. The sun was reflecting off a bay window in the brownstone across the street, so I knew it was morning. My t-shirt clung damply to my skin and my eyes were crusty and pasted shut. When I went to rub them, I felt something heavy, hard and cold in my right hand.

"Now what?" I mumbled through crusted lips.

I opened my hand to find a worn, triple-bladed arrowhead made of a bluish-silver metal I didn't recognize resting in my palm. I didn't own an arrowhead and I had never seen one like this before, but there was no question of how it got into my hand. Clees could manipulate my dreams and screw with my reality—materializing a solid object out of thought molecules would be nothing but an elementary magic trick to him.

I sat up and turned it over a few times, then carried the metal relic to my kitchen area where the light was brighter, reflecting off the birch-wood veneer of my cheap, drop-leaf table. On the arrowhead's shank, one word was clearly embossed: ESTIA. The word was Greek, I knew that, but I checked a translation app on my phone to be sure of its meaning.

"Focus," I said out loud, as I studied the definition. It was the ancient Greek term for *focus*. I studied the arrow tip closely for additional markings, but there were none.

I remembered every detail of the nocturnal visit I'd had with Clees in the Borderland, right down to the frenzy of passing faces at the end and how disoriented I felt. But I didn't recall his using the word *focus* and I couldn't connect it with anything he had said while we were together. There was no doubt, however, that this was another clue in an unfolding puzzle, a missing piece that Clees would surely integrate into our next encounter.

I put the metal bolt down on the table, got up and grabbed my cell phone off the kitchen counter. I pressed in the number for my best friend, Verilee Fulbreth. I vowed early on that I wouldn't tell anyone about Clees, his recent visitations, or his unconventional worldview until I could verify what was happening, or until I couldn't take it any longer. And at that moment, I couldn't take it any longer.

Vee—I rarely call her Verilee—didn't answer and as the phone rang, I debated whether to leave a message. What would I say that would make any sense, that I'd been hanging out with a 2600-year-old Greek illusionist who defied death, could prove reincarnation, and believed that everything we know and care about in this world is a worthless fiction meant only to distract us from our true reality? Then I heard her familiar voice message, "Vee here. Keep it short." I told her to call me as soon as she got my message and hung up.

Vee and I grew up in Scotch Plains together, although we had vastly different childhoods. My family was solidly middle class and quite close. Her's lived on the wrong side of the demographic divide and seemed to be at constant war with each other. Vee used to tell me that she would never have survived her family if she hadn't spent half of her days and nights hanging out at my house through middle and high school. This didn't strike me as an exaggeration. It was rough, maybe even a little dangerous for her at home, although she was tight-lipped about the details, even with me.

I should also mention that Vee was and still is one of the most attractive women I know. By the time my adolescent hormones were firing on all cylinders, I was tormented by her daily proximity, and I frequently dropped hints about my non-platonic interest. Vee, however, always seemed completely neutral and uninterested in me, other than as good friends, and either didn't notice or chose to ignore my awkward attempts at flirtation. When she told me during our sophomore year that she preferred girls to boys, manifesting at that moment in a crush on a mildly appealing but timorous wallflower named Hannah Karvash, I was bummed out but not totally surprised.

After high school, our close friendship took a semi-hiatus for four years, long enough for me to earn my applied linguistics degree from the University of Wisconsin in Madison while she earned a graphic design certificate from Parsons School of Design in New York. Almost immediately after my graduation, Vee and I decided to become roommates in the city together. She had just broken up with her third girlfriend in about as many years, and the woman I was living with in college for the past two gave me a graduation present that she didn't need to wrap—a very delicately worded, farewell letter. I wasn't devastated. To be honest, I never felt fully committed to the relationship either and probably would have given her the same graduation gift had she not beaten me to the good stationery.

So, a month after my return from the midwest, Vee and I left Scotch Plains and moved to an apartment on Washington Street in Brooklyn where our faithful friendship resumed.

This was before the waterfront Dumbo neighborhood got insanely hot, prohibitively expensive, and overrun with hipsters and tech start-ups. We were able to find a decent-sized, two-bedroom apartment with good light for $1750. I covered three-fifths of the rent since my first job translating communications materials into Spanish for the New York City Department of Health paid reasonably well. In exchange, I also got the larger bedroom, which I estimated had 18-square-feet more space. Enough for a dresser that I pilfered from my parents' guest bedroom.

Vee and I were ideal roommates and our friendship deepened during our four years of sharing house keys and dog-walking duties. She had brought her mixed-breed rescue, Homer, to Brooklyn—a four-legged feeding frenzy that she adored, and I tolerated. But I knew that Vee's old wounds and insecurities, kept at bay with her chilly social bearing and highly flammable temper, were soothed by Homer's benign, warm-blooded companionship. So, he and I conspired to keep Vee reassured, safe and cared for. Ours was an odd but functional family.

After four years of working for the city, I made the leap to my current job at the software company with a hefty salary hike. Vee, who is a gifted and versatile graphic designer, was successfully freelancing after a few bust-ups at some of the city's more progressive digital ad agencies. Her social media expertise and web design were always first-rate, and she was a perennial award-winner, but her people skills didn't quite match her technical expertise. She would eventually butt heads with her bosses or creative directors and wanted no part of management herself. She was more peaceable and productive on her own, picking the projects and people she wanted to work with and making her own schedule, which often meant starting her jobs after midnight. Her circadian rhythm never quite jived with the world's conventional workday, and I would often hear her booting up her computer at night just as I was turning off my reading light.

Around that time, Vee also started dating a human rights lawyer named Justina Thompson, a brilliant, self-possessed woman ten years older than we were, who I thought was awesome, and who handled Vee's mercurial moods with unflappable composure. Together, the three of us decided it was a good time for Justina to move in, for me to move out, and for Homer to manage the testosterone imbalance on his own. He seemed amenable to the idea.

That's when I found my third-floor walk-up apartment on Grove Street in the West Village. I was staring out its rear window at the tree-filled backyard, watching a red robin urge one of her nestlings into flight, when my phone vibrated. Her name appeared on the touchscreen and I answered.

"Verilee, hey, where are you?" I said.

"Verilee? Must be serious. Who croaked?" She knew me well.

"No one, Vee, I just have to meet you," I said, with some urgency in my voice. "Where are you?"

"At home dude, it's eight in the morning. I'm practically still sleeping." But she was clearly awake, because I heard her stirring her ever present chai tea, bringing the honey up from the bottom. I knew her well, too.

"Can you meet me for lunch today by my office?" I asked.

"I'm working on a pitch at Massoud's," she said, "but it's a shit show and I have a tight deadline. Let's meet tomorrow after work, somewhere near the High Line." My office was on 16th Street and 8th Avenue in the Chelsea neighborhood, near the iconic High Line elevated park, so she'd suggested the meeting spot for my convenience.

"I was hoping to see you sooner."

"Gimme a hint, Rog," she said, sipping.

"It's important, but I can't explain it on the phone," I said. "How about later today, maybe five-thirty at that café on the west side of Chelsea Market? The one with the booths in the back."

"Alright, I'll try to make it happen, but I hope this is about that chick you met at the gym last week, the one with the tat of Felix the Cat on her shoulder." Vee was always knee deep in my pathetic love life. Plus, she liked tattoos—at the time she had five of her own. "Wait, I know, you slept with her last night, she is multi-orgasmic, and you're not sure if Jerry is up to the task."

"My Jerry is fine, Vee," I replied, feeling antsy to get off the phone, "and this isn't about a girl. It's crazier than that."

"Crazier than romance? Nothing's crazier than romance, Rog" she said, the cynic always poised at her shoulder, eager for a quip. "Alright, the place with the booths at five-thirty. Unless I text you that the Ayatollah's henchmen have chained me to my Aeron chair and have threatened to beat me with their sandals until I finish the wireframes."

Vee's current gig was working for this Iranian American dude named Massoud Phipps who I could tell she really liked although she complained about him frequently. She had been freelancing for Massoud and his ad agency, located near Grand Central Station, off and on for the past couple of years. Two years was like employment servitude to Vee, so Massoud had to be both very patient and extremely smart. Vee hated stupid.

Plus, his agency had recently won a big piece of the Harley-Davidson digital media business, in large part due to Vee's strategic thinking and design, so I'm sure he calculated that it was more prudent to batten down the hatches and wait out her hurricane force mood swings than tangle with her violently shifting weather patterns.

She once told me that she'd never met anyone who could manage difficult clients as well as Massoud. As she put it, "He has the charm, sophistication and diplomatic skills of Anwar Sadat." I'm not sure if she realized that Sadat was Egyptian and Massoud was Iranian, and just lumped the entire Middle East into one darker shade of the melting pot, or whether she understood that she was also commenting on his tactful handling of *her*. Either way, coming from Vee, that statement was a full-throated endorsement of Massoud.

"Okay, but if you can make it any earlier let me know. I can slip out anytime." I hung up and checked my kitchen clock—8:10.

My own boss was a genial Belgian woman named Manon Lepere who was not a stickler about arrival time, but I still hated to waltz past her office after 9:00. So, I showered quickly, packed an apple into my shoulder bag and started walking out the door. Then I turned back and grabbed the three-bladed arrowhead off the kitchen table and zipped it into one of the side pockets. It was 8:40 when I finally left the apartment.

Usually, when I had plenty of time to get to work and the weather cooperated, I would take a leisurely stroll to the river, walk north along the waterfront promenade, and east on 16th Street. But that day I was short on time, so I grabbed a Citi Bike a block from my apartment and jumped on the buffered bike lane extending along Hudson Street that turned into 8th Avenue.

I don't suppose it would have mattered if I'd chosen to walk up 7th Avenue that day or gotten lazy and went underground to the subway—Clees would have found me anywhere.

And that morning he snatched me off the bikeway as I was crossing 15th Street.

CHAPTER SEVEN

I had just spent what seemed like the entire night with him at the Borderland and didn't expect another encounter with Clees for days, if not weeks. But as I was halfway through the intersection at 15th Street, the traffic light changed from green to orange. I was in third gear, accelerating past a determined-looking woman on a cargo bike with two small children harnessed into the front carrier box, when a hole was punched into the panorama of moving pedestrians, cars, and delivery trucks directly in front of me.

My bike lifted off—Elliot and *ET* style—into the perforation, and just like Elliot, I yelped in a histrionic display of amazement and fear, wide-eyed, mouth agape, white-knuckles on the handlebars.

As I slipped through the gap at a sharp upward angle, I had the stupidest thought ever—that I wouldn't get the Citi Bike back within the allotted timeframe and would have to pay the inflated, late-to-dock penalty. There I was, literally rupturing the space-time continuum, and all my brain could process was that I was in danger of breaking some petty bike share rule.

Without realizing it, I had closed my eyes and when I opened them again my bike had become an intergalactic cruiser traveling through deep space. I saw so many stars in every direction, generating so much light, I had the impression of more starlight above, below and all around me than there was sheer black space.

"Metis, fancy meeting you here!" Clees was approaching on my right side riding another blue Citi Bike, sitting upright, hands-free, the ever-present smile on his handsome Greek face. He was wearing a well-tailored dark gray suit, crisp powder blue shirt, a perfectly knotted, expensive looking necktie, and stylish black buckle loafers.

"Like the suit?" he called out. "My homage to the professional career man." I wasn't sure if he meant me, because I never wore a suit, or was just making a general comment on the international uniform of business convention. "Not a NASA-approved space suit, of course, but just as uncomfortable."

When he said that, my baffled brain suddenly registered that I was in outer space and that it was impossible to breathe in zero atmosphere. In a panic, I clamped my mouth shut and started peddling frantically, like I might catapult myself back to 8th Avenue. I shot a look towards Clees, trying to communicate my alarm, and reached out to grab his bike for support.

"Just relax and breathe, Metis. This is as much a made-up figment of your imagination as the lighthouse or the West Village. Breathe like you were sitting at your kitchen table."

I didn't listen. He might have been an expert in unassisted interstellar travel, but I wasn't. I started a last breath, seconds-from-death gyration atop my bike seat. Clees quietly laughed at this.

When my lungs began to sear, I buried my face in the crook of my left elbow in an attempt to suck up whatever remaining oxygen molecules might be trapped in the fibers of my shirt. Clees grabbed my hair gently from behind, pried my head out of my arm and turned my face to his. "Stop. You're okay. Just breathe normally."

After another few seconds I had no choice and inhaled in horror, ready to do a face plant into my other arm if necessary. But the air was cool and crisp and completely breathable. I swallowed several gallons of the oxygen-rich atmosphere before my brain caught up to my lungs.

"There, not so hard, was it?" He smiled again, then abruptly turned away and steered towards a small celestial body floating nearby that I hadn't seen seconds before. My bike followed his as though I was tethered to his seat post, and together both bicycles landed silently on the hard, lumpy surface of the little asteroid.

Clees adjusted the kickstand so his bike was securely parked and walked thirty feet to the edge of space. I rolled mine next to his, lowered the kickstand, then moved alongside him as more absurdities raced through my head.

"Clees, I'm going to be late for work and we're both going to be slammed with the twelve-hundred-dollar fine for the lost bikes."

"What bikes?" he said, as his eyes tracked a fireball of atmospheric debris racing across the heavens a thousand or a million miles away.

I whipped my head around, but the bikes were gone. *Oh, great,* I thought, *how are we going to get home now?*

"The bikes didn't get us here, Metis," he spoke this quietly into the total silence of space, not turning to look at me, "and we won't need them to return to New York."

Then he made a theatrical gesture with both arms, looking like a Broadway impresario introducing his most dazzling show ever. "Behold, your magnificent universe at a mere two-hundred-million miles from earth."

I looked out again at the 360° span of twinkling brilliance and my knees got rubbery. I sank to the gritty surface and flopped down on my butt. In that moment, there was no marvel or excitement, just growing confusion and a creeping anxiety—the default mode for most of my life.

"Come now, Metis, cheer up. Last stop, I promise." He unbuttoned his suit jacket, then squatted down to sit next to me. "It's just that your call to Miss Verilee this morning forced me to accelerate our sightseeing tour."

"My call? Look, Clees, I'm sorry but I had to talk to someone," I said, a twinge of guilt in my voice. "Every certainty of my life has been shattered in the past two weeks. I don't know what truths to trust anymore. You don't expect me to go through all of this alone?"

"No, I don't. In fact, Miss Verilee is very much a part of our plan." He turned to me and placed a hand on my shoulder. "A call to our talented collaborator was not only predictable, it was inevitable. I just didn't know exactly when you'd make it. Free will and all that."

He withdrew his hand and as he did the sleeve of his suit jacket inched up and I saw that he was wearing cufflinks—tiny, three-sided, silver arrowheads. Exactly like the larger one I'd found in my hand that morning that was now in the pocket of my shoulder bag lying a few feet away. He saw that I noticed but didn't say anything.

"Vee already knows? About you… about all of this?" I asked.

"No, not in the way you mean," he said. "Like you, she has temporarily forgotten me and her role in our grand adventure. But she agreed to do her part and, once we meet again, she'll eventually remember. Miss Verilee was another of our talented co-conspirators and a master illusionist in her own right. Brilliant treasure hunter, too."

"She's smart, for sure," I responded.

"I'm not speaking of intelligence now—that's not the characteristic most critically required when it comes to mastering what we're about to do," he said. "Intuition and sensitivity—employing all of the senses at once to see past the illusion—that's the key, and more valuable for this work than intellectual acuity."

"Well, she's definitely sensitive," I said. "In fact, she can be a little uber-sensitive."

"You're speaking of Miss Verilee's tendency to take offense quickly, retaliate sharply, and generally maintain a highly defensive emotional posture?"

"Yeah, that about sums it up. Your first meeting with her probably won't leave you feeling all warm and fuzzy; let's put it that way."

"When Miss Verilee re-embodied in her current life, she chose some circumstances that have been challenging and that not everyone could manage. But she did so willingly and in doing so she has learned some useful lessons that will serve her, and all of us, well," he said.

"Willingly? I doubt that Clees," I responded. "I don't have all the details, but I'm pretty sure she was abused, maybe even roughed up at home. I don't know who's served by that."

"As I said, very challenging, and only a few could have managed it as well as she, but Miss Verilee is quite extraordinary, as well as psychologically strong and capable."

"That might be true, but if I can make a suggestion, I wouldn't mention her childhood when you meet," I said. "She might take that fancy tie you're wearing and use it as a hangman's noose."

He laughed. "I'm glad to hear she hasn't lost her spunk. But just to be safe, I'll leave the necktie behind."

There was a burst of brilliant light in the canopy above us and I thought to myself that the massive explosion that caused it probably happened a few million years ago. Clees was staring up at it, too, as he spoke. "There's another reason why she chose the incarnation and circumstances that she did."

I thought I knew what he was going to say next. "So, we could be together?"

"Yes, that," he responded, "but also so she could look after you."

I chuckled. "Look after *me*? Sorry, I think it was the other way around, Clees. Vee came to our house almost every single day. She took refuge there. It was me and my parents who kept an eye on her, made sure she got out of her crazy house alive."

"That's certainly how it looked."

"What are you talking about?" I said defensively. "I was there. You have no idea how vulnerable she was or how vigilant she had to be just to stay in one piece."

He changed the subject completely. "So, tell me, Metis, how did we get here?"

"How did we get here?" I said, not understanding the sudden shift, but looking around at our seat in the center of the solar system.

"Yes, how?" He was surveying the heavens again, hands on his hips, an entitled property owner taking in his vast domain.

"I really have no idea," I responded, feeling a wave of irritation mixed with vertigo, wondering how long my mind and body could withstand the mental and physical gymnastics of this Greek galaxy trotter.

"Please, Metis, humor me," he said, "last question and you can return to the city that never rests."

"Never *sleeps*," I corrected him. "The expression is 'never sleeps.'" Even here, in the depths of outer space on the verge of being permanently cleaved from all touchstones to reality, I felt a neurotic need to edit his malapropisms.

"Oh, it sleeps," he said, "it just *never truly rests*. Like everything and everyone else in your world of bad dreams."

I didn't know what he meant and I didn't feel like pulling it out of him, so I leaned back on my elbows to consider my surroundings.

"Metis, once we begin our work in earnest, I won't have the opportunity for these refreshers. So, I must ask for your full attention a little while longer. Focus is the key."

There it was, he said it—*focus*. He even seemed to emphasize it. His eyes danced away from mine, but I was coming to understand that nothing Clees ever said or did was an accident. He had injected that word into our conversation at that moment for a reason. I was sure of it.

Despite his demand for my attention, I was still feeling irked by the cavalier way he spoke about me and Vee. It was irritation mixed with fear, and a strong desire to go home. I wanted to return to my predictable translation job that I didn't like, my shoe-box apartment that was too tight and expensive, and my jittery existence before the sudden retinal splits and Clees' reality-buffeting appearance. I wasn't happy with my life on earth, but it was strange how quickly one could long for the boring, insipid, and familiar, faced with a complete rupture of everything considered reliable, grounded, and predictable. Or as Clees might have put it, I wanted to linger by the bars of my cell awhile longer.

"Try to focus on my question, Metis, because this will be one of the foundations of our current work together," he said. "Tell me, how do you think we traveled this vast cosmic distance in an instant?"

I spoke. "Okay… somehow you understand that the reality we live in isn't what it seems and, therefore, you can bend the incontrovertible laws of physics to your whims. You have a way of warping the field so you can be anywhere you want, whenever you want, in whatever form you choose."

"All that goes without saying, but…"

I interrupted him. "Or, maybe I'm just dreaming. Let's say that I never actually woke up this morning from the dream in the Borderland at all. Maybe I am still dreaming at this very moment, waiting to wake up from this dream of outer space, too."

"Ah, fantastic, Metis. All true… with only minor corrections needed here and there. That bit at the end about everything in your universe being a dream—spot on!" He seemed truly proud of me. "So, extrapolating from that, how was it possible for us to arrive here in a virtual instant, seemingly two-hundred-million miles from your precious metropolis, when so many of your most esteemed physicists agree that we can travel no faster than the speed of light? How is that?"

"I really don't know, Clees," I answered. "Maybe you could just tell me."

"Thought is faster," he responded.

"Thought is faster than what?" My own thinking felt murky and slow, maybe the lingering effects of limited oxygen to my brain.

"Faster than the speed of light. Superluminal. So, when you thought about this place, you arrived. Presto! No lag, no drag, no delay. Thought is everything, Metis. The mind is all there is. You can see how this is going to save us a lot of time and effort when we put our operation into place." He sat back on his own elbows, looking content.

"What are you talking about? I wasn't thinking of this place," I said, unable to follow his thread. "*You* brought me here. And now I need to go back to New York."

"Sure, anytime you like, Metis, ruby slippers and all that… three clicks, there's no place like home—bang, you're there. Remember, matter doesn't matter… or exist. The physical world is all just thought energy crystallized to appear solid. This entire cosmos, just layer upon layer of thoughts. But, aside from that, aren't you enjoying this spectacular view of vast nothingness?"

He was playing fast and loose with the scientific facts and I felt that an immediate clarification was warranted. "Our observable universe has billions of galaxies in it, Clees, and while it's true that it's mostly empty space, calling it nothing wouldn't be accurate at all."

I had been a bit of an amateur astronomer growing up, and on my 11th birthday my parents had given me a Meade ETX-90 telescope—a beautifully made instrument that offered ridiculously detailed views of spectacular superclusters. My father would take me up to Packanack Mountain after dinner in the summer and we'd stay out close to midnight some evenings.

I loved that classic telescope, the way it brought the constellations to life, and how my dad would thumb through *Nightwatch*—our favorite stargazing guide—using his old Army flashlight to help us identify certain galaxies and star clusters that I'd sight in the eyepiece. I still have that well-thumbed copy of the *Nightwatch* guide on my bookshelf somewhere, although I never use it anymore. You can't see more than a handful of stars on a summer night in the city, plus I'd lost interest in astronomy by the time I'd moved there. But that didn't mean I was going to let Clees dismiss an entire field of natural science, a study as ancient as the henges—at least 6,000 years old—simply because it didn't conveniently fit into his arcane conception of the world.

He was sitting up looking at me with an expression of mock alarm. "But what happened to your brilliant reasoning of just a few seconds ago?"

I was trying to remember what I said. "What brilliant reasoning?"

"When you told me it was all a dream, a persistent fiction, nothing but a complex and convincing creative construction of the Worldborns' collective thoughts."

"I said it was *maybe* like a dream… maybe. I never said any of that other stuff."

"Metis, I have made this point repeatedly, now let me make it firmly: *there is no earth, no solar system, no Milky Way, no Proxima Centauri… it is all a grand illusion.* Everything and anything you can see, touch, hear, smell or taste is just an elaborate 3-D hallucination… all of it. Or as you said yourself, it is just a dream." He gestured in front of him, pointing towards the endless heavens. "What you think you see before you, this infinite universe, exists nowhere but in your mind—change your mind, along with the content of your thoughts, and you'll change your entire reality in an instant."

As he said this, I could feel a slight tingling starting below my navel, spreading up into my chest. "Worldborns have so much knowledge about nothing," he said wistfully, staring up towards the heavens. But he was a little out of focus, cosmic dust in my eyes probably. I blinked several times to clear my vision.

"Don't forget, Metis, you have invented everything you see… all of it… making it up out of inner mind clay with each thought you have."

"Okay, I'll try to remember," I said, straining to stay focused.

"One last thing… I believe the time is right for me to meet Miss Verilee again. This Friday evening would be perfect, at nine near your home—northeast corner of Bedford and Commerce."

My vision got even blurrier and the tingling in my chest became more intense.

"And don't forget to bring the kila on Friday," he said, his voice now seeming faint and far away.

"The what?" I asked, my own voice sounding like it was being projected from a distant star.

"The silver blue kila," he said, "that three-edged arrowhead in your bag. Bring it on Friday."

I think that's when I blacked out.

CHAPTER EIGHT

The next moment I was back on 8th Avenue, leaning on the handlebars of my Citi Bike, pedaling steadily, almost through the intersection at 15th Street. The mom with the kids in the cargo bike was there on my left and the traffic light was still changing from orange to red.

"No goddamn way," I said under my breath, as my eyes darted from side to side, and I fought to keep my front wheel steady in the green painted bike lane. "You've got to be shitting me, Clees," I called out, in a voice loud enough for the cargo bike woman to hear and veer away from me. I don't like to swear, but that moment warranted a full recitation of every word of shock and awe at my disposal. I had just traveled 200 million miles from earth and back and not a millisecond of time had elapsed.

I looked over my shoulder to see if Clees was riding up behind me, then stared hard at the roadway in front of me just in case he tried to slice another slit into my reality. "Leave me alone, Clees, just let me get to work." I spoke this nervously into the air, not caring who heard me.

After another minute of pedaling, I passed in front of my office building, turned the corner at 17th Street and docked the bike at my usual rack next to a small playground. When I dismounted, my knees were shaking, and I had to grip the bike seat to steady myself. I stood for a half a minute, my feet firmly planted on the asphalt, breathing deeply and fully into my belly, a yoga trick to slow my heartbeat and regulate my nervous system.

When I felt more grounded, I walked around the corner to the building entrance and checked the time on my cell phone—8:50. Not only had I hyperdriven to the heavens and received an early morning, extraterrestrial lecture on life and illusions, but I was actually early for work and my bike was docked on time. I wouldn't get hit with the bike share penalty after all.

Clees would have to worry about his own bike.

My office was on the 6th floor, and I was too wired and weirded out to wait in the queue for the elevator, so I headed towards the south staircase instead. A half-dozen floors and a handful of breathless "good mornings" later, I pulled open the fire door and passed quickly through a warren of low-slung cubicles. I sped up as I approached the glass walls of Manon's office, but didn't see her at her desk. I stepped into my own small workspace a few enclosures down from her's and closed the door. I hadn't gotten my bag off my shoulder before I grabbed my cell phone and punched in Vee's number.

She picked up after one ring. "You've decided to tell me about the gym chick's other tattoos?"

"Vee, if I told you that I was leaving my body on a regular basis and going to other places that we shouldn't be able to go to, would you think I was crazy?"

"No, but I'd tell your parents," she snickered and waited.

"I mean it. Something's been happening to me that I don't know how to explain. It's both strange and amazing, and shouldn't be possible at all."

"Alright, well, that's not so strange. We used to read about that astral travel and out-of-body stuff all the time. Remember when we tried to do it up on Packanack that one night? But we smoked way too much weed and you had a panic attack while I fell asleep."

"There's a man involved, too, Vee," I said. "Not like anyone I've ever met."

"A man? Look, Rog, you know I'm totally cool with anything alternative—the whole LBGTQ option pool works for me." She was clearly not getting my meaning.

"No, not a man I'm interested in romantically, Vee. This guy is some kind of omniscient immortal, an all-knowing super aware, something like that. He seems to be controlling or initiating the out-of-body experiences I'm having."

"He better not be a religious nut, Rog. You know how I feel about religious fanatics. They're usually preaching, and when they're not, they're spreading virulent crap about anyone who doesn't look or think like them."

"No, Vee, definitely not a religious nut. And it's hard to imagine him rejecting anyone or anything, frankly. It's difficult to explain, but he doesn't really care about anything on earth. He only cares about stuff beyond earth, energy dimensions and places we can't see."

There was a long pause. "Wait, is this about psychedelics? Is that it, you've been quietly tripping without me? Or… I know… you've joined up with another one of your goofy gurus and he's been spiking your brain with crazy talk."

While she was blessed, or cursed, with the same metaphysical curiosity I had, Vee was not naïve and preferred verifiable science to my mystical wish list. She had a phrase she was fond of repeating whenever I put forth some empirically soft idea. "Prove it, Swami Sillinanda," she'd say, employing the name of a fictional guru she'd made up.

"Is this guy fueling another one of your alien visitation fantasies?" she asked, and I could feel her winding up. "Don't forget that last fiasco, dragging me out to Mount Blast-Off to wait for an extraterrestrial shuttle pick-up because of some 'planetary convergence.' I missed one hell of a graduation party back home because you were convinced it was time to vacate earth."

"Mount Shasta. And in the end, you liked that trip."

"Because I met some very cool, very stoned hippies who turned me onto Burning Man, where the following August, as you recall, I met the absolute love of my life. Only lasted a few days, but it was a two-hundred-twelve-degree affair. Best sex I ever had. And don't tell Justina I said that. Don't tell Homer, either."

"This guy isn't an alien, Vee, at least I don't think he is. And I know he's not affiliated with any religious movements, because he doesn't give a damn about that stuff. He's not a spiritual charlatan or Svengali either."

"I kinda like Svengalis. Remember Mola Ram from *The Temple of*

Doom? That guy was sick."

"Okay, then he is a Svengali… and he wants to meet you."

"Wait, what? Why does he want to meet *me?*"

Just then, Manon walked by my office and waved two fingers, her signal to meet in her office in a couple of minutes. I gave her the thumbs up and started rustling some papers like I was speaking with a client.

"I have to get off in a sec, Vee," I said, "but he says that the three of us have some sort of global mission to complete and that we have to start now."

"Definitely a nutcase. You are, too, Rog, but you're my adorable nut job." I could hear her zipping compartments closed on the fancy backpack I got her for her birthday in March. It cost a bundle, but it was worth it—it was built for abuse, made Vee happy, and she used it every day.

"Look, you'll see what I'm talking about when you meet him. He's definitely out there, but he's about as sane a person as I've ever met."

"So, you set up something with him already?" She had put the phone on speaker, probably to throw her coat on or pour water for Homer, and her voice sounded hollow and echoey.

"He sort of arranged it. For Friday night at nine."

"Oh, Rog, I don't think I'm up for meeting your jolly Svengali just now, really. Besides I'm pretty sure Justina and I have plans for Friday night." I could hear her leaving the apartment, keying the bolts on the four locks we'd installed on our industrial front door. "You go by yourself, tell him I say hello and that maybe I can help him change the world after I finish this pitch."

She was lying about Justina. "Uh, excuse me… Justina told me she was leaving for D.C. on Thursday morning for a symposium on prison reform and was staying the weekend to visit her roommate from college."

Vee responded in an exasperated tone. "Bitch is always blowing my cover. Okay, I'll go but I'm only staying an hour—that's sixty minutes and not a second longer. I mean it, Rog, I'll be watching the clock." I heard her footfalls on the sidewalk and her breath quicken. She was walking uphill to the York Street subway station. "So where are we supposed to meet him?"

"At the corner of Bedford and Commerce."

"Sure, of course, a nabe where he knows we won't get pissed when he ghosts us," she said.

"What are you talking about?"

"He's going to blow us off, Rog, it's so obvious. And he figures at least we'll find a good bar in that neighborhood. It's queer central over there. You've probably already told him mine's a girl's world."

"I didn't tell him anything about you, Vee. Besides, I don't have to, because he knows everything already. He reads your mind."

Manon peaked through my front window again and pointed to her watch. I mouthed "PARIS" and held up my index finger to indicate one minute. She smiled and turned away. Manon was cool.

I heard Vee stifling a laugh on the other end of the phone.

"What?" I said, and as soon as I did I regretted it.

"Dude, this reminds me of the time we did mushrooms in Ricky Saunder's backyard and you got super paranoid and thought his pool was the ocean."

"Yes, Vee, I know, you bring up this story like every other month."

"And you dove in with all your clothes on because you said there was a talking horseshoe crab in the deep end, and it was trying to send you a message."

"Verilee, this is getting so old."

She was chuckling out loud now. "And when you came up, you were holding the robotic pool vacuum."

"Yup, that's what I did."

"And you said it had spoken to you in… oh, I always forget."

"In Chibcha," I reminded her for the hundredth time.

"Chibcha, right, right, the ancient Incan language." She had told this story for more than a decade and it still made her crack up.

"No, not Incan, Muiscan," I corrected her. "It was the ancient language of the Muiscan people."

"Whatever. Anyway, you kept saying the 'horseshoe crab,' aka the pool vacuum, gave you the coordinates for the Lost City of Eldorado and that we all needed to go down to Peru and dig up its hidden gold… the vacuum told you that!"

Now she was howling with that same hyena laugh that would send Homer diving under the couch in the Brooklyn apartment. When Vee slipped into one of these fits, the sound came from some high-decibel dimension that barely sounded human. Her cackle could smash the bombproof glass at the World Trade Tower.

"Are you done?" I asked.

"… you sound the same way now!" She was gasping for air.

It took her a half minute to settle down before I could speak. "These experiences I'm having are not drug induced, Vee. And this guy is real, solid flesh and blood, not a ghost or a delusion—at least not totally anyway. And what he's been showing and telling me about dimensions beyond this one is going to blow your mind."

I knew, despite her resistance, that this was the kind of enticement that Vee would get off on. Ever since we were kids, she would say that while her home was hell, she knew there was another place that wasn't hell, and she was somehow going to get there in this lifetime. I told her I was determined to find that place with her, one where I could live free of angst and apprehension.

But I still found myself wondering if I *could* share my recent experiences with her. Would my Clees visits become her new Chibcha story? Would she believe any of it?

Did I?

This thought triggered a new wave of anxiety, but I kept talking. "Anyway, I just called to say that if there is any change in your schedule, can we please get together earlier than five-thirty?"

"Yeah, you asked me that already," she'd calmed down. "Look, I'll get in at ten, talk to Massoud, see if there are any IEDs hidden in the roadsides, and call you to confirm by one, no later. That work?"

"Sure," I said, "Thanks, Vee."

"I'm ducking into the subway." Then she disconnected.

CHAPTER NINE

It was a strange morning and equally unsettled afternoon. Manon and I had our daily briefing, then I went back to my office and daydreamed, my mind turning over and over about my trip to deep space and, before that, the Borderland. Vee called just before 1:00 and confirmed for 5:30. She said she was kicking butt on her project and might even get out a few minutes early.

The rest of the day crawled by. I don't think I got anything done that was worthwhile, and I remember the hours passed so damn slowly I wished I'd had Clees' ability to effortlessly collapse time. At 4:30, I couldn't sit any longer, left the office without saying anything to anyone, and walked down to Chelsea Market well before Vee was due to arrive. I puttered around a bookstore and sat on a stone bench staring at a pipe-fed indoor waterfall for a few minutes. I was eyeballing some coconut-topped madeleines in a pastry shop when I saw Vee walking towards me from the 9th Avenue entrance.

"Hey, why the long face, horse breath?" she said, as we exchanged a brief side hug.

"I'm good, just have a lot on my mind."

We walked together to the café at the far end of the food court. At this time of day there were several booths open in the back, so I chose one, stripped off my shoulder bag and sat down.

Vee slid in across from me and looked animated and happy. "Almost finished it," she said.

"The pitch?" I responded distractedly.

"The creative concepts, the digital tactics, all of it," she said. "It was like the design gods reached into my brain and injected epinephrine directly into my right hemisphere."

"Sounds awesome," I said, but with little enthusiasm.

"Yeah, and when I presented the linchpin concept to Massoud over lunch, I thought he was going to spit-take his lentil salad, he was so blown away." Vee had a way of referring to various ethnic groups in terms that could sound stereotypical, but it really wasn't malicious. While her humor was often irreverent, it wasn't bigoted. In fact, while she was never syrupy sweet with people, she was very tolerant of every culture and character. It was one of the reasons I was so fond of her.

"Well, you're the best, that's why Massoud always hires you for the big projects," I said, looking around for the waiter.

Vee started waving her hand in front of my face, a half-dozen silver bangles on her right wrist jangling as she did. "Yo, Rog, where are you, dude?"

"Sorry, Vee, it's just been the strangest day ever," I said.

"You're not the only one," she responded, laughing with nervous energy. "If I told you what happened when I ran down to get lunch, you wouldn't believe it."

It was the way she said it, her voice lacking its usual swagger and certainty, that made me instantly curious. A faint electrical charge coursed through my body.

"What happened?" I said.

The waiter came over just then and we both ordered—Vee, an iced tea and a pulled pork sandwich, me the portobello mushroom wrap with a ginger beer. The waiter thanked us and walked away.

"What happened at lunch?" I asked again and this time she had my full attention.

"So, I'm waiting to cross Madison at the corner of Forty-Fifth Street, and you know how Con Ed sets up those big, orange and white stove pipes, the Cat-in-the-Hats, to vent steam from below the street?" She was becoming more animated as she went on. "Well, I'm looking up at this thick white plume and suddenly I see a guy standing in the steam. I didn't see him super clearly because of the mist, but he wasn't a utility worker, and he wasn't getting singed—he was just kind of floating up there."

"No… it can't be," I responded, as I started fidgeting in my seat.

"Wait, that's not even the craziest part," Vee said excitedly. "I'm just standing there staring up at him and I realize nothing else on the street is moving, everything's frozen. The people waiting next to me at the corner, the cars, the buses… everything except that steam was stock-still. And I couldn't hear anything, Rog, no noise. Midtown Manhattan at lunch hour—the loudest place in the western freakin' hemisphere—but there's total silence. It was whacked."

"The guy, describe him to me," I said.

"No, you're not getting it… there wasn't anything special about the guy, he was just a mirage. The whole thing must have been a bizarre brain belch or something," she said.

"What did he do, Vee?" I said it with more intensity. "Tell me what he did next."

Her face changed when she heard my tone. "Why do you think he did anything next?"

"I think this is my guy, Vee," I said, as my brain seemed to click into a higher gear. "I think you saw the same avatar shaman guy I've been trying to tell you about. What did he do next?"

"I'm not sure, it was quick, maybe only ten or fifteen seconds."

"What did he do?!" I was getting worked up.

"Well, he never raised his arms or anything, but all of a sudden this projectile thing came flying out of the steam cloud towards me. I was so startled I didn't have time to react. It stopped dead about two inches from my forehead and just… hovered there."

"What did it look like?" I asked with urgency.

"The projectile? Kind of arrow-like, I guess," she responded. "I don't know, I didn't study it."

"Did you see the whole arrow or just the tip, you know, the arrowhead part?"

"I guess just the metal tip," she said. "I hadn't seen one like that before. It had three sides, not two. And it was a silver gray-color, but sort of bluish, too."

"Did it have writing on it?"

"Rog, what's with the twenty questions? I'm telling you it was all just a hyper real hallucination or something."

"It was *not* an hallucination, Vee," I responded. "Not exactly anyway. Did you see if the arrowhead had any writing etched into it?"

"I don't think so. I went to grab it and suddenly everything came back to normal. The noise, the traffic, the people jostling to get across the street," she said. "The arrow disappeared and so did the apparition in the steam."

"What then?"

"I don't know… it took me a few seconds to recover, I guess. Honestly, it was so strange and happened so fast I just assumed it was some kind of crazy peyote flashback. I certainly ate enough of that stuff with those derelict mushroom caps I called 'friends' back at Parsons. Besides, I've had vivid flashbacks before. Anyway, I picked up the salads, went back to Massoud's office and got absorbed in the pitch again. The whole street episode was freaky, sure, but it didn't bug me out all day like it's doing to you now."

I grabbed my shoulder bag off the bench, lifted it into my lap, and fished around in the side pocket. I pulled out the arrowhead and held it up a few inches from her face, the tip pointed directly at the bridge of her nose.

"Did your arrowhead look anything like this?" I asked.

She pulled her head back, reached up tentatively and took the weathered bolt from my hand.

"Yeah, exactly like this," she said. "Where did you get it?"

"It's a long story."

The waiter arrived with our food and while he put the plates down, Vee was turning the heavy chunk of metal over in her hands, running her index finger along the blades, studying the shaft. As soon as the waiter walked away, she said, "He gave this to you?"

"Sort of… I know it came from him anyway."

"ESTIA," she said, tracing her finger across the engraved letters. "Do you know what it means?"

"It's Greek for *focus*," I said.

"Is your guy Greek?" she asked.

"He was once. I guess he still is."

"What the hell, Roger? An old Greek arrowhead? I didn't even know the Greek's used arrows."

"They had archers, so I assume they had arrows. We'll find out for sure on Friday, because he asked me to bring it," I said. "And you have to be there with me."

"Roger, is this some sort of macho war games thing?" she asked, placing the arrowhead back on the table in front of me. "Because, you know, I'm not into that crap."

"Yeah, well, I'm not either," I said. "All I know is that every time I see this guy, he chips away at the plaque growing around my imagination. He completely blows my mind. It's *Fantasia* on steroids."

"*Fantasia*? I love that movie. I'll bet we watched it fifty times together as kids."

"And you snuck in a dozen more viewings that faded in a cloud of hemp smoke," I said.

"Amen to that," she responded, chuckling and seeming more relaxed. I thought it was a good time to tell her something I thought could raise her hackles.

"You're going to really like this guy, Vee, I'm sure of it."

"He better impress me in an hour, Rog, because that's all he's got. I told you, sixty minutes and I'm outta there."

"Right, I understand," I hesitated a moment, "there is one thing I should probably mention."

She must have picked up on my tension because her body stiffened along with mine.

"I'm listening," she said.

"Well, he sort of knows everything… or he seems to know everything about everybody."

"Yeah, you mentioned that—he reads minds, you said."

"Yeah, that. But he also knows about your life, like… everything about your life. He knew that I haven't had a serious relationship in almost two years. He knew about the stuff I like to read, and that I canceled my Netflix subscription to make myself read more."

"You canceled your Netflix subscription?"

"That's not the point. What I'm saying is that he doesn't just give you the generic fortune teller stuff, 'you're about to come into a large sum of money.' He knows specific things, too, all the little details about your life… along with the big things."

She said nothing, just waited for me to continue.

I hesitated, then spoke looking down into the dregs of my ginger beer. "What I mean is, he seems to know about *your* childhood, that it was tough and all."

She went rigid and leaned in slightly. "He says one word to me about it and I walk."

"He probably isn't going to say anything, Vee, but I just thought I should mention it."

She wasn't done. "If you think I'm going to have a conversation about my happy home with some… *sham-man* you pulled out of your goofball woo-woo wish list, Roger, you're warped."

She was tapping the table with her finger, the bangles slapping hard against the wooden surface. "I buried that life, it's dead to me, you understand. If this guy wants to play amateur shrink, you can be his pop-psych punching bag, not me."

"I'm on your side, Vee, really I am. He says one word about it, I walk with you."

"I know what you think, Rog, you think that I've stuffed it all. You think I put it under my dumping rug."

"Under your what?"

"You know, you read that book once about people who shove all their emotional stuff under their inner mind rugs. You think that's what I do, you think I'm in denial, that I'm too scared to face it."

I suddenly remembered what she was referring to and thought it was fascinating that she'd held onto a casual reference I'd made long ago and had practically forgotten. It wasn't a book, it was an article written by a psychologist who believed that we can't heal and evolve personally before examining our old psychological wounds—an idea shared by many serious traditions of self-knowledge and discovery.

The author used the metaphor of a living room rug in our internal houses; as we go through life, people suffer emotional trauma that is deeply painful and grievous, sometimes nearly impossible to look at, so we sweep the hurts under the rug to keep them hidden.

Over time, these emotional dustballs grow larger, and by the time we reach our 30's and 40's, we're unconsciously stumbling all over them. They unknowingly trip us up, impede our progress, interfere with our ability to form attachments to *anything*—people, jobs, our communities—until every relationship in our lives becomes soiled and infected. And, still, we expend an enormous amount of energy, every day, to keep this inner debris covered up and out of sight.

The author's theory was that eventually it becomes so problematic that a decision has to be made—either clean our inner houses of this emotional detritus or let it pile up under the rug until we can't move anymore. The longer it stays buried, the more it stinks up the house and taints everything—inevitably leading to serial emotional crises and lives of emptiness, anxiety, depression, even physical illness.

Some people will choose to pull the rug back and face their fears and self-limiting expectations, this psychologist wrote, usually through psychotherapy, a spiritual practice, a psychedelic experience, or some other kind of self-investigative approach. But it can be a perilous journey, never easy, and terrifying for many. Even if the hard choice of self-examination is made, the outcome is uncertain.

Many people who begin to explore their emotional debris discover that it has been rotting under the rug for years, that it's fairly toxic, and that their inner houses appear to get dirtier at first, before they get cleaner. They conclude that their lives had the appearance of more order and manageability *before* the self-assessment and clean-up effort began, so they metaphorically drop the rug back in place and try to forget that they ever looked under there.

This psychologist's conclusion was that if a person can stick it out till the end, with a heroic commitment of time and energy, true healing can take place. Our inner houses can be largely purged of the toxic clutter that thrives under the rug and seeps into the floorboards. Release from the emotional muck, along with increased energy and creativity, are just some of the rewards for persevering. A greater sense of freedom, the personal power derived from self-actualization, and the ability to more fully focus on one's own potential and purpose are also possible.

The author even suggested that without the emotional static and enervating internal clutter, some people can come into contact with unseen forces beyond the physical—mysterious helping hands that they previously had no idea existed.

"I'm right then, aren't I?" Vee sounded angry. And loud. The waiter glanced over from his serving station and a woman put down her e-reader a few booths away and shot us a look.

"You already know what I believe, Vee," I said, keeping my own voice low. "You have every right to your privacy. I have never pushed you about your past and I've never accused you of running away from it."

"But you think I have, right? Don't lie to me." I was quickly wishing I hadn't said anything about Empedocles or his peek into her past.

"Vee, please, come Friday for one hour. If he messes with you, we both leave, and I will never mention him again. I promise."

She stared hard at me, and I could see that she was on the fence about coming. I kept my mouth shut.

"I'm gonna try to get a few more hours in on this pitch," she said, getting up and reaching into her pocket for a wad of bills. "I'll swing by your place at eight-thirty on Friday. If I'm not there, go without me." She tossed two tens onto the table and turned away. I stretched for her arm, but she had already moved quickly towards the exit before I could think what more to say.

Now, I just had to wait—there was nothing more I could do to try to convince her. Vee would either show up on Friday when she said she would or Clees would have to find another way to reach her. He had cast the city into a state of suspended animation and shot a dart at her face to get her attention. If that wasn't enough, there was little in my feeble arsenal that could alter Vee's resolve.

I reached over and finished her iced tea.

CHAPTER TEN

In the forty-eight hours after Vee stomped out of the Chelsea Market, I tried with limited success again to concentrate on my work. When I wasn't at the office, I had the arrowhead in my hand almost constantly, turning it over, hefting it, tossing it to feel its weight, rubbing my fingers over the inscription again and again.

I bought a cheap magnifying glass at a corner stationery store and spent a good part of Thursday night going over every square millimeter of the object, looking for microscopic markings I may have missed, pocks or abrasions in the worn metal, anything that might offer a clue to its origins or how it had been used.

I tried to remember the name that Clees had given it right before I vanished from the asteroid, but the word was unfamiliar, and I couldn't recapture it. I had already done a search for "arrowheads," "spearheads," "ancient Greek archery," and "Hellenic weaponry," but I had come up empty. It didn't appear, however, that archers played a significant role in Greek warfare. I concluded that this talisman was going to remain a mystery until I saw Clees again on Friday night. Which had come at last.

I hadn't called or texted Vee, and she hadn't contacted me either. So as 8:30 approached, I was doubtful that she was going to show. But five minutes before our designated meeting time, the street door buzzer rang, and I released a swallow of breath I didn't know I was holding. I rushed over to the wall box to let her in and saw her scowling face in the security monitor. She was there, but she wasn't going to make this easy.

"Come on up," I said into the intercom, but she didn't move.

"You come down," she said, "I need to walk and talk."

Walk and talk. Since we were teenagers, whenever Vee was agitated, angry or confused, she would say, "I need to walk and talk." We'd stroll slowly around the half mile residential loop near our homes, around and around for what sometimes seemed like hours, until Vee got whatever it was off her chest and the walking meditation settled her nerves.

I came to believe that these circumnavigations of our Scotch Plains neighborhood were another necessary ritual that helped Vee survive her childhood. With these repetitive steps she was carving her own personal mandala into the pavement, inscribing a circular path that could bring her back to a semblance of sanity and calm.

One night when we'd first moved to Brooklyn, Vee and I were talking about these reparative walks, and I said that Scotch Plains should re-name that circular drive *Verilee's Loop*. She got a kick out of that.

"I'll be down in two minutes," I said into the wall box, then grabbed my wallet, cell phone, and the heavy arrowhead that I'd wrapped tightly in a paper towel and secured with a rubber band. I dropped it into a car-go pocket of my pants, snapped the pocket securely closed and slipped out the door.

Vee was standing by the curb when I stepped outside and didn't turn around, although she certainly heard the door open and close. Someone had tried to jimmy open the lock on the building's heavy glass and metal entrance a few weeks earlier and it was never fixed properly. The only way to get it to close and stay locked was to force it with a firm tug, an effort that always caused a loud metal-on-metal scraping sound that I was sure must be driving the ground floor tenants crazy.

"Hey Vee," I called down from the top step of my front stoop.

"Hey," she said, glancing up at me, then turning back to watch the pedestrians and a few cars passing by on Grove Street. I descended the stairs, walked a few steps and stood next to her. Neither of us spoke for a few beats. Then she turned to me. "Can we walk to Seventh, maybe come back on Barrow? I like that street," she said.

"Sure, Barrow's good," I answered, and we started to walk slowly, side-by-side, heading east.

"I'm sorry I got so worked up on Wednesday," she said, not looking at me.

"I understand," I said, "no need to apologize."

"It's true that you haven't pushed me about my past and that you've respected my boundaries," she said. "It was bad in that house, Rog, I mean ugly, shameful, disgusting bad. And I made a decision when I left that I was nailing the box shut." We had to walk single file past a gutted brownstone under renovation that had stacks of black garbage bags out front. Then we came shoulder-to-shoulder again.

"I get it, Vee, really. And I meant what I said the other day—if you feel pushed tonight, just walk away, and I'll walk with you."

"Okay, cool," she said, as she slowed her pace, then cleared her throat. "There's something else… it's hard for me."

"Let me guess," I replied. "I owe you big time for agreeing to come tonight."

"No, that's not it. Well, yeah, that's true, you do owe me, but that's not what I wanted to say," she continued, eyes averted. "I… uh… wanted to tell you how much I… um… appreciate you."

"Thanks Vee. I feel the same, you know that. You're the best."

I'd barely gotten my words out when in one smooth gesture she turned, reached up, and threw her arms around my neck, squeezing hard. The hug came so abruptly I was thrown off balance and nearly fell into a tree pit behind me. I curled my arms around her and hugged back, as much to steady myself as to return the gesture.

You have to understand, as long as I've known Vee, and as much as I adore her, she didn't express herself this way. She just wasn't one for public displays of affection—or private ones for that matter. And I learned early on that physical contact wasn't her go-to method for expressing intimacy, at least not with me. So I barely initiated hugs or even casual cheek pecks with her. I often wondered how Vee engaged sexually in her early pick-up encounters or in her current relationship with Justina. I never asked.

She held me for a moment longer, then spoke something quietly into my ear. But her lips were so close, the words were muffled.

"Sorry?" I said.

She pulled back an inch, but not enough that I could see her eyes or face. "L-word. I just used the L-word, that's how I feel about you."

Vee and I had agreed long ago that love, the "L-word," was dumb, that it was used so casually and superficially, so overused and misused, often in manipulative and disingenuous ways, that it had come to mean nothing. She'd express an approximation of the sentiment on birthday cards and on the little tags stuck to Christmas gifts, but always framed in some sort of crude joke or she spelled the word with a *u* instead of an *o*, with no *e* at the end.

I knew that admitting she loved me in that moment was major for her, so much so that it was actually unsettling for me to hear.

"You've been an amazing friend," she continued, "and I know that I wouldn't be standing here if it weren't for you."

I tried to put some breathing room between us so I could look at her, but she had a tight lock on my neck, and I knew I wouldn't be able to break her grip. Vee was deceptively strong, and this embrace would end when she decided it was over.

"You're an incredible friend, too, my go-to emotional anchor," I replied. "Whenever I'm freaking out, which is pretty often, you're there. And you saved me from an equal amount of trouble and tedium growing up. I love you, too, Vee. So much."

The hug lasted a split second longer, then she stepped back a foot.

"Okay, then," she said, taking a deep breath, "this meeting of the Scotch Plains Mutual Admiration Society is adjourned. Let's go find your Svengali."

She turned and started walking away, and just like that, the most emotionally expressive moment of our shared lives was over. But I will always remember that unsolicited hug in the street near my home as a turning point—as consequential and significant as any of the bizarre, fantastic, and other-wordly things that were about to happen. It was a gesture that seemed to yoke our destinies as spiritual adventurers, putting Vee and me together on a single trajectory that was as challenging and frightening as it was ecstatic and thrilling.

CHAPTER ELEVEN

As we walked to the designated rendezvous point, I wondered again what more I should tell Vee about Clees. I didn't want to give her any more specifics about the strange and surreal things I had experienced with him, because I was afraid she'd dismiss them as folly, and leave. I also didn't want to prejudice their first meeting in any way, and I assumed Clees would be more skilled than I was at managing the mercury that was Vee should she get riled. In the end, I decided that sharing as little as possible was the best approach.

"So, what does this master of manipulation look like?" she asked.

"You saw him in the steam, remember?" I answered.

"No, I didn't see him, Rog, I told you that. I saw a guy, or the outline of a guy, who didn't really have any features at all. He was Vapor Man, that's it."

"Well, he has kind of a changeable look. He's probably in his late sixties, with short, salt-and-pepper hair, but he's lean and fit and moves like he's half that age."

"Sounds like every old, gay dude in the city," she said.

"No, you can't miss this guy. He has fiery eyes, a gold color with green flecks. More feral cat than human."

"That sounds attractive," she said sarcastically, as we arrived at the northeast corner of Bedford and Commerce, as Clees had directed. It was a little before 9:00, but I wanted to get there early so there was no chance that we'd miss him.

It was a perfect late spring evening, warm with just a hint of a breeze, and this part of town always attracted tourists and evening strollers, so there were plenty of people about. As we both kept our eyes out for him, I wondered if there was a reason beyond proximity to my apartment that Clees had chosen this spot. Just west of us, fifty yards up Commerce Street, was the distinctive awning of the historic Cherry Lane Theater. It was well-known for introducing emerging playwrights and staging experimental productions, but I couldn't imagine why that would interest Clees. This block was also celebrated for its stately Greek Revival buildings, but my Hellenic friend didn't seem like the nostalgic type, so I ruled that out.

After a couple of minutes, I gave up trying to guess his intent and realized that Vee was staring at a group of five or six women across the street who were talking quietly near the entrance to a popular bar Vee knew well. Suddenly, a long-haired brunette, probably in her late 20's and seductively dressed, turned to look at us, then broke from the group and started to saunter over. As she stepped off the curb into the soft light of a Bishop Crooks streetlamp, I could see that her gaze was unmistakably fixed on Vee.

"Damn, she's coming over," I said. "You've got to get rid of her."

"You sure?" she said. "This one's pretty cute. If your alien doesn't show up, she could fill in nicely."

She was kidding. Vee was steadfastly loyal to Justina. But as I mentioned, she was also extremely attractive and every time we'd go out together this would happen—women and men of every age, ethnicity, and sexual stripe would hit on her. Vee knew the magnetic power of her physical appeal and seemed to enjoy drawing people in before snubbing them with a rejection. It wasn't her best quality. I really don't know how Justina ever penetrated Vee's prickly defenses—a testament to her lawyerly poise and patience, I guess.

"I don't think he'll approach us unless we're alone," I said softly. "Lose her or she'll screw up the whole night."

The young, long-haired woman was almost upon us, and I saw then that she was both alluring and self-confident. When she got a few feet away, I noticed her eyes.

"Hello, Metis. Good evening, Miss Verilee." The woman's feline eyes were reeling us in, but it was the rich timbre of her voice, a velvety vibration, which was most impactful. It was slightly accented and hit me like a shot of exotic cognac—warm and smooth and out of the ordinary.

Vee turned on me. "What the hell is going on, Roger? Is this a joke?"

I spoke quietly. "I'm not sure. I've never seen this woman before. This isn't Empedocles... exactly."

"Emped... who? Are you screwing with me?" Vee stepped back and stumbled at the edge of the curb, but managed to reorient herself quickly.

The woman spoke again in that sultry, almost regal voice. "Miss Verilee, I can assure you that Metis knows nothing of my physical transformation. I thought it would be useful in getting your attention, which it was, while also demonstrating that I could care less about your sexual preferences, something you were concerned about. In addition, it reinforces a point that I have been trying to make to Metis—that bodies don't matter and are completely interchangeable, that you have been male many times in past lives, and that he has been female in just as many. We are all without age, race, sex, or gender."

Vee's head was tennis balling back and forth between this female version of Clees and me.

"Wait, who's Metis?"

It was my turn to answer. "Metis is me, Vee. At least that's what he... or *she* calls me," I said, gesturing in the direction of Lady Clees. "He says we all met in another life and that Metis was my name back then."

Vee looked flustered, a rare state for her. I don't think I'd ever seen her so off balance. "What the hell, Rog, this is nuts. Who is this chick?"

"This is Empedocles... uh, I call him Clees." I was talking hurried-ly. "But... um... this is him in disguise or something. She's usually a guy."

The female Clees spoke directly to Vee. "May I suggest that we postpone further introductions or explanations, Miss Verilee? Right now, I think we should go to a quieter place to talk."

Vee had wildfire in her eyes. "Look, Claus... Closs, whatever your name is, we're not going anywhere..."

But before she could say another word, the feminine version of Clees cut her off, speaking again in that Courvoisier voice with its mesmerizing quality.

"Miss Verilee, I think you will be very interested in what I have to say and what I'm going to show you. I assure you that if you remain for another fifteen minutes, you won't be disappointed. In fact, this may be the most pivotal meeting of your heretofore very painful life."

That pissed Vee off. I knew Clees was a bit of a miracle worker, but you crossed Verilee Fulbreth at great risk to your personal safety. Even he might not have an antidote for the venom in her bite. Vee practically spit her next words.

"You don't know a goddamn thing about my life, bitch, okay. Roger told me you might pull this shit and I'm not sticking around for it. Let's go, Rog."

Lady Clees put up a manicured hand. She wasn't angry, and looked completely at ease, but the raised hand froze Vee like it was a loaded stun gun.

"Indulge me for just a few more minutes," she said. "I'd like to show you something." Then the female version of Empedocles turned and immediately began walking north along Bedford, her long dark hair glinting under the streetlights.

It was a charged moment. I didn't expect Vee to remain silent, much less to follow. But after a few seconds of hesitation, and to my astonishment, she began trailing Lady Clees at a brisk pace. It occurred to me then that Vee might be intending to assault her from behind. But after a dozen quick steps, Vee stopped suddenly, like she'd slammed into a hidden lamp post or an invisible tree trunk. She folded in half and clutched her head as I ran over.

"Vee, you alright?" I asked, reaching around her waist to steady her.

"She threw something at me, that witch," she yelled, "did you see that?" She slowly straightened up and put a hand on my shoulder to steady herself, wincing and rubbing her head.

"Threw something? She never even turned around."

"She threw something, Roger. It hit me right between the eyes. And whatever it was, it hurt," she cursed and began a faltering half-run in the direction the female Clees had gone.

"Where are you going?" I asked.

"She's not getting away with it," Vee said, and I didn't like her tone at all.

As we walked north together at a hurried pace through the intersection at Barrow Street, I tried to reason with her, the heeled summer sandals of Lady Clees clicking and clacking a hundred feet ahead of us. Then we saw the black hair disappear as she turned sharply right on Grove Street and I wondered if she might be headed towards my apartment. Before we reached the corner to follow, a group of eight or ten, tipsy, college-aged kids came out of a restaurant on the corner and gathered on the sidewalk blocking our way. We had to detour into the street, and when we finally turned the corner at Grove, the attractive female version of Empedocles was gone.

"Where'd she go?" Vee asked.

"*She* is now a *he*," I replied.

Leaning against the wall of an Art Deco apartment building about forty feet ahead of us was Clees, the man—late sixties, thin, curly graying hair, short beard. He was wearing a pink, tie-dyed T-shirt, lime green pants with rips at the knees, and well-worn desert boots—the perfect caricature of a vintage West Village hippie.

Vee's mouth dropped open. She was clearly unprepared for Clees' quick change act, but even this stunning transformation could not quell her fires. She moved quickly to where he was propped casually against the beige brick wall and pointed a finger at his nose.

"Look, dude, your amateur smoke and mirror tricks might impress Roger, but you're just a fraud as far as I'm concerned," Vee shouted, apparently readying for a fist fight. "And what was that back there, what did you throw at me?"

Clees never changed position or moved a muscle, but he appraised Vee with a look that, despite the circumstances, I can only describe as adoring.

"I threw nothing at you, Miss Verilee," he said, in the soothing male voice that I recognized. "I believe you were hit by a bolt of recognition, a distant memory, if you will. And lucky for me, it came when it did."

"Don't pull that on me," Vee barked, moving another half-step closer to Clees. "You clocked me with something in the forehead back there. No one does that to me and gets away with it."

I stepped over and put my arm between them. I knew Clees wouldn't strike Vee, but I couldn't say the same for her.

"Vee, I don't think you were hit, really," I said, "but, either way, can we take it down a few notches?"

She wheeled on me. "Shut up, Roger, this is between me and Clueless."

"Clees," I corrected. "Look, there's a café on Perry Street that should have a quiet table at this time of night. Let's talk this out over there."

As I started to move, with Vee still glaring at Clees, he smiled reassuringly and said, "I have a better idea."

Then he slid past Vee and took a few steps farther east along the building's outer wall. He walked directly to a four-inch gap where the light bricks of the Deco building approached the darker bricks of an adjacent Tudor residence and, without hesitation, turned abruptly into the seam and vanished.

Vee's face turned ashen. As I reached the point where he had slipped through the narrow gap in the masonry, I saw a shaft of faint light coming from the far end of the deep aperture. I felt a flush of fear and hesitated at first. Then, with a sudden, "what-the-hell" impulse, I grabbed Vee's hand and without waiting for her to react or resist I dove headfirst into the crevice where Clees had evaporated.

CHAPTER TWELVE

We landed awkwardly and stumbled a few steps along a wood-chip-lined path. It ran parallel to the banks of a stream that was six or seven feet deep and about twenty-five feet wide. It was daytime, a cloudless blue sky overhead, the temperature so ideal I could barely feel the shifting air against my skin.

Upstream, one-hundred feet away, Clees was sitting on the edge of a small wooden footbridge, boots off, his electric green pants rolled up to mid-calf and his feet dangling into the water. There were large trees on the far side of the bridge where the pathway continued and disappeared into a dense conifer forest.

"Not the West Village," I said, my voice trembling.

Vee said nothing and I turned to look at her. She was squinting in Clees' direction, her face pale and expressionless. Despite a noticeable wobble in my own knees, I took her arm to urge her forward. But she was rooted to the ground.

"How is this possible?" she asked.

"It's crazy, I know, that's what I've been trying to tell you. It's been like this from the moment I met him—totally unreal and totally amazing at the same time. Little scary, too."

"So, he made this happen?" she asked, still studying him on the bridge.

I thought for a moment, then answered. "He'll say we did it, that we temporarily forgot how to manipulate our illusory environment, but now that we're remembering, we aren't powerless anymore, that we made it happen. But, yeah, he did it."

Her combative tone of a few moments earlier had disappeared, and her confidence seemed shaken. I knew what was going on—I had experienced what these instantaneous, stomach-wrenching dimensional shifts in Clees' presence could do to a person, too.

"I'm not sure I can handle this," she said, looking pensively behind her, apparently trying to locate the crack in the wall in case she needed to make a hasty exit.

"Come on," I said, and held her hand as we started walking slowly towards Clees, side-by-side on the narrow path. He was staring down into the water and didn't look up. The sleepy branches of a large willow on the far side of the bridge trailed over the stream, its tips kissing the surface of the water, creating puckered creases and wakes.

Clees didn't seem to notice us until we were twenty feet away. As we reached the wooden planks of the gently arched bridge, we stopped, and he spoke to us without lifting his eyes.

"Metis to *my left*, Miss Verilee to *my right*, please. And you might want to slip off your shoes and pull up your pant legs. The water is delightful."

I started to move forward but Vee tugged firmly at my arm. She had a clenched, snarly look on her face that I was very familiar with, one that always signaled anger or resentment at being told what to do. The first time I saw it we were about ten years old. My mother had brought us to an ice cream shop famous for its exotic flavors in a town called Westfield, near our home. We'd gone there mostly because Vee loved ice cream and my mother was good at reading when she needed a special treat.

As Vee peered excitedly into the frosty glass case filled with tubs of colorful, creamy blends, the guy behind the counter nonchalantly said to her, "Get the mango, honey, you'll love it. I'm going to set you up with a double scoop in a sugar cone." The counter man was just being friendly, and mango was one of her favorite flavors, so no problem there. He wasn't even being insistent, just playfully engaging with her.

But she looked at him with that tense, squinched, facial expression and said sharply, "Lychee Nut. One scoop. In a cup."

There was no reason for her to oppose him except to be contrary. The ice cream guy didn't care, he was making his buck fifty a scoop either way. She just couldn't stand being told what to do—even when it was only about flavored frozen milk.

Back on the bridge, she whispered into my ear. "*You* sit on his right, *I'll* sit on his left."

Instead, I stood there paralyzed. While I assumed Clees had a reason for asking us to settle where he wanted, I knew Vee would start a row if I didn't do what she said. That's when Clees looked up and stared directly at her. Had he heard her? He didn't look angry or ruffled, but I felt anxious anyway. She was still irritated about the perceived forehead strike, and I knew Vee would snap if he challenged her again. I wasn't sure I wanted to see Clees upset either, even if I knew nothing bad would happen—as I've said before, I'd never seen him so much as raise his voice a few decibels.

When Clees opened his mouth next, I understood immediately that he had planned his first comment to elicit exactly this reaction and resistance from Vee, and that he was already half a dozen chess moves ahead of her.

"Miss Verilee, your home was not a nice place to grow up in, was it?"

It was hard for me to believe he was pursuing this line of inquiry. Vee seemed surprised, too—I don't think anyone had ever challenged her with such persistence, equanimity, and kindness before, and her face changed from her signature look of irritation to one of confusion.

"In fact, it was a rather miserable place for a curious, creative, and sensitive girl to spend her first sixteen years," he continued.

She struggled to answer and while her tone was recalcitrant, it had lost most of the hostility it had on Commerce Street. "It wasn't a Disney childhood, if that's what you mean."

"Ugh… Disney again." He said it under his breath, shaking his head slightly, but I heard him.

Vee continued. "Look, I learned to take care of myself in the world and that's what matters." She said this with even less conviction, a quaver in her voice.

"So, *that's* what matters?" Clees spoke without derision, a tone that was empathetic and caring, and Vee picked up on this. As I said, he was so many moves ahead of her, it was as though he knew what she was going to say next, as if he'd already had this conversation with her before.

"Miss Verilee, I wouldn't ask you to do anything without a reason and I am not challenging your power or your free will. I have no need to demonstrate my strength or superiority, because we are precise equals. It is only the illusion of time and space that separates the expression of our talents, abilities and knowings. Everything that I do is to help you awaken, so that we can help other Worldborns to do the same—something they very much want to do whether they are fully conscious of it or not."

Vee hesitated and seemed unsure of herself, not something I'd witnessed often, yet she tried again to parry his invitation. "I've heard that 'everything I do is to help you' crap before. It doesn't ring true for me, okay? I don't trust it and I don't trust you, even if Roger says I can. That's what's kept me alive until now, so I'll just keep doing it my way."

Clees turned his head slowly back towards the water. "Your tolerance for pain may be high, Miss Verilee, but it is not without limits. In any case, if you want to sit on my left, with Metis to my right, you are free to do that. I won't stop you. But my request has nothing to do with my personal preference or need to dominate you, and everything to do with principles of energy transfer that neither of you can understand at the moment. I can assure you, however, that the intensity of what I want to share with you, and the benefit it will bring to you, will be markedly richer if you sit where I suggest."

Vee glanced at me. I saw fear in her eyes, yet another look that was unfamiliar. One of the reasons I liked her so much was that she always seemed to be fearless, even ferocious, at times when I thought I'd pee in my pants. She made me feel braver than I often do. As I continued to look at her, trying to process this version of Vee that had no precedent, she did something that was also so rare for her, I realized that I'd never seen it before—she started to cry. And as she did, my throat tightened, and my own eyes welled up with tears.

Clees saw this and extended his right arm in a mid-air half hug, beckoning her with a tilt of his head and a flick of his fingers to fill the empty space that he'd just created. Her tears flowed soundlessly, but more intensely, and she covered her eyes with both hands, but for only a moment. Then, without further hesitation, she moved towards him and sat down on his right. *On his right*, just as he had asked. He put his arm over her shoulder and pulled her closer as her sobs deepened and her shoulders began to rise and fall.

What was happening to my Vee?

I waited a moment, then moved over to Clees' left, stopped to remove my socks and sneakers, laid them on the plank boards, then reached down to cuff my pants, watching Vee the entire time. I wanted to reach out to her, too, hug her reassuringly along with Clees, but he seemed to be rocking her slightly and I didn't want to interfere with these palliative motions.

I let my feet dangle over the bridge as he did, but they barely touched the water. Vee left her motorcycle boots on. Clees might have gotten some seating cooperation from her and even put a chink in her emotional armor, but those heavy black boots were staying on. I knew that and apparently so did he, because he didn't press the point and started talking as soon as I'd found a comfortable position. Vee was still cupped against his side.

"You have it?" Clees looked at me.

"The arrowhead?" I responded and reached into my cargo pocket. "Right here."

I unwrapped it from the paper towel as he extended his left hand. He slowly let go of Vee who was wiping tears from her cheeks and sniffling. I started dabbing tears from my eyes, too, using the paper towel.

"This is called a *kila*," Clees said, addressing us both, "a silver-blue, three-bladed arrowhead. Sometimes called a phurba. It was carried for centuries, over the course of eight successive lifetimes, by a Tibetan sorcerer and mystic by the name of Calabris."

"Tibetan, not Greek," I said. "That explains why my Hellenic arrowhead searches came up empty."

"The inscription on the shaft is Greek. The kila itself comes from Tibet," Clees said. "But it's made of a material that is best described as… mental matter."

He paused and shifted his head slowly back and forth between us, studying our faces. Then he continued. "The kila was symbolic of Calabris' considerable powers, and everyone who came into contact with him knew instantly when they saw it that this man was beyond human, an all-aware who did not live by the world's physical laws and was completely beyond its control."

Clees held the silvery bolt higher until the sun glinted off the engraving on its side.

"ESTIA, as Metis has certainly discovered by now, means *focus* in Ancient Greek. Calabris had the word engraved into the shaft before he gave this kila to me as a token of trust."

"You traveled to Tibet to see him?" I asked.

"No. Calabris came to Acragas." Clees turned to Vee. "Acragas, Miss Verilee, was a Greek city located in what is now Sicily. I lived there as Empedocles more than two-and-a-half millennia ago."

"Tibet is halfway around the globe from Greece," I said, scanning a mental map in my head. "A hell of a journey back then, even on horseback, and over some really forbidding terrain. That must have taken him months."

"Calabris did not travel by foot or by horse," Clees said.

"What, then, boat?" I asked. "Was it even possible to circumnavigate Asia and Africa in ships of that period?"

"Maybe he flew," Vee said under her breath. We both turned to look at her.

"Yeah, on Tibet Airlines," I said smiling, happy to see Vee returning to her wisecracking ways. "And he got free yak butter on his barley biscuits in first class."

"It wasn't flying exactly," Clees said, ignoring my quip and speaking mostly to Vee. "It was more like… materializing. Calabris could go anywhere he wanted, in an instant, just by thinking of a place." Then he turned to me. "Sound familiar, Metis?"

I remembered our intergalactic travels by Citi Bike a few days earlier.

"As I said, Calabris was a mystic and unconfined by the laws of physics that most Worldborns consider so immutable," Clees continued. "He came to Greece so we could combine our energies and construct a unified plan that would focus all of our power on one shared goal—to make the leap beyond this illusion. You were there, too, Metis, working together with us on this plan."

My mind was trying to digest and integrate all that Clees was sharing. Vee was looking at him, too, appraising him closely. She appeared to be working as hard as I was to process the torrent of information that he was delivering, but since she'd just met him, I knew she would need more time to grasp even a small part of what he was saying.

I was bubbling with questions. "So where is Calabris now, Clees? Is it possible that we'll meet him? How does…"

He touched my arm to silence me. Then he lifted the kila from his lap and extended it forward so we could see it better. "I gave this kila to you a few days ago, Metis. And it was originally a gift to me from Calabris a couple of thousand earth years before that."

Vee and I stared at him waiting for him to continue. He turned to Vee.

"I got the kila from you, Miss Verilee. You were Calabris."

CHAPTER THIRTEEN

There was silence, just the sound of the gurgling water beneath us.

I looked over at Vee and saw tears in her eyes again. Were they tears of recognition? Was she recalling her life as Calabris, the Tibetan mystic?

"Vee, you knew about this?" I asked, feeling slightly resentful. "Why didn't you share it with me before?"

Again, Clees answered for her. "Memories of Calabris are as distant for Miss Verilee in this moment as your previous lives are for you, Metis. Although I do believe something started to take shape in her unconscious awareness as she was chasing me down Bedford Street. Thoughts are potent—even long-forgotten ones—and I believe a trace of recognition stopped her in her tracks."

"It felt like you cold-cocked me," Vee said through her tears.

"Thoughts are powerful—you could even say they pack a punch. In fact, they are more than powerful, they are the only things that exist."

"But when we caught up to you, Vee stormed over and got in your face," I said. "If she had remembered being Calabris and working with you in Acragas, even if they were long ago memories, how come she acted like a charging banshee back there, oblivious to your previous relationship?"

"Miss Verilee is strong-willed and determined, even stubborn at times, as was Calabris," Clees said smiling, glancing at Vee with that look of doting admiration again. "The young Metis I trained was also imbued with an indomitable spirit and energy. Those qualities are deeply embedded in your energy fields and have been carried over lifetimes. For both of you."

"So, what happened to my indomitable spirit?" I responded. "Seems to have wilted over the last couple millennia."

"Not at all, Metis. In fact, when the time came for us to leave Greece, an exit we needed to make with some urgency, it was you and Calabris who agreed to take on the challenging assignment to follow. Executed with great success and courage, I might add. A quality which continues to thrive within both of you to this day."

"Living in New York without getting assaulted, you mean that challenge?" Vee asked, as she emerged from her restrained tone of a few minutes before.

"That wasn't your next assignment," Clees replied, "although you have mastered the big city with characteristic command and confidence."

Vee was looking at our surroundings, at the bridge, the fast-moving stream, the forest beyond, then changed the subject. "How is any of this possible? How does a pastoral place like this appear on the other side of a brick wall in downtown Manhattan?"

"Solid barriers are fictitious, Miss Verilee, as is any hindrance in your ability to pass through them. None of this pastoral beauty exists anywhere except in our collective imaginations—which are becoming aligned now once again. This is, however, a convenient meeting place, no?"

"I could have suggested a nice cafe, saved us the trouble of shimmying through cinder blocks," she replied.

"Nevertheless, managed with aplomb," Clees replied, wrapping her in his right arm again. "In any case, the three of us made a pact when we were last together in Greece, Miss Verilee. We agreed on a comprehensive plan, and we have been waiting for the right time to execute that plan. This is the right time."

"And what does the kila have to do with all this?" I asked.

"It's a prompt. A recognizable and reassuring symbol of a radical shift in human destiny that we, and many others, are working to usher in together."

"I don't get it," Vee said, speaking softly from the crook of Clees' arm. "I'm completely lost here."

"Not completely. Remember when I launched the simulacrum of the kila at you on Madison Avenue? That was an intentional bit of mirage theater to light the fuse in your subconscious. Metis showing you the actual arrowhead in the café later that day intensified the effect. It was originally yours, remember, and deeply tied to your identity as Calabris. So, when you saw it floating in front of your face, and held the kila again at the café, the wheels of your subconscious started churning, whether you were aware of it or not."

"I wasn't intending to bring the kila to the restaurant that day," I said. "Lucky I did."

"You knew exactly what you were doing on one level, Metis. There are no coincidences involved in any of this. Luck is irrelevant," Clees said.

After another few seconds, Vee reached over and took the kila from Clees' hand. She balanced it in the middle of her left palm, then closed her hand around it, careful not to drop it in the water. Clees watched her appraise the object, then spoke. "The kila is a symbol of the focus required to do many of the marvelous feats that you were able to accomplish during your life as Calabris—feats that I am certain you will do again. But it is important to remember that it is only a symbol, a reminder, and, as such, has no power in and of itself."

As I was listening to Clees I was starting to feel envious, maybe even a little competitive with Vee. Clees had come to *me* in the mews, and I had brought Vee to *him*. Now she was the one getting all the attention and it bothered me.

Clees spun quickly to look at me and smiled. "You don't need to hide those feelings, Metis. And there is nothing you should want to hide even if you could. One mind, remember? All access for everyone." He was listening in on my private thoughts again. "But let me assure you, your role is no less or greater than Miss Verilee's or my own."

"I'm okay," I said, but the words came out sulky.

"Feel free to puff up your chest a bit if you want to, Metis," Clees continued, "it was you who offered the basic outline of our future plan. You had the clearest vision of what was to be done once we reunited."

"Me?"

"Yes, and it was also you who suggested that I use the kila to shake the two of you awake, so to speak, when the time was right."

"But I don't remember ever seeing the kila before," I said. "I had no idea what it was. And I can't remember anything about my life as Metis or any sort of plan we conceived together. Vee already remembers about flying."

The mention of her name seemed to draw Vee back to the present, and she swung her head out from the cradle of Clees' arm. "Flying? No, I don't, Rog. Nothing's clear to me at all. I just have a weird feeling every time Clees mentions that Calabris dude."

"Well, the name Metis means nothing to me," I said, frustration in my voice. "Not the tiniest flutter of recognition. I feel like I'm the slow student here, dragging behind, missing out on something important."

Suddenly there was a hissing sound, then a powerful churning in the stream below us. I looked down as a long, greenish-brown tail broke the surface, whipped around crazily and sprayed the three of us with chilly stream water. Vee jumped up in one athletic burst and started cursing as the hose-like tail lashed around and sent another jet of cold water her way. Clees didn't seem surprised or disturbed at all. He just watched us both and laughed.

The tail sunk again beneath the surface of the water. I leaned over and spotted a dark silhouette a few feet below us in a shallow eddy, moving in slow, desultory circles.

"Recognize that sea monster, Metis?" Clees asked, then he immediately turned to Vee. "How about you, Miss Verilee, have you ever seen that unruly serpent before?"

Vee was unamused, wiping her face where the spray had mixed with her drying tears. I kept one eye on the circling creature ready to leap out of the way if it surfaced again.

"Yeah, I recognize it," Vee said. "It's the shit-eating son-of-a-bitch that's going to have the tread of my motorcycle boot etched into its obnoxious fish forehead if I get the chance."

For some reason, I was relieved to hear Vee vigorously swearing again. Clees just smiled at her profane outburst. "Perhaps if you refrain from threats of violence, Miss Verilee, and ask it nicely, the mischievous bottom feeder will reveal its secrets to you."

"If you have something you want to share, Clees, maybe you could just tell us, instead of dousing us with a goddamn arctic stream to make the point," she said.

He ignored her and turned to me again. "Metis, you speak a half dozen languages. Maybe you should dive down and ask it what it wants?"

"I'm with Vee on this one, Clees. How about you tell us what's going on?"

"You were talking about being a slow learner," he said, and looked down at the stream, "and that impudent water creature provided a counterpoint to your unflattering self-appraisal."

"A counterpoint? By spraying us? How?"

"Why don't you ask it?" he said. "In Chibcha."

Vee had been staring into the water and whipped her head around to look at Clees.

"Chibcha?" she said. "What does Chibcha have to do with anything?"

"Ah, so you remember your peyote-induced adventure at the poolside of Ricky Saunders?" Clees asked, smiling broadly.

"Why the hell does that matter?" Vee was getting agitated. "That was like fifteen years ago and Roger was totally baked anyway."

"I was pretty high, Clees, it's true, and just acting stupid, that's all." I could feel myself getting flushed.

"Do you recall what you heard that night, Metis?" Clees asked.

"Oh, come on, you've got to be kidding?" Vee cried out. "You're not going to tell us that a mechanical pool cleaner *spoke* to Roger?"

"Let Metis talk, Miss Verilee, he was the one who received the message."

"Message? *Deep Thoughts From A Pool Vacuum*," she snapped, "that's the great wisdom you brought us here to learn?" She placed both hands on her hips for emphasis.

"Miss Verilee, you saw me freeze traffic on Madison Avenue, metamorphose from an exotic young woman into a bearded old man, and appear to walk casually through a solid barrier to get here. Which, I might remind you, you did as well. But it's the vacuum incident that has pushed the limits of plausibility for you? Walking through walls, okay, talking to vacuums, no way?"

Vee stared down at him for a moment, then her lips quivered, and she snickered. Within seconds the snicker had turned into *the laugh that can move mountains* and even Clees seemed startled by its ear-piercing intensity—but only for a second, then he joined in. I watched them both go at it till their eruptions died to titters and Vee could speak clearly again.

"Okay, you make a decent point about plausibility," she said. "You just freaked me out bringing up that Chibcha thing. It's always been a big joke to me. Still a big joke."

"I know you enjoy retelling that story, Miss Verilee, but don't confuse amusing with meaningless. Nothing that has ever happened to you, or to anyone else, is meaningless. Nothing is random. Not even a sneeze is an accident."

I heard Clees say this kind of thing before and never quite grasped what he meant.

"Well, 'nothing' is an exaggeration, right?" Vee said, "I mean, if I stub my toe, it's just a random accident, no big deal, and I just go about my day."

Clees responded in that intense way that imbued his words with physical force, one that knocked around inside my chest. "Let me say it again so I'm clear, Miss Verilee. Every moment of your every day, even the briefest interaction and most innocuous incident have profound meaning. No moment is more important than any other and every moment, in the context of our mission, is laden with incalculable consequence and no shortage of the miraculous."

"Even Roger's eleventh-grade, drug-addled delusions?" Vee asked sarcastically. "They matter, too?"

Clees looked up at Vee standing over him, her hands back on her hips, and held her gaze firmly. She sighed audibly and started shuffling her feet on the bridge but stayed quiet.

"So, if I have the facts right," Clees continued, "the pool vacuum told Metis that he should go to the Lost City of Eldorado in Colombia and uncover the hidden gold there?"

Clees was actually validating a confounding experience that had happened to me more than a decade before and that I was mocked mercilessly about ever since. I could hardly believe my ears.

"Actually, what I heard was Peru," I corrected him, "that we should go to Peru. And there were coordinates, too, for where the gold would be hidden, where we could dig it up."

"The hallucinogenic mushrooms you ingested that night, Metis, created some static in your internal receiver, so you didn't hear the message quite right," he said. "If you had checked those coordinates, you'd have discovered that the ruins of the Lost City of Eldorado are actually in the Andean range of southwestern Colombia. And while there is no precious metal hidden there, there is buried treasure… located in the caves that surround the lost city. I believe information about the caves was included in the message you heard?"

Vee rolled her eyes and shook her head with incredulity, but said nothing.

"Yeah, I do remember something about caves, but it wasn't *caves* exactly," I said, trying to think back. Then I had it. "LAIRS… that's what I heard, lairs, not caves."

"Exactly right," Clees said enthusiastically. "The caves around the Lost City were used as human lairs—places of darkness, absolute quiet, and stillness—from where tribal priests would guide the devoted to dimensions far beyond any they could imagine."

"Oh, geez, is this leading somewhere?" Vee said, appearing agitated again, "because, if not, I think I'll go look for a gap in the bricks back there and head home." She took a few halting steps towards the wood-chipped path.

"Yes, Miss Verilee, it is leading somewhere, somewhere quite significant," Clees said firmly. "Back to another one of *your* former lives, actually. The next 'assignment' after Greece that we spoke about earlier. One in which you tried to spread a powerful teaching that would have impacted all of humankind if it had ever made it out of Colombia."

That seemed to get her attention. She hesitated, then slowly returned to Clees' side and plunked herself down on the bridge. She kept the soles of her boots on the planks, hiked her knees up against her chest, and hugged them.

"I'm listening," she said.

CHAPTER FOURTEEN

"In the early sixteenth century, you were the Zipa, the supreme leader, of the Muiscan people of Colombia," Clees said. "You were actually the last Zipa to rule before Spanish conquistadors wiped out your people through conquest and the inadvertent spread of disease."

"Zipa? Is that a Chibchan word?" I asked.

"Yes, the Muiscan people spoke Chibcha," Clees said, "but as you know, it is now an extinct language."

"I've read about the Muisca," I responded. "They were known for their sophisticated gold-working techniques. It was so advanced and so far superior to gold tooling anywhere else on the planet, European explorers who arrived in South America were astounded by its craftsmanship and quality."

"That's correct, Metis, but the Spanish occupiers who invaded the Muiscan civilizations didn't care much about their artistic metal work—they melted down most of the gold pieces they plundered anyway."

Vee was laughing quietly to herself. "Chibcha... such a funny word," she said.

"What you didn't find so funny, Miss Verilee, was the gruesome way in which you were executed in the early fifteen-hundreds," Clees said.

"Really? Do tell. Spanish sword through the heart?"

"No, you were hanged."

"Hanged? That's not so gruesome," Vee said.

"Then your body was cut into little pieces and sent to Muiscan and Incan tribes throughout Colombia, Peru and Ecuador as a message—a warning."

"Those conquistador bastards," she said, amused.

"The Spanish were after your gold, Miss Verilee, but you withheld it, believing you had something much more valuable to offer them."

"Tequila?"

"No," Clees responded, "wrong culture anyway."

"So, what did I have that was more precious than gold?"

"Incubation," Clees said. "You both knew about incubation."

"Incubation? Like what they do in hospitals with premature babies?" Vee asked.

"No, this kind of incubation was about something else entirely, Miss Verilee, a way to access answers to all questions from dimensions beyond this one through intense focusing of the senses."

"You lost me back at tequila," she responded.

"Well, you're in luck. Because as the Zipa of the Muiscans, you had an extremely enlightened priest and incubation master at your side— an old friend who also acted as your trusted counselor and confidant," Clees said smiling, then he turned to me. "Care to guess who the high priest of the Muiscas was, Metis?"

"Dude, you were my sham-man!" Vee yelled out, suddenly laughing. "No wonder you could talk to pool vacuums!"

"He could do much more than that, Miss Verilee. You both could by bringing knowledge from your previous lives to Colombia, including ours together in Greece."

"So, were you there with us in Colombia, Clees?" I asked.

"Of course he was," Vee said. "He was my personal goldsmith. Pounded my stockpile of the yellow metal into kinky handcuffs."

"You have a wonderful imagination, Miss Verilee," Clees said evenly, her ribald humor not seeming to ruffle him. "But, actually, my expertise was in gold-handled spanking rods."

She laughed her big laugh in response. Clees' quick wit matched Vee's own, and I could see that it was winning her over. She appreciated his sense of humor and his intelligence. Like I said, she would never have tolerated stupid.

"No, Metis, I was not in Colombia when you and Miss Verilee

were enlightening the Muiscas, although that would have been enjoyable. I was spreading preparatory pixie dust elsewhere during your lifetimes in South America, one that as I said, ended up being quite challenging for both of you."

Vee turned to Clees. "Okay, so let's get back to incubation and how it's going to help me get the answers to all the questions I've ever had."

Instead of launching into an explanation, Clees turned to me. "Perhaps you would like to expound, learned priest?"

"I know nothing about incubation," I said, perhaps a little testily. "Never heard of it."

"Metis, with your permission, I might be able to reactivate some neural pathways that have been dormant for a time. It should help you retrieve some of those memories."

"Uh… yeah, I guess. What do I do?"

In one fluid motion, Clees brought his legs up onto the arched bridge, shifted his body to the left to face me, and sat in a casual cross-legged position.

"You know that yoga breathing technique you use to calm yourself?" he said, placing his left hand lightly on the back of my head, the other on my chest. "Try that now."

I shut my eyes and began a slow, deep diaphragmatic breath. Clees applied gentle pressure at his fingertips, maybe his version of a recalibrating Vulcan mind-meld, and as soon as he did a slow-motion film began to tick past my closed eyelids. I was watching a Muiscan version of myself inside a dimly lit cave. I was wearing a primitive, black jaguar mask and a purple hooded cape, ornamented with small jewels. My arms were heavily tattooed in black and red inks, but I did not recognize the designs. I was holding a votive candle in one hand and a ceremonial bowl burning with smoky incense in the other.

As shadows jumped on the cave walls from the light of my candle, I moved deliberately between a dozen or so blanketed Muiscan men and women in native finery, lying motionless, flat on their backs, about ten feet apart and breathing lightly. As I approached each one, I knelt down and blew a cloud of heavy incense from the bowl over their motionless bodies.

At first, nothing happened. Then, as I continued to watch the scene from behind my inner eyelids, I observed a slightly larger, spirit image of the prone person rise up from his or her body and pass through the smokey cloud, ascend slowly, then accelerate quickly beyond the lair's ceiling. It wasn't clear to me whether the incense was facilitating the conveyance or if it just allowed me to observe the astral navigation as it happened. But I watched as each person was able to achieve this teleportation. Once their specter body was clearly visible in the smoke, the jaguar priest version of myself moved onto the next person.

After another minute of this visit to the Muiscan lair, Clees dropped his hand from the back of my head. I took a few more deep breaths and opened my eyes.

"Whoa, what a rush," I said. "Like my brain accelerated to hyper-drive."

Vee tapped Clees' shoulder and bowed her head forward. "My turn, Clees. I'll take one of those brain rush things now."

"I'm sorry, Miss Verilee, but as a lowly metal worker in your royal court, I am not permitted to touch the Zipa."

She laughed hard again. It made me happy to see Vee light up like this as she verbally jousted with Clees. He seemed to understand her in ways no one did, especially not upon first meeting her. He was tender and compassionate while also being firm and unflinching, and I think this made her feel more secure. Whatever it was, Vee appeared to be molting a layer of hard shell right there on that enigmatic bridge.

"I like the sound of all of this nutty stuff," Vee said contentedly, inhaling deeply as a light breeze came off the water and the willow branches downstream did a lively dance, dipping in and out of the fast-moving creek. What a change in Vee's demeanor. It was hard to believe that this was the same thorny woman who'd been looking for a fistfight on the streets of the West Village not minutes before.

Clees then asked me to relate what I had just seen, which I did in all the detail I could recall. After I'd finished, he shared more about incubation and how it related to our current situation.

"The incubatory tradition is ancient, dating back to the seventh century BC, where it was regularly practiced at the Temple of Apollo in Delphi," he explained. "It was not considered mystical back then, it was an entirely practical technique for divining answers to the most important questions regarding existence, reality, and consciousness. But, in those times, incubation was reserved for the wealthy and for those connected to powerful citizens of Delphi.

"I should mention that I myself was a practicing priest of Apollo. Few people are aware of this, but the inner chambers of the sanctuary at Delphi were filled with incubation lairs. Priests would go there to lie in isolation and silence for days, even weeks, journeying to far away places, communing with knowledge keepers on other planes, receiving prophetic visions. Apollo was actually referred to as the God of Lairs."

"Were you ever in the lairs at Delphi?" Vee interrupted.

"Yes, many times," Clees replied. "And I modeled the incubation lairs in Acragas on the ones in Delphi. It was in those caves below Acragas that you—as Calabris—along with Metis and others, perfected the incubation techniques that you eventually introduced to the Muiscas and Incas, and that you had hoped to teach the Spaniards."

Vee looked thoughtful. "But you said these incubator people had to lie in isolation and silence sometimes for weeks to get the guidance and truths they were after. That doesn't seem realistic for the times we live in today, Clees. I don't know anyone who can sit still or in silence for more than a couple minutes—everyone is so distracted."

I was pretty sure that Vee was raising this point for personal reasons.

He nodded. "Yes, there's been a change. A need to speed things up. Incubation training was effective, but to your point, Miss Verilee, slow. And it was reserved for the elite and privileged. That won't get the job done any longer with the immediacy or breadth that's now required."

"So, Rog isn't going to get to put on his purple cape again? No jaguar mask?" She looked over at me and snickered. Clees reached back playfully and admonished her with a soft tap on the top of her head. She winced and feigned pain. I had never seen Vee act so coquettish around a man before and it was fascinating to watch.

"Worldborns have evolved in the past twenty-six hundred years," he continued. "As a result, incubation as it was previously practiced is no longer necessary or desired. But what hasn't changed are the principles of hyper-focused attention and dedication to mind training that was necessary for incubation to occur, and that must be relearned now for a critical mass to be reached."

"Whoa, go slow here," Vee said. "I want to understand this." Clees smiled at her, then turned to me to make sure I was also listening.

"As you saw for yourself, Metis, during a Muiscan incubation ritual the men and women of the Zipa's inner circle attempted to use *all of their physical senses simultaneously,* with a kind of hyper intense awareness, to transcend this illusory world."

"What do you mean by using all the senses at once?" Vee asked.

"Miss Verilee, the idea of coordinating all the senses simultaneously is not as foreign as you might think. In fact, you have a familiar expression for it."

"We do? What?"

"*Common sense.*"

She smiled at his naivete. "That doesn't mean using all your senses at once, Clees. It just means paying attention to what the hell you're doing and not being a brain-dead idiot."

He swung his legs effortlessly over the side of the bridge again to better face her, while extending his toes to touch the water. He churned them briefly in the current before continuing.

"I realize that the expression has taken on a mundane and trivial meaning. But, originally, the ability to exercise *common sense* was viewed as an extraordinary achievement—the foundation for a profound and powerful transformational technique practiced during incubation. Those who could activate and coordinate all five senses simultaneously—touch, sight, taste, smell, and hearing—held the key to emerging from this persistent dream *by transcending those five senses.* They could tune into and enter an expanded state of consciousness that encompassed all other dimensions and revealed the most deeply coveted secrets about this perceived reality."

Vee was staring down at the moving water but concentrating hard on Clees' words. "You're saying that the combined action of all five senses makes it possible to experience a kind of… *sixth sense?*"

"Quite right," Clees said, "an *extra* sense. Extra sensory. And by attaining this heightened perception and greater awareness through a state of totally focused attention—a magnitude of attention that few Worldborns have ever given to anything—they can use their infallible intuition to bring about massive changes at speeds no one can yet imagine. The possibilities are enormous… and endless."

"My Aunt Aurelia claimed to have extra sensory abilities," Vee said then. "She called from Dallas one night when I was twelve during one of her 'ESP spells,' said she had this vision of me and my stepfather and… well… she said she saw something that bothered her and was calling to check on me."

Vee's voice trailed off as she shared this, but her facial expression did not betray any sense of agitation or anxiety.

"The abilities that accompany that subtle realm of the all-encompassing sense, Miss Verilee, are natural for all Worldborns. And they're needed now. Seemingly mysterious powers like future vision, instant self-transport, and psychic insights are just the tip of the experiential iceberg. Any paranormal ability you can imagine, literally any that you can think of, are part of that alternate reality. There are no limits in the thought dimension. None."

"So, if it's so natural, why aren't we all astral projecting to Bali without Jet Blue?" Vee asked.

"Or manifesting gold bullion out of thin air to cover not-so-illusory rent payments?" I added.

"I said the abilities were natural, not necessarily well understood or widely used," he responded. "But thought travel to Bali, manifesting objects at will, co-creating reality, and doing many other so-called 'miracles' are the potential of everyone… for what that's worth."

"Let's get on with it then," Vee said with genuine enthusiasm.

"The answer to reaching that potential, Miss Verilee, and slipping out of the prison that is the illusory world, lies right before your eyes. I mean that literally."

Vee leaned back and dropped herself flat on the bridge, staring up at the cerulean sky overhead.

"Right before my eyes, right up there in the clear blue sky?" She rolled her head slightly to look at him. "Show me."

"It all comes back to the message held by the kila," Clees said, holding out the three-sided arrowhead again, cupping it in his right hand which was poised a few feet over the creek. From where I sat, this looked precarious, like the precious relic could accidentally slip from his palm and drop into the fast-moving current. I wanted to reach out and pull his hand back.

But, as it turned out, there was no need for me to worry about him inadvertently dropping the kila. Because in the next moment, Clees tightened his grip around the treasured object, drew his wiry arm back, and in one quick and intentional motion, hurled it into the current sixty feet downstream.

The ancient, weathered arrowhead that Vee and I credited with having magical powers, that traveled from Tibet to Greece and then to America over the course of two millennia—the silver blue kila that even made an unscheduled stop in outer space—sank instantly into the deep silt of the cold creek and disappeared.

CHAPTER FIFTEEN

Vee snapped upright with unnatural speed, and I almost dove in head-first after the discarded relic before Clees extended his sinewy arms and held us both in place.

"What the hell did you do that for?" Vee shouted. "I thought that thing was the key to exiting the world?"

"I've been guarding that arrowhead for the past two weeks like it was the most sacred object on earth," I added. "Now you go and toss it like it's just some meaningless trinket?"

I was staring downstream, trying to fix my eyes on the spot where the kila had melted into the riverbed, but my focus kept shifting along with the fast-moving current and I couldn't steady them on the exact point of entry.

Clees was characteristically nonplussed to the point of being annoying. "I never said the kila was sacred, Metis, nor did I ever tell you it was the key to exiting this dream world, Miss Verilee."

"You said I brought it to you as a gift, that I hauled it all the way from Tibet to Acragas," Vee said. "I wouldn't have done that if it didn't have some serious power."

"Before you came to me in Acragas, you were already applying common sense to achieve one-pointed focus. This single-pointedness opens the door to limitless answers and observational abilities—eventually it will allow you to do anything you can think of, like materializing anywhere instantly. Instructing others in that kind of focus will also facilitate a global awakening. The kila is merely a symbol of that focus, nothing more. It has served its purpose."

"So why did I carry it to Greece, why did people associate it with mystical powers?" Vee asked. "And what the hell do you mean by a global awakening? Why are you being so vague?!"

"When you brought the kila to me, you were merely acknowledging that you fully understood the rewards of focused attention, and that you were ready to join me in showing others how to change their minds," Clees said. "A global awakening through this transformative shift in thinking is the reason you're both here in this lifetime."

"Wait, slow down," she said. "So, it wasn't the kila that helped me materialize or teleport?"

"As I said earlier, Miss Verilee, only insofar as it reminded you to pay attention, to be fully alert in the present moment, and to stay as sharp and focused as the point of an arrowhead is on its intended target. I have said this to Metis, and I will repeat it for you. Anything you can see, taste, hear, touch or smell—anything that you think exists in the physical world—is an hallucination, pure smoke-and-mirrors, a vast and intricate illusion. Including the kila."

"Including me, you and Vee then, too," I replied.

"Correct Metis. There are no exceptions. This is an all or nothing proposition. We are all dreaming a collective dream from a different point of view. And since our bodies are manifestations in that dream, we don't exist within these walls of flesh. We're not here. However, I am inviting you both to become infiltrators within the hallucination to help other Worldborns escape and find their way out of it. You'll both remain in the world for a short time longer, with your bodies in tow, but you'll be fully aware of our benign deception."

"Okay, I'm totally lost now," Vee said.

"Me, too," I added. "Can you go back to the common sense part and how it can lead to radical change?"

"I think we've had enough talk and theory for today," Clees said, quickly drawing his legs up and reaching for his shoes. "As I mentioned to you once, Metis, conversing about ideas can be fine for foundation building, but the real learning is in practicing these concepts. Doing, not deliberating."

He had his boots on in a flash, stood up, glanced once downriver in the direction of the now irretrievable kila, then turned and exited the bridge from the other end, walking briskly along the path towards the pine forest beyond. I reached back and fumbled for my socks and sneakers, almost dropping one shoe in the creek, while Vee tugged at my arm to get me moving. Her boots had never come off.

"Hey, wait up," she called out as Clees reached the forest's edge.

"Clees, hold on!" I said and began hopping next to Vee with one shoe still in my hand.

"I must leave the two of you for awhile," Clees said, half turning towards us, smiling brightly, "but it was wonderful to be together again, was it not?"

"How the hell do we get back?" Vee said.

"Look around you, Miss Verilee. Your mind is capable of creating entire worlds, you can certainly use it to depart from this one. Don't think your way out, feel your way out. Be attentive to every moment and use every fiber of your intuitive being to do this. Stay focused and look for helpful clues using a little common sense."

Then he turned away and just before he disappeared around a particularly massive tree trunk, he called back, "Remember, it's all an illusion, just a dream, and you are the creator of the dream."

<h1 style="text-align:center">CHAPTER SIXTEEN</h1>

The previous times I was with Clees in other dimensions—at the Borderland and on the little asteroid—I was yanked away, then thrust back into my own world in a kind of swoon, with no apparent effort on my part. Now I was alone with Vee, standing on a bridge over an unfamiliar creek, stranded in some other dimension, unsure of how we got there and clueless as to how we were going to get back. And to make matters worse, Clees had ditched us, taking his formidable bag of travel tricks with him.

"What the hell?" Vee said, expressing in her no-nonsense way my own unease. "What kind of goodbye was that?"

"He's a little weak on exit etiquette," I replied.

"He should be careful vanishing like that on a person with my childhood abandonment issues. I might end up irreversibly traumatized."

She was kidding, but maybe not.

I stopped to slip my other shoe on properly, then looked around. Maybe this was some sort of elaborate theatrical set that Clees had contrived simply to deliver the evening's lessons and now the stage doors would appear and the clearly marked exits would suddenly spring open.

"What are we going to do now?" Vee asked, with more curiosity than concern.

I had no idea and was feeling responsible for getting Vee home since I was the reason she was there on that bridge in the first place.

"Do you think maybe we should try to get the kila back?" I asked, looking downstream.

"Why? It's lost in the muck somewhere, maybe pushed another

fifty yards downstream by the current. Besides, Clees said it never had any magical powers to begin with."

She was right. He chucked it to make the point that we didn't need it and hadn't known what to do with it in the first place.

"Want to head back along the path where we came from?" I asked. "Maybe find that seam in the buildings, inch our way through to Grove Street?"

"Are you kidding?" She was getting upset, probably feeling a little apprehensive, too. "We didn't walk through a friggin' four-inch crack in the bricks, Roger, we dematerialized, then reconstituted or something like that. Do you know how to reverse that process? Because I sure as hell don't."

"I'm just trying to come up with some suggestions here," I said defensively.

Vee turned abruptly and started walking determinedly in the same direction Clees had gone, up the path's mild incline towards the trees.

"Where are you going?" I asked.

"I'm following him. If Clees walked out that way, common sense dictates that the escape hatch is somewhere through those trees."

"Common sense? He just got through telling us that common sense doesn't mean what we think it means."

"If you have a better idea, speak now." She started picking up the pace. "Otherwise, shut up and hurry up, I don't want to lose him."

We reached the forest's edge in seconds, then we both began running along the wood-chipped path, sidestepping fallen pinecones and serpentining between tree trunks. It turned out that the forest wasn't as dense as it looked from the bridge and, after only a couple of hundred yards, we could see light coming through the trees ahead and the path emptying into a clearing.

"Okay, here we go," Vee said, practically sprinting now, "we'll catch him in that field up ahead."

But when we emerged into the clearing, we both stopped dead in our tracks. About a hundred feet in front of us was a wooden foot-bridge, crossing a twenty-five-foot stream, with a big willow on the far bank, its branches brushing the top of the water.

"That's not the same bridge, is it?" Vee asked. "That's not possible, right?"

We both turned at the same time to look back the way we came, but now the forest was gone and in its place was a thin scrim of fog.

"What does common sense dictate now?" I asked her.

"That you close your trap. It also dictates that when I see Clees again, I'm going to rearrange his flawless Greek nose." It was an interesting image, but Vee was clearly more intrigued than angry at that moment.

"What did he say when he headed towards the forest, something about focusing and using common sense?" Vee asked.

"And paying attention. And not thinking."

"Weird, but alright, let's try it his way," she said, taking my left hand in hers and leading me slowly towards the bridge. "See, touch, taste, hear and smell, activating all the senses at once, paying attention as we go, not relying on our intellects."

"So, what are we looking for?"

"I have no idea, Rog, but apparently we already know how to do this, so let's concentrate."

"How do we know how to do this?"

"Geez, Roger. Clees just said we were ready to spread this knowledge around the world, remember, until I was chopped up into little Zipa chunks. So, yes, we can do this."

"I don't know, Vee…"

She dropped my hand and wheeled on me, and I flinched. "Roger, that little rendezvous just now on the bridge, that was the most insane thing that has ever happened to me… and also the greatest. I know it started a little bumpy, but in the end, I loved it. Clees is amazing and I owe you forever for bringing me to him."

"Okay, but what does that have to do…"

"Years ago, I told you that I didn't know how, but I was going to find a better place than the psycho house I grew up in, remember? A *Fantasia* kind of big possibilities place? Today I found out that it exists. And if that dude, Clees, holds some of the clues to getting us there, and wants us to play the hyper-focused, common sense, intuition game, I'm going to play it, all out. And you need to play it with me."

I could see the hope dancing in Vee's eyes and heard the excitement in her voice. And even if I had little idea about where or how to start, I was going to try. If anyone deserved to have that hopeful feeling stay alive in them, it was Vee, and I wasn't going to be the one to snuff it out. Besides, she was certainly right about one thing—this was the most remarkable thing that had ever happened to either of us. And even if it straddled the edges of sanity as we understood it, I wanted what Clees was promising just as much as she did, and we probably had a better chance of getting out of this predicament together than either of us did alone.

Without another thought, I took her hand and started walking slowly towards the bridge, repeating a kind of mantra to myself, "Pay attention, stay alert, be aware… the clues are everywhere."

"Right," she said in response. "Focus is the key."

CHAPTER SEVENTEEN

Trying to activate all of my senses at once to find invisible clues was basically impossible. I wished Clees had given us more instruction before he disappeared, and I felt irritated with him for telling us that we already knew how to do this. I certainly didn't and I kept looking over at Vee to see how she was going about it. She just seemed to be squinting her eyes and looking around intensely, taking a deep inhalation through her nose every few seconds.

The best I could manage was aligning my vision with my hearing to some extent, but it took so much effort I wasn't really paying attention to my surroundings.

"Are you getting anything?" I asked Vee sheepishly, expecting her to pounce on me again.

"A mild headache from squinting."

We both laughed at that which released some tension. The next few minutes were more relaxed, and I immediately felt more aware of my environment.

"Did you notice those carvings on the bridge poles before?" Vee asked, looking up ahead. I hadn't, and I was surprised that I hadn't because they weren't tiny or insignificant. On the left-hand post, which was round and about the width of a small utility pole, the wood was marked with deep cuts. As we got a little closer, I could see that they were letters. And the right-hand post had some sort of metal trail marker nailed to it, circular in shape, about five feet up from the base. It was three inches across, painted a deep blue, with the number "4" at its center in bold black type. How had I missed this before?

As I began to walk towards the etchings on the post, I saw Vee stop and reach down for something half-buried in the woodchips under our feet. It was a coin.

"An old penny," she said, then scratched hard on the date side with her fingernail. "1989."

"Year we were born," I said, and she flashed a quick smile.

"I like this, it's fun," Vee said, clutching the penny in her right hand and scanning the woodchips for more lost change. "It's like a treasure hunt."

I had this vague memory just then of Clees telling me that Vee was a terrific treasure hunter.

"What?" she asked, because I must have been staring at her.

"Nothing, I was just thinking about something Clees had said."

"What? It might be important. Look for clues, he said, remember? It might be a clue."

"He told me you were once a brilliant treasure hunter."

"What did he mean by that?"

"Not sure, but you just said you were having fun because this is like a treasure hunt."

"Finding coins makes me brilliant? Must be about other stuff."

"Let's go check out the markings on the bridge posts and see what else you come up with, Most Esteemed Treasure Hunter."

I said this with a pinch of salt and Vee heard it.

"Drop the tone, Rog, okay, that isn't going to get us anywhere. We have to work together. Besides, treasure hunts are supposed to be fun, so let's aim for that."

She was right, of course, but I couldn't shake the feeling I had earlier, that Vee was processing stuff that I wasn't, and doing it more quickly.

"Sorry, I don't know why I'm letting this get to me, but I just feel like I'm lagging behind."

"Look, let's regroup here. Let's try to focus and use the common sense thing."

"And not use our thinking minds," I added pointedly

"Yeah," Vee replied, "that part was strange. I'm happy with my brain and the way it works. How do I not think?"

I had no idea, so I stayed silent. We reached the bridge together and I walked over to the carvings on the left side, while Vee studied the blue trail marker on the right post, circling it slowly.

"It's definitely the same bridge," she called over. "I see that splashing thing swimming around. Its tail is really long, more than three feet."

"Don't piss it off. I've finally dried out."

She went back to examining the marker, while I looked at the scars in the wood beside me. One set of deep scratches seemed to be more prominent than the others, it jumped out at me more. It was a crude heart with some initials inside: C.E. + A.F. I thought about who I knew with those initials but couldn't come up with anyone.

"Hey, you know anyone with the initials C.E. or A.F.?"

She stopped her inspection and her eyes rolled up as if she was concentrating. "Aretha Franklin, that's A.F. Not sure about the C.E."

"Clees is a C. And his full name is Empedocles. Maybe that's the C and the E?"

"Yeah, maybe, maybe not. Keep looking."

Instead of looking, I closed my eyes and sniffed the air and listened hard. I heard the willow branches rustling downstream and simultaneously caught a whiff of something fresh and herbal. At first, I thought I smelled sage, then I decided it was more lightly aromatic. I was trying to zero in on it, poking my nose in the air like a beagle targeting a scent, when Vee blurted out, "I smell mint."

"I was just going to say that."

"Where's it coming from?"

"Not sure. Downstream, I think, judging by the light breeze," I responded. We both looked in that direction and saw the willows swaying gently on the banks of the stream. "I picked up the scent at exactly the same moment I heard the willows swishing in the wind."

"That could mean something," Vee said, "let's go check out those trees."

We crossed the bridge, made a sharp right and started to walk along the soft banks of the creek. At one particularly squishy spot, I almost stepped out of my right sneaker, which made me look down and behind me. Out of the corner of my eye, I spotted a greenish hue gliding alongside us in the water.

"We're being followed," I said.

Vee turned towards the bridge, then looked down, noticed the water creature and harrumphed. "You get me wet again, Cecil, even a drop, and I'm going to rip your goddamn hose off."

That made me laugh. Cecil was a lovable sea serpent from a kid's cartoon called *Beany and Cecil* that Vee was obsessed with when we were kids. I think the program originally aired in the 1960s, but they brought it back briefly in the '80s and Vee would watch those revival episodes over and over. My mother found a special edition VHS tape of those rare '80s shows at a now defunct Blockbuster store and gave it to Vee one Christmas. But she never took the tape home. Vee always watched the show at our house, then tucked the tape in the back of our media console until the next viewing.

I'm not sure why she liked that cartoon so much. Beany was a cute kid with a propeller on his two-toned beanie cap who was always getting kidnapped or into some sort of trouble. Cecil was his loyal serpent sidekick who was big, green, not too smart, and spoke with a comical lisp. I remember being fascinated with Cecil's nostrils because they looked exactly like the little suction cups on the back of my dad's shaving mirror in the bathroom shower.

Anyway, whenever Beany got into a jam, he'd call out to Cecil for help and the green galoot would famously yell, "I'm a-comin' Beany-boy!" Every time Cecil said that and sprang into action, Vee would smile at the TV and sort of rock back-and-forth on our couch until Cecil managed to rescue Beany.

I kept one eye on Cecil, our newly christened water creature, until we reached the willows, where I immediately spotted a patch of wild peppermint growing on a sunny slope behind the largest of the old trees.

"That explains the mint smell," I said as I walked up the slope a few steps, picked a stem of mint, broke off a leaf and started chewing it. I turned to see Vee squatting low to the ground, running her hand along the willow's exposed roots, carefully studying every knot and knob like she was one of those Sioux trackers trying to determine when the last buffalo had passed. I walked over and was following the movement of her hand when I saw water churning in the creek and the tail of our sneaky sea monster breaking the surface. It shot a powerful jet of chilly liquid in our direction.

"Mother f… !" Vee yelled out, leaping back towards me. "That's it, you soggy son of a bitch!" She started to yank a heavy rock from between a gnarled fork in the aerated root tangle.

"I don't think Cecil was aiming for us," I said, watching the dark creature swim across the creek, then turn slowly to face us again, staying close to the surface.

"Not aiming for us? Really? He got us pretty damn drenched before," Vee said, standing up with the rock poised in her throwing hand.

"That's my point, he didn't miss before. Perfect aim. But this time, he was off by ten feet," I pushed Vee gently aside and moved towards the big willow's trunk where the plume of water had landed. "Clees told us that nothing is an accident, right? Maybe Cecil's errant aim was no fluke either."

I stepped over some large roots to the far side of the tree trunk. "Check this out," I called over to Vee, who dropped the rock and joined me.

Two massive roots radiated out from the base of the tree forming a wedge above ground. In the middle of the wedge, well-protected and close to the willow's trunk was a hole, maybe eighteen inches across. The packed dirt along the rim was wet where Cecil's concentrated geyser had soaked it.

"Animal den?" Vee asked.

"Yeah, I guess. Most likely raccoon or fox—assuming that they even exist in this alternate reality. An animal that likes fish, apparently, judging by the lair's proximity to the creek."

Vee came closer and sat on one of the two exposed roots, using it like a bench. I sat down on the other. "Lair, Rog, you just said lair."

I had, without noticing it.

"You think this hole has something to do with us getting back to Grove Street?" I asked.

"Possibly," she said, turning towards the creek with a soft look that made her appear more approachable. "Maybe Cecil isn't such a bastard after all. Maybe he was directing us here."

"To help us?" I said.

"Or rescue us," she said with a wistful smile.

We both sat there for a while, looking out towards the creek, back down at the hole, at each other. Vee was doing something that she seemed oblivious to, rocking gently back-and-forth on the sturdy root.

"Okay, so what do we have so far?" I asked.

"A penny from the year we were born," she said, opening her hand and laying it on the dark soil between us. The tarnished copper caught the sun and glinted. "A blue trail marker painted with the number '4.' Young lover carvings on the bridge post with the initials C.E and A.F., some fragrant mint, and a deep burrow under an old willow tree that you called a lair."

I took the sprig of mint I'd picked and laid it next to the penny.

"Alright, so the penny was clearly meant for us, minted in 1989, our shared birth year."

"Minted." Vee said. "That's like mint." She picked up the sprig, plucked off a leaf and began to chew along with me.

"Okay, I'll buy that connection. Mint and minted. The mint got us here to this burrow. Alright, what about the initials then? Should be R.S. and V.F., if it's logical and we're the ones being guided."

"Nah, that would be too easy," she replied. "If the clues were that obvious, we'd be noticing and deciphering them constantly, every day, everywhere we went."

"Yeah, true. Okay, C.E. and A.F.? I think I gave that my best shot with Clees and Empedocles."

"You're giving up too fast."

I shuffled my feet on the dark soil below my root bench. "Clint Eastwood and Anne Frank?"

"Clint Eastwood and Anne Frank? What the hell is that?"

"They're clues, right?" I replied. "Clint Eastwood is a famous macho actor and Anne Frank was a young heroine of the Holocaust. So, what does that tell us?"

"It tells us nothing, Steiner, because that is friggin' dumb. There's no connection there at all."

It was rare for Vee to use my last name, but when she did, it almost always foreshadowed an argument between us.

"Well, you haven't come up with anyone but Aretha Franklin," I said.

"Alright, let's table the initials for a second. What about the trail marker? A bold black '4' in a bright blue circle."

"Maybe it's like a billiard ball?" I responded.

"It's not a billiard ball, you idiot. Besides, the four ball is purple, not blue."

It made me angry when she called me an idiot and I stood up quickly, dislodging some rocks under my feet. One of the larger ones dropped into the hole. There was no rolling rock sound, no clamor, no thud at the bottom.

Vee registered this immediately. "That must be a pretty deep hole."

I leaned over the edge of the earthen cavity and looked down but couldn't see anything. I sank to my knees and peered in, but it was pitch black. I reached in with one hand but couldn't find the angled sides of the descending walls. There were no angled sides—the hole just seemed to fall away into a bottomless chasm.

"What animal builds a burrow sixty feet down?" I said, pushing myself back up, standing a few feet away to take in the opening from another angle. I looked for a bigger rock and found one wedged loosely below my root bench. When I dropped it into the hole it was the same thing. Total silence.

"What do you think?" I asked her.

She got down on her belly and put her face over the rim. "HELLO!" she yelled. "CLEES, ARE YOU DOWN THERE, YOU SON OF A BITCH?!" We both snickered at that. Vee sat up and brushed the dirt off the front of her jacket. "Looks like it goes all the way to China."

Then her expression changed, and I could tell that she was calculating.

"I don't think that's a good idea," I said.

"Me either," she responded. Then she scooted her butt to the edge of the hole and swung her legs into it. "But what do we have to lose?"

She raised both arms straight overhead, jerked her butt forward, let out a whoop, and dropped like a stone into the coal-black emptiness.

I saw this coming, but Vee's quick plunge still jolted me. I was not eager to follow her and as I slumped down to the edge of the hole and looked in, I was already thinking of alternate strategies.

"Vee," I called down. "VEE!"

There was no answer, no echo, no sound. I pushed myself back onto my knees, feeling weak in my arms, a burst of panic invading my chest. I looked up and saw that the wall of misty fog on the other side of the stream was rolling closer. I decided to hurry back to the bridge and hunt for more clues, but as I stepped over Vee's root bench to move in that direction, Cecil broke the surface again and discharged a single globule of water directly into the earthen shaft.

"Oh, man, really?" I said out loud.

Cecil had already descended and was swimming away, but there was little mystery in his liquid message. Reluctantly, I turned back, stepped over several exposed roots and inched my way to the rim of the hole, but not before reaching down and picking up our birth year penny and jamming it into my pocket. Then I aligned the tips of my sneakers with the burrow's edge, compared the width of my hips to its diameter, pressed my left hand solidly against the side of my body, and pinched my nostrils shut with my right. I closed my eyes and stepped off.

I'm sure I felt a splatter of icy water hit the back of my neck just as I began to drop.

CHAPTER EIGHTEEN

The moment my descent began, it abruptly ended. I landed on pavement and when I opened my eyes, I saw that I was on a West Village sidewalk, but I wasn't sure exactly where. Then I spotted Vee standing on the corner about twenty feet away and quickly walked over. She turned before I reached her, a radiant smile on her face.

"What took you so long?" she said.

"I went for a quick dip with Cecil… thought he seemed a little lonely."

"Look where we are."

My legs were wobbly but I took a few steps forward so I could see around the corner. I recognized it as the intersection of Waverly Place and 6th Avenue, just a few blocks from where we had followed Clees into the masonry.

"Damn, this is so crazy," I said, placing one hand against the side of the building to steady myself. "How is this possible?"

"That's my line," she responded playfully, still looking victorious.

"Okay, so we made it back, but I thought maybe we'd land on Grove Street."

"Come on, for our first astral voyage, we kicked ass," she said.

"What time is it?" I asked.

She took her phone out of her back pocket and tapped it on. "Little after two."

"More than four hours have gone by, and we're blocks from where we started."

"Gimme a break, Rog, we did great."

"But the other times, with Clees, I ended up exactly from where I had taken off and not a millisecond had passed."

"At least we returned to New York and it's the same night. We could have landed in Siberia during the winter of eighteen-ninety-two. I think we rocked it. And look where we are," she said again, pointing north up 6th Avenue.

"A block from Eighth Street, so?"

"No, the subway station is right there."

The West 4th Street subway entrance was a half-block away, two police officers standing sentry at the top of the stairs as dozens of people in their 20s and 30s entered and exited. The Village was always hopping on weekend nights, even at 2:00 in the morning.

"Yeah, so what?"

"What subway is that?"

"All of them. The A, C, D, E… " I got as far as D and stopped. "Oh, man, the blue and orange lines are here, the A, C, E, F from the West 4th Street station."

"Yup, C.E. and A.F." She seemed positively elated. "A little common sense and here we are—home sweet home, baby!"

She was right. We didn't do it the way Clees did, with seamless precision, zero effort, and no time-lapse, but by using our collective senses simultaneously, sort of, as well as by paying attention, following the clues, and getting an assist from Cecil, we had made some progress.

"I don't want to go home, Rog. I'm too wired. I want to stay at your place tonight, talk, put some of these pieces together."

"Sure, but what about Homer?" I asked, as we crossed the avenue and started walking west on Waverly towards my apartment.

"I left him a bunch of food and peed him before I came over. I'll leave early in the morning, but he'll be okay. He's got a massive bladder for a small dog."

"I could go out to Brooklyn with you. Stay at your place tonight if you want?"

"Nah, I want to stay here. Maybe Clees will show up again. Maybe tonight's adventure isn't over yet."

We walked quickly back to my place barely saying a word. When we stepped through my front door, we realized we were both ravenous. We raided the refrigerator, ate hummus and eggs and avocado, shared half a cantaloupe, and finished off a vegan chocolate cake that I'd bought at an organic bakery on Carmine Street a few days before. After the frenetic food consumption, we remained at the kitchen table, our birth year penny lying between us, and talked about every moment of our encounter with Clees.

"We both know that everything we saw tonight can't happen, right… but it did happen, I didn't imagine it… please tell me it happened." Vee was wiping cake crumbs from her lips as she spoke.

"It sure felt real to me," I responded.

"Because I keep wondering if maybe Clees hypnotized us before we went into the wall, you know, put us into a trance somehow. It felt so damn real, but what if that bridge and the brook and Cecil were all just elaborate hallucinations? He's a sorcerer, right? A magician, so he could have definitely put us under some sort of spell."

I listened to her try to rationalize the night away for the next twenty minutes and I understood. I had been doing much the same thing after each visit with Clees. But why? Was it too frightening, too much for our brains to work out, so we diminished it, tried to make it go away? Or was it because Vee and I wanted so desperately for Clees to be real and true, for his promises to be kept, for the hope he raised in us to stay alive, that neither of us would be able to bear it if he went away and left us forever? Maybe we were already lowering our expectations, convincing ourselves that we made it all up just to protect ourselves.

"Yeah, it could be a trance, a spell of some sort," I finally said when she'd slowed down enough for me to slip a word in. "Maybe he is a Svengali, after all, and we're under his mesmeric powers right now. But what if that isn't it, Vee? What if our longing for a *Fantasia* kind of place is possible and it's revealing itself to us right now, through Clees? That would be even better, wouldn't it?"

She didn't answer, she just stared at me. Then her eyes started to glisten, and she turned away to stare out the front window.

Over the next hours our chatter turned to wonder and whispers until there was light in the sky. I hugged Vee goodbye at around 6:00 a.m. and stumbled to my couch where I instantly fell asleep, dreaming of winged wizards who could carry people beyond the stars.

<h1 style="text-align:center">CHAPTER NINETEEN</h1>

Vee and I saw each other almost every day in the two weeks that followed. We met for either lunch or dinner, she'd hang out at my place after work or I'd head out to Dumbo and join her for walks with Homer, taking roundabout routes along the East River parks. The evenings were mild, the sunsets were beautiful, and we had so much to talk about, revisiting all of our shared life experiences through the filter of what Clees had shared with us on the mystery bridge in that unnamable land.

But there was always that asterisk, both of us tempering our excitement and hopes by reminding each other that it could all be a ruse, that Clees could be a charlatan, and his magic an illusion. Still, I think Vee wanted to stay close in those ensuing days because she had the idea that if he did materialize again, it would be in proximity to me and she didn't want to miss any of the action. I was just glad to finally have someone to talk to about all of the far-out stuff that was going on.

Reading from the Mews Man entries on my iPad, I filled Vee in on the details of each of my encounters with Clees before she met him, from that first afternoon on Hudson Street until the night we walked through a wall together. She made me read and retell each story in painstaking detail, then had me repeat it again from the beginning.

"There might be some details you're leaving out," she'd say, as she jotted down key points in a small, black notebook that she'd bought specifically for this purpose. "Let's just go over it one more time."

"Again?" I'd whine.

"Remember what Clees said—the clues are coming at us every second, whacking us in the head constantly. We can only catch the express train out of here if we pay attention to our present experience with every fiber of our being."

If this thing called *escape* was possible, if there really was a way to get the answers we needed to wake up and walk out, Vee was hot on its trail. She had written "Clees Encounters of an Absurd Kind" in block lettering on a carefully cut, three-inch square of blue paper that was taped to the cover of her notebook. Underneath that, on a smaller square of yellow paper, she'd written "ESTIA," with the notation "PA, SA, BA" just below that. I had no idea what that last bit meant, so I asked her.

"ESTIA, of course, means focus, it was etched onto the kila. You discovered that. And the kila was all about staying focused, right?"

"Right, but what about those other letters, the PA, SA, BA thing?"

"That's my own reminder. You uttered it on the bridge. *Pay Attention, Stay Alert, Be Aware.'*"

"Huh, I like that, glad I thought of it." I started to repeat it in my head so I wouldn't forget my own mantra.

I was happy that we were both recording our Clees encounters. We would pour over my iPad and her little notebook every time we met which, as I mentioned, was often. Vee had also been drawing pictures from memory of the kila that Clees had unceremoniously cast from the bridge. She was an excellent freehand illustrator, and her renderings were lively and realistic. Despite Clee's insistence that the kila was only symbolic, it had made an impression on both of us, and we liked remembering it.

After weeks of these near-daily rendezvous, Justina got suspicious and flat-out asked Vee if something was going on between us, whether Vee was having an affair with me. Vee assured her that nothing had changed. She told Justina that I was remembering some traumatic events from my past, and asked for her support with any recollections from our shared childhood. It was a bit of a lie, but harmless enough and far more believable than the truth would have been. Besides, being able to discuss all this Clees stuff with Vee was validating for me and having another witness became essential to preserving my sanity.

Almost a week after the bridge experience with Clees, on a Thursday afternoon after I returned from work, I opened my hallway mailbox to find a letter addressed to Roger M. Steiner. I got chills. My middle name is Joseph—a tribute to my grandfather—so I immediately suspected the "M" was for Metis, and that this was a letter from Clees. But there was no return name or address, so I couldn't be sure.

I slammed the metal box shut and bounded up the interior stairwell two at a time rather than wait for the unreliable elevator. When I got inside the apartment, I threw my jacket and shoulder bag on the couch and took the letter to the kitchen table. I wanted to tear it open immediately, but Vee and I had been trying to heed Clees' directive that we take in our surroundings with extra attention, which usually meant exercising patience and avoiding hasty action. So, I took a long, slow breath and gave the letter a careful inspection.

The nearly square envelope was invitation-sized, an ochre color, and addressed to me with blue ink in an elegant script. I had never seen Clees' handwriting before, but the more I looked at the penmanship, the less it seemed like the letter could have come from him and I felt deflated. The writing was too precise, each of the three lines written along a perfectly straight rule, with each letter having a dramatic flourish that was almost calligraphic. It occurred to me that Clees was capable of addressing this note without ever picking up a pen and could have just as easily written in hieroglyphics or in ancient Sumerian as calligraphy, but it nevertheless seemed too graceful and meticulous to be his.

The postmark was from Salinas, CA, which meant nothing to me, and the upper left corner, where you'd expect to find the return address, was left blank. When I turned the letter over, there was a pressed circle of light brown wax sealing it shut. A pineapple-like image was stamped at the center of the dollop, absent the leafy stalk. Details of the small wax imprint were difficult to make out, so I got up and retrieved my magnifying glass. On closer inspection, it didn't appear to be a pineapple after all, although it definitely had that oblong shape with a pattern of crisscrossing squares on its surface, like the fruit.

I knew that once I opened the letter the wax seal would crack into pieces, and that Vee would kill me if I didn't show it to her first. At the same time, there was no way I was waiting to open that letter. So, I retrieved my phone from my jacket pocket, tapped the camera feature and took a few photos of the seal in high definition using the flash to lift the image impression. This seemed to bring out more detail, but it was still no clearer to me what the image was exactly.

I put the letter down on the table, got an X-Acto knife from my utility drawer, and tried to open the envelope by cutting precisely around the seal. I did a careful job of leaving the wax circle intact, only breaking off a few tiny pieces at the edge. Then I slid the letter out.

There was a good reason why the envelope was invitation-sized— the note inside was an invitation. It was a folded tent card, a light yellow color on the exterior panels and white on the inside. The words "YOU'RE INVITED" were printed on the front in a traditional serif font. Below the words was an illustration of a small pot of purple hyacinths.

The message on the inside was handwritten in the same elaborate script as the envelope address and covered the top and bottom panels:

> *Dear Roger and Vee,*
> *Our mutual friend has asked me to invite you both to join us in California during the second week of July. It would be ideal if you could arrive on the 12th, booking your flights into the Monterey airport. You will know what to do once you get there. Just pay attention. We will arrange for your accommodations during your stay. There is no need to RSVP.*
> *Our mutual friend will know whether you'll be coming and exactly when you'll arrive. I do hope you can make the trip.*
> *Oh, the places we'll go!*
> *Looking forward to hugging you both.*

There was no closing, no signature. Just the promise of hugs from somewhere near Monterey, CA, by someone with whom Vee and I shared a friend—obviously Clees.

I read the note again maybe six or seven times. The invitation itself was fairly straightforward, but the line that kept popping out at me was the one near the end, *"Oh, the places we'll go!"*

Maybe it was just a coincidence, maybe it meant nothing at all, but those words were almost exactly the title of a classic Dr. Seuss book that I loved as a kid—*Oh, The Places You'll Go!* Someone had given it to me as a fifth-grade graduation gift the summer before I entered junior high school. At first, I was offended at receiving a silly old children's book at the advanced age of eleven years, and I didn't look at it for months. Then one afternoon towards the end of the summer, I was cleaning out my room on my mother's orders, putting things together for a charity donation, when I opened it and started reading. It never made it to the contribution box.

This was the last book Theodor Geisel, aka Dr. Seuss, published before he died in 1991, and I've always imagined it was his parting shot of whimsical advice on getting through life. Eventually, the book came to mean as much to me as *Beany and Cecil* did to Vee, and I knew every rhyming, image-rich line by heart.

There was one section, about *"The Waiting Place, for people just waiting,"* that I always thought was totally dead on. Even as a kid, it seemed to me that practically every adult around me was bored, despondent, feeling kind of useless and clueless, and just waiting around for something to happen—something bigger, something better, something more fulfilling and fun. Those particular lines I can call up instantly:

> *Waiting for the fish to bite*
> *or waiting for wind to fly a kite*
> *or waiting around for Friday night*
> *or waiting, perhaps, for their Uncle Jake*
> *or a pot to boil, or a Better Break*
> *or a string of pearls, or a pair of pants*
> *or a wig with curls, or Another Chance.*
> *Everyone is just waiting.*
> *NO!*

That's not for you!
Somehow, you'll escape
all that waiting and staying.
You'll find the bright places
where Boom Bands are playing.

Waiting was definitely *not for me*, and I was determined to escape from the trap of boredom and despair that seemed to weigh on everyone around me. That was part of the agitation, anxiety, and feeling of emptiness that had been with me so tenaciously since before Clees appeared. I was someone who wanted to get to the Boom Bands.

Now, as I was staring at the invitation in front of me, I started to wonder if I had been waiting all these years for Clees to show up? Did that make any sense? I tried to recall who had given me that book... was it a kid from my class? An aunt? A teacher? I did like my English teacher a lot, and she liked me, but I can't remember her or any other teacher giving kids gifts back then. So, who was it? I was lost in this question when my cell phone started vibrating on the kitchen table and startled me. I turned it over, saw Vee's name, and answered it.

"Hey, what's going on?" she asked pointedly, as if she sensed something.

"Can you come over?"

That's all I needed to say.

"Be there in an hour," was her clipped response.

And I waited.

CHAPTER TWENTY

"You shouldn't have opened it without me," Vee was saying as she sat at my kitchen table, turning the invitation over in her slightly clammy hands. My apartment was on the top floor, it was the last week of June, and even in the early evening my window air conditioner was straining to keep the place cool. "I might have seen something on the wax seal that you missed. Now it's wrecked."

I had predicted this rebuke. "Vee, it's exactly the way I found it in my mailbox, and I was really careful opening it."

"There are wax pieces missing right here at the edge," she said, pointing to minute nibbles of absent wax along the seal's perimeter. "Are you sure nothing else fell out when you excised the invitation?"

"Excised? Now it's surgery?" I was getting annoyed. "You're making too much of this, Vee. The important message is in the words, not the way the note is sealed."

"Hey, I'm only doing what Clees told us to do, okay? Pay close attention to the details. Besides, you're not going to tell me that this symbol is meaningless."

We'd both been looking at the pineapple-like impression for the past half hour but couldn't determine what it was. Neither of us had seen anything quite like it, and we didn't even know how to begin researching it. She was right, though, it had to be significant.

"You think if we took it to the library, they could help identify it?" I asked.

"The library? Dude, that's pretty old school," Vee said. "Do they even do research like that at public libraries anymore? Are there still librarians?"

"What are you talking about, of course there are still librarians," I replied. At least I thought there were.

I took out my phone and searched for hours of operation at the Jefferson Market Library on 6th Avenue, just a quick walk from my apartment.

"It's six forty-five now, the library is open till eight tonight," I said.

"Call them, see if they have a librarian."

So, I did and, yes, there was one on duty until closing time.

"Come on," Vee said, standing up and putting the small envelope into a larger manilla one that she found on my makeshift writing desk in the corner of my cramped living room. "I've got to find out what this thing is, or it'll drive me crazy all weekend."

The Jefferson Market Library is one of the most eye-popping buildings in Greenwich Village, looking more like a Gothic church than a library. Built in the 1870s, it was actually a courthouse with a women's jail attached for a long stretch of its life. In 1927, it famously housed the actress Mae West for eight days after she was arrested for "corrupting the morals of youth" with her play titled *Sex*. But its prison and courthouse functions were later moved downtown in the late 1950s. After an uproar by local residents to prevent its demolition, the intricate red brick building, with its iconic clock tower, became a branch of the New York Public Library.

It was a few minutes after 7:00 and we were rushing up the circular stone steps in the building's tower, climbing towards the main research floor. We were hoping to find a knowledgeable and cooperative librarian, and as it turned out, Mr. Peter Howe was that and more. Tall and blonde and not much older than we were, with a welcoming smile and a playful disposition, Mr. Howe seemed as delighted to see us as we were to find him.

"Hey there," he said quietly and casually as we approached his big oak desk that looked like it might have once resided in a judge's office, a relic from the building's courthouse days, "need some help?"

"It's a strange request, really," Vee said, pulling the invitation envelope with its waxed seal from the manilla sleeve, holding it out to Mr. Howe. "We have a feeling that the symbol on this seal might have some significance, but we don't know how to even begin researching what it is."

He took the envelope, glanced at the wax seal, turned it over, noticed the flourish in the penmanship, saw that it was personal and not promotional, and looked back at us.

"I assume you've already considered asking whoever sent this to you about the seal?"

"We don't know who sent it to us exactly," I said. "They're being sort of mysterious."

"Well, we think we might know," Vee corrected, "but we're not one-hundred percent sure and learning more about that symbol could be an important clue."

Mr. Peter Howe studied our faces, gave a half-smile, and seemed immediately engrossed along with us in the mystery of the wax impression. He pulled his desk lamp closer to cast more light over the seal's surface.

"It's not a pineapple," I said helpfully, leaning in from behind Vee. She shot me a look that told me to be quiet. Mr. Howe studied the seal carefully for another half minute, then reached into his side drawer and took out a loupe and set it over the seal to get a closer look.

"No, it's definitely not a pineapple," he said. He moved the loupe around to the edges of the wax seal, then back to the center, and didn't speak for what seemed like a very long time. Vee was getting fidgety and started tapping her foot against Mr. Howe's desk.

Finally, he looked up. "I can't be sure, it's pretty small, but I think it might be an omphalos."

The second he said the word, my neck hair prickled. Not because I had any idea what an omphalos was, but I knew for sure that the word was Greek, and that alone was enough to start my mind spinning.

"What the hell's an omphalos?" Vee had grabbed the envelope back from Mr. Howe and was staring at the wax dollop again, as if by naming it, it would have changed appearance and gathered new meaning.

"It's a Greek thing," he replied, "a religious stone artifact associated with the Oracle at Delphi. Wait, I can show you."

Vee glanced back at me. Her eyes were electric.

Mr. Howe didn't get up or go over to any dark stacks to pull a dusty tome from a high shelf. He did what we would do. He shifted his body to his keyboard, tapped in a few keystrokes, stared at the results of his online search, then turned his monitor to face us. There on the screen was a very large version of the image on the brown wax stamp. The object was sitting on a heavy stone pedestal in what appeared to be a museum.

"With the naked eye I can understand how you might have interpreted it as a stalkless pineapple," he said. "But with the loupe I noticed something else, that the pattern was more intricate and had a braided rope appearance, common with the omphalos."

The goosebumps rose on my skin again. If this was, in fact, a stylized wax impression of a Greek artifact it meant that this fourth person would be entering our adventure with full knowledge of Clees' past. And very likely a Greek backstory of his or her own.

"How would you know about this?" Vee asked. "I've never heard of an omphalos. It's obscure as hell."

He shrugged. "You managed to find the right librarian. My master's degree is in Greek mythology. I even did a semester abroad in Athens. I was kind of obsessed with the oracular legends. Guess it was no accident that you found me."

No, Mr. Howe, guess not.

He printed out the omphalos page from the screen and handed it to us as we thanked him profusely. Vee stuffed it back in the envelope and we headed towards the exit. We started to descend the granite steps to the street, got to the first landing, then stopped and turned to fist bump each other.

"Wait, why exactly are we celebrating?" I said. "How does the omphalos help us?"

"It's not the omphalos per se, Rog, it's the fact that it is certainly connected to Clees."

"We already knew that."

"Right, but the person who sent this is also telling us that he or she is not just a messenger but has a vital piece to add to this wild story."

"And likely lived in Greece once, too," I said. "Most likely with us in Acragas, and now out there scheming with Clees in Monterey, California."

"Right, and that's where I'm going. In two weeks. And you're coming with me, so don't even think about saying no."

"Oh, I'm there. I just wish Clees had left us the kila. We could have flown out without bothering to purchase plane tickets."

CHAPTER TWENTY-ONE

The next couple of weeks, Vee and I both got caught up in figuring out the logistics of the California trip; me booking the time off from work and wrapping up some pressing projects, Vee mollifying Justina about taking a trip to the west coast without her and trying to explain our sudden urgency to go.

"What's so important that you have to rush out to California in the middle of the summer?" Justina had asked Vee. "Let's just go next January when our bones are cracking from the cold and the west coast sun will lift our spirits."

"This trip isn't for me," Vee explained to her. "I was telling you about Roger digging through his past, remember? Well, he found an old relative out there who has promised to shed some light on a nasty family secret and Rog is freaked out about going alone. You know how he freaks out about everything."

"I thought you told me that Roger's childhood was storybook perfect compared to yours?" she said. "What did he stumble on in his thirties that he didn't know ten years ago?"

"You have no idea," Vee responded. And neither did Vee, because she was fabricating all of it. But we were both allowing ourselves tremendous leeway on the truth spectrum, because we figured that our transgressions would be forgiven once we came back with tangible gold to share with those we cared about.

After a brief discussion, we decided that since the omphalos-sealed invitation specifically mentioned July 12th, we might as well arrange to arrive in California on that day. And since the 12th was a Thursday, and the invitation didn't specify how long we should stay, we calculated that returning on a red eye flight the following Sunday probably made sense. We figured a long weekend would be enough to wake up the world.

As the departure day got closer, I started getting nervous about our next steps once we arrived in California. The invitation's instructions clearly stated that we'd know what to do when we got there if we paid close attention. But, despite our relative success getting home from the mystery bridge by staying alert for clues and synchronicities, I was suddenly feeling woefully unskilled in this intuitive approach and worried that we'd be stuck twiddling our thumbs at the airport before tossing our hands up and stumbling our way through Carmel Valley the old-fashioned way, with Google Maps and Yelp hotel recommendations.

Vee, on the other hand, had no such concerns.

"Come on, they're not going to lure us all the way out to California, just to abandon us at the airport," she tried to reassure me. "All we have to do is stay focused and keep our eyes open… along with our ears, noses, hands, and taste buds."

Since the day we'd booked our flight, Vee had been on a self-administered crash course in applying focused attention. The answer to every question and challenge was to remain intensely aware of her surroundings to spot any useful clue. And she was, at least by our amateur standards, getting really good at it. She was quick to notice coincidences and connections that eluded me and seemed to piece everyday puzzles together quickly. I was observing Clees' brilliant treasure hunter in action, and it was fascinating and fun.

The night before our very early departure on the 12th, I didn't sleep a minute, partially because I couldn't turn off my mind in anticipation of the trip, and partially because Vee had passed out in my bed next to me wearing just a loose T-shirt and underwear. She had decided to sleep at my apartment so we could make a faster exit to Newark Airport in the morning and, despite our decades old and well-established platonic understanding, a combination of her extremely close proximity and my desperately dormant hormones, left me feeling preoccupied all night. So, suffice to say, I was relieved when the alarm clock went off with its chirping insistence at 4:45am and I could get busy with the logistics of departure.

Although Vee appeared to have slept soundly for five hours, she was in a kind of fugue when I tried to rouse her, seeming confused about where she was and why she was waking up in the dark. When I reminded her that we had to leave for California to solve the mysteries of life, she grunted once, threw her feet on the floor, and pitched herself towards the bathroom door.

We were out of the apartment in thirty minutes, got a car service to the airport which took another half hour, and were through security and sitting at our gate by 6:15, at which time Vee passed out again. I nearly carried her through boarding and down the jetway, and as soon as our flight had lifted off at precisely 7:00, she was sound asleep once more, snoring lightly.

Only after we were at cruising altitude did my own fatigue take over and within minutes my head flopped onto Vee's shoulder. We both were out cold until the flight attendant tapped my arm and asked me to put my seat back upright for our landing in San Francisco. There was no direct flight from Newark to Monterey, so we had a short, 45-minute layover at SFO before catching our connecting flight down the coast. I leaned over Vee to get a closer look at the greater San Francisco area as we approached. I saw Alcatraz prison sitting forlornly in the bay, spotted the Oracle Park sports stadium nearby, then the brown hills of the California coast came into view as our plane made its final descent.

We had both slept well on the cross-country flight, although it was unusual for me to sleep even one wink on a plane. As we waited at our gate for the commuter hop to Monterey, we began to chat animatedly about the prospect of seeing Clees again and meeting his mysterious associate with the pristine handwriting.

Vee was in high spirits and speaking with a lovely sparkle in her eyes as we made the short flight into Monterey Regional Airport. She had apparently been working on common sense strategies in her transcontinental sleep because the moment our tires touched the tarmac, she bombarded me with a number of carefully considered tactical approaches.

"Now, Rog, when we get down the ramp, don't just go rushing into the terminal, willy-nilly," she exhorted as our commuter aircraft taxied to the front of a featureless, beige-and-brown terminal building. "Walk slowly, look around, stay present and engage the baggage handlers if they make eye contact with you. Keep all your senses at the ready because it's entirely possible that the first sign we receive will be outside the terminal, not in."

But she was wrong. Because the first sign we saw was the one Clees was holding up to his chest with both our names written on it in thick black marker: "Fulbreth/Steiner."

CHAPTER TWENTY-TWO

He was standing in the small airport terminal between two drivers with similar signs, just past the glass-walled security area. He was dressed in a kind of old-school chauffeur's get-up—black suit, white shirt, thin black tie, with a snappy black cap on his head. His face was beaming in sharp contrast to the other drivers, who looked bored, gray, and impatient as they waited on arriving passengers.

We both stopped short when we saw Clees in front of us. Vee looked almost disappointed that she wasn't going to be able to string together obscure clues to puzzle our way out of the airport. I, on the other hand, felt relief mixed with mild annoyance that I'd been in distress for two weeks wondering if Vee and I would be up to the task of locating Clees somewhere on the coast of California, when here he was waiting no farther than a wingspan's distance from our plane. Luckily, her disappointment and my annoyance quickly gave way to excitement and good cheer the moment Clees opened his mouth, "Metis, Miss Verilee, I see you survived the drop through the center of the earth. How wonderful. Let's get going, shall we, there's someone eager to see you."

Clees must have known that neither Vee nor I had checked our bags in Newark because he bypassed baggage claim, skirted the rental car counters, and led us directly out of the airport. We followed close behind, making small talk as we walked, exiting the double glass doors at the front of the terminal building and crossing a narrow driveway to a short-term parking lot built in the shadow of a steep embankment. I was dying to see what kind of car our Svengali had chosen to drive. I half expected him to transport us to our next destination by spiriting us through a terminal wall or pulling us into a crack in the sidewalk.

But, no, he was driving a car—well, not exactly a car, an ambulance. An old one. Painted a brown-bronze color with plenty of dents, scratches, rust patches, and the remnants of a municipal decal on the driver's side door. As we approached the rolling relic, I turned to Vee with a what-the-hell expression and could see Clees grinning impishly.

"1959 Cadillac Miller-Meteor," Vee blurted out. Despite the fact that we grew up in the suburbs where everyone drove everywhere, Vee didn't have a driver's license and had never owned a car. Yet she had this bizarre ability to identify almost any vehicle type, even foreign cars, and could even guess their vintage with astounding accuracy.

"Correct, Miss Verilee, a fine automobile with a distinctive cinematic history."

"Ecto-1 from *Ghostbusters*," she added. And as soon as she did, I realized that our vehicle's silhouette matched those of the ambulance used in the original 1984 movie classic. Clees' car, however, lacked the roof racks used to carry unidentified ghost-detecting equipment, and instead had a single, rusty bubble gum light mounted on top.

As I got closer to the vehicle, scenes from the film flashed through my head and I smiled. When we were in our teens, Vee and I would watch that movie over and over in my basement den, laughing hysterically. *Ghostbusters* and *Fantasia* were regular Saturday night fare.

I quickly surveyed the other cars in the lot, spotted a perfectly restored classic Jaguar, a couple of late model BMWs, and a sleek new Tesla, and remembered that Californians were both proud and very particular about their automobiles. I was already feeling embarrassed for us, and I was glad that Clees would be driving this brown bomb instead of me. I would have hated to be seen at its steering wheel. But as we reached the car, he turned and tossed me the keys, "Maybe you should drive, Metis. My license expired a millennia ago and I don't want to flirt with a traffic ticket. That's a three-point deduction, you know."

I doubted that he had an expired license or a driver's license of any kind, but I wasn't going to argue with him. I just threw my carry-on bag through the wagon's rear door, opened the one on the driver's side, and slid in.

The interior wasn't dirty exactly, and when I turned the key, the instruments seemed to be operating normally, but the entire automobile was fairly run down, and I wondered if the dilapidated rolling boat was going to be safe on California's busy highways.

"Not to worry, Metis, I recently had it tuned up. It also went through an exorcism, so it's completely ghost-free." It had been a while since I had a mind-reading from Clees, and his sneak peek into my mental musings reminded me that this wasn't going to be any sort of conventional vacation. He seemed tickled at his quip and was laughing quietly to himself as he buckled up in the back seat, then took off his tie and tossed the limo driver's cap to the side. Vee had thrown her bag in the rear compartment with mine and taken the passenger seat.

"Exit the airport, Metis, and follow signs for Highway 68 to Pacific Grove," he said.

I pulled out of the parking lot, up a short hill and around a bend to a traffic light on 68. A sign indicated that Pacific Grove was off to my right.

"Neither of you is going to ask why we're traveling by ghost mobile?" Clees said, once I was safely on the highway and headed west.

"Because you're a kooky spook whose sole purpose here on earth is to get a lucrative contract from the Cartoon Network?" Vee responded.

I saw Clees smile broadly in the rearview mirror.

"And you chose the two of us as business partners because we logged more time on Nickelodeon than most sane kids of our era, therefore we will make excellent co-producers?" she continued. "And you've summoned us to California because this is the center of the television universe and we'll be making a long drive to LA, during which time we'll be negotiating our partnership agreement? Am I getting warm?"

"If by kooky spook, Miss Verilee, you mean a figment of the imagination who is no more corporeal than your *Casper* of TV cartoon fame then, yes, that would be getting warm. Of course, I have no interest in an acting career or television stardom at this time."

It had been a few weeks since Clees had vanished into the forest thicket above Cecil's icy stream, but he and Vee had picked up their playful verbal sparring right where they had left off and I was enjoying hearing them go at it.

"So, if you're not angling for a television deal, what, pray tell, would our friendly ghost be up to?' Vee asked.

"An ambulance is what type of vehicle?" he countered.

"Emergency," I responded.

"Correct. Employed for what purpose?"

"Saving people from serious injury and death," Vee answered.

"Precisely. This illusory world that you appear to inhabit is in the midst of an acute emergency—a dangerous bottleneck in understanding to which we must urgently respond," he said, his eyes fixed on a passing grove of eucalyptus trees. If the fate of mankind was at stake, you wouldn't have guessed it from Clees' demeanor, which was utterly calm. "Our job is to rescue Worldborns from a terrible accident of their collective thinking that is threatening their peace, well-being, and survival. I thought this vehicle would help underscore that point."

"Oh, that's all then, we're just saving humanity?" Vee said sarcastically.

"Yes, Miss Verilee, that's all for now. Perhaps we'll tackle related calamities occurring in remote galaxies and parallel universes at another time." He clearly enjoyed Vee.

"How about filling us in on how we're going to go about this global salvage mission?" I asked.

"I intend to do so without delay, Metis, which is why we're bound for Pacific Grove."

We drove for fifteen minutes, came to the exit, and passed through a neighborhood of Victorian Gingerbread style homes, several turned into bed-and-breakfasts, along with colorfully-painted cottages that looked like adorable, vintage dollhouses. We turned left onto Lighthouse Avenue, a wide, two-lane thoroughfare several blocks from the ocean that appeared to be the town's main commercial strip. We cruised past quaint gift shops with seashore-inspired merchandise, boutiques

selling sundresses and flip-flops, art galleries filled with sea otter paintings and whale sculptures, and real estate offices with appealing photo-
graphs in their windows of oceanfront properties.

"Park wherever you can find an open spot," Clees said as we passed
the last of the tourist cafes at the far end of town. I angled into a
space in front of a medicinal herb shop, threw the big jalopy into park
and watched as window-shopping pedestrians turned in our direction
wondering what kind of local eccentrics or tie-dyed hippies were going
to emerge from this ancient rust bucket. As the three of us got out of
the ambulance, the look on their faces was mostly disappointment.

"We'll head to that ice cream shop over there," Clees said.

I looked to where he was pointing and saw that the store was actually called *The Ice Cream Shoppe*. I suddenly remembered a friend
from college with a skewed sense of humor telling me that you should
never eat at a place called *Mom's*, never date a Greek girl, and never
patronize a store that spells "shop" with a double "pp" and an "e" at
the end. I wasn't sure why any of those injunctions mattered to him
or me, but I was thinking of this as we approached the cheerful glass
storefront which was decorated with ferns, off-season candy canes, and
multi-colored streamers.

Clees entered first, followed by Vee, with me bringing up the rear.
As he pushed open the front door, a string of small silver bells jingled
from the top of the doorframe. The light inside was dim compared to
the strong California sunlight and my eyes needed a couple of seconds
to adjust. And what a sight when they did. The entire colorful, vaguely
chaotic shop was covered in vintage music posters and original album
covers from Wood-stock-era performers and 60's bands. Every inch
of the walls from floor to ceiling was a tribute to music legends, from
Chuck Berry to The Animals, Buddy Holly to the obscure Spencer
Davis Group. All of this memorabilia was protected in cheap plastic
wrap or by clear zip bags, with other band and rock-n-roll collectibles
similarly displayed on every other surface of the place.

The owner appeared to have a particular fondness for The Beatles,
judging by the number of Fab Four images staring at me from every

corner of the shop. Beatle-mania filled the air, too, with songs from the band's *Abbey Road* album playing at high volume from a sleek turntable by the cash register. People were sitting at a half-dozen Formica topped tables which were surrounded by a hodge-podge of wicker seating and old, metal soda fountain chairs. A family with two toddlers was laughing at a table up front, the children appearing ecstatic as they ate their ice creams, most of which was plastered to their cheeks.

Clees walked us slowly to a table in the rear whose top was decorated with a large, laminated Elvis image. The table was tucked up against a long banquette upholstered in striped fabric and also covered in heavy plastic. Sitting with her back to us was a small, lean woman, maybe in her early 60's, with silver hair pulled into a loose ponytail. As we got a few feet from the table and I saw her face, my breath caught, and I felt faint.

I could not believe who was sitting in front of me.

CHAPTER TWENTY-THREE

"Rebecca?"

"Hello, Roger," she said, beaming as she rose to embrace me, "it's been a long time."

It was my grandfather's former secretary, clearly older, but with eyes and mannerisms even more sparkly and youthful than how I remembered her sixteen years before. I had spoken with her a few times since my grandfather's death, but we had lost contact and I had not seen her since the day of GeeJay's funeral.

As she stood up to hug me, I gave her a weak embrace in return, not knowing quite what to make of this or how to react to the woman standing before me.

"I don't understand," I said, "How is this possible?" That question, again, asked in the face of a series of impossibilities.

"It's not easy to explain," she said, "and it won't make sense if you use any normal frames of reference."

Vee reached out a hand to introduce herself.

"Hi, I'm Verilee Fulbreth, Roger's friend from New York. But everyone calls me Vee."

"Yes, hello, Vee," Rebecca said, shaking her hand and putting the other on her shoulder, gently squeezing. She seemed to know intuitively that Vee wasn't a first-minute-you-meet sort of hugger. "You're Roger's best friend, if I recall. I'm Rebecca Blix. I knew Roger a long time ago, when he was just a boy, really. I was his grandfather's secretary in Pennsylvania."

"Yeah, I remember your name. You gave Roger that dumb Liberty Bell." Vee sucked in a breath. "Sorry, that came out wrong. The bell was okay, it was just dumb because he kept it on his desk for like fifty years."

"I still have that bell." I half whispered this, in a voice that sounded like I was sedated. I was feeling off balance and I could sense Clees watching me closely. "I don't understand," I said out loud, then turned to Rebecca, "how could you know Clees?"

"I realize this must be disorienting, Roger, but I'm hopeful that in the next few days, I will be able to offer you an explanation that you can accept, if not fully understand." As she said this, Rebecca moved closer to Vee so that her left arm was brushing lightly against Vee's right. I don't know why I noticed, but it seemed significant, as though Rebecca closed the gap intentionally. Vee seemed completely oblivious to this. Clees took my upper arm and began to move me towards the counter, where a bone-thin older man, probably the shop's owner judging by his "Imagine" tee shirt, was waiting silently.

"Let's order some ice cream," Clees suggested. "We'll have time to close any information gaps afterward." That helped to break me out of my trance, and Clees shepherded me slowly towards Vee who was already at the counter reading the flavor board.

"They serve Lappert's ice cream here, good stuff," Clees said, "Miss Verilee, you should try the mango. I think you'll love it. I'll order you a double scoop in a sugar cone."

I have no idea how Clees knew about that revealing and long ago ice cream shop incident with Vee, me, and my mother, but he apparently said it for my benefit, because Vee didn't react at all, just said no thanks, that she was in the mood for chocolate chip mint and would have her scoop in a cup.

I shot him a quizzical look. He clearly wanted to make a point about Vee's former obstinance, but I wasn't sure what it was exactly. I was still reeling from the sight of Rebecca, now standing only a few feet away from me. He took my arm again, pulled me in closer, and quietly said, "We can start our history anew any time we want, Metis. We are not at the mercy of the past, it doesn't exist. The point of power is in the present."

I could not process what he was saying, and my attention went to the man behind the counter who was generously scooping out Vee's mint order. I started thinking about a double chocolate peanut butter cone, probably as a way to distract myself from the confounding circumstances that I found myself in. Or maybe it was just the bewitching power of ice cream. A sage can be whispering ancient wisdom into your ear, something you've waited lifetimes to hear, but if ice cream makes a sudden appearance, there's faint hope of absorbing the message.

I got my cone, Rebecca hers, and as Clees took his pistachio ice cream from the outstretched hand of the taciturn counter man, he pulled out a wad of cash and paid for all of us. He must have materialized the roll of tens and twenties just seconds before he reached into his pants pocket, because each bill was crisp and new. He then urged us all back to the Elvis table.

I sat on the banquette against the wall, my arm against a faded, cellophane wrapped issue of *Teen Life Magazine* with the Rolling Stones and a young Donovan on the cover. Clees took the seat to my right under a huge *Hard Day's Night* movie poster, with Vee sitting to my left and Rebecca across from me.

"This is a special day," Rebecca said with a look filled with so much compassion, I started to tear up. I was trying to think of a way to respond when Vee began to speak, and I was glad for it because I was getting progressively more emotional. I feigned concern about rivulets of ice cream dripping down my cone and let her talk.

"So, you're the one who wrote the invitation?" Vee asked.

"I did, yes."

"Nice handwriting."

"Thank you," Rebecca replied. "Calligraphy was a specialty in one of my past lives."

As she spoke, and I stared at her, I suddenly had a revelation. "Wait, you were the one who gave me the Dr. Seuss book for my fifth-grade graduation."

Rebecca looked at me and slowly nodded. "That's right. *Oh, The Places You'll Go*. I slipped the words into the invitation message as a prompt. I wasn't sure if you'd remember. I guess I didn't give myself away after all."

"I loved that book, but I couldn't recall who had given it to me."

Vee was itching to ask a question. "We were actually more curious about the image on the invitation's wax seal," she said. "Why the omphalos?"

"You figured it out. That was quick," Rebecca said appreciatively, glancing over at Clees who acknowledged her with a quick nod.

"Never underestimate the power of a good librarian," Vee said.

"Or two superb treasure hunters," Clees added.

I felt myself recovering and was energized by Vee's sudden mention of the omphalos. "You need to know anything Greek, especially regarding oracles, we recommend Mr. Peter Howe of the New York Public Library."

"Noted," Clees said.

"So, why the obscure image?" Vee asked again.

"Did Mr. Peter Howe tell you anything about the significance of an omphalos, what it symbolizes?" Rebecca asked.

"Just that it was culturally important, sort of sacred, and was connected to the temple in Delphi," I answered.

"The word omphalos is ancient Greek for 'navel' and was intended to symbolize the center, or origins, of the physical world," Rebecca said. "Omphalos stones like the one depicted on my wax seal were placed at several points along the Greek coast, the most renowned being the one in Delphi."

Clees interjected. "The omphalos signified power, particularly feminine power. The large omphalos stone in Delphi was placed at the exact center, the most sacred part of the temple, and was believed to facilitate direct communication with the deities."

"So, it was like the planet's belly button," Vee said, "where divine information came in?"

"Or went out," Rebecca answered. Vee smiled back at her.

"What's the connection to you?" I asked Rebecca, still trying to wrap my head around the fact that the woman sitting in front of me was the same person who chatted about alternative realities and meta-physical mysteries with my grandfather.

"Before my current life, and others before this one, I lived in Greece, specifically at the temple in Delphi. My name was Ismene. I was considered a Delphic sibyl or priestess—an oracle able to hear and communicate with the gods."

"Oracle?" Vee asked. "Like in *The Matrix*?"

"That analogy has been made before," Rebecca responded, "but the matrix of the movie was child's play, mere kindergarten stuff compared to what we're speaking about now. And I surely wasn't smoking cigarettes and baking cookies. I would sit near the foot of the omphalos and offer insights, glimpse the future. People would come from all over the world to receive this guidance and the prophecies."

"Did you hear that?" Clees asked, looking from me to Vee. "People from the far reaches of the globe were aware of Ismene's divinations and would travel impossible distances to pay homage to her."

I thought I knew where he was leading with this. "People like Calabris." I said.

Vee sat up an inch taller and fixed Rebecca with a steady gaze. There was something happening between the two of them that seemed to be coalescing as I watched.

"The sibyls were considered legends and were revered for their spiritual insight and the guidance they offered," Rebecca said. "Of course, a man or woman with an oracle's gifts today might simply be considered a skilled psychic, medium, or channel—or even just someone with very good intuition. Times have changed and so has society's willingness to accept these sorts of latent abilities."

"But what about Calabris?" Vee asked again, as if she sensed evasion on Rebecca's part. "Did you know him?"

"I did," Rebecca replied and glanced over at Clees again, an appeal in her eyes.

"Miss Verilee, this is the moment when intrigue can become disorienting. You and Metis will have to suspend all sense of what you think you know."

"I can do that," Vee insisted.

"Metis?"

"I'm not sure what you could say now that would be any more un-settling than what's been upending my world for the past eight weeks," I glanced over at Rebecca, "or the past eight minutes."

Clees snuck a quick look at Rebecca, who responded with an almost imperceptible dip of her head. At the same moment, the shop owner came around from behind the counter, asked if we needed anything else, cleared our table of used napkins, and seemed to linger a few beats longer than necessary before walking away. Clees stretched the pause, punctuated it with a substantial bite of his waffle cone, wiped his lips with a new napkin, and directed his next comment at Vee.

"Ismene was married to Calabris. The strange truth is that the two of you were once man and wife."

Vee laughed nervously. "What… how does that work?"

"Very secretly, actually," Rebecca responded, "Oracles were not le-gally allowed to marry since we were effectively considered property of the temple. Not human, not fully spirit—existing in a sort of in-be-tween state."

"No, I mean… how were we… how did we…," Vee was getting flustered. I suddenly remembered Clees at the Borderland cycling through dozens of my previous lifetimes, showing me just as many lived in a woman's body as those I spent in a man's. I was beginning to understand exactly how this could be, and how it could work.

"There's more," Clees said to Vee, as butterflies took flight in my stomach, anticipating another bombshell. "You had a child together, a boy."

"Spawn of the Oracle," Vee said, "I think I saw that movie." No-body laughed. I felt a rising tension in my chest as Rebecca turned to me and held my gaze.

"No way," I said.

"Yes, Metis, you were the son of Calabris and Ismene," Clees an-swered for her. "An adored and talented child from a most extraordi-nary bond."

My heart started to pound and the psychedelic shapes of a Peter Max magazine cover on the wall seemed suddenly trippier and more surreal. "Okay, I'm having a hard time with this."

"As I said, Metis, it is best to suspend judgment about what we're discussing until you're both better versed in the true nature of this nonpermanent reality."

Vee didn't seem to hear Clees' last remark. She was staring down at the laminated Elvis image, then back at Rebecca, her forehead scrunched in concentration all the while, both hands gripping the table with her ice cream melting in between.

"So, Rog was my... I mean Ismene's and my... we had a child together?" There was bewilderment in Vee's eyes as she looked at Clees, then scrutinized Rebecca.

The two of them let her question sit.

My mind was jumping from one thought to the next. I turned to Clees, "But you said Calabris and I were living with you in Acragas, planning stuff together?"

"Yes, Metis, we were all together, the four of us, Ismene, too," Clees responded. "Although her involvement was more secretive—it required more cunning to keep it safely hidden from temple authorities. Until now, I have never shared anything with you about our personal histories or given any indication as to how much time passed in Delphi and Acragas as we devised our plan. We remained in close proximity to one another for almost twenty years. We needed to wait for you to grow older before we could fully manifest what is now unfolding. Your role, as I have previously indicated, was not insignificant."

There wasn't much more I could take, and Vee was looking overwhelmed and befuddled, too. She was just staring into the slushy remains of her ice cream as she stirred it around in the cup. Clees clearly registered that we'd had enough because after a moment of silence and the last bite of his cone, he put both his hands on the table and lifted himself out of his seat.

"Well, Rebecca, I think we've succeeded in making the start of this California weekend memorable for our guests. Shall we retreat to your lovely home and let these two rest up a bit before our evening's activities?"

"Yes, sounds good," she glanced down at the watch on her wrist. "If we leave now, we can make it to Carmel before the worst of the afternoon traffic." She stood, taking a lilac-colored sweater off the back of her chair and moving towards the exit. Vee and I rose slowly, turned to each other expressionless and started to follow Clees and Rebecca out the door.

As the four of us stepped into the California sunshine, the owner of the shop followed us out with his gaze. What would he say if I told him that he'd just served his frozen treats to a 2600-year-old Greek sorcerer and a former Oracle of Delphi?

He'd have to rethink that "Imagine" tee shirt.

CHAPTER TWENTY-FOUR

Rebecca was driving a red, late model Volvo wagon, which was parked just a few spaces from our junker. She indicated that we should follow her, and just as we were stepping into the dilapidated ambulance, Vee announced that she would ride with Rebecca. Before waiting for a response, she slammed the passenger door and ran up to the Volvo. Clees walked around and climbed into the front seat next to me.

"An auspicious beginning, wouldn't you say, Metis?"

I didn't respond, just angled out onto Lighthouse Avenue, keeping Rebecca's rear bumper in close view. We drove in silence while I tried to sort out all I'd seen and heard in just the past half hour. But instead of wrapping my head around it, I felt more confused.

At a stoplight before we reached the highway, we pulled up close to the Volvo and I noticed Rebecca's vanity license plate: "CALISONE." Any casual observer would have assumed that the Volvo was being driven by an ardent fan of the Golden State: "California Is Number One." But as I stared at it, I started to see something else in the plate's inscription. "Calabris and Ismene are one," I said under my breath. After a few seconds, this interpretation became so apparent to me that it was all I could see, and I was sure this was the meaning Rebecca had intended.

Clees evidently heard my inner musings. "Yes, Metis, I also thought that was a clever fusion. You might want to point out the license plate to Miss Verilee if she hasn't yet taken notice. I think she'll get a kick out of it." I wasn't so sure about that.

"This is all pretty insane—you realize that right, Clees?"

"How do you mean?"

"It's too weird, all of it," I said. "Rebecca resurfaces after almost twenty years, she knows you, she was once married to Vee—but when Vee was Calabris a couple thousand years ago. To any normal person, this is all insane."

"You forgot to mention the part about you being their beloved off-spring."

"See, that's what I mean. Why should I believe any of it? It's crazy. Disturbing even."

"Crazy. Insane. These are subjective observations, Metis, not useful in accurately defining our current situation at all. What you regard as *normal behavior* in the world of time and space, I would call unnatural at best, psychotic at worst. Either way, exactly one-hundred-eighty-degrees from true reality."

I was feeling frustrated speaking with him, convinced that he was being intentionally evasive. And if there were more surprises coming, I wanted to know about them.

"How many more surprises can I expect? Who else is going to show up from my past?"

"Which past?"

"You know what I mean."

"Rebecca is enough for one afternoon, don't you think? But with the four of us together again, things will accelerate. There will be other notable moments, along with general amazements and life-altering events—these are a natural by-product of the heightened vibrational activity that's reconstituting between us. Even I cannot predict all that will unfold going forward—but more surprises can certainly be expected."

"What if I don't want to play along? What if I just want to head back to New York right now and pretend we never met?"

"Is that what you would like to pretend?" he seemed unconcerned by my grousing, as if he knew I was behaving more peevishly than I felt.

"Maybe."

"You agreed to this, Metis. We all did, a long time ago. Don't forget that."

"Says you. I have no idea if that's true or not."

"Oh? Do you think it is possible then, that you wandered into this life with no purpose at all, content to be buffeted by the vagaries of this existence, only to slip away when the bruising was over, stone-cold dead, making no sense of this strange world or your reasons for being in it? That is a rather feeble life plan, Metis, don't you think? Not fitting for you or any other Worldborn."

"Maybe you could do one of those brain acceleration things again, help me to remember."

"Not necessary. Useful memories will come back to you as needed and, as I said, faster now that we've reunited. But understand this, Metis, the relationships the four of us had in lives past only establish how deeply connected we are, how well we work together, and how much we enjoy one another's company. Beyond that, they have no relevance to the present moment or our current mission."

I stayed silent, watching the road ahead of me. Each time we slowed and approached the Volvo, I could see Rebecca speaking animatedly in the driver's seat. Vee glanced over from time to time, acknowledging her in a way that suggested agreement. I was eager to know what they were talking about. Casual catch-up chat spanning the lifetimes since they'd been apart? Heart songs from the lovesick after a two-thousand-year separation?

"So why us, what makes us so special?" I asked, truly bothered by this. "Who decided that we would have an exclusive role in this awakening thing? It feels elitist. Arrogant. I don't like it."

"Who said it was just us or that this mission we're undertaking is exclusive? I told you before that people all over the world have been called on to help. Ancient friends are reuniting for this same purpose, realigning their destinies in the same way as we are."

"Everywhere? People regrouping now?"

"As we speak."

I glanced out the side window at the brown hills, took a deep breath, thought about what that could mean, other people in other places also preparing for... what?

"Okay, let's say I believe you, that there's some sort of destiny shift coming, and all these secret cells are reforming to make that happen. Why now? What's so special about this time in history that it's happening now?"

"I mentioned in the mews that the Covid contagion was no accident, that it set the stage," he replied, still gazing out the window at the passing California landscape. "As difficult and challenging as it was for so many, the global pandemic put all Worldborns into a state of collective readiness for what is to unfold next. A radical shift in human destiny would not have been possible without it."

"The pandemic had a silver lining?"

"Yes, but this can only be understood in a broader context. For the time being, let's just say that mankind has dug itself into a cavernous hole and circumstances are dire enough that an intervention is necessary. A kind of cosmic course correction is now underway, a speed-up happening on a number of vibrational dimensions at once, directed at this crystallized pattern of distortion and despair that's consuming Worldborns and threatening to become irreversible."

"But you keep telling me that this world is an illusion, that's it's not even here," I paused for a moment, "if that's true, then what does it matter if we all die in a pandemic or burn a mirage hole in the non-existent ozone layer and fry ourselves? Who cares if we blow each other up with fictional dirty bombs or dabble in some other form of make-believe annihilation? If there's no world, there's no problem."

"I assumed you would take that tact and it sounds logical enough to a confused mind. On one level, it's even true. But what you don't realize, Metis, is that this drift towards destruction being reflected at the level of form is also occurring at the level of thought, in our collective mind. As I've often repeated, thought is all that matters and all that exists."

He stopped briefly to take in new views of the ocean that had burst through the trees as we sped along. "The shared thoughts of all Worldborns have moved so far from their right minds, and are so profoundly mistaken, that healing the one mind that we all share is growing more onerous. Great fear and pain have been the result, tired hearts have voiced a collective cry for help, and an answer has presented itself. Our mission, undertaken in unison with many others, is that answer."

I was quiet for a moment. "Well, I'm definitely not happy about that child-of-the-oracle thing," I said petulantly, my voice shaking, "maybe this just isn't the right mission for me. You don't know for sure, maybe I'm in the wrong place."

"Then you're in a pickle, my friend," he turned to face me, "because now that your eyes are open, it will be impossible to close them again. There is nowhere to run, Metis."

His last words made me feel anxious and trapped. I wanted to believe that I had an out, or at least that I could slow things down if I needed to.

"Even if what you're saying is true and there really are people everywhere coming together to fix things, it took about a million years for the world to get this screwed up, so unscrewing it is going to take some time."

"Correct, it will take time," he replied, and I felt momentarily validated. "About a second," he added.

I took my eyes off the road and glanced at him to see if he was joking. He wasn't.

"Did you say a second? One second to make this world right with all its endless troubles, trials, and tragedies?"

"Or less," he shrugged. "Once we bring healed thinking and forces of infallible help together, then it will get right in a cosmic instant."

While most everything that Clees had shared with me in the previous weeks was wondrous and welcome, this last statement was so far off base, I had to challenge him. "Clees, I respect you so much, I do. But I think you have a big problem—you really don't know how the world works."

He countered instantly, swatting away my comment without a care. "And your problem, my friend, is that you don't know there's another world."

Just then, Rebecca signaled to exit, which came as a relief because I felt utterly baffled by what Clees was saying. Instead, I put all my focus on the Volvo weaving through a bottleneck of traffic that had formed near the exit.

Monterey, Pacific Grove, and Carmel are charming coastal cities situated close enough to each other that you can drive from one to the next in twenty minutes or less, barring one of California's epic highway snarl-ups. We hadn't been on the road for long before Rebecca made the turn off Highway 1 onto Ocean Avenue in Carmel. I guided the ambulance down a sloping hill following the Volvo towards the sea.

We drove through the downtown commercial district and when we were just blocks from the ocean, Rebecca made a left on Casanova, a north-south thoroughfare dotted with small bungalows and hand-crafted storybook homes, typical of the architecture in the area. These classic Carmel cottages, along with the picturesque setting and quaint commercial district filled with galleries and gift shops, made Carmel a popular destination for weekend tourists arriving from San Francis-co, and an ideal point of departure for sightseers driving farther south along the undeveloped coast. This enchanted village is the last bit of civilization before heading into Big Sur country, a stunning, rustic area of Central California that has drawn nature lovers and spiritual seekers for hundreds of years.

Rebecca drove a couple blocks along Casanova, slowed the Volvo to a crawl, and pulled into the gravel driveway of a small, but appealing off-white bungalow that looked to be impeccably well-maintained. It had a pitched roof, a front door painted deep blue, matching shutters, and lush window boxes filled with tiny white flowers that gave the en-tire place a cozy, inviting feel. From my vantage point on the street, it appeared that a white picket fence at the front of the house extended along the sides of the small parcel into the backyard. I eased the am-bulance onto a narrow, gravel shoulder that ran along her front fence.

The women got out of the Volvo first, walked to the front door and stopped. They waited for us to retrieve the luggage from the ambu-lance's rear bay, pass under an arbor covered in pink roses at the fence entrance, and walk up the short path of blue flagstones bordered by fragrant lavender plants.

"I remained in Pennsylvania for a few years after I saw you last,

Roger," Rebecca said as we approached. "My husband Ken became quite ill with pancreatic cancer. He passed within months and, with both your grandfather and Ken moving on, I decided it was time for me to do so as well. I felt strongly guided to come west, specifically to Carmel, and bought this home about ten years ago. I've never felt so comfortable in a place, both in Carmel and in this house. I hope you'll both enjoy it as much as I do."

She took a step onto her front stoop, turned the brass doorknob that was already unlocked, and led us into her home. The moment I walked inside I could see why she felt so content here. Despite two big coastal oaks and an enormous pine tree towering over the house, the interior was not dark, but spectacularly light-filled, almost gleaming. It was deceptively spacious inside, too. The front vestibule opened immediately onto an open kitchen and a large den with a stone fireplace. Sliding glass doors at the far end of the house revealed a handsomely-built cedar deck, with sitting nooks and benches along its sides, and tiered levels that descended into a carefully landscaped backyard.

And, just as I thought, the white picket fence ran along both sides of the backyard and extended at least another forty or fifty feet past the rear deck. The far side of the fence bordered another dense and well-maintained garden, but I couldn't spot a neighboring house within it. A rear gate in Rebecca's fence opened onto this adjacent plot, but it didn't appear to be part of her property.

Clees crossed the length of the room, opened the sliders, and stepped onto the deck as Rebecca spoke to us. "There are two small bedrooms upstairs to the right of the landing. Pick whichever one suits each of you and make yourselves at home. The guest bathroom is right at the top of the stairs. Why don't you take a few minutes to freshen up, then join Clees and me out back for some iced tea?"

Vee and I dutifully grabbed our carry-on bags and retraced our steps towards the front entrance where there was a carpeted staircase leading up to the second floor. The twin bedrooms sat at one gabled end of the house. There wasn't much more than a double bed, a chest of drawers, a soft-pile area rug, and a sitting chair in each, but both were quite comfortable with several fine seascape paintings on the walls, all signed "R. Blix." Calligraphy was not Rebecca's only artistic talent.

I chose the bedroom on the right, facing the street, while Vee took the other, with a view overlooking the backyard. After placing my bag on the chair and looking out the front window at Clees' ambulance parked next to the road, I walked over to Vee's room, kicked off my shoes, and sat upright on her bed. She was unpacking her bag and placing her clothes in a pinewood dresser.

"Might as well settle in," she said, flattening out some tee shirts on the bed, refolding them, and placing them in the top drawer. "What the hell was that back there at the ice cream place? Some wacky stuff, huh?"

"I'm kind of freaking out, Vee," I said. "Maybe we need to rethink what we're doing here."

She didn't stop her folding or even look up at me.

"It was the kid thing," I continued, "I'm not sure what to do with that. Maybe Clees and Rebecca are delusional… or just plain nuts."

"They don't seem nuts to me. You told me once that you thought Clees was the sanest person you'd ever met. I'd say the same for Rebecca—and they're both smart, too." She hesitated for a second, then pointed to her shoes that she'd left near the window. "Oh, son, could you grab my boots and place them under the bed for me?"

"No, Vee, don't do that. Honestly, that's too much… don't mess with me right now."

But I had the sudden thought that this might explain something Clees had said a few weeks back—about Vee choosing her challenging lifetime in Scotch Plains so she could watch over me, not vice versa. Could that be what he meant? Could he have been referencing some sort of past-life, paternal protection?

"Well, one thing for sure," she said, "this trip ain't gonna be no tipsy, California wine country tour."

She placed the last of her clothing into a drawer while I slipped my stocking feet under her bedspread, leaned my head back on the pillow, and felt a sudden wave of fatigue. I shut my eyes and promptly fell asleep.

CHAPTER TWENTY-FIVE

I woke up to find Vee on her side, breathing deeply, sprawled horizontally across the foot of the bed, her head facing the window with half open lips. I was thinking how attractive she looked, then remembered our recently reported father-son connection and suddenly felt glad our relationship had never turned physical. If you want to bust up a tenacious fantasy in a hurry, just introduce the prospect of sex with your Pop from a previous life.

I pulled my phone out of my back pocket to check the time—6:00pm. I was feeling hungry and wondered if Rebecca's earlier promise of iced tea came with some dinner. I got up slowly from the bed trying not to wake Vee, but she stirred, opened her eyes, wondered aloud what time it was and asked if I thought it was okay for her to sleep for the rest of the night. I told her no, that it was too early to go to bed and that it would screw up her internal clock for the rest of the trip—besides Clees and Rebecca were waiting for us downstairs. She grumbled but pulled herself up onto her elbows.

I slipped my shoes back on, told her I'd meet her down in the kitchen, and headed towards the bathroom to splash some water on my face. Then I went to my room and pulled a fresh shirt out of my bag; the one I'd taken off smelled a bit transcontinental. Before I left the bedroom, I looked out the window towards the street and noticed the ambulance was gone and thought maybe Clees had driven off somewhere.

But when I descended the stairs, I heard the TV on in the den, and as I stepped into the kitchen, I saw that Clees had changed out of the black chauffeur outfit into his West Village attire and was now sitting comfortably in a sleek, modern-looking recliner, casually watching the screen. There was a reporter talking about a resumption of clashes in the Middle East after the collapse of a recent ceasefire between Palestinian factions and the Israelis.

"I don't think of you as a CNN guy, or a news guy at all," I said, as I came up alongside his chair.

He looked up at me with a flicker of a smile, "It's always a good idea to know what the children are doing so they don't end up burning down the house." I guess by children he meant most of the world's population, some of which were engaged in scenes of bloody violence on the screen.

"Hey, where's the ambulance, you park it somewhere else?" I said.

"We aren't going to be needing it anymore. It has served its purpose," he responded.

"Right, but where did you move it to, down the street?"

"We don't need it anymore." He repeated this calmly but gave me a look that said he'd spoken the last word on the subject of the ambulance. My mind flashed to that early morning asteroid visit and the way he'd made the Citi Bikes disappear just by the saying of it.

Vee came down moments later, poured herself a glass of Rebecca's iced tea from the pitcher on the counter, and walked over to us, "Hey, where's the ambulance?"

"We don't need it anymore," I answered.

She glanced over at me. "Okay, but where is it? It wasn't out front."

Clees turned off the television, got up from the recliner, took a few steps out the sliders onto the deck and walked slowly into the backyard.

"The ghost mobile didn't get us here, Vee, and we won't need it to get back to the airport."

"What the hell does that mean?"

"Just don't ask him any more questions about the car," I said, and followed Clees outside, stopping to admire the rear deck. The cedar boards were arranged in a way I'd never seen before, sort of spiraling from the outside edges of the platform towards the center where I stood. The pattern had a whimsical, somewhat hypnotic effect. Clees had moved to a woven hammock that hung between two medium-sized trees in the yard, untied his sneakers—which I recognized as the same blue ones I admired the night of the impossibly large lighthouse—and lifted himself into the string cocoon.

"That was very Cleesian of you," Vee said, joining me on a slatted cedar bench built into the deck architecture. Ever since our time on the mystery bridge, whenever I'd say something that was unclear to her, or abstract, she'd call it "Cleesian."

"That looks good," I said, staring at the reddish-brown liquid in Vee's frosted glass.

"Get your own," she responded in a stony tone that was quintessentially "Veesian."

Before I could get up, Rebecca came out of the house with a tray containing three brimming glasses, each with sprigs of spearmint resting at their lips, along with a plate of fruit, cheese, and crackers. One glass was presumably for her, the other two for me and Clees. She rested the tray on the top step of the deck for a moment, handed me one of the glasses, then moved to where Clees was resting in the tree cradle.

"Grab a couple of those folding chairs and join us down here," she said, indicating a cluster of wooden lawn chairs stacked against the side of the house. I hopped up and grabbed two heavy teak folders, while Vee made her way into the garden.

Rebecca's backyard wasn't carpeted like an East Coast lawn, not green or cropped fairway short, nothing like that. I didn't see many verdant lawns on our drive over, I guess because much of California is a desert and keeping one's yard golf course green would require an irresponsible amount of groundwater.

Instead, Rebecca's eighth of an acre was covered with stands of lush beach grass and clusters of colorful flowers—bright red bougainvillea, some type of white lily, more pink roses, along with thickets of purple lavender. In between the indigenous growth was a meandering walking path softly blanketed in dark woodchips. The path branched off in several directions but the widest led straight from the cedar deck to the gate at the back fence, passing the hammock along the way. I was crunching along this footpath with a chair in each arm while Vee carried my drink.

As I approached, Rebecca was maneuvering a teal blue Adirondack chair, the kind that was common back east, so that it was facing the rear of the house. Clees rolled out of the hammock, more deftly than I would have imagined he could, and pulled a second Adirondack, this one forest green, next to Rebecca's. Neither of them sat down but, instead, stood behind the raised chair backs waiting for us to get settled. I casually placed the two folders in an arc in front of them, so that the four chairs formed an approximate circle and Vee and I sat down.

"Are you sure about those spots?" Clees asked. "It would be prudent to place yourselves in the most advantageous positions for a productive dialogue."

I looked at Vee, then towards the garden, the side fences, and the back of the house. I studied the placement of the chairs and thought that each was situated well enough for easy conversation, along with good views of our surroundings.

"I'm not speaking about positioning yourself for pleasant scenery, Metis," Clees said. "I'm suggesting you both discern where to sit based on something more subtle."

"This is like on the bridge," Vee said, and I remembered exactly what she was talking about. Clees had directed us to specific places at his side, suggesting that this would impact the intensity and value of our dialogue. He said it had to do with the way energy moved between us, something like that.

"Yes, Miss Verilee, same dynamic as on the bridge," he responded, "and just like then, this is not personal, it is not about you sitting where I want you to sit, it is about each of us intuiting where we might derive maximum benefit from our exchange."

"So how do we do this?" I said, hovering over my chair.

"You find your seat in the same way that you found your way successfully off the bridge that day and back to your restless city," he said.

"Focused attention and common sense?" I asked.

Rebecca answered for him. "Helpful hints and useful clues are coming at us constantly, Roger, but most of us aren't paying attention.

If we did, we would begin to align with these signs and enter a percep-tible energetic flow that would make everything we did in life easier, almost effortless—as well as facilitate our preparation to take a bigger step."

"Doors will open," Clees added, "and you will be propelled forward in ways that offer the highest possible outcome for all Worldborns. Consciously and consistently piecing together meaningful clues, coin-cidences, and synchronicities will allow Worldborns to make a conse-quential shift forward."

"*May the Force be with us*," Vee said in a slightly sarcastic tone in her best Yoda-like impression as she turned to me. Neither Rebecca nor Clees reacted to this.

"We want you to practice heightening your sensitivity to the pres-ence of these clues, which can come in many forms, many different ways, so you'll need all your senses at the ready," Clees said. "Above all, you must try to avoid using the intellect, it will never give you the answers you want. In fact, it will only get in the way. For the mission we're undertaking, brainpower will be of little use. One-hundred per-cent intuition, no intellect, one-hundred percent heart, no head should be your goal going forward."

"So, again you're telling us, don't think?" Vee asked.

"Don't try to mentally work this out," Rebecca responded. "Feel where to sit, using all of your senses to collect and decipher signs and clues."

"What's the point of this?" I asked, feeling my frustration build. "If I did this for every decision I had to make, it would waste an incredible amount of time and I wouldn't have any way of verifying if I was right anyway."

"Actually, both of those statements are incorrect," Clees said. "Once you learn to use your feeling senses, your intuition, in place of your intellect as your primary decision-making tool, you will save vast amounts of energy and time. Lifetimes."

"But how can we tell if we're really in the flow and getting the right signs, not just making stuff up?" I added. "It all sounds so vague and wishy-washy."

"It won't happen instantly, it takes practice," he responded, "but once you achieve a degree of mastery, you will always know whether you are on track because the results will be undeniable. As well as extremely comforting. You will feel this as a certainty, you will know this unassailably."

"I'm kind of with Roger on this," Vee said in a tone that also sounded exasperated, "what difference does it make in the big picture where we park our butts right now? How is picking a damn chair going to help the world from tipping over the edge?"

"It is not your chair selection that matters per se, Miss Verilee, it is about retraining vital, inner mind muscles that have atrophied since we last convened. You can begin to stimulate and strengthen those deeper senses once again through the process of locating the chair that is most optimally suited to you, the one most energetically aligned with the rest of us."

"Clees is saying that choosing a seat to sit on, like all other things that we do in our everyday lives, should not be undertaken unconsciously," Rebecca added, "but with an awareness that there are no accidents and no coincidences, and everything is interconnected."

Vee shrugged and looked at me. "Okay, let's just do this, Rog, let's pick us some ass targets."

With no more conversation, Vee and I repositioned our feet slightly and made solid contact with the ground. Then I tried to focus on bringing my sense of smell, sight, hearing, taste, and touch into alignment. Vee must have been doing the same because I could hear her smacking her lips and taking some deep breaths.

I must have gotten better at the common sense technique since that first time on the bridge, because almost immediately I caught the scent of eucalyptus and spotted a sprig of leaves floating down to a patch of dried grass behind Rebecca's chair. I assumed this was significant because there were no eucalyptus trees nearby that I could see. Then, as soon as the leaves touched down, I heard a rustling at the grass's root base. Nothing happened for a moment, and I was about to turn away, when a small gecko darted out, stopped, tilted its head to look me directly in the eye and scurried off under Rebecca's chair.

"Wow," I said, and Rebecca and Clees both followed my line of sight.

"What happened?" she asked.

"I think I just got a message from a gecko. Sight, sound, and smell at the same time, drawing me to that patch of grass there, then towards the blue Adirondack by Rebecca. Is that stupid?"

"No, not at all. Triple play, well done, don't ignore that," Clees said. "You take Rebecca's chair, see how that feels to you."

I took a few steps, plopped myself into Rebecca's Adirondack and, curiously, felt more relaxed and calmer than I did by my folder.

"What do you notice?" Rebecca said.

"I'm comfortable. And feel kind of peaceful," I responded.

"That's exactly what you're looking for, a lightness, a sense that all is aligned, all is well," Rebecca said. "Stay exactly where you are."

Then she, Clees and I turned our attention to Vee. She shuffled a bit and looked awkward as our eyes bore in on her.

"Do you have to stare? I'll get this, just give me a sec."

Then, after a few moments of uncertainty, she started to walk slowly around us in a kind of musical chairs parody, breathing deeply through her nose as she did, eyelids closed to mere slits. After two revolutions, touching each chair back as she passed, she returned to the seat where she started.

"Here, I belong here," she announced decisively, then sat in her original spot.

"How did you come to that conclusion?" Clees asked.

"It's just where I felt most comfortable, like Rog said. Each time I walked by, this was the chair that spoke to me. None of the others did."

"Excellent," Clees said. "And correct. I felt the energetic flow ease the moment you made your decision."

He then dropped where he was standing at the green Adirondack chair as Rebecca came around and took my original seat, next to Vee. Now the men and women were sitting opposite one another.

"I knew where my seat would be as soon as I rolled off the hammock," Clees replied. "The color green makes me happy." He gave us both a look filled with equal parts mischief and delight.

"Applying this new understanding of common sense and carefully noting useful coincidences will reliably reveal the next pieces of our unfolding puzzle," Rebecca said. "This process is testable, verifiable. But start small and practice consistently. Don't feel like it all has to come together at once—it's not a one-and-done event. Just pay attention, stay alert, and follow any inspired guidance you receive—no matter how insignificant or innocuous it may seem. This alone will accelerate the number of meaningful synchronicities in your day."

I settled into my seat and looked around at the others. I became aware of how easy it felt to be in this foursome. The connection seemed to go deeper than friends, more like the intimacy of family. Clees said often that we shared one mind and there in Rebecca's backyard, at that moment, I felt that the four of us also shared one body. It was a strange, yet reassuring sensation.

When Clees spoke next, I knew that I wasn't the only one having this feeling.

CHAPTER TWENTY-SIX

"Our true family is reuniting after a long absence, renewing our commitment to an ancient pact," Clees said, looking at me and Vee, pausing to let that sink in. I felt a shot of adrenalin course through my veins. Vee reacted, too, shifting in her seat.

"I have been speaking to you both about a great awakening," Clees continued. "I have said that it is inevitable, as well as something that all Worldborns deeply want—whether that is a conscious awareness or not. Any discussion of a universal wake-up should prompt two questions from you—what are we waking up from and why is this critically necessary now?

"In answer to the first question, as I've suggested to you both before, Worldborns are currently lost in a mass hallucination of their own making. Everything experienced through the senses is a fabrication of the sleeping mind, every element of this universe, down to the smallest and most intricate detail, is a thought construct created by all Worldborn minds operating together. If you had even an iota of understanding about how this one misguided web of thought makes up the world, and keeps it riveted in place, it would stagger you. But virtually no one realizes what's going on here at all."

"You're saying that we are making everything up together, nanosecond by nanosecond," Vee asked, "and there is nothing permanent or objectively real here at all... and that we're all in on it?"

"Not consciously, but I assure you that this is true, Miss Verilee," Clees answered. "And the implications of this, while astonishing at first, are also extremely promising. If the truth of what I'm saying is universally accepted, escape from this hallucination can be universally employed."

"Think of it this way," Rebecca chimed in, as if repeating something she had heard Clees say many times before, "if we dreamed all of this up together, we can undream it together… but we'll need help."

"Which brings me to the second point, why this is critically necessary now?" Clees continued, with another measured inhalation and another deliberate exhale. "Mankind has reached a crossroads, a decisive moment. For eons, Worldborns have explored a million paths to escape their endless troubles and taken countless detours, but no road has alleviated the emptiness or suffering, no pathway is free of despair and, ultimately, the perception of death, final and forever."

He had touched on these points during our car ride to Rebecca's and I found what he was saying just as dispiriting sitting in her backyard.

Then it got worse.

"There is a creeping awareness among a growing population of Worldborns, magnified by the global pandemic and the ubiquitous presence of pointless wars, that the situation has become entirely futile, that they have reached the darkest hour. Utter chaos appears to be gripping the planet and its people. All life feels out of control, dysfunctional, in a permanent state of decline—and the cry for help has never been more deafening or insistent. You are aware of what I'm speaking of, Metis, Miss Verilee?"

"The world does seem totally chaotic right now and people have plenty of worries, if that's what you're asking," I responded.

"Yes, and this can be useful—a shared sense of doom among Worldborns can actually spur meaningful and inspired action. In fact, the only good use for pain is that it can propel change, finally driving Worldborns to say, 'There's something very wrong with this picture and we need to choose another way.'"

"That's twisted about pain being helpful," Vee said.

Clees ignored her comment and continued.

"The physical world's temptations will never offer a way out, nor will they ever provide an ounce of sustainable joy. It's all seek and do not find here. There is no point any longer in pretending otherwise—

any possibility of finding an answer to the heartache and wretched gloom people experience on earth is doomed. The world holds nothing that you want. It's a complete dead end."

"Okay, Clees, this storyline is getting *really* dark," Vee interrupted. "It's going to bum out a lot of people—like it's doing to me now."

Rebecca put a finger up before Clees could respond. "If the narrative stopped there, Vee, there would be justification for abandoning all hope and giving up. Many throughout history have done exactly that upon exhausting the world's external answers for filling the void—financial success, political power, religious devotion, material rewards, sexual pleasure, and romantic relationships, to name just a few. Only to discover that all eventually fall short and lead nowhere."

"But the story does not end there," Clees continued, with even more vigor in his voice. "In fact, this is the point where all hope is restored, at exactly the point where this senseless world of bitter nightmares disappoints so utterly and inexorably. When you no longer turn to it for relief, when you cease to pin your dreams for satisfaction and salvation on false idols and choose instead to shun the world's shiny but momentary allure… only then is it possible to find a way out."

He sat back and smiled, looking radiant. I had no idea why he appeared so buoyant because I'd heard nothing yet to make me feel anything but miserable. He'd just proclaimed, and Rebecca concurred, that there is no hope of finding happiness in this world.

I wanted to get up and run from the backyard.

"Stay put, Metis," Clees said, raising a hand that seemed to glue me to my seat. "I'm not done yet. Leave now and you'll miss the part where Acragas, Colombia, New York, and California come promisingly together."

I realized that I was gripping the arms of the Adirondack chair and lightened my hold just enough to start the blood flowing through my fingers again. As I tried to settle, I was briefly distracted by the sound of an animal, maybe a cat, mewing loudly in the yard behind the back fence. I saw Clees' ears prick at the sound as well, but then he resumed talking which refocused my attention.

"It's time to connect the dots between our years together in Acragas, your experiments with incubation in Colombia, and our preordained reunions in present day New York and California… as well as gatherings of a providential nature yet to come."

"Thought you'd never get around to it," Vee said, and Clees silenced her with that same look he used on the mystery bridge, one equally adoring and reproving.

"So, what is the common denominator between Ismene's oracular gifts, Calabris' instant travel talents, and the insights you shared during your Colombian incarnations?" he asked.

"Focus," Vee answered, "it's obvious. In every case, their abilities involved an intense level of focused attention."

"Focused attention, good, training the mind to stay alert, yes," he said, "but there's more to it. They all understood that what they were seeing with their eyes was not the truth, had nothing to do with real vision, and completely missed the point. They also had the awareness that they could use their heightened senses to look past the lie and the illusion to the real world. They were able to increase the number of meaningful coincidences in their days, which in turn facilitated their ability to actively participate in their unfolding futures—thereby shaping their own personal destinies and finding their deepest purpose, while pointing the way for others. To say it slightly differently, Ismene, Calabris, the Zipa, along with her jaguar priest, understood how to remove the blocks to waking up. And what they came to know is teachable."

"Clees is saying something really important here, the crux of which has brought us together again across the span of so many lifetimes," Rebecca said. "There is a profound level of possibility now, truly transformational and unlimited, that those who are joined across the globe in pockets of activity like ours are comprehending. Our age is ready, and a critical mass of consciousness is crystallizing as we speak. Clees and I believe—along with many others—that lifetimes of learning are converging at this moment, that radical change is upon us, and a quantum leap in understanding is about to trigger an unprecedented awakening."

"You guys are driving me crazy," Vee said, stamping both feet for emphasis and almost taking out a thatch of lavender by her chair. "It's all stick and no carrot with you two."

Clees and Rebecca both smiled, and Clees reached out to touch Vee's knee as if to underline his appreciation of her. I wasn't sure how I felt at that moment. Overwhelmed, I think. Scared, for sure. A global movement? Radical change? Quantum leaps? And I was supposed to join others, clusters of strangers worldwide intent on paving the way somehow?

"You're absolutely sure we signed up for this?" I asked.

As all three turned to look at me, the feral cat sound, more like a wail or cry this time, drifted over us again from the back fence.

"What's with that cat?" Vee asked, shifting her body to see past Clees' shoulder.

"Maybe in heat," I responded. "Sounds sort of like the alley cats prowling behind my apartment building at night."

Clees completely surprised us then by standing up, turning without saying a word, and walking purposefully towards the obscured back gate.

"Wait, Clees," Vee stood up and called out after him, "what happened to connecting the dots between Acragas, Colombia, and California? I've waited like a thousand years for this."

He didn't turn around or respond, just opened the gate, and stepped silently into the adjacent garden where the yowling sound was coming from. Within seconds, we lost sight of him in the fading light. I got up to follow him, but Rebecca touched my arm as I went to step past her. "It would be best if you left him alone."

"I don't get this guy," Vee said to no one in particular, but in a way that let us know she was annoyed, "his timing is the worst."

Rebecca revealed a whisper of a smile, one that made me think she'd experienced this same frustration with Clees herself in the past.

"One of the drawbacks of staying in the present moment," she explained, "and acting on the messages that reveal themselves in that moment, is that our best laid plans often get waylaid. Clees responded to an impulse that needed to be addressed now, not later, not when it was convenient. *Now.* Neither life nor miracles unfold according to our schedules. You're going to have to adapt moment by moment. This level of spontaneity will clash with your accustomed routines and the world's accepted rules of behavior, but eventually you'll find it exciting and marvelously rewarding."

"I'm not sure how well this is going to go over at work," I said. "Sorry, Manon, I'd like to make our morning meeting but the present moment calls. Gotta run, be back when the spirit moves me."

Rebecca flashed another quick smile before responding. "Yes, this will test you. You're going to find out in a hurry how radically spontaneous you're willing to become. And how committed you are."

"So, what now?" Vee asked, still staring off into the rear garden thicket.

"Dinner," Rebecca answered, and without hesitation stood up and headed back to the house, with us following.

I turned once, still curious about what caused Clees to leave us so abruptly, but by then I couldn't see or hear anything coming from the abutting garden. I soon learned, however, that the keening sound that called out to him, the feral yowling that made Clees suspend his much-anticipated explanation of what we were all doing there together, was no cat in heat at all.

CHAPTER TWENTY-SEVEN

After a home-cooked meal, consisting mainly of fresh produce grown in a small but productive vegetable patch at the side of Rebecca's house, the three of us retired to the back deck. A half-dozen battery-operated, flameless candles flickered pleasantly in the night, casting a soft light onto the spiral pattern of the deck boards which had again captured my interest.

At some point between preparing dinner and us eating inside, Clees had returned to the green Adirondack chair where he was sitting now, silent, and barely moving. Rebecca again urged us to let him be.

While we breathed in the cool night air, talking in soft tones, Rebecca filled us in on the lush plot lying beyond the back fence, the garden into which Clees had hurried off. She told us that a few years before, she had turned the 100'x100' lot—with the City of Carmel's approval and with her own money and labor—into an impeccably tended garden, "a place where people can go to break down or break open and, eventually, break free," she said.

We asked her what that meant, and she explained that she'd always dreamed of a living sanctuary, a refuge, filled with growing things that wouldn't judge, wouldn't interfere, and wouldn't try to make things better as people dove into their dark places. "I wanted the garden to be there to absorb the melancholy, the anger, and the despair carried into it, with no attempt to change it. It's an ideal place to go deep, pulled into the fertile darkness where we can explore all that is blocking us."

Open to the public, she explained that the handsome garden was not only accessible by the secluded gate in her backyard, but also by a more welcoming public entrance on the street side. As I found out during several explorations in the days that followed, the garden was dense with branches and leaves, tree roots and shoots, all tangled together to form a kind of "organic, emotional shock absorber," as Rebecca put it.

There was a split rail fence lining its perimeter, covered in crawling vines so lush you could barely see the garden's demarcation. There were paths thick with woodchips underfoot, just wide enough for two to walk side-by-side. Weathered teak benches were tucked inside stands of swaying beach grasses and Weeping Cherry trees. More Adirondack chairs were placed here and there throughout the bursting growth, lying low and solitary, so that sitting in them put you at eye-level with violet snapdragons and calming lavender plants. An enormous eucalyptus tree, probably the one that had dropped the sprig that helped me "locate" my energetically optimal seat a few hours earlier, anchored the far end of the garden leaning slightly away from the ocean.

Rebecca called this place "The Wailing Garden," and as you entered on the street side, there was a neatly lettered sign hanging over the entrance which I recognized was painted in the same precise, calligraphic hand that she'd used on the invitation sent to me and Vee. It read:

> *The Wailing Garden is a place to drop to your knees.*
> *You can shed tears here, face your fears here.*
> *You can confront the rage that fills you, or grieve your losses.*
> *No one will ask questions.*
> *No one will interrupt.*
> *Hold nothing back, leave no box unopened.*
> *Stay as long as you like, leave when it feels right.*
> *Return again.*
> *The garden will pass through its seasons, as you will pass through this,*
> *Cleansed, cleared, and ready to awaken anew.*

Rebecca told us that from the first day the garden was open, people came. First out of curiosity, then for more. Somehow, she managed to get the city to allow her to keep the street gate unlocked twenty-four hours a day, and she said that from her bedroom window at night she could hear hushed voices, and weeping, along with the occasional howl of anger or wail of grief—what I had thought were cats mewling. She called these "the sounds of repair," and told us that only through this honest process of laying bare and engaging with one's "concealed shadow" was personal acceptance, healing, and release possible.

"It takes courage to look deeply at the hidden dark side," she added, "to bring your hate, grievances, and judgments to light—but it's the only way forward. You must look within, expose it all, even the most difficult parts. This part of the journey is rarely pleasant but dropping into the underworld of your own screaming darkness is essential for the reparative journey to begin. You must feel it to heal it."

"But cold caves? A dark side? The howling underworld?" Vee responded. "Why would anyone volunteer for that?"

"It's not for everyone, Vee, definitely not for the faint of heart," Rebecca replied. "At times the healing process can feel more painful than the original wound. That's why so many people on spiritual journeys bow out at this point, avoid the inner forest, take a long detour. They'd prefer more unicorns and rainbows, more heart emojis and feel-good stories. There is nothing wrong with that but, in the end, there's no escaping this thorny step and no alternative. It's the dark places inside us that close the door to light and love, and that's where we must go to open them. It's the only way to remove the emotional obstructions that make it difficult, even impossible, to stay alert for transformational signs and synchronicities. If you are busy hiding your hurts, and locked in the past, you can't find the clues that only reveal themselves in the present."

"So, when you and Clees make this pitch for a plunge into Pandora's Box, you actually get takers?" Vee added. "I'd probably opt for a thousand-mile detour myself."

Rebecca paused like she was trying to decide whether to comment on this. Then she spoke. "Do you know the whole Pandora's Box story? Have you ever read it, all of the allegory, to the end?"

"Everyone knows it—basically, it's a bad idea to open Pandora's Box. The bats fly out, all the evil escapes, and the world is swamped with demons."

"That's not where the story ends. That's just where people stop, at the warning—'Don't open Pandora's Box, it will kill you.'"

"Right, excellent argument for keeping the lid closed."

"Wrong. Read the full allegory, it's the conclusion that no one talks about. After all the evil and darkness is released, one thing still remains at the bottom of the box."

"Dead bodies?"

"No… *hope*. Hope lies at the bottom. Isn't it a wonder that almost no one tells you that? In our world, we're discouraged from exploring the underlying cesspool of our dark thoughts; from truly diving in. But that's where all the gold lies, below the surface, just waiting for us."

Rebecca stopped so we could take this in. Vee glanced at me, but I didn't respond. I was already prepared to join her on that thousand-mile detour.

"You don't look convinced," Rebecca said with a smile. "I understand, I've been there myself. When Clees and I reconnected some years back, and he explained to me what had to be done, I resisted. Even with some understanding gained in my lives as a guide and oracle, I had skeletons in my past I wanted to keep buried. I also felt like so many people do when awakened beings like Clees show up in the world and share what they know—I was terrified. That is why mystics and metaphysical savants like Clees have been condemned and crucified throughout history. Way too frightening. Way too demanding, their light too bright."

"So, how do you get past the terror and resistance?" Vee asked.

"It's definitely made easier if there's someone nearby who has gone into that cold, dark cave themselves and survived. It's important to know that you're not alone and safe while you make your way through this arduous, but life-altering passage."

"Safe? How do I know I'm safe? Sounds scary as hell, like I'd be in great danger."

"Shadows cannot kill, Vee," Rebecca answered obliquely, "and I can promise that you'll have plenty of help." She held Vee's eyes for a moment longer, before turning back to the calm of the garden's dense flora.

In many ways, Rebecca's garden seemed sad to me, but she said it was precisely all those tears shed and deep emotions felt there, as well as the mindful removal of inner debris—"the hidings we hold onto, the undiscussables"—that made it such a beautiful and hopeful place.

A few more moments passed before she half-whispered something that made me want to cry, words that have stayed with me ever since. "You think that all of your dreams are broken, all of your hopes dashed, and every cherished promise ever made to you will not be kept. In fact, all are intact, none have been diminished, and not one is ever lost. Not one."

I was thinking about this, looking off into the garden, green and deep and for the moment, quiet, when I noticed Clees shift in his seat, his hands still hanging loosely in his lap. His head was bowed a few inches forward and he appeared to be either sleeping or staring down at something in the flower bed.

"Is he sleeping?" I asked Rebecca.

She looked up and shrugged, "I doubt it."

"Does he sleep?"

"There are better ways of resting than sleeping, Roger."

"Like what… meditation?"

"Like waking up," she replied. "That's the better way."

Vee cut in. "How does waking up help you rest?"

"There is only one thing to do in any lifetime," Rebecca responded, "and that is to awaken from all your lifetimes."

No one said anything for a minute, then Vee stood and stretched. "Well, sorry to disappoint you, but I'm going to get some rest the old-fashioned way—asleep in a bed. You staying down here, Rog?"

"No, I'm going to head up, too," I said, and stood. "Thanks, Rebecca, for everything. It was a pretty weird day, I won't lie to you, but I'm glad we've reconnected after half a lifetime. See you tomorrow if the world's still here."

"Sleep well, you two. I can pretty much promise more eye-opening revelations in the morning."

I followed Vee to the top of the stairs where she stopped on the landing and turned to me. "That Wailing Garden, I don't know, pretty heavy," she said, peering out the window.

"Yeah, agreed. It sounds like Rebecca was tying visitors purging in her garden to the 'wake-up' thing… and to us being here. It's a lot to process, at least for me."

Vee shuffled slightly and the light from a streetlamp caught dew forming in her eyes, maybe The Wailing Garden's influence touching Vee from a distance.

"Good night, Rog," she said quietly, retreating to her room and closing the door.

As I stood leaning against the landing rail, I saw that it wasn't a streetlight that had illuminated Vee's tears, but a full moon shining into the upstairs window. It was pretty and hypnotic. Eventually, I tottered the few steps into my bedroom, eased the door shut, and collapsed onto the mattress without removing my clothes.

I was so tired, I wondered if I would ever wake up.

CHAPTER TWENTY-EIGHT

My eyes opened at 7:00, an hour I thought was impossibly early until I realized my body was still on east coast time. When I opened my bedroom door to check on Vee, I saw that she was already up, her curtains pulled open, and her bed neatly made. I heard her animatedly talking with Rebecca in the kitchen, the pleasant smell of something baking drifting up the stairs.

I wandered into Vee's room to look out the window into the backyard. Clees was no longer in the Adirondack chair but instead was standing at the far end of Rebecca's yard talking to a young, solidly built man who stood a few inches taller than him. I hadn't even showered yet and our first full day in California was off to an intriguing start.

After I washed up and changed into fresh clothes, I went downstairs. Everyone was sitting outside on the deck, including the newcomer. As I passed through the kitchen, I spotted the source of the fresh-baked aroma—blueberry muffins left out on the counter to cool, along with a carton of orange juice next to a small teapot.

I reached for a muffin, grabbed a napkin and put both on a plate, then poured some tea into a mug, adding a dollop of honey and milk from a porcelain pitcher. I slipped an apple from an overflowing fruit bowl into the pocket of my sweatshirt, then carried my food spoils towards the sliding porch door.

Before I stepped out, I stopped to take in the new arrival who was now sitting next to Clees on one of the benches built into the deck. I guessed he was a little older than Vee and me, probably late 30's, muscular and athletic-looking, with a movie star's good looks—almost intimidatingly handsome.

He had short, thick black hair with a shock of striking silver at the front, offset by alert blue eyes. His eyes were unusual, an azure color like those brilliant skies you see in postcards of alpine ski resorts. He also had a high forehead over a prominent nose, with a noticeable scar near his right temple. His skin was a lightly baked, reddish-brown that I was sure didn't come from a tanning bed. He was dressed casually in a plaid, jacquard Western shirt, denim jeans, and a pair of battered brown cowboy boots that looked like he might have actually worn them wrangling horses.

The man had an easy manner, punctuating the air with casual hand gestures when he made a point and smiling amiably as he did. I continued to watch him for another half minute; he looked vaguely familiar, and I wondered if I'd ever seen him before. But I concluded that we had never met and stepped outside to introduce myself.

"Hi, I'm Roger Steiner," I said walking over to him and extending my hand after putting my mug down.

"Hey, man, Kyle Ferguson, nice to meet you," he said in a warm, genuine way, pulling me in for a half hug. "I hear your first day in California wasn't boring." He chuckled at this, something I soon learned that he tended to do at the end of almost every sentence. This might have seemed like a nervous tic, annoying coming from some people, but with Kyle, it just made him more approachable. I liked him immediately.

I took a seat next to Vee as Kyle asked us a few questions—how we first met, if we liked New York City, what kind of work we did. But as we exchanged pleasantries, I suspected that Kyle's conversation with Clees at the back fence earlier had included more vital information about our visit than he was letting on.

"Kyle lives down the coast in Big Sur," Rebecca said then, seeming to intentionally shift the dialogue. "He drove up this morning to hang out with us for a couple hours before he gets going with his workday."

"My family owns a ranch about forty miles south of here," Kyle offered. "My great grandparents immigrated to the west coast from Scotland in the late eighteen-hundreds, bought three thousand acres cheap, ten dollars an acre when nobody else wanted it, and started a cattle ranch. About twenty years ago, my parents decided that they weren't interested in raising cattle anymore, so they sold the herd and turned our spread into a dude ranch of sorts. We run horseback riding trips into the Big Sur backcountry now, mostly for tourists and San Franciscans who can't get enough of the big redwoods down there. It's some of the most beautiful wilderness on the planet, as far as I'm concerned."

"Kyle left out some important pieces," Clees interrupted, putting his hand on the rancher's shoulder as he spoke. "There's more happening at his place than horses, something more aligned with our current mission. Why don't you tell them about it?"

Kyle smiled, then shifted his powerful frame on the bench so that his face and those bright eyes were illuminated by an early morning sun burning through the coastal fog. A blanket of cool morning mist was typical along the Pacific coast in the summertime. It was why I had zipped my sweatshirt up to the neck and pulled my hoodie up over my head. Vee had done the same with the hooded cotton sweater she was wearing.

"Our ranch is on old Esselen lands," Kyle began, "the Native American people who lived in the Big Sur hills and Santa Lucia mountains for ten thousand years before the Spanish arrived. There were a couple thousand Esselen living in these parts at their peak, but their population dwindled, and then mostly disappeared somewhat mysteriously in the early eighteen-hundreds. Today, no full-blooded Esselen natives live in California."

"Tell them about the caves," Rebecca urged.

"So, our ranch was basically a sacred site for the Esselen clan," Kyle continued. "There are several hot springs on our property which were used in tribal rituals and medicine healings. There's also a string of deep caves and underground chambers on the land, with ancient pictographs on the rock walls that few people have seen. Shortly after he bought our spread, my great-grandfather was out surveying the property and stumbled upon the caves. Later, exploring them with my great-grandmother, they found the pictographs."

Vee looked over at me when Kyle mentioned the caves and he noticed.

"Yeah, exactly, caves like the ones you guys experienced in an action-packed past life of your own, from what I hear," he said, punctuated by that easy chuckle again. His face betrayed no circumspection or doubt.

"So, you know about the Muiscan lairs in Colombia?" I asked.

"Just what Clees has shared with me," Kyle answered, "but the whole thing sounds completely consistent with what the Esselen were up to on our property during their own out-of-body rituals. At least that's how we interpret the cave drawings and our own experiences inside the underground chambers."

"You've incubated?" Vee asked, pulling the hood off her head to see Kyle more clearly.

"No, not that exactly, but everyone in my family has had some kind of…" he hesitated, glanced at Clees, then continued, "mind-expansion or revelatory experience happen to them up there. As far back as the first Fergusons, there have been family stories related to the caves that most people would find incredible… or unbelievable. My grandmother was an intuitive and had frequent contact with long dead Esselen elders and tribal medicine men when she visited the caves. I would often go with her as a kid, as early as I can remember, and the sort of channeling she did, communicating with the departed, never seemed odd or strange to me. It was perfectly normal. Now my daughter seems to have inherited her great-grandmother's gifts—Feather has powerful visions that are always heightened when I take her to the caves."

The plot thickened. Kyle had a daughter. Named Feather.

"I believe that Kyle's daughter is an indigo child," Rebecca said, "although Kyle doesn't like me using that term."

I read about indigo children once in a magazine article. The piece focused on a group of kids in Romania, but all indigo children are supposedly born with amazing paranormal abilities. Some people believe that these highly creative kids, who seem wise beyond their years and can perform unexplainable feats—like appearing in two places at once—are here to usher mankind into the next stage of human evolution.

"Nope, not much into labels," Kyle responded, but with a smile. Something about his tendency to not take anything too seriously reminded me of Clees. "I just worry that you make too much of her abilities. Feather is an amazing kid, no doubt, but I'm pretty sure what she does, any of us could do if we had her upbringing and her total suspension of disbelief. She's not 'special.' Most people are just totally tuned out and simply not picking up on the messages coming at them rapid-fire, sunup to sundown. Feather notices them all."

This was beginning to sound a lot like one of Clees' riffs and I was going to question Kyle about that when Vee spoke.

"Your kid is named Feather?"

"Yeah, Feather," he responded. "I know, very California. But she actually told us the name she wanted before she was born. My grandmother communicated with her when she was still in the womb. It happened when we were visiting the caves a month or two before my wife gave birth."

"Your daughter told you what she wanted to be called? Like, she spoke to you… in utero?" I asked, just to be clear.

"If Clees and Rebecca haven't told you yet to put everything you think you know on hold, this would be a good time to do it," Kyle said, smiling broadly, "because it's probably only going to get weirder and wilder from here."

"Yeah, they've warned us, more than once," Vee said, "but some stuff needs repeating before it goes in all the way."

Kyle laughed at this and slapped his knee. I didn't think what Vee said was so funny, but he found it sidesplitting.

"So does your wife work on the dude ranch, too?" I asked, to bring him back from the Land of Glee.

"She did," Kyle answered, "not anymore. She was thrown from her horse and hit her head on a corral post. It was a bad fall. She went into a coma and died a week later. That happened when Feather was only four, so five years ago."

"Oh, man, I'm so sorry," I responded, wishing I hadn't asked. Vee started fidgeting in her seat, obviously discomfited by this news, too. But Kyle seemed untroubled, even serene reporting this. Maybe the passage of time mediating his loss?

"It's okay, really," he assured me. "It was initially sad, of course, and left a huge gap in our family, especially for Feather. She was really attached to Laura… that was my wife's name. We were in communication with her while she was comatose and immediately after she left her body. Actually, it was Feather who helped us understand my wife's passing, the reason for it and that it was okay, even meant to be."

"What do you mean she helped you? She was four. What kind of child understands about death at age four?" Vee asked this with intense interest. As she did, scenes from my visit to the Borderland flashed through my head. What kind of child can understand loss and grief at that age? Maybe one with a full understanding of the unreality of death because she's visited the landing place in-between lives that Clees had shown me… and remembers it.

As Kyle was about to answer Vee's questions about Feather, he shifted his weight in a way that stretched his torso and exposed his belt buckle. It was one of those big silver and brass affairs with elaborate designs stamped in high relief that rodeo cowboys wear. I had to look closely to be sure that I was seeing it correctly, but then the morning light caught the buckle squarely and there was no question what I was looking at—a kila, about two inches long, beautifully crafted in great detail, with its three-bladed tip pointing boldly towards a radiant sun.

CHAPTER TWENTY-NINE

"What you have to realize about Feather…" Kyle was saying, but I interrupted before he could get another word out.

"Your buckle. That design. Where did you… why are you wearing that?"

Clees answered before Kyle could.

"I told you in the car yesterday and will repeat it for Miss Verilee's benefit—we are not alone. Thousands of years of experimentation, evolution, and discovery are converging now. People the world over, even forces in dimensions beyond this one, are pulling all of their experiences and abilities together to create a connected field that will allow Worldborns to participate in their unfolding future. Through that joining, and in that field, extraordinary things can and will happen."

"Okay, but how could Kyle know about a kila? How many did Calabris give you, Clees? How many other people have one?" The sight of Kyle's belt buckle had propelled me to my feet. I was standing just a yard from him.

Rebecca answered for Clees.

"There's a chance now to work as a unified collective, Roger, passing clues to one another as we get them. This will redefine what is possible, open doors to new insights, and usher in radical change through an extraordinary era of intentional miracles. Ultimately, this will prepare us for a deliberate shift into a world beyond the one you think you know."

Vee cut in then, speaking directly to the rancher who was listening placidly to our animated back and forth, "Kyle, why is there a kila on your belt buckle?"

He smiled, took a deep breath, seemed happy to address a question that had originally been directed at him.

"Clees didn't give me a kila, Roger, and as far as I know, he only had one," Kyle said, while passing a thumb over the metal buckle at his waist. "This design, almost exactly as you see it here, is taken from one of the Esselen pictographs found in the caves that I mentioned. My great-grandparents were fascinated with all the rock art and petroglyphs, but this particular image affected them both deeply, so much so they named the ranch after it. We call it the Soaring Arrow Ranch."

There was a pause as Vee and I tried to assimilate what Kyle was saying. "So, the Esselen hunted with three-bladed arrows?" Vee asked.

"The pictograph that this arrowhead appears in is not a hunting scene," Kyle responded. "It is something else entirely and hard to explain. The visual themes relate to elevation, transformation, transcendence… something like that. From what Clees has told me, it sounds like the scenes resemble the out-of-body exploratory journeys your Muiscans were having centuries ago."

"So, the Greeks, the Muisca, and the Esselen were all engaged in the same paranormal phenomenon even though they had different belief systems, lived thousands of miles apart, and across big gaps of time?" I asked, trying to make sense of this.

"The truth of reality is the truth, Metis, it does not change based on place, time, culture, or country," Clees responded. "Remember what I have been telling you, that all thoughts are shared. All minds are one. The Greeks, Muisca, and Esselen all being aware of the same universal, metaphysical truths, along with other peoples, too, like the Incas and Mayans, is not at all far-fetched."

"So, you're saying that the Esselen knew what a kila was?" Vee pressed, looking uncertain.

"I doubt they called it that," Kyle replied, "and I never heard the word 'kila' myself until Clees mentioned it to me about a year ago. What the Esselen did apparently understand was the idea of one-pointed focus, represented through their own three-edged, ritual daggers. The Esselen rock art tell us that their medicine men and elders were involved in directing the tribe's fate by staying intensely aware of clues in their environment, looking for signs and following this guidance exactly. There is every indication from the cave drawings that they were actually trying to leave this reality together—to dematerialize as a group by using their own techniques of hyper-alertness, probably to escape Spanish aggression."

"The Mayans were supposed to have done that, too, raised their vibrations together or something and vanished—just mysteriously disappeared," I added.

"That's exactly what they did do," Clees said, his tone leaving no question that he had inside information on this point, "and what the Mayan and Esselen figured out, all Worldborns can know now, too."

I stepped back, sat down, and was mentally processing all of this as I picked up my mug and stared mindlessly into my now cold tea.

Rebecca spoke. "The value in the universality of this image, the kila, a soaring arrow, whatever you wish to call it, is that it can be used today to help us identify each other, so we can immediately recognize those mighty companions who walk the world as we do, those we can trust who share our mission."

"So, are we looking for people carrying kilas now?" Vee asked.

"As you've both learned, the physical kila itself is not the point," Clees said, "it's just a symbol, but a powerful one… unmistakable even. As you suggested to us a couple millennia ago, Metis, we can use the message behind the kila as a way to identify others doing exactly what we're doing."

"Hence, the belt buckle?" Vee asked, looking over at Kyle who just smiled in return.

"Yes, exactly," Rebecca responded, answering for him. "Or you might see someone wearing the three-edged blade as a lapel pin, a button, a neck pendant, earrings, even a kila tattoo…"

"Or cufflinks," I said.

"Or cufflinks," Clees acknowledged.

"That's how Kyle and I found each other actually," Rebecca said. "I was hiking in Andrew Molera, a state park down in Big Sur… I guess it was three years ago. I had reached a bluff with a great view of the ocean when I saw Kyle and Feather sitting on a rock outcrop nearby, eating picnic sandwiches. I walked over and was chatting with them for about twenty minutes, falling quickly in love with Feather, when I noticed Kyle's buckle. That changed our conversation in a hurry and it hasn't stopped since."

"I think I need to meet this Feather," Vee said, speaking to Rebecca before turning to Kyle. "Is your daughter around? Can we visit your ranch at some point? I've never ridden a horse." I realized that I'd never been on horseback either.

"Yeah, I think we can make that happen," Kyle responded. "Clees and Rebecca want you to see the caves anyway, and Feather always likes to go up there with me."

"Cool, can we ride horses then, too?" Vee asked.

"It might be easier to take an ATV if you've never been in a saddle before. You city slickers might get pretty butt sore after a day of riding."

Vee looked disappointed, but I was relieved. "Off-road vehicle sounds good to me," I said, not feeling like the horsey type.

"I need to head back and get ready for our first group of day trippers," Kyle said. "Fridays are busy with guests but I don't need to ride with them. I can send out other guides to take them around. I could meet up with you later today, if that works? At the main house, say, one o'clock? We can spend some time exploring the backcountry as we head up to the caves. You all would be welcome to stay for dinner afterwards. That sound doable, Rebecca?"

She nodded. "Sounds perfect, and that'll give Roger and Vee time to look around town a bit before we get in the car." She turned to us. "You'll like Carmel, and there's a fun bookstore I'd like you to see."

Kyle stood up and brushed off his pants, despite them looking perfectly clean to me, maybe a horseman's reflex. Then, as we all got up to see him off, he took a few steps towards Vee and put his hand on her shoulder. "Feather's going to know stuff about you."

Uh-oh, I thought.

"She does about everyone," he continued. "She can't help it, she just sees things, has access to more information floating in the air than most people. You can ask her about it when you meet her, she doesn't mind talking about it."

I waited for Vee to bristle, but instead she smiled.

"I can't wait. I like a girl with moxie."

I exhaled and just stared at the two of them. Only the second day in California and already the world had shifted on its axis.

We walked Kyle to the front yard where he climbed into an old pick-up truck that was parked where the ambulance had been.

"1960 Ford F100," Vee blurted out when she saw it. "I'm guessing 292 V-8 Flareside, three-on-the-tree?"

This made an instant impression on Kyle, who broke into his signature, five-star grin. "You got that right, city girl," he said, as he turned the key. "Belonged to my grandpa way back when, but she still runs real good. Okay, see you folks later."

He pulled away from Rebecca's picket fence with gravel flying. As he did, I saw his vintage, black and orange California tag—"ARROW." I guess everyone in this state had a license plate story to tell.

As the four of us were walking around the house to the back porch, Vee returned to the subject of the kila on Kyle's belt buckle.

"Sorry to fixate on this, Clees, but I thought you said the kila wasn't necessary, we didn't need it, let's chuck it in the river. Now it's back, taking on even more importance."

"Once more, for the fixated," Clees responded with a half-smile. "The physical kila has no power in itself, it is not where the answers lie. Worldborns are always confusing form with content. Besides, you were both getting obsessed with the thing and that did not serve us. Better to discard it. As an identifying shibboleth, however, yes, it's back and it's useful."

"So, what about you two?" Vee pressed. "Where are yours?"

Rebecca stopped abruptly on the steps of the deck, turned her back to us and used her right hand to pull her hair up. At the nape of her neck was a tattoo of a three-bladed arrowhead, small, not more than an inch-and-a half long, this one bluish gold with a bright red tip. It was pointed down, not up as one might expect.

"Nice ink," Vee said, then turned to Clees. "Can I do ink?"

"As you wish," he responded casually. He was standing at the deck's edge looking in the direction of The Wailing Garden again, turning his head slightly to listen.

I wondered out loud about the directional incongruity of Rebecca's tattoo. "I assumed arrows would fly upward, towards the sky, and elevated consciousness would travel the same way."

"Arrows do, but focus can be directed wherever it's needed," Rebecca said, dropping her hair and combing it back into place with her fingers. "For many people, preparing for their awakening is facilitated by going down and in—not up and out—to the void many of us feel deep inside. This connects to The Wailing Garden and what I'm good at."

"Does anyone ever see it back there, your tattoo?" I asked. "It's kind of invisible."

"We notice what we need to notice, when we need to notice it," she answered cryptically. "Besides, I often wear my hair up. I had my hair in a top knot that day at Andrew Molera when I met Kyle and Feather. I also had it in a ponytail yesterday when I met you at the ice cream shop, but your minds were in other places."

Clees headed back down the steps and started to walk towards the adjacent garden again. "I'll meet you back here at noon for the ride down to Kyle's," he said, waving behind him. "Enjoy Carmel. It's a sweet town."

"I'm still waiting to see your tattoo, Clees," Vee called after him playfully. "Don't think I'm going to forget."

He half-waved again but kept walking. I wanted to follow him but felt Rebecca's gaze keeping me in place.

"Isn't he just bothering people slinking around in your crying garden like that?" I asked.

She took her previous seat on the deck, pinched off a nibble of the muffin I'd been eating and popped it into her mouth.

"We've noticed a dramatic increase in people visiting the garden in the past year. It's been written up in some alternative travel guides and on spiritually oriented websites, even mainstream travel sites, and people are coming from all over the world to experience it. This is an exciting time for us—an important time."

She took another morsel of the muffin, chewed thoughtfully, then resumed. "If you haven't guessed by now, Clees is thrilled to have reconnected with the two of you again. He's excited about the possibilities in front of us. He views all that is currently happening as an inevitable continuation, maybe the culmination, of our work together in Acragas. The clearing or unblocking going on in The Wailing Garden is part of our work now and he can help accelerate that process for people by being close to them. They probably aren't even aware that he's there, frankly. He's operating on an energetic level, not wiping tears from crying eyes or offering hugs. Although, hugs aren't off limits."

She smiled at the mention of hugs and that made me wonder, not for the first time, if there was something intimate going on between her and Clees. But sex between the sorcerer and the sibyl was too much for me to wrap my head around, so I filed the thought away and decided to ask Vee what she thought about it later on.

But she wasn't waiting.

"Are you and Clees fooling around?" Vee asked Rebecca.

"All the time," she answered, not missing a beat. "We're always fooling around, every minute. That was something Clees and I missed when we were all together in Greece… to play with this illusion, not take it too seriously, and enjoy the ride."

Rebecca got up, finger hooked the handle of my mug, grabbed the plate with the muffin crumbs on it and stepped into the house.

I followed her with my eyes, then turned to Vee. "What just happened?" I asked, confused.

"The world's one big orgy, didn't you know?" Then she hopped up to follow Rebecca inside, but not before tousling my hair as she passed.

CHAPTER THIRTY

Rebecca gave us fifteen minutes to wash up and get ourselves together before walking into town to explore Carmel. The fog had burned off and the day was brilliantly sunny. As we passed bungalows planked in redwood and cedar, I smelled woodsmoke in the air, unexpected on a summer's day, but pleasant, nonetheless. California in July was full of surprises.

"I've been thinking," Vee said as we walked three abreast on a quiet, uphill road within earshot of the ocean. "It's about Ismene and Calabris."

I was sure I didn't want to hear whatever was coming next but turning around and walking back to Rebecca's at that moment seemed like bad form. And I had to admit to some curiosity about the relationship that resulted in my former life as a Greek wonder child.

"If Ismene was a gifted seer and Calabris was this super advanced being," Vee continued, "then they probably were aware of each other somehow, right, they would have known about the other?"

"I don't remember all the details, but Clees does. He said that just after Calabris arrived in Acragas, a messenger came from Delphi. He gathered people at the main temple and shared a prophecy that Ismene, that was me, had made just days before. The oracle spoke of the arrival in Greece of an 'almost-human who would arrive on the shaft of an arrow.' So, yes, Ismene knew about Calabris, and he was aware of her reputation in Delphi."

"Okay, so if they were both buzzing on this higher plane, and they hooked up, then they must have been soulmates, right, destined to be together?" Vee continued.

"That's a messy term, soulmates, and I don't want to say 'yes' without some clarification," Rebecca answered, stopping at the top of the hill to point out a view of the ocean a short distance off. Surfers in wetsuits were paddling on their bellies, positioning themselves to catch a string of six-foot waves breaking a hundred-fifty feet offshore. I knew that the Pacific Ocean was a lot colder than the Atlantic and it was obvious from the floating cluster of black-clad boarders that neoprene protection was necessary, even on a mild summer day.

After a silent half-minute of surfer watching, Rebecca started walking again and we fell into step with her.

"This idea of soulmates is grossly misunderstood by people here," she continued. "It is generally used to describe a special romantic relationship, one where two people come together to create a bond at the exclusion of all others. 'You and me against the world,' that sort of thing. This is considered very positive, very desirable. But it isn't truly helpful to anyone at all. It isn't connection, it's separation, because it fundamentally excludes others."

"But I thought the big goal in life was to find your soulmate," I said, "you find your soulmate, you've made it, you get to live happily ever after."

Rebecca gently tsk-tsked me and I knew she wasn't buying it.

"Sorry to disappoint you, Roger, but it's quite the opposite. If you create a relationship where you and your partner are intent on becoming one impenetrable duo, blinders to the rest of the world, you're in big trouble. That's a prison, not a paradise. The relationship that Ismene and Calabris created was a very different kind of bond, much more powerful and transformative in that it embraced others and invited them in. It had a higher purpose and was built on conditions of service that transcended the two of them and their individuality or personhood. Do you know anything about that kind of union between partners?"

I looked over at her and said nothing. Vee kicked a fat pinecone lying in the road.

"No, you know nothing about it because it's never talked about, rarely seen, and not understood here. And what I'm describing certainly is not the stuff of top forty love songs. A true soulmate bond is not a gift for just two people, it is not personal, it's for all Worldborns to share. It is not built on a 'partner savior dynamic,' it is about union with autonomy and independence. Ismene and Calabris had that kind of connection—one that transcended fleeting human love, or a worldly romance that comes and goes uncertainly with no promise of stability. So, yes, they were soulmates, but probably not in the way you mean."

"No such thing as a simple answer from you or Clees, is there?" Vee asked.

"Thoughtless answers to mindless questions are what landed Worldborns where we are today," Rebecca said.

"Ouch," Vee responded.

"I'm sorry, Vee, but it's better to get clear on what works rather than continue to reinforce what has failed us all miserably throughout time, and always will. I still adore you, though, don't worry about that."

She wrapped both hands around Vee and gave her a quick side hug. Vee leaned in, not out, and I felt confident that peace would prevail.

As we approached the commercial district, a concrete sidewalk appeared that was crowded with strolling tourists looking into shop windows and entering galleries that had their doors flung open to let in the summer air. Carmel-by-the-Sea was like Pacific Grove, but even more picturesque and storybook charming.

Vee walked into a gift shop on Ocean Avenue with interesting t-shirts prominently displayed on a rack outside. I left her to her browsing and checked out the menu posted in the window of a Middle Eastern restaurant a few storefronts down. Rebecca had slipped into a yarn shop and was talking animatedly with a saleswoman who she appeared to know well.

After a few minutes, I took a seat on a curbside bench to people-watch and wait. There was a vintage Mustang convertible parked directly in front of me that was getting a lot of attention from passers-by. California was filled with these immaculately restored, classic cars. Everyone seemed to have one, but I noticed that this cherry red Mustang had Vermont license plates. Either it was a recent import, or someone had been tending to it lovingly on a daily basis. I made a mental note to point it out to Vee. Five minutes later Rebecca walked over from the yarn shop and sat down next to me. As she was settling in, Vee appeared behind us.

"Wow, sweet," she said, walking right past us to appraise the pristine car. "1966 Ford Mustang Sprint Special, mint condition. Looks like a six-cylinder, too, kind of rare." She took a few steps closer, speaking mostly to herself. "Wonder how they kept it like this through Vermont winters?"

We listened to another half-minute of Vee's automotive commentary before Rebecca stood up and ushered us down the block towards the bookstore she mentioned.

"The owner of this shop is tuned in," she said. "Clees calls him the Paperback Warrior. He wears the sign, and you won't have any trouble spotting it."

We entered the bookstore through a narrow alleyway off a side street that made it seem even more mysterious and served to heighten my sense of anticipation. Vee charged ahead apparently determined to develop her kila detection skills. I had no doubt our excellent treasure hunter was going to find the owner and apply all her common sense muscles to find him first. Rebecca walked a few paces behind her, and I brought up the rear.

The spacious store had several large rooms as well as a tented outdoor area and no shortage of unusual merchandise with a decidedly esoteric bent. If Rebecca and my grandfather had ever opened a bookstore together, these were the titles and trinkets that would have been on their shelves. Here was everything you ever wanted to know about meditation, astral travel, alien visitors, death, near death, past lives, mysticism, metaphysics, psychic powers (and how to develop them), the history of religion, the Aquarian Age, esoteric philosophy, plant medicines, paranormal phenomena, quantum physics, tantric rituals, opening the chakras, the I Ching, and every form of yogic practice you could name.

There were also books on alchemy, vampirism, the Dark Arts, neo-paganism, Christianity, the Knights Templar, how to connect with angels, biographies of every spiritual leader who ever lived and some who just "hovered," plus everything else ever written on spirituality, mythology, and astrology.

But that was just the books. If you were in the market for wind chimes, gongs, purifying sage sticks, singing bowls, tarot cards, Buddha statues, dream catchers, crystals, yoga mats, meditation pillows, detoxing bath salts, herbal teas, healing magnets, bonsai plants, or inspirational greeting cards, this was the place for you.

I was smelling a dozen attractively displayed, essential oil candles, with Rebecca a few feet away drawing pleasant sounds from a small Tibetan singing bowl, when Vee came around the corner pulling a small, middle-aged man with a friendly face and round, wire-rimmed glasses.

"This is Martin Newbold, folks, wearer of a kila ring," she announced, and I immediately looked at the man's hands.

"Hi, Marty," Rebecca said as she gave the Paperback Warrior a hug. "I guess you've figured out that this is Vee."

"Yes, and this is Roger, no doubt," he said enthusiastically, reaching out to shake my hand. Clearly, our reputations had preceded us.

"How are you guys liking California?" he asked, making small talk.

"Just arrived really but, so far, it's lived up to the hype," I answered.

"I'm from back east originally, too," Martin said, "but the sunshine and outdoor living seduced me, and I couldn't leave once I'd been here awhile."

"You grew up in New York?" Vee asked.

"No, born in Burlington, Vermont, actually, moved out here to attend UC Berkeley and basically never left."

"Vermont?" I responded, "so, that's your vintage Mustang parked up the street?"

"Mustang? No, wouldn't be mine, I drive a rickety old Subaru," he said, and I thought that this was a strange coincidence. Then my attention went back to the ring on his finger.

"Did you design that?" I asked, looking at the intricate band. It was a circle of bluish silver, shaped like an arrow with one end fashioned into the now familiar, three-bladed arrowhead.

He beamed at the question. "Not only is it my design, I tooled it, too. I like to work with precious metals. I've made quite a few kila and phurba pieces. Not just rings, but necklace ornaments and tokens for charm bracelets, too. I keep them here, although I don't display them prominently. It's more interesting to see who comes in asking for three-edged arrowhead jewelry. In the past year, more and more people have discovered the significance of the symbol and have come here asking for them. I always give the pieces away, since I know that these visitors are ambassadors for an emerging world movement. So far, I've given kila pieces to people from twenty-seven countries and counting. Can you believe it? This new awareness is galvanizing globally."

Martin said this last bit with such a surge of excitement, I thought he was going to lift off the floor. He then invited us to have a cup of tea in an upstairs office with a balcony overlooking the main room of his busy operation. As we stepped into the aromatic space, where he was burning some woody, hypnotic Palo Santo incense, it became clear that our visit wasn't so spontaneous, and that Martin had been expecting us. Four teacups were arranged on a low table with three folding chairs spread out around it. He wheeled his high-backed office chair over to fill the fourth space.

"Grab a seat," he offered, and I got nervous that this was another test of our skills in common sense. Vee must have had the same thought because she hesitated before plopping down herself.

Rebecca saw what was happening and intervened. "Vee and Roger are practicing using their intuitive muscles, looking for clues to help them make decisions," she said to Martin. "We emphasized to them yesterday that even picking a chair, particularly in an energetic dialogue with others on the same journey, can make a big difference."

Martin laughed. "I know it can seem a little neurotic and crazy-making at first, but once you get the hang of it, searching for signs is not only really useful but enjoyable and entertaining as well. It's like *Candy Land* for grown-ups."

He was referring to the old school, kid's board game where you race around trying to find King Kandy, the lost ruler of Candy Land. I played it with my sister when we were really young, but I didn't remember much about the game except that it was absorbing and, Martin was correct, quite a lot of fun.

As he poured a fragrant herbal liquid from a steaming, black stoneware teapot, Martin continued. "Did Rebecca tell you how we came to learn about each other's interests?"

"Judging by the theme of your bookstore," I replied, "I just assumed she was a frequent customer."

"No, not at first," he responded. "About five years ago she called here early on a Saturday morning, before we opened up. I was the only one in the store, so I answered the phone. She wanted to know if we had a particular title, one on ancient Greek poetry. The book in question included remnants of writings attributed to the philosopher Empedocles. Incredibly, I was reading that very book at the time. It was sitting right here on my desk. You have to understand, it was an impossibly obscure title. This was much more than a coincidence."

"I had just reconnected with Clees—that's a longer story for another time—and I wanted to acquaint myself with his prophetic poetry," Rebecca said. "I thought Martin's esoteric bookstore might have the title in stock. Once he shared that he was reading it at that moment, I knew we had entered another dimension."

"Rebecca introduced me to her friend Clees shortly after that," Martin continued, every word infused with his unique brand of infectious excitement. "He actually schooled me in the dynamics of focused attention, among other things. I had Empedocles as my personal trainer. Pretty special, huh? It took a while, more than a year I guess, but eventually I learned his common sense technique, and how to consistently stay alert for clues in my environment; more or less anyway, it takes a lot of practice."

"Yeah, we know," Vee said sarcastically, taking a sip of her tea. I was already deep into my cup. It was very good, licorice mixed with something else.

"Vee and Roger have created a sort of mantra to help them remember the message behind the kila," Rebecca told him. "Pay attention. Stay alert. Be aware. Because the guidance and clues are everywhere."

"Oh, I like that," Martin said, reaching for a pen and yellow pad on his desk. "I need to write that down. I'm going to share that with others if it's okay with the two of you?"

"Totally," Vee answered. "The original kila that Clees showed us also had the word 'ESTIA' engraved into its shaft. That means 'focus' in Greek. So, we added that to our mental mantra, that focus is the key."

"Yes, very good," Martin said as he continued to write. "The need to stay focused is a strong argument for not wearing earbuds constantly or burying our noses in front of our devices all day long. I fight the urge to check my phone constantly. The curse of this age, in my thinking, is overstimulation of the senses blocking out awareness of all the unseen help coming to us moment by moment. 'The sidewalks are littered with postcards from God,' Walt Whitman wrote, but most of us never seem to notice. Shame."

Martin sat back in his roller chair, placed the pen and pad back on his desk, and seemed to slip away for a moment. Rebecca touched his leg gently, "Remember what we talked about, Marty?"

"Oh, yes, sorry. So, Rebecca thought I might share with you a little about the work of David Bohm. Do you know who he is?"

"Physicist, right?" I replied. "Quantum physicist, I think."

"That's correct," he said, "brilliant thinker. Albert Einstein once said that Bohm was the only person who could explain quantum theory to him. So, Bohm certainly had the brain power, but more than that, he understood about using focused attention to accelerate human evolution."

"Is he still alive?" Vee asked, reaching over for the teapot, and pouring herself more of the licorice brew.

"No, Bohm died in nineteen-ninety-two. But not before leaving a voluminous paper trail that hints at the same ideas Empedocles was trying to communicate as far back as Greece."

"You've read all of Bohm's books?" I asked.

"His books *and* his academic papers, actually; I admit to being a bit of a geek when it comes to quantum ideas. I've read most of the books in the store on the subject."

"Martin has read most of the books in the store, period," Rebecca said, taking Martin's hand and squeezing it. Vee glanced over the balcony to the rows and rows of bookshelves containing thousands of titles and let out an exhausted sigh.

"Clees has been telling me to stop reading and start applying. 'Time for action,' he says, so, I'm trying to do that more," Martin added. "The jewelry making gets me out of my bookish head somewhat. Making the pieces is very engaging and it also attracts new friends." He paused, appraised me and Vee and smiled in his high-spirited way. "This is all so fascinating, isn't it?" His roller chair bounced a centimeter in the air, propelled by his buoyancy.

"Back to Bohm," Rebecca said, reminding Martin about the physicist.

"Oh, yes, Bohm. Amazing mind, way ahead of his time. He wrote about a 'generative order,' basically how we can all work in flow with one another, as a single intelligence, to manifest massive change in this quantum illusion—the world we think we see. He spoke of a phenomenal power that we all have inside us, a creative force that will allow us to do amazing things and have extraordinary experiences collectively. He also wrote about how to release this power."

"In part by paying close attention to what's blocking it," Rebecca interjected.

"Right," Martin continued, "Bohm talked a lot about the remarkable potential we have to pass cues on to one another and work in unison towards an active unfolding, but that we also have something blocking that potential. He wrote passionately about this—that we need to give attention to this block with everything we have, with our muscles and bones, to break free of these obstacles."

"I don't understand, what exactly was Bohm referring to?" Vee asked.

"I'm not entirely sure, Vee. I've read every word of Bohm and I'm not sure that *he* was entirely clear on what he was talking about," Martin said, "but he mentions the blocks frequently. He said that they kink the hose in the flow of idea sharing and interfere with our ability to receive help. He may have been referring to emotional blocks from past experiences or even past lives, if he believed in that, I don't know. But what he does emphasize is that these internal distractions keep people from staying in the present and prevent them from knowing what is needed of them in the immediate here and now."

We sat silently working over what Martin had just shared when his desk phone beeped. He picked it up and listened for a moment, responded with a quick "Okay," then came back to us.

"I've got to go downstairs in a moment, check on a delivery. Would you like to take a peek at my kila creations, see if one of the pieces speaks to you?"

"I'm going with a tattoo actually," Vee responded, "but I'd still like to see them."

"I'm not much of a jewelry guy," I answered, but then I thought about the mysterious "Vermont" coincidences coming in such close succession and thought I should follow this one to its conclusion, as Clees had been urging us to do. Maybe Martin Newbold, native of Vermont, had a piece to add to the puzzle. So, I quickly added, "but if you have a pin or something, maybe I'd be interested."

"Let's take a look," Martin answered and stood up. "I've been playing with some new designs, maybe there's something that will appeal to you."

The three of us followed him downstairs to the main desk where he signed some papers as we browsed the bookshelves. How was it possible that Martin had read all these books? It would take me several lifetimes.

He finished up with his delivery, then directed us to another sales counter where he pulled out a velvet-lined display box from a locked cabinet. In it was an assortment of fifteen or twenty, finely tooled jewelry pieces, some were silver-blue in color, others were gold, in addition to silver kila necklaces, bracelets, rings, and pins. There was also a tie bar and a pair of cufflinks that looked just like the ones Clees had been wearing in the cosmos.

Vee picked up a small nose stud that I might have grabbed, too, if I had a piercing in the right place. She held it in her palm and looked to be considering it, but after half-a-minute she laid it down next to the cufflinks. "These are all amazing, Martin," she said, "but I know exactly where I want to put my kila tattoo."

I was curious to hear what part of her body would be indelibly marked with this inspiring new image. I was about to ask when I noticed Martin staring at me, waiting to see if I was interested in a piece. Before I could say anything, Rebecca spoke up.

"Martin, what happened to that amulet necklace you had, the one on the leather strand?" she asked.

"Oh, yes, I have it in another display roll." He leaned down and brought up a handkerchief-sized square of navy velvet that he unfurled on top of the counter. "I had it out a few days ago to show a fascinating young fellow from Belarus who studies string theory. He tried to explain why string theory is a *theory of everything*, but Clees assures me that it's the theory of nothing. Confusing. Anyway, here's the pendant."

Along with another half-dozen, carefully crafted rings and pins was a chunky, two-inch, three-bladed kila hanging from a twenty-inch cord of brown leather. I liked it immediately.

"This is cool," I said, picking it up and hefting it in my hand. The bolt was not pure silver but made of a heavy silver or iron alloy that seemed to be the same metal as the original kila, the one that appeared in my hand after the visit to the otherworldly lighthouse and that Clees ended up tossing from the bridge.

"What kind of metal is this?" I asked. "A type of silver?"

"It's not pure silver, I've tested it," Martin answered. "It's not an alloy of any metals I'm aware of. Clees gave me a couple of nuggets last year and asked me to shape them into kila pieces. This amulet is one. I made a ring with the other that I've already given away."

I slipped the simple necklace over my head, snapped shut the lobster claw closure made of the same bluish silver alloy, let it fall over my sweatshirt and turned to Vee.

"It's you," she responded and smiled.

I spun to my left to show Rebecca.

"Definitely you," she concurred, a noticeable sparkle in her eye.

"Yeah, maybe. Can I buy it?" I asked Martin.

"No, no, a gift," he responded. "I want you to have it, Roger. My pleasure."

I objected, insisting that I would pay for it, but Martin clearly wasn't having it and Rebecca assured me that it was okay to take the necklace, suggesting that it had found its rightful owner.

We lingered for a few more minutes as Martin put the jewelry roll and display box away, then he walked us through the alley passageway and out onto the street.

"Please come back and see me before you leave Carmel," he said, still buzzing and bubbly. "Your visit here will certainly yield more clues, and every day that someone comes in from a faraway place, they bring another piece of the puzzle for me to ponder. Stop by and we'll compare notes."

Vee and I assured him that we would as Martin briefly hugged us both goodbye and we left. As we were walking back to Rebecca's house, I picked up the kila hanging at my chest to admire it. It was plain and unpretentious, which I liked, and it felt substantial around my neck, formidable despite its modest design. I was surprised at how comfortable it was to wear, never having owned a pendant or piece of jewelry of any kind before.

After Vee watched me lift it up and roll it over in my hand a few times, she turned to Rebecca. "Looks like Roger's got a new good luck charm. Maybe now he can get rid of that damned Liberty Bell."

They were both laughing good-naturedly as we walked out of the commercial district, but not before I noticed that the last store in town was a Ben & Jerry's ice cream shop with its famous slogan prominently displayed in the front window: "Vermont's Finest."

CHAPTER THIRTY-ONE

By the time we returned to the house, making a quick detour to walk along the beach where Vee gathered a few shells and an oddly shaped stone ("This one looks like Homer!"), Clees was back from The Wailing Garden, his latest mission of comfort-offering having concluded for the time being.

He was leaning against the kitchen counter eating an apple when he spotted the kila pendant around my neck and responded with a half-second smile. "You got it," he said, and I suddenly felt set up.

"Wait, how'd you know I'd… but I don't like jewelry."

"That's not jewelry," he said, pointing to the pendant. "That's a wake-up call."

I took it in my hand and looked at it again and it struck me that this really wasn't for decoration or personal adornment; it was to send a message, or receive one, and suddenly my new pendant took on added significance.

"Well, I like it," I said, "and I'll keep wearing it. Martin said he got the metal for it from you. What is it?"

"I told you once before… mental matter." Then he pushed himself away from the counter and announced that we all had ten minutes before we would leave for Kyle's ranch. With the day turning warmer, Vee and I headed upstairs to drop off our sweaters. We also both slipped into shorts and ankle-high hiking boots that we'd brought along for the trip. It sounded like we were heading into rugged terrain, and this seemed like appropriate footwear. Precisely ten minutes later, the four of us piled into the Volvo with Rebecca driving, me riding shotgun, and Clees and Vee sharing the back seat.

As we drove, Rebecca told us more about the history of Carmel and pointed out various points of interest on the route to Big Sur. The rocky coast became more spectacular as we headed south, and we stopped at a few lookouts to take in the scenic views. At one turnout we saw several humpback whales breaching, which Vee found amazing, yelping each time one of the big gray bodies surfaced, sending a cloud of mist from its blowhole into the air.

After a half hour on Highway 1, with Vee snapping photos of memorable seascapes and me commenting on rockslides around almost every turn in the narrow roadway, Rebecca announced that we were close to Kyle's ranch.

She slowed down two minutes later as we approached a deep canyon. Fifty-feet off the highway on a rock-strewn, single lane path was an open wrought iron gate with a large, rectangular piece of weathered metal about 15-feet up, welded horizontally across two stanchions. In big capital letters, cut neatly into the metal, it said, SOARING ARROW RANCH.

Below that was a whitewashed, roughly 5' x 5' wooden sign with precise black lettering and red highlights secured to one of the stanchions that read: "HORSEBACK RIDING. Big Sur Backcountry. Family Trips. Day Excursions. Spectacular Views. TOURISTS WELCOME." A phone number and website address appeared below that. The signage looked hand-painted and professional, and I wondered if Rebecca might have played a part in creating it.

We turned in and Rebecca slowed even more as the Volvo lurched over and around deep ruts and washed out areas of the dusty approach road. We bumped along for another five minutes until we came to a big clearing at the bottom of two steep slopes that cradled the heart of the Soaring Arrow Ranch. The first thing I noticed was Kyle's vintage Ford pick-up parked alongside three large corrals with a dozen or so horses inside each, some huddled under substantial lean-tos built to offer relief from the midday sun. Large troughs of water stood between several corral posts and a few of the smaller ponies were taking long drinks.

It was a morbid thought, and I was a little ashamed for thinking it, but I found myself wondering which corral post Kyle's wife Laura hit her head on, if there were many tourists around when it happened, and if Feather saw her mother thrown from the horse to what would be her eventual death?

When Clees spoke from the back seat, I knew that he had listened in on my thoughts.

"Laura was an expert rider and on her own horse the day she was thrown," he said. "She was trying to calm a nervous older man visiting from overseas who was making his own mount jittery. The fellow panicked and tried to jump onto Laura's horse when she came close, knocking her off her saddle. She went over headfirst near that third pen over there, coming down hard on the top rail. She was out cold before she hit the ground. They airlifted her to a hospital in San Francisco, but as Kyle told you, she died a week later without ever regaining consciousness."

"Where was Feather when it happened?" Vee asked.

"Down in Monterey Bay with Maggie, her grandmother," Rebecca answered. "They took a day trip to the aquarium. Maggie told us that Feather was staring into a big fish tank when she turned and casually said, 'Grandma, Mommy's hurt.' Even at age four, Feather had demonstrated enough of her extrasensory aptitude that Maggie took it seriously. She called Kyle immediately and found out about Laura's fall. Instead of driving back to the ranch, Feather and her grandmother drove straight up to UCSF Medical Center and arrived an hour after the medevac helicopter. Kyle, Feather and Maggie basically camped out at the hospital until the doctors took Laura off life support with Feather's encouragement."

"Her encouragement?" Vee asked skeptically. "What kind of four-year-old is giving counsel to adults on pulling life support from her own mother?" More astonishment from Vee over the remarkable child and her extraordinary gifts. I was afraid Vee might explode if she didn't meet this budding phenomenon in the flesh soon.

"If you can temper your fascination with Feather for just a few more moments, your curiosity will be rewarded," Clees assured her.

Rebecca drove slowly past a small wooden building on our right with a "Check In" sign over the weathered door. A group of ten or twelve visitors wearing matching green t-shirts and carrying similar daypacks over their shoulders were standing out front. They were loosely gathered around a young woman in traditional Western gear and a tan cowboy hat. There was a saddle on the ground in front of her and she was swinging a lariat back and forth as she talked, probably briefing them on the afternoon's outing. The cluster of adults and children, maybe members of the same family, started laughing as the affable guide playfully lassoed one of the younger members in their party.

I was looking back over my shoulder to see what other tricks the female buckaroo could do with the lasso when Clees spoke again.

"There she is."

On the porch of an enormous log and timber frame home, half a dozen steps up and standing next to her father, was one of the most radiant girls I'd ever seen. Feather was smiling from ear-to-ear and every bit as beautiful as Kyle was handsome, rocking happily from heel to toe in anticipation, as though she'd been waiting there to see us for months.

As we parked the Volvo under the shade of a big oak tree at the side of the house, she bounded down the stairs ahead of her father and flew into Rebecca's arms as soon as the car doors opened. "What took you guys so long? We've been waiting like forever. Daddy says we're going up to the caves later, yay." She clapped for emphasis.

Then Clees came around the hood of the station wagon and Feather ran to him. He picked her up in his arms and she hugged him hard, both arms wrapped around his neck with her legs scissoring his waist. He responded just as enthusiastically, kissing her on both cheeks. They were obviously well-acquainted.

"Empedocles," she said, "will you ride up to the caves with me? I have stuff I want to tell you. You can take Licka, and I'll ride Duncan. Licka will love that."

She used Clees' full name, his formal Greek one, but in the sing-song kid's way she said it, it sounded even more familiar than the nickname I had been using for weeks.

"If Licka doesn't slobber all over my face like she did last time then, yes, we can ride up together," he laughed.

"She just licks you because she's so happy to see you," Feather giggled back. "Besides, that's why we call her Licka. How would she ever earn her name if she didn't try to lick your face off, you silly?" It was fun to hear their light-hearted banter and watch their easy rapport. Clees put her down and they held hands as she pulled him towards Vee and me. We had been standing off to one side of the car watching their high-spirited reunion.

Feather's mother must have had lineage from far to the east of California, because her daughter had distinct Eurasian features: round face, high cheekbones, eyes with epicanthic folds but large and bright that only made her seem more exotic. Her hair, which was dark brown, had two streaks of color dye in it, one purple and one pink on either side of a middle part. Her thick, straight tresses would have fallen below her shoulders if they weren't pinned back on both sides with decorative floral barrettes.

Feather shared something else with Kyle that made it difficult to turn away from her—the unusual color of her eyes, a hyper-blue that was stunning against her dark hair and tanned skin. Belying her name, she was neither delicate-boned nor wispy thin, but fit and athletic-looking. Not tall, but sturdy like him.

Even more than her physical features, though, Feather had a kind of uncommon charisma and natural ebullience that made her, and this is hard to explain, mesmerizing. When she talked, you were compelled to listen, and if those crystal blue eyes bored into you at the same time, you were transfixed. You simply couldn't turn away. And this wasn't just my impression; Vee was spellbound by the girl, too. From the moment Feather appeared, Vee was watching her bounce around the yard with a bedazzled smile as the young girl held court and flitted between enchanted adults.

I thought from the stories of her preternatural gifts that Feather might be a spacey kid, her thoughts off in the clouds, lost in a reverie as she divined the future; but she was more present than any kid I'd ever met. She seemed totally alert, never missing a passing detail of anything that happened around her. In every way, she appeared strong, clear, and capable. Her presence was powerful.

She dropped Clees' hand and marched closer to us.

"Hi Roger, hi Vee, I'm Feather and I'm a hugger," she announced, as she moved towards Vee. She threw her hands around my friend's waist and squeezed. Reflexively guarded, Vee wasn't expecting this and threw both her arms up before bringing them down around Feather's shoulders in a noncommittal embrace. The spunky girl wasn't going to let that slide.

"Alright, not the best hugger, but we'll work on that later," she said, smiling at Vee disarmingly as she pulled away and came to me.

"Let's start again, city boy," she said, standing directly in front of me and almost breaking into laughter. "Hi Roger, I'm Feather and I'm a hugger."

Then she leaned in, and I embraced her with conviction, almost afraid not to. This kid knew where she stood and what she wanted and pleasing her seemed to be the best approach.

"There you go," she said, as she stepped back and assessed us. "Okay, the shorts and hiking boots are doable because dad says you'll go up in the ATVs. They wouldn't work on the horses. But it's chilly in the caves. Did you bring hoodies or something?"

"It had gotten so hot we dumped them back at Rebecca's house," I said. "I guess we should have realized the caves would be cold."

"Sorry," Rebecca said coming towards us, "that's my fault, I should have warned you."

Just then Feather turned towards a middle-aged woman who stepped onto the porch of the house without my noticing and called up to her.

"Grandma, look, the Carmelites brought a couple of New York newbies. No sweaters for the caves. Do we have something of Laura's for Vee and maybe one of Dad's sweatshirts for Roger?"

Laura, Feather said, referring to her mother by her first name. I always thought it was odd when children used a parent's given name, but I would soon learn to discard any preconceived ideas I had about Feather and normal childlike behavior.

Feather's grandmother descended the stairs with the same strong, fluid motions that her son and granddaughter possessed. She was a beautiful, vital woman, a green-eyed, red-headed Maureen O'Hara look alike. This whole Ferguson clan was off-the-charts attractive.

"Hi there, I'm Margaret, Maggie to my friends," she said, reaching out to shake hands. Her grip was firm, her voice sure. "Has Feather hugged you both into submission yet?" she asked and laughed, settling in behind her granddaughter and placing both hands on her shoulders.

"I tried but they seem to be unfamiliar with hugging," Feather said to her grandmother, "maybe a New York thing. We'll give it another go again later. I'm sure they'll get the hang of it."

Everyone laughed and Feather poked me playfully in the belly. Confident kid. Maggie wrangled her mischievous granddaughter and pulled her back. As she did, I saw a conspicuous silver-gray bracelet on her left wrist that, unsurprisingly, was festooned with a stylized three-bladed arrowhead. The kila was fashioned into the thickest part of the metal and had a small black jewel, maybe an onyx, set into the tip. Judging by the precision and quality of the metalwork, it could have been one of Martin's creations. Or maybe an Esselen hand-me-down.

Maggie caught me staring at it.

"Yup, I run in Clees' pack, too," she said, smiling, "ready to track down more who want to assist in our mission. We alpha females are really good at it." She shot a knowing look towards Rebecca and glanced at Vee.

I sensed that Maggie was also telling me in her quietly confident, Scotswoman's way, that she answered to no one but herself and kept her own counsel. I gave her a quick nod to let her know that I understood.

Feather broke from her grandmother's grip and took Vee's hand. "Come on," she said, starting to skip away with Vee in tow. "I'll show you guys the stables, and we can saddle up Duncan and Licka."

As we dutifully followed Feather towards the Soaring Arrow's large, well-maintained barn and horse keep, Clees and Rebecca started towards the house with Maggie and Kyle. For the next half hour, we got an extensive tour of the girl's domain as a few more carloads of tourists drove up with people eager to ride horses and see the coastal California views. It was a bustling, pleasant scene and Feather was a charming guide, stopping to introduce us to a handful of friendly ranch staffers, all of whom scooped the girl up for an embrace, clearly schooled in Feather's idea of a proper greeting.

It seemed that whatever else happened at the Soaring Arrow Ranch that afternoon, we would leave well-hugged. But that isn't what Vee and I would remember most.

CHAPTER THIRTY-TWO

Feather showed off her natural equine skills as she led Licka and Duncan, two solid quarter horses, into the smaller of the three corrals to saddle them up. One of the younger ranch hands, a short, wiry Spanish-speaking teenager named Victor, followed her lugging saddles, stirrups, halters, and more gear for the horses, which Feather informed us was called "tack."

I had been watching Feather closely as she engaged a succession of arriving guests, as well as a half-dozen ranch workers, to see if she performed any miracles around them or pulled off any Clees-like magic tricks. Her playful ribbing and comedic timing got a smile out of everyone, and her natural charisma was apparent, but I didn't see anything especially mind-blowing or unusual from the nine-year-old.

Then, as she was brushing down Duncan and Licka with Victor's help before throwing a cloth pad over their withers and hefting the saddles onto their backs, Vee came close and whispered into my ear.

"What are those other horses doing?"

I peered around Licka's big hind quarters to see what she was talking about. With my attention fixed on Feather, I hadn't noticed that several of the other horses inside the corral had wandered over and were standing in a semi-circle around us.

But that wasn't the weirdest part. They were facing out, not in, with their heads away from us, forming a phalanx, like they were guarding us from the growing crowd in front of the check-in cabin. A few clusters of people had come closer to watch, including some young children who were excited and vocal, but none of the tourists presented any danger. That didn't seem to matter to the horses, whose heads were raised high and at attention—sharp-eyed equine sentries.

"Uh, is that normal?" I asked, pointing to the close formation of swishing tails hemming us in.

Victor said something to Feather in Spanish that I couldn't hear, and they both laughed. She could obviously speak the language well because she answered back with fluency and a chuckle of her own, then spoke to us.

"After Laura died, she told the horses, the big mare mostly because that was her horse, to watch over me, you know, to keep me safe," she said, without looking up from the heavy leather straps that she was securing under Licka's belly. "They'll stop if I tell them to, but the tourists think it's neat and they like to take photos of the formations. I don't need the horses to protect me or anything, but if it makes my mom feel any better, it's fine with me."

Vee and I glanced at each other, then stared at the half circle of protective horses for a few more seconds.

"You talk about your mother as if she's still here, Feather, like you're communicating with her even though she's... not around anymore," Vee said a little hesitantly.

"That's how it is," Feather responded with a matter of fact, nonchalant shrug, cinching the black strap even tighter through some metal rings with Victor's help.

"And your mother is able to give the horses instructions from... wherever she is now?" I asked. "And you can talk to the horses, too, give them silent commands?"

"Or loud ones," Feather responded. Then she turned to Victor. "*A veces puedo hablar en voz muy alta, verdad?*" They both laughed again as I loosely translated for Vee—"Feather says she knows how to roar, too"—then she and Victor spoke Spanish to each other for another minute as they made some final adjustments to the riding tack.

"Done," she announced and brushed off her pants in the same way that her father had back at Rebecca's house when he rose to leave. Feather reached up for Licka's reins, urged the saddled horse to one side, and came around to face the phalanx.

"Sorcha, go back," Feather called out, and the largest of the mares, the one that she identified as her mother's horse, whinnied, broke from the pack, and walked lazily towards the shade of the lean-to as the others followed.

Victor handed Duncan's reins to Feather and after she gave him a quick hug goodbye, the uncanny girl led the two saddled horses effortlessly out of the corral's gate and towards the main house.

"That was interesting," Vee said to me as we walked side-by-side, fifteen feet behind the young horse whisperer. "Not your average, Tik-Tok-obsessed, twerpy little kid."

"She could have trained them to do that," I said, looking back at the corral, "a show for the tourists."

"Yeah, she could have, but we both know she didn't."

Vee was right. Feather didn't seem like someone who would have bothered to grandstand for us. And the bit where her dead mother instructed the horses, while it sounded a little crazy and improbable, it no longer seemed impossible.

As I watched her secure Licka and Duncan's leads to a post under the big oak tree near the main house, I was thinking that we probably hadn't witnessed the last of Feather's surprises for the day.

"*Vamos, mi amigos!*" she called to us with an exaggerated flourish, and we knew Feather wanted to get going. She ran towards the steps of the big timber home, took them two-at-time with practiced movements, then vaulted over the last one onto the wide porch. Before we had reached the main door, which had the traditional flag of Scotland painted on its lower half—a blue-and-white saltire cross—Clees and Rebecca emerged from the house. Maggie followed holding a large wicker basket brimming with sandwiches, snacks, and bottled drinks. I was hoping that we would have lunch on the porch before heading off, but Kyle appeared next carrying a fully loaded duffel bag slung over one shoulder and made it clear that he had other ideas.

"Okay, Rebecca and mom in one ATV," he announced, "me, Roger and Vee in the other. Feather and Clees on the horses. We'll stop on the big bluff for a quick picnic before heading to the caves."

"Beat you there," Feather squealed as she grabbed a brown felt hat that Kyle was carrying in his free hand, then bounded back down the steps. "Come on, Empedocles, the horses are right here. We can reach the bluffs long before the ATVs."

Clees laughed out loud, clearly delighting in the girl's presence. We watched as Feather raced over to Duncan, threw her left foot into a stirrup, and mounted the handsome black gelding almost without breaking stride. She put on the cowgirl hat and cinched it under her chin as she waited for Clees to climb onto his horse.

The friendly Licka neighed when Clees reached her and as predicted, nuzzled his neck and face with gusto as he reached under her chin to untie the reins securing her to the fence post. He scratched her forehead affectionately, then pulled her chestnut head close and spoke something into her ears, each of which tipped forward to listen. Licka gave a short whinny, then swung her head up and down as if to affirm whatever he had just said.

As Clees set his foot into a stirrup and mounted Licka, Feather steered Duncan around, then showed off a bit by having him pirouette in a tight circle in front of us before she whooped, gave him a light kick in the flank, and sent him galloping off on a dirt trail that climbed a hill behind the house.

I was curious to see how our Greek sorcerer, thrown into this Wild West adventure, was going to handle a horse, but there was no hesitation whatsoever as Clees began to ride off after Feather. In fact, he looked completely at ease, a born equestrian, barely holding Licka's reins and not doing much at all. He flashed us a peace sign as he passed, with the powerful horse kicking up some fine dust as she picked up speed. They were out of sight in seconds.

Kyle then took long strides as he led us towards a weather-beaten outbuilding with two wide, wooden doors that I assumed housed the ATVs. Vee fell into step with him and started to chat while I walked beside Rebecca and Maggie and eyed her basket of treats.

"Not till later," she said without looking up. "It will all taste better up on the ridge."

"I'm okay, I can wait," I said, then continued. "I noticed the Saltire on your door and I heard Feather call out to a few of the horses—Sorcha, Angus, Fennela. All Scottish names. You're keeping the family heritage alive?"

Maggie threw a glance towards the corrals. "Innis, Logan, Cody, Duncan, Morag… that's right, lots of Scots in those pens. We're citizens of this illusory world, the Fergusons, but we also like to keep grandpa's spirit alive. He likes it, too."

I looked at her when she mentioned her grandfather, but she wasn't smiling and didn't seem to be joking. Maggie had a forthright, no-nonsense style, but I could feel her big-heartedness. She was not unlike Rebecca, and I thought then that they both must be about the same age.

When we came to the ATV shed, Kyle dropped the duffel bag off to one side, turned a latch on the double doors and swung them as far as they would go. At the threshold stood a rugged looking, all-terrain vehicle with side-by-side seats and a roll cage. A four-seater, equally heavy-built, also with a roll cage, was parked just behind it. I guessed this was the machine that Vee and I would be riding in with Kyle.

Maggie climbed onto the smaller of the off-road vehicles, turned a key that was already in the ignition barrel and slowly pulled it out onto a flat clearing in front of the shed. Her ATV was painted forest green with another blue and white saltire flag on its nose and a decorative decal fixed to either side that read "SOARING ARROW RANCH." The decal included a stylized kila displayed over the name.

After Kyle had secured the duffel bag to the rear rack of the larger ATV, also painted dark green and emblazoned with the Saltire and ranch decals, he climbed in and gently inched the wider vehicle forward as Vee made sure it didn't clip the door frame. Once he'd cleared the entrance, he gave the vehicle some throttle and pulled it expertly next to Maggie's, both ATVs pointed towards the trailhead where the horses had gone.

Using bungee cords to tie down the basket of food, Rebecca secured our lunch, then climbed in next to Maggie. I quickly took the jump seat behind Kyle and Vee on the four-seater and strapped myself in. The ATVs started moving gradually past the house and up the trail in single file, the older women leading the way, their bodies bouncing to and fro ahead of us.

For the first quarter mile, the track appeared to be dual use for vehicles and horses. Then as we came to a small plateau with an expansive valley view, we took a right onto a narrow, much steeper trail that was rockier and bumpier, and judging from the droppings that appeared every few yards, primarily used by the horses. We scooted past patches of sharp thistle bushes along the trail with bright pink flowers, as well as fragrant purple sage. Kyle also pointed out the reddish-green leaves of poison oak, coupled with a stern warning not to touch it. Despite the occasional pop of color, most of the vegetation in these hills had been baked brown by the summer sun, dried reed grasses occasionally dotted with a tenacious blue, orange, or yellow wildflower.

The ATVs had plenty of power and no problem pulling around sharp corners and climbing sudden grades, but despite the secure seat harnesses, I was holding onto everything I could get my fingers around, including the metal frame of Vee's seat in front of me, the steel supports of the roll cage, as well as grab handles bolted onto the sides of my own cushioned seat, clearly built for this purpose.

I wasn't finding the off-road trip to be a lot of fun, but Vee was getting into it, whooping with gusto whenever we'd hit a big bump that sent us briefly airborne or yelling for Kyle to hit the gas when we'd come to a short stretch of gravelly straightaway. Rebecca heard Vee's yelps and hollered in response a few times, raising an arm and giving her a fist pump. I was longing for the promised bluff and the picnic lunch.

Ten minutes later I saw the horses up ahead grazing on a hillock. Feather and Clees were sitting nearby on a dry, grassy promontory overlooking a truly breathtaking view of the coastal hills dropping into the Pacific Ocean a half-mile beyond. Suddenly, the Soaring Arrow's promise of "spectacular views of the California coast" didn't seem so much like hyperbole as an understatement. This was almost worth all the jostling and borderline nausea triggered by the ATV.

"Wow," Vee and I exclaimed in unison as the all-terrain vehicles stopped together at the top of the promontory, twenty yards from the picnic spot that Clees and Feather had chosen. It must have been a common destination for the ranch's riding groups, because the grass here was beaten down almost to dust, dung droppings were plentiful, and there was a loose cluster of cedar, cypress, and pine trees off to one side of the clearing that offered some dappled shade from which to take in the vistas without getting roasted. The sun was intense up in these hills at midafternoon.

I hopped from the vehicle and stretched out the kinks in my back and legs before walking over to the other ATV to help Rebecca with the food basket. Feather left her shady spot and ran up to meet us, undaunted by the heat. "Catch any air?" was the first thing she asked as she approached, directing the question at Vee.

"Yeah, we went airborne a few times, but your dad kept us on the ground for the most part because Roger was behind me with a death grip on my seat."

I shrugged in mock sheepishness and Feather laughed. She came over and patted me on the back.

"That's okay, Roger, the women tend to be the ass-kickers around these parts," she said with a bit of Western twang. "You just put your boots up and let the ladies lead the way."

"Language, Feather," Kyle said, but without much conviction, as he grabbed the duffel bag from the ATV and started downhill towards the shady patch. I had the picnic basket firmly in my grip as I followed. I wanted to be the first to dive in once we'd settled down and dumped its contents.

Before I got a chance to slake my hunger, Kyle zipped open the duffel and pulled out two red checkered drop cloths with a tough synthetic coating on the undersides. He handed me a corner as Maggie took the basket from me and we spread the ground covers out wide. When that was done, Maggie laid out an assortment of wrapped sandwiches, along with individual bags of veggie chips. She then took out bottles of water and fruit drinks that she had swathed in cooler sleeves and placed them on the picnic blankets.

Kyle reached back into his bag and produced two pairs of high-end, compact binoculars, handing one to me and the other to Vee. I thanked him but put the binocular case aside as I reached over for one of the sandwiches. I was starving. Vee was already scanning the horizon with her binoculars, marveling out loud at the expanse of ocean in front of us and the rolling hills to either side. "This is sick," she said, looking through the high-powered specs with a tone of genuine appreciation for what Kyle had earlier called "some of the most beautiful wilderness on the planet." Taking in the panorama of Big Sur sky, blue ocean, and dramatic coastal scenery between bites of a very good egg salad sandwich, I had to agree.

Clees was situated at the front edge of one of the blankets, staring out towards the Pacific. He seemed to have slipped into an avatar's trance. It felt as though he and I hadn't spoken all day, and I had some pressing questions to ask him, but I didn't want to interrupt his reverie. Just then, he half-turned to me and spoke, "Metis, would you pass me one of Maggie's fine egg sandwiches if you haven't eaten them all already?"

I sorted through the remaining sandwiches until I found another wrapped egg salad and tossed it over to him. It hit his back and landed on the blanket behind him, and he reached around for it. I asked him if he wanted a drink, and he chose water. I rolled a bottle over the ground cloth. Then I resumed eating the last bites of my sandwich as the others dug into their lunches and Maggie told us a bit more about the ranch and its history.

As I was listening, I had a sense that Feather, who had flopped down two feet to my left, was staring at me. I ignored her and kept eating, but after a half-minute, I snuck a glance over and she still had her eyes fixed on me.

"What?" I asked, turning my head to face her.

"Do you know why Empedocles calls you Metis?"

I wasn't sure exactly how to answer that since the truth would involve the mention of a past life, but I assumed this unusual girl was prepared to hear just about anything, so I gave it to her straight.

"He says that was my name a long time ago, when we knew each other in another life, a former life when we were together in Greece."

"Yeah, I know that part," she responded with indifference. "I mean, do you know why you were given that exact name, why you were called Metis in the first place?"

"No, not really," I answered, wondering if she was getting ready to tell me and how she would even know. "Clees never really said."

"Hey, Empedocles, you never told Roger why you call him Metis?" she asked, simultaneously throwing a fallen twig from an overhanging branch at his back.

"Apparently slipped my mind," he answered in the cheerful tone that he seemed always to use when addressing the girl.

She turned back to me. "Want to know? It's pretty cool."

"I guess, yeah."

By now the other conversations around us had stopped and all eyes were on me and Feather. Clees didn't turn around, but he slumped back so that he was lying on the blanket, his head just inches from my outstretched legs, situated so he could hear what the girl was going to say next.

"Metis isn't usually a person's name, it was more like a thing in old time Greece, a word that meant, like… paying close attention but with a little cleverness and trickery," she said, gesturing with her hands as she spoke. "Trickery, right, Empedocles?"

"Intense awareness and attention with characteristics of the clever trickster, that's correct," he responded from his prone position.

Then she continued. "So, someone with metis can stay super-focused even if there are tons of distractions around. The metis person is on the lookout for hints and clues all the time and can figure out how to use the signs and stuff to find the exact right way to go next."

"It is a special quality of supreme attentiveness," Clees added. "The metis gift allows the holder to focus on many things at once, anything that can be used as help and guidance, no matter what form it takes. The person possessing metis can see beyond the visible to what's invisible, and they miss nothing, ever."

"It's fun to have a tricky metis person around because lots of magical stuff can happen when they're with you," Feather continued. "If you think of this world as getting made up every single second, like in a video game with new stuff coming at you around every corner, then metis people are really good at playing the game. You want them on your team."

"And how does this connect to me again?" I asked her.

"Because you're a metis person, you silly" she answered, and the way she said it made it all seem so obvious, "and so am I. But I didn't live in Greece, so I was never called 'Metis,' just you."

Vee adjusted herself to better face the little wisdom teacher with her rapid-fire revelations.

"Roger and I are working really hard to remember things, Feather, but we don't have very strong memories of our past lives in Greece or anything like that the way you do," she said.

"We totally believe in it, though," I was quick to add, "you talking to your mother and all this other mystical stuff. We don't doubt it, but it's still kind of far out and new to us."

"New to you? What do you mean new, you silly?" Feather said, sounding mildly impatient while again employing her favorite term for the slow learners. "This isn't our first rodeo together, bud. You guys really need to speed it up a little here. The shifts are going to happen really fast now, and you have to be ready."

Maggie abruptly changed the subject then, sensing that Feather putting her spurs to us might be arousing some discomfort. "Tell these guys about your mom being in the hospital, and how you were talking to her normally, blabbing away together even though she was in a coma and no one else could hear the conversation? Remember that?"

"Sure, I remember," Feather responded. "Laura told me about the machines and turning them off."

"Right. And do you recall how the doctors got all spooked and told your dad that you were in shock? Tell Vee and Roger what you said to the doctors then, it might help them understand some things better."

Feather eyes came alive. "I told them that they don't know what anything means, and that all their ideas about bodies were wrong. That's when they really thought I was crazy because they were doctors who thought they knew everything about life and death and human bodies and stuff. Right, Grandma?"

"They sure did. And what did you say to that really concerned doctor about why your mother died when she did?"

"Oh, yeah, so this one doctor, this lady who was crying, she was saying that my mother would always love me and be there for me and not to be sad, and I said, 'Yeah, I know, that's what I'm trying to tell you. My mom had to die now because I'm old enough and she knew that she could help me better if she wasn't in a body, because a body is really heavy and hard to work inside of, and so I'm not sad.' That's what I said to her."

"And you were four when you told the doctor that?" Vee just couldn't let go of the age detail.

"Was I four, Grandma?"

"Almost five, but still four, yes," Maggie replied.

"The medical team at UCSF was really worried about Feather, even told me to find a trauma therapist immediately because she was in shock," Kyle added, while Feather munched on chips from one of the open bags as she listened, obviously enjoying this part of the story. "They gave me some names of child grief counselors, but they had no frame of reference for what Feather was saying, or why we weren't freaking out about it or falling apart. Like I told you this morning, it was Feather who helped us understand what was happening and why it all made sense. She also acted as a go-between with Laura, so we could ask my wife questions and communicate with her in real time, so to speak. We got so much verification about things that Feather could never have known unless she was in direct dialogue with Laura, there was no doubt for us about the truth of what Feather was saying—that her mom wasn't truly dead, and never would be. Zero doubt."

Vee spoke next. "Okay, but let's say I'm not super sharp like Feather…"

"Not super sharp?" the girl burst in. "You're the Treasure Hunter, Vee. You were Calabris! Rebecca, Vee she says she's not very sharp. That's so silly, right?"

Rebecca put her hand on Feather's shoulder before she answered.

"Feather has a full grasp of everything that happened in Acragas and how it all connects to what's happening now," Rebecca said, looking from Vee to me. She seemed to be speaking more slowly than usual, confirming my suspicion and concern that Vee and I were holding up the works and that our picnicking companions were prepared to hasten our progress even if they had to drag us through horse dung to do it.

Feather poured the crumbs from the chip bag into her mouth, then announced, "I remember all my past lives and most everybody else's, too."

"So, I'm guessing you're not scared of death, then?" I asked her.

She sighed, glanced up at the horses in a way that suggested she was getting bored and antsy, then answered. "Death is dumb. The truth is going to come out really soon. Everybody is going to think about dying like they do about a flat earth—that it's just silly. Little kids will say to their parents, 'Huh, you mean people thought the body went away and died forever… why?' See, it's so silly."

Clees made a throaty sound that seemed to affirm the girl's words. "Worldborns believe that to die is to gain release from conflict and hell," he added. "When someone dies, they say, 'Finally, he's at peace.' This is what most children here are taught, that there is no chance of obtaining peace in life, only in death. This is a terrible misconception. Nothing is accomplished by dying. The answer is life, not death."

Feather was staring at Clees as he spoke, seeming to lose herself in some memory before she came back to us. "Anyway, I remember all my past lives, some of my futures, too, because it's all there in the cloud."

"Not the Google cloud," Kyle cut in, laughing hard. Feather started laughing, too, a joke between them that I didn't understand. Rebecca came to the rescue, speaking in that slow learner's cadence again.

"You've heard Clees repeatedly say that we are all connected, and not in some airy-fairy way, but literally, scientifically, atomically, irrevocably, and forever," she said.

"You can ask any quantum physicist about that," Clees interjected from his prone position, now sounding dozy.

"There is the illusion of separation between us, and individuality, but no separateness," Rebecca went on. "So, if we accept that we're all part of a unified whole and inseparable—what Bohm hinted at in his writings—then it follows that we all have access to everything that makes up that whole. Everything. Including every memory and thought from all Worldborns, through all of time—past, present, and future. All the information is available to us if we can learn how to extract it, how to pluck it. Feather was born knowing. She can pluck at will."

"Pluck, pluck, pluck," Feather tucked her hands under her armpits and started flapping like a chicken, while bouncing around on the cover cloth. I'm pretty sure Rebecca had just told us that this nine-year-old girl beating her wings in front of us was some kind of quantum wunderkind—like Clees, but in a smaller package—yet Feather seemed to find the whole thing funny and didn't seem impressed with herself at all.

I looked over at Vee, wondering what she was thinking. I could see her eyes calculating, taking in what Rebecca said, staring at the girl, absorbing, organizing. All I was feeling was overwhelming bewilderment, that the important stuff was just revealed and went clear over my perspiring head. Kyle must have picked up on my agitation because he stepped in without missing a beat. I knew I liked the guy.

"The good news is, Feather isn't special," he said, crawling behind her and corralling her flapping arms in both of his, holding her tightly. "What I mean is, she doesn't have any gifts that are exceptional, that we can't all experience. And, if everything goes to plan, soon will. These abilities are totally natural and available to us all."

"It's easy," Feather said from inside her father's embrace, and she wasn't bragging. She seemed genuinely perplexed by what all the fuss was about.

"Well, I'm definitely going to need some help," I said to no one in particular, and the supplication in my voice made everyone crack up.

"You act all bound and bewitched, Roger, but deep down you know what's real because you're metis," Feather said, while picking up twigs and tossing them at Clees. "You'll pick up the game again soon. I swear, it's really easy, and so fun, you'll see."

I wanted to say something that would restore my credibility, so I added, "Fun isn't the point, though, is it, when we're talking about something as consequential and serious as a worldwide awakening, saving mankind, all that stuff?"

Everyone except Vee turned to me in unison, even Feather.

"That is what we missed last time, Metis, exactly that," Clees said, suddenly sitting up and turning around to face me. "It took Feather to expose a gap we completely overlooked in Greece, in Colombia, other ensuing lifetimes, why the path had been so difficult for so many Worldborns and mostly unreachable until now."

"Because we forgot to have fun?" Vee asked, now seeming as unsure as I was.

"Yes... well, the playing together part," Clees answered. "People quit back in Acragas when I tried to teach them because I approached it all rather humorlessly. I made it seem like a chore, a solo slog, and frightening for many... not enjoyable at all."

We just looked at him. He tried again, more merriment in his voice. "You've heard the adage that people must change and become like little children to find true peace and happiness? Do you know this proverb, do you have any idea what it means?"

I continued to stare at him. Vee shrugged. He was on a roll now and didn't wait for an answer.

"It has nothing to do with adults taking on childlike obedience or a willingness to submit to some all-powerful force, and everything to do with a child's curiosity. The whole point of that famous instruction is that in order to see what's true, we have to view the physical world *exactly as children do*—noticing everything, touching everything, smelling and tasting everything that's put in front of us... *using all of our senses at once,* always alert and aware all the time, exploring and enjoying every moment.

"That is the way Worldborns will unwind from this illusion," he continued, "in the way little children do, using their imaginations and playing at the hints and clues game. You see now? To become a child again is to be in a natural state of constant engagement, noticing the littlest things with undivided attention, believing that the impossible is possible, that whatever we can imagine is true… and *not believing* that we don't know how this world works. Joy, wonder, and fun, that's what it is to become like little children. That's what we neglected to factor in all the other times, and that we must embrace moving forward. That it's hopeless here, yes, but it's not serious."

I felt so muzzy at that point it was a relief when Feather put an end to our conversation, and the picnic, saying, "What's the point if it isn't fun?"

From the mouths of babes.

She hopped up, wiped her britches off with that gesture I'd come to recognize as a predictable Ferguson quirk, planted her feet on the downside slope of the hill in front of Clees, extended her right arm and said, "Come on, old man, let's beat them to the caves."

Clees grabbed her hand and got to his feet, then they both started to move towards the horses. Feather called back, "See you guys up there, don't get lost," as Duncan and Licka raised their heads, turned, and trotted down to meet them.

The man and the girl—separated by their ages, but spiritual twins—mounted quickly, directed the horses to an unmarked trail behind us, and headed east before disappearing behind a large rock outcropping with a single gnarled pine at the top, forcing its way between two boulders to reach towards the sun.

The five of us watched them recede from view, then began gathering the remnants of lunch and putting whatever we hadn't eaten back into the picnic basket. Kyle picked up one of the spread cloths, shook off the crumbs, and began folding it up. Maggie did the same with the other ground cover. I was still in a daze, and I could see that Vee also had a lot on her mind as she carefully replaced the lens cover on her binoculars and put them back in the case.

"Is Feather an ascended master, then?" she asked out loud. "Would you call her an enlightened being, something like that?"

Kyle grabbed the other blanket from Maggie, scratched his chin, then took the binoculars from Vee and put all of it back in the duffel bag before answering.

"Names and labels like that don't mean much really, so I try to avoid them." I remembered him saying something similar back at Rebecca's when she called Feather an indigo child. "Those terms are mostly misunderstood and create a lot of confusion. And they can get people, people like Feather, into a lot of trouble."

"Trouble? How?" Vee asked, and Maggie answered.

"Calling Feather, or anyone like her, a mystic, a master, or an enlightened being just makes her seem different than the rest of us, strange even, and she's not either of those things. What she's able to do isn't out of reach or odd, as she told you, it's easy, if we can just fully believe it is."

"Feather came into her physical life with the same capacities we all have but have rarely seen used," Kyle said, picking up on his mother's thread. "She doesn't accept what most people consider physical limitations, and she has told us that she lives outside the confines of her body, beyond her form. Her exact quote to me once was, 'This isn't the real me, daddy, but you can think of it as me while I'm here.'"

Vee picked up a juice bottle from the ground that had slipped under one of the blankets. "I mean, okay, so we can all do what she does, I believe that, but we don't, right? We don't."

"That's one of the reasons we wanted you to come to California," Rebecca added, as we began trudging up to the ATVs. "You've both seen and experienced Clees' wonders during the past couple of months, but it's easy to think of him as an extraordinary outlier, a one in a billion exception. Watching Feather match him marvel for marvel, someone we all would agree looks like a child, makes it seem a little more attainable, doesn't it? At least it does for me."

"Of course, that's just another illusion, the child part," Kyle laughed. "Clees once informed us that Feather is the oldest of the Fergusons. Or as he put it, 'she's had many more cycles than any of you have had.' As her father, that was a wild piece of information to digest."

We reached the ATVs, and I was eager to get in and get going. I knew my body was about to take a pounding, but it seemed almost welcome compared to the bulldozing my brain had gone through during that past half hour.

As we waited for Rebecca to secure the picnic basket onto the smaller ATV, Kyle let us in on a family confidence. "Where we're going next has been just for us, a private place for the Ferguson clan, I mean, and for a few other people who understand the way things are set to unfold. We never bring ranch guests up here, and supposedly great-grandpa showed only cued-in family members because he understood that the caves could be misused if they became public knowledge. When he and my great-grandmother were still alive, there were also a handful of mixed-race Esselen descendants living in the interior mountains, and they had free access to the caves and hot springs whenever they wanted. My great-grandparents acknowledged that the Esselen were here first and that they had dominion over these sacred sites, even though they were located on Ferguson lands. We were the intruders, not them."

Maggie started up her vehicle and shot a quick glance over her shoulder, which Kyle understood to mean she wanted him to pull up alongside. As we came even with Maggie's ATV, she called out in a voice loud enough to be heard over the low growl of the two vehicles, "We'll only gain another couple hundred feet of elevation in the next twenty minutes. The track isn't steep, but it can get a little lumpy. We'll take it slow, but you might want to tauten that harness, Roger."

I gave my seatbelt an extra tug.

"Don't worry," Rebecca said with the kindest of smiles, "the trip up to the caves is the easy part. The journey once we get there, that promises to be the real roller coaster."

"Wonderful," I replied, forcing a smile, then added, "it had better be fun."

Rebecca laughed, then looked directly at me and said, "Oh, the places we'll go."

CHAPTER THIRTY-THREE

Not open to ranch visitors, as Kyle had informed us, also meant that the overland approach to the caves was a spartan affair—a rough, rocky, extremely bumpy passage. Every inch of the journey registered in my tailbone, and I don't know what Maggie was using as landmarks, because I couldn't see any distinctive features as we made our way across the backcountry terrain. It occurred to me that Ferguson family members had been visiting the caves for well over a hundred years, so the invisible trail must have somehow been mapped into their DNA.

About ten minutes in, Kyle indicated a pair of red-tailed hawks that were circling a hundred feet above the ATVs. "The locals know we're coming," he called out, and I took it as a joke. But when we arrived at the site, two hawks were perched together on a low tree limb close to where we parked the vehicles.

Before I could ask about them, Vee pointed to the raptors. "Are those the same hawks as before?"

"Could be, probably," Kyle answered. "Every so often we're met up here by a pair of them. Feather says they're the spirits of my great-grandparents watching over us and the sacred site. Calls the hawk couple by their first names, 'Fraser and Gwyllyn.' But the prey birds aren't alone—we've seen lots of unexpected wildlife near the cave entrance. As a kid, my grandfather would tell me about a mountain lion, claimed he saw it for years, swore the big cat was guarding the caves. Never bothered him or any other Ferguson, but it would sit on that crag up there overlooking the footpath to the chamber opening as if it was the gatekeeper. Myself, I've seen coyotes do the same thing, poised high on that rock, but we politely chase them off because they make the horses nervous."

I was looking at the rock face that Kyle had pointed out, trying to imagine a mountain lion or a coyote peering down at us, and I was glad the only greeters we encountered were a pair of high-flying hawks.

Maggie and Rebecca started to climb out of their ATV, and while Kyle and Vee were unbuckling their harnesses to step out, I scanned the area looking for the cave entrance. While I didn't expect a conspicuous sign like the one down on Highway 1, "Welcome to the Ferguson Lairs," there was nothing here to mark the cave entrance, and I didn't see Clees, Feather or the horses around either.

"Where's the entrance?" I asked him. "And where are Feather and Clees?"

Kyle was hefting the duffel bag onto his shoulder and took another small backpack, one that I hadn't seen before, out of a rear well. Maggie came over and took it from him. "We have to walk a couple hundred yards uphill from here," she said. "The path weaves between rock outcroppings and it's too narrow for the ATVs. The horses can squeeze through but not the vehicles. Ready to walk a short ways?"

"Yeah, I like to hike," Vee said, retying one of the laces on her hiking boots. "Will we need those sweaters?"

"Got 'em right here," Kyle said, indicating the duffel bag, "along with some other things we'll need inside the caves, like flashlights and water bottles."

I offered to carry the bag, but Kyle assured me it wasn't heavy, and Maggie pushed my hand away when I attempted to take her backpack.

"You just stay focused on the footpath," she said. "No stepping on rattlesnakes."

I didn't realize we had to worry about rattlesnakes. Even if she was kidding, talk of mountain lions, coyotes, and venomous snakes had me sticking close to Maggie and Kyle as we started our ascent into a maze of light-colored rock formations. I had pulled the kila necklace out from inside my shirt and was fiddling with it as we started off. Vee had called it my new good luck charm, and this seemed as wise a time as any to unleash its protective powers.

"How'd Fraser Ferguson ever find this place?" Vee asked, referring by name to Kyle's great-grandfather.

"When I told you this morning that he was surveying the land and stumbled upon the caves, that wasn't exactly true," Kyle replied. "He was led up here."

"Guided, more like," Maggie chimed in, "by a dream, just a few months after he and my grandmother moved to the property. They were living in a temporary shelter—a canvas yurt—while they built their first cabin, and that's where he had a vivid dream. He was following an Esselen tribesman on foot from the valley floor into these hills and up to the caves. When he woke, grandpa said he could envision the entire route, 'stone for stone, twig for twig,' he used to say. He decided to retrace the path a few days later, following the exact route that was shown to him in the dream. That decision deeply impacted him and my grandmother, and every Ferguson generation since."

"We think now might be the time for the messages contained in the rock art and the kinds of experiences made possible at the caves to reach a lot more people, to go public," Kyle continued, "but we're trying to be careful and conscious about how that will happen and Clees has been helping us work it out."

"Maggie and Kyle are also concerned about Feather," Rebecca added, a little breathlessly. "We all are. That's one reason why Clees has been working so closely with her." She'd been walking at the tail end of our single file procession through a tight passage and closed the gap so we could hear her more clearly as our breathing got heavier and more audible with the climb.

"Clees believes Feather could play a major part in what comes next, especially with her generation, and he's been coaching her along those lines, to prepare her," Rebecca continued. "But he doesn't want Feather to get overwhelmed by people focusing on her, turning her into a spectacle, or even turning against her, instead of staying alert and focusing on their own guidance and their own destinies. That happened to him back in Acragas, and with me as the Oracle of Delphi, and it doesn't work, it's problematic. When people see what someone like Clees or Feather is capable of, it's easy for them to forget their own roles and to fixate on the parlor tricks—demand miracles, insist they make blind men see, cure them of cancer, all that nonsense. When a feverish crowd starts looking for fixing, it can get ugly."

"How do you avoid it?" Vee asked. "She's kind of a mind-blowing kid, after all, fascinating to be around and marvelous to watch."

"Clees says it's a matter of getting people to understand that everything she has, they have," Rebecca answered. "But more importantly, to impress upon them that everyone has his or her own unique part to play in this mission, a function that only they can perfectly fulfill. We can't make the shift if a single person is left out of the plan. Once we align our specific contributions and get in flow with each other, an extraordinary change will take place—a new perception so powerful, it will be undeniable."

"That's where the caves come in," Maggie added. "Things seen, heard and felt here, experiences which Empedocles assures us can be duplicated around the globe, will accelerate the awakening by putting Worldborns in touch with forces that exist far beyond what they are aware of now. I believe it to be so soul lifting, people will gladly put everything else they're doing on hold to share in that feeling and fulfill their unique purpose."

She certainly had my attention, and I was eager to hear more. But, instead, Maggie picked up the pace and accelerated past Kyle through a narrow passage with high walls that I was surprised even the horses were able to navigate. Most of the walk my eyes were fixed to the ground on rattlesnake watch, but here I let myself stare up at the sheer face of the glacier-polished, thirty-foot granite walls on either side of us. I couldn't help but think about the Esselen elders and shamans who must have passed this way for centuries. As I was looking up, I saw our raptor friends flying above us again, calling out with their distinctive screeches.

Moments later we came to the end of the tight portion, made a sharp turn to the left, another to the right, and emerged onto a large circular opening about sixty feet across with uneven stone walls reaching forty feet high in some places. Clees and Feather were sitting on a ten-foot ledge, directly across from where we entered. The horses were off to our left in a shaded area, standing idly, barely reacting when they saw us.

The space seemed to be completely enclosed, like a miniature stone stadium, and I couldn't see any way in or out other than the way we entered. For all intents and purposes, it would be impossible to find this hollow in the maze of rock that we'd just traversed unless you were a bird, or a drone… or were led there.

Maggie and Kyle walked across and dropped their bags at the base of the stone shelf where Clees and Feather were propped, both sitting with their legs dangling over the edge. Vee started walking the perimeter of the rocky ring, looking up and marveling at its natural dimensions. I was standing close to the spot where we came in, scanning the base of the walls trying to find an aperture that might be the cave entrance. Nothing.

"Pretty cool, huh?" Feather said as she stood up on the sill and got ready to drop into her father's strong arms. He caught her in a tight embrace, twirled her once, then set her down. She marched over to us and crossed her arms, the boss of the place. "So, have you spotted the cave entrance yet?"

Vee and I both surveyed the walls again but to no avail. I couldn't see any shadow or recess that might be the entryway. We both stood there dumbly, not saying anything.

"This is the neatest part, watch," Feather said. With a mischievous smile and her eyes fixed on us, she walked backwards to a place in the stone wall about twenty feet to the right of where the others were clustered. She stood still for a moment, her back to the rock face, then raised her arms dramatically.

"Now you see me," she announced, quickly sliding to her right, "and now you don't." She had vanished as we watched, while her voice, clearly audible seconds before, became muffled. Vee and I walked purposefully to the spot where Feather had disappeared. When we got a couple yards from where she had passed from view, she jumped out, arms held high again, and yelled, "TADA!"

I had to get within a few feet of the opening before I realized what I was looking at. The rock here formed a kind of layered, vertical curtain, and because of a trick of the light, or the longitudinal striations in the stone, or both, it was virtually impossible to see, even from mere steps away.

"That's a good trick," Vee said as she passed her hand over the rock, then stepped in and out of the opening to test it for herself.

Feather watched, applauded, and laughed. "So cool, right?" she said, then hopped around, her body unable to contain the excitement of sharing this optical illusion with first time cave visitors.

I moved into the crease after Vee slipped out and took a few steps deeper in. I was in front of a tall triangular opening, clearly the access to the grotto because the air was twenty degrees cooler when I peered inside. But I couldn't see much else because it was pitch black beyond a few feet of my face. There was a faint smell coming from the opening, too—sulfur, for sure, but a smoky scent, too. Burnt sage? Cedar? Then I heard Kyle's muted voice calling out to me.

"Come on out, Roger. You're going to need a flashlight if you don't want to smack your head or slip into an open shaft."

I had no intention of going any farther without the others, so I dutifully retreated from the refreshing coolness of the dark opening and rejoined them. As soon as I did, Clees began a preamble to our imminent journey into the caves, one that put Vee and me on notice that this was not going to be any garden-variety spelunking expedition.

"As you've heard me say repeatedly, there is not one second of your life when hints, clues, and messages aren't being rained down upon you," Clees said, his lion eyes coming to life with more golden fire in them than usual. "A prolific shower of revealing signs is available to anyone who's paying attention and inviting in the guidance."

As his voice echoed faintly off the walls of the stone bowl in which we stood, Feather impatiently kicked up some dust with her boot and Maggie told her to stop. In that moment, Feather seemed just like any other restless nine-year-old. But she wasn't.

"For the next phase coming," Clees continued, "we'll be working closely with like-minded friends around the world, but we'll also require the help of an invisible multitude amassing now—the writers of the postcards, so to speak."

Postcards? I couldn't remember the words of the Walt Whitman quote that the Paperback Warrior had shared at the bookstore in his off-hand way, but judging by the intensity of Clees' eyes as they bored into me and Vee, I knew that had to be the reference, and that it was important.

"Kyle, treasures await, please lead us in," Clees said, stepping off the boulder that he had used as a makeshift stage.

"Treasure hunters, unite!" Feather yelled, giving Vee an arm poke, which Vee returned with a rib tickle. Despite the importance that Clees was clearly attaching to this journey into the caves, Feather wasn't going to let things get too serious. She remained as cool as a California cucumber standing in that summer heat. This was all a big game to her and her unwavering lightness helped me relax.

Kyle spoke then. "I'll go first, but we'll all have flashlights, so you won't have any trouble following the path to the main chamber. Just watch your skulls on the low points and we'll give you a heads-up before we come to a couple of sharp drop-offs on the left side."

"Don't scare them, daddy, they're not really drop-offs. The furrows are only like five feet deep."

"Okay, honey, you make sure they don't fall in. As we said, it can be chilly in the big chamber, and we'll be hanging out for a while, so you can grab the sweatshirt and sweater now and I'll have some blankets for your legs later if you need them. But we can sort that out when we get there. We'll be single file for about ten minutes as we head deeper into the mountain, so don't step on the person in front of you."

Then he unzipped the duffel bag to pass out the flashlights and sweaters and Feather started bouncing around again in anticipation. As we slipped on the warmer clothes the Fergusons had lent us, and started to move towards the triangular entrance, Clees fell in between me and Vee and spoke at a whisper. "It is possible to go beyond this world you think you know, to another world where you'll give up nothing to get everything."

Clees' words hung between us, another puzzle both enigmatic and alluring. As we reached the cave entrance, I saw Kyle flip on his light and take the first step inside. Before I ducked my head to enter, I noticed the pair of hawks soaring above again, wingtip to wingtip, sending us off with a salutary screech.

CHAPTER THIRTY-FOUR

Kyle was twenty feet ahead, talking quietly to Rebecca who was directly behind him. Feather was next with Clees behind her, then Vee, me, and Maggie bringing up the rear.

My flashlight was ready to illuminate cave drawings that we passed, and I was poised to receive any messages transmitted by long-gone Esselen elders who first consecrated these caves. But we hadn't been inside the dark passage for more than two minutes before I realized that the footpath was narrower than I had anticipated, the ceiling lower, and despite Feather's assurances, the drop-offs on either side alarmingly deep in some places. My efforts at using common sense quickly gave way to a preoccupation with watching Vee's feet in front of me and following in her steps.

At one point, my left boot slipped a few inches into an open pit at the side that appeared deep enough to cause injury, but Maggie grabbed a handful of my sweatshirt and steered me quickly to firmer ground. Her grip was strong, and I was thankful that the steady Scotswoman was behind me. They weren't kidding about it getting colder either. I pulled the hood from Kyle's sweatshirt up over my head and wished someone had suggested long pants and a wool cap. But just as I had that thought, a wave of warm air washed over me along with the sulfuric odor.

"There are some hot springs off to the right on a side vault that warms things up a bit at this junction. Did you feel it?" Maggie asked me.

"Sure did. Smelled it, too. Will we get a chance to soak later?" I asked her.

"There are better springs in the cave complex for that," she responded, "but let's see how you feel about soaking after we spend some time in the main chamber."

That sounded vaguely ominous, but I didn't have time to think about it because the crown of my head bumped into a hanging stalactite as my nose picked up the faint smell of incense again. It was familiar, certainly not sage alone and definitely not cedar, and while it burned my nostrils slightly, it also left me feeling a little lightheaded. Or was I simply growing anxious about falling into the not deadly, but definitely precarious pitfalls?

I turned slightly to ask Maggie about the smoky odor, but she jabbed my shoulder and rotated me around so I was headed straight again.

"Eyes forward, Roger. Sorry, but the path tapers here and you don't want to have a misstep into the furrows. Never can tell where the boo-by-traps might be."

Feather heard her grandmother and called back to me. "Yeah, don't fall in, city boy, you need to use your little feet here."

"Can I borrow yours?" I parried, as I wished for cloven hooves and wondered what Maggie meant by booby-traps. While the packed earth beneath me seemed solid enough, it wasn't much wider than a gymnast's balance beam and I slowed down to get over that attenuated stretch without incident.

"This part of the path approaches the main chamber and was intentionally narrowed by the Esselen," Kyle called out, as I turned my body to sidestep my way along. Maggie reached out to steady me again and I assumed that she and the others were also taking it easy along this ribbon of raised earth. Vee was doing approximately the same side shamble as I was, but with a decidedly surer step.

"Why'd they narrow it?" I asked. "You'd think they would have wanted the widest footing possible here, what with it being so dark and all."

"Fraser Ferguson was told that Esselen tribal elders used no torches or candles to find their way inside the caves, only what they called an 'inner sight,'" Kyle responded. "This heightened sensory ability would not have been available to uninvited visitors or Spanish mission soldiers, so it was a way for the Esselen to protect this sacred site and limit access, their version of an early warning system."

"But if intruders did fall into these gaps, big deal," Vee said, pointing her flashlight into the furrows on either side of us. "They'd just take a tumble and get scratched up, eventually climbing back out and continuing on, so what?"

"Back when the Esselen used these caves for ritual ceremonies and as a portal to other dimensions, they rigged the border ditches with snares, deadfalls, and leghold traps, as well as primitive noisemakers," Maggie responded. "If an unwanted visitor fell in, they'd be quickly discovered and disabled."

"Primitive noisemakers?" Vee asked. "Like what, Esselen whoopee cushions?"

Everyone laughed but I was distracted by something else Maggie had said, that the caves were used as a portal to other dimensions. That's the first I'd heard anyone mention that.

We got past the narrow section quickly and after an uneventful few minutes, and after I'd scraped my head once more on a low-hanging ceiling section, more space appeared above and around me as we walked into a large, circular-shaped chamber. Immediately, Kyle stepped over to a tall, ancient-looking woven basket to our right and pulled it away from the wall. Behind it was a small car battery lying on the dirt floor. He fiddled with the electric cell for a few seconds until, following a faint humming sound, about twenty dim bulbs, six feet apart and strung high around the interior walls, lit up the roughly oval cavern we were in.

"As you might have guessed, the string lights are a post-Esselen addition," Kyle said. "The tribal elders probably would not have approved, but we've asked for their forgiveness. You can turn off your flashlights now."

"Come see," Feather said, as she pulled at Vee's arm and gestured for me to follow. We passed two other waist-high, woven reed baskets pushed against the side walls, then we saw what the youngest Ferguson was so excited about—the Esselen pictographs. I had imagined that they would be crude stick figures, unsophisticated depictions of tribal life, but I could not have been more wrong. The ancient rock art was elaborate, detailed, and beautifully rendered, drawn with great skill using natural dyes and inks.

Feather launched into a high-spirited, but clear and revealing description of what we were looking at. As Clees came over to listen, she explained that the drawings told a coherent story of transcendence and transformation, "like directions for how to skeddadle from this dream world altogether." Beginning to the left of the cavern entrance and moving clockwise around the entire space, she shared a lucid narrative, one that seemed almost personal to her.

"See these handprints?" she said. "They belonged to the artists who made the drawings, like signatures." I looked closely and they were not just painted handprints, they were sunken indentations, like you might see a child make in wet concrete.

"But this is solid rock here," Vee interrupted, speaking my own question. "How did those handprints get in there without chipping them into the stone?"

"You think stone, they thought liquid," Feather answered, matter-of-factly. "There are other caves, too, with different pictures and different hand marks."

"Liquid stone?" I said to Vee at a whisper, as Feather advanced a little farther along the wall. She shrugged as we both followed the girl.

"Here you see tribespeople searching for something, trying to understand what the heck we're doing here and what does this crazy world even mean?" She spoke this in a chirpy kid's voice that didn't match the existential importance of her commentary.

As we made our way around, Maggie, Kyle, and Rebecca came over after lighting thick wax candles that sat in sconces mounted to the walls. It was odd to see the adults hanging on a child's every word. Even stranger to see Clees—who I took to be the keeper of all knowledge—looking like a proud teacher appraising his star student.

"Here's the first drawing of an arrowhead," she pointed to a precisely drawn, three-edged blade soaring through the sky. I recognized it as the same image that was on Kyle's belt buckle. It was sailing over the heads of a half-dozen Esselen staring up at it. "But you don't see any wild animals, and nobody's carrying bows or spears. So, if there's no game, and no hunting gear, it can't be a picture of a hunting scene, right?"

"Maybe the Esselen were preparing for a fight against the forces of evil?" I offered helpfully.

Feather stopped where she stood and looked over at Clees. I heard him clear his throat behind me, "You can tell them."

"There are no forces of evil to fight, you silly," Feather said smiling.

That's sweet, I thought, that Kyle and Maggie were working hard to protect Feather's innocence, keep her in the dark awhile longer and shield her from all the horrific evil in the world. Of course, at some point, she would have a rude awakening, but it was kind of them to let the truth come out slowly.

Feather interrupted my mental musing, a knowing look in her eyes. "Evil is nothing but living backwards, Roger. That's all. If you're not going with life's natural flowing, that's the evil."

I said nothing, just stared back at the girl, nodding solicitously.

"No, really," she said, then repeated her words more slowly, in a slightly different way. "*Evil... is... when... you... live... in... reverse.*"

My mind jolted and suddenly I understood what Feather was trying to tell me—that the word *live* spelled backwards is *evil*.

Vee got it the second that I did, and Feather was thrilled when she saw it register on both our faces. Her next words tumbled out, "And you can do the same thing with *devil*. Flip it. That's what the devil in you is all about, Roger, just living an entire life going in the wrong direction, *thinking* in the wrong way. So fun, right? Cosmic joke for the language guy." She started laughing, hopping around, her shadow coming alive, bouncing against the cave walls.

Where did she get this stuff, this little girl? I had studied words and languages all my life and was completely unaware of these etymological gems that she was tossing around. I started to feel like the slow learner again, that Vee's progress had shifted into turbo-drive at the mystery bridge, and that this nine-year-old had lapped me by lifetimes. I could feel some resentment building in me, too, the "it's not fair" feeling asserting itself again. At the same time, I was desperate to hide those feelings from Clees.

That's when he came up behind me, his mouth next to my ear: "Hang in there, Metis, you don't have all the facts yet, you can't see the whole picture."

Oh, man, I thought, what is he going to spring on me next? That Feather was my kid in a former life? A long-lost uncle? How about my executioner? You certainly rattled a lot of skeletons hanging around with these people and their mind-cracking ideas.

Feather resumed her commentary, oblivious to my wounded ego. "Okay, so we know these aren't hunting or evilness pictures and the Esselen are zeroed in on the sky trail of the kila. See that?"

Vee and I nodded; diligent students enthralled by their midget schoolteacher.

"And here's a tribesman lying face down, with half of his head buried in the ground," Feather continued. "Weird, right? He's what you call an ash chewer."

"Cinder biter," Rebecca corrected her.

"Okay, cinder biter, whatever… it means that he's gone down into the dark to search out old fears and whatever other stuff is buried down there distracting him, messing up his focus so he can't find the tricky clues for escaping."

"Feather is underlining this point because the only way to emerge from the darkness, from a form of blindness, is by uncovering the blocks and obstructions to light and aliveness," added Rebecca, seeming to drill this point into us every chance she got.

Vee took the flashlight out of her sweater pocket and aimed its beam at one of the final cave images. "What's happening here, Feather?"

"That one's super important. You see how all the tribal people are locked arm in arm, floating over a bright sun and silvery stars? The

Esselen got so good at catching synchronicities and finding important clues, they were able to rise above the earth and all the galaxies. They scooted out of this phony physical world together into the never-ending world."

"They've disappeared from here for good?" Vee asked, stepping closer to study the image more carefully.

"Well, not totally," Feather answered.

As she said this, I heard a faint sound coming from near the entrance to the cave, an impression of feet treading on ground. I turned and so did Vee, but none of the others seemed concerned. The sound stopped, then started again, and grew more distinct, and I was sure it was the sound of soft footsteps.

"There's someone coming," I said, reflexively stepping back and bumping into Kyle whose solid body didn't budge. I wondered if one of the tourists had followed us on horseback or if a ranch hand, maybe Victor, had come to deliver a message to Maggie or Kyle.

But what I saw next stopped my breath. Silhouetted in the arch of the cavern entrance was a big cat, and no house cat, a mountain lion.

"I don't think the snares worked," Vee said, strain in her voice. "What should we do?"

"Stay calm, Miss Verilee, don't run," Clees said. "Be still."

I fished around in my pocket for my flashlight, wondering if it had enough heft to inflict damage, and decided it didn't. Then I wondered if Kyle had a pistol in that duffel bag or a knife in his boot.

The lion snuffled loudly, looked calmly to the left and right, then took a few leisurely steps farther into the cave. I got weak-kneed and nervous and did something I felt embarrassed about later—I reached around Kyle's waist and pushed him in front of me. He didn't seem to mind, instead I heard his muted chuckle.

"Is someone going to do something?" I said, with a noticeable tremor in my voice. No one answered. Instead, Feather nudged me aside and skipped directly over to the big cat.

"Don't be scared, Roger," the intrepid nine-year-old said, "this is an old friend."

It's difficult to describe what I saw next. The light was dim, and the candles were flickering, projecting a slow, orange strobe effect over the entire scene. But Feather placed her right hand on the shoulder of the muscular mountain lion which seemed to be a cue for the tawny-colored cat to stand on its hind legs.

And then it changed.

"A shape-shifter," Vee said under her breath, and I realized she was seeing things exactly as I was.

In the span of about sixty seconds, the mountain lion morphed into a man—an old man with deeply tanned skin, a wiry physique and black hair, streaked with silver, which fell to his shoulders. Two dried cattails were tied into his hair with reddish sinew. He wore a loose, greenish-brown skirt made of supple reeds and beach grass with a hare skin over his privates. His chest was bare and there were ink markings on his shirtless body, but I couldn't make out what they were. On his feet were simple leather coverings bound with the same ruddy-colored sinew. His face was serene and pleasant, and at the risk of sounding completely cliché, he looked like a caricature of a Native American medicine man.

When his body had reorganized fully from cat to man, he stood almost six-feet tall with no slouch in his shoulders and no geriatric bend in his back or knees. There were no leftover patches of fur either. He placed his left hand gently on Feather's head, smiled at her, and greeted us all by nodding once while lifting his right arm slightly. In his raised hand, he was carrying a simple leather bag with loose straps that was bulging against its contents.

Feather looked fondly at the man and spoke a few words that I didn't recognize or understand. It sounded like she said, "*Kokezil, kokezil,*" maybe a greeting in his language. He didn't verbally respond, just nodded, and continued to smile sweetly at the girl.

"This is Manec," she turned to us and reported. "He is an Esselen tribal elder, a medicine healer and a jumper. I mean, a space-time jumper. He's also a shape-shifter, but you saw that already."

My knees were still shaking as Feather and Manec came towards us, and I thought I might crumple to the ground in front of them. Clees met the man halfway, embraced him and uttered more unfamiliar words, which I recall phonetically as, *"Kokezil, ni tish ekee."* Again, the man smiled serenely, squeezed Clees' shoulder, and replied with a few hushed syllables. Then he turned to Vee and me and seemed to be doing an appraisal.

He scanned us both from forehead to foot, then walked closer and cupped the crown of my head with a rough, weathered hand. He reached down and lifted the kila necklace from my sweatshirt, studied it, and said a few words in his language to Clees before letting it drop to my chest. I could see that Manec was human, just like me, and tender, but his arrival as a very large predator moments before hadn't entirely left me, and I'm sure I cringed at his touch. He patted my cheek soothingly, as if to say, "Steady, man, I won't hurt you."

He stepped in front of Vee and, breathing deeply and in tandem with her, held her eyes with his for what seemed like minutes but may have been thirty seconds. He lowered the leather satchel to the ground, reached up with both hands and pulled her face close, touching his forehead to hers. The old man's internal medicine must have been strong, because it seemed to bypass Vee's head and travel the fifteen inches to her heart. I doubt many people in her life, if anyone, had ever done this before, and she was clearly moved by the gesture. I heard her sniffle, clearly fighting back tears. It reminded me of when Clees gave her the tender, avuncular hug on the mystery bridge.

Manec lifted his head away, held her dewy eyes again in his, shared brief greetings with the others, then turned and looked to Clees as if to say he was ready. Clees nodded in response and Manec moved purposefully across the cave floor to one of the large conical baskets against the wall as if he'd done this a thousand times before.

With his back to me, I saw that Manec had a large tattoo between his shoulder blades and even in the faint light I recognized it as a kila. It was about the size of the ones we'd just seen on the rock walls and orientated in the same direction—upward. He had at least a dozen or so other ink markings on his body, but these were smaller and less discernible.

"Cool tattoo," Vee whispered to me. "A tad predictable, but cool."

"Manec has agreed to lead you on a ritual journey in the Esselen tradition, a great honor, with which I will assist," Clees announced as the cat-man got busy removing items from the first basket. He then lifted the lid from another, pulled out several long, braided ropes and proceeded to lay them on the ground. "If all goes as intended," Clees continued, "you will experience a dimensional jump. As the Fergusons and Rebecca already know, no one comes back from a jump the same person. Your mind cannot return to its previous confinements and will recalibrate to these new dimensions."

It's weird when someone tells you that something you're about to do is going to change you forever. When I first met Clees, I wanted nothing more than for my life to be dramatically altered and me along with it. Now, here I was, just eight weeks later, the changes coming at a furious pace, and I wanted to put the brakes on. Or, at least, have Clees review the risks of a "dimensional jump" and warn me if there was any chance I was about to fry my brain or go insane. But he didn't, and no one else voiced any concerns or appeared to need comforting. Reluctantly, I kept quiet.

Manec was carrying several of the basket items into the center of the cave space, and Feather skipped over to help him arrange the lengths of rope. As six of us would be journeying, she laid out six pieces of rope, each fashioned into a loose circle on the ground, side by side. Inside those, Manec laid down a tightly woven grass mat and Clees took blankets out of the duffel and put one on top of each mat.

Manec then drew an ancient-looking mask made of corn husks from his leather shoulder bag and put it to the side. Next, he took an animal skin, coyote I think, from the third basket and tied it around his shoulders. Finally, he removed a big abalone shell from the basket and filled it with a cluster of small sticks from his own satchel. Then he lit them using a candle that he had pulled from one of the sconces on the wall. They smoldered, then began to release a pungent incense into the air. It was the same scent I'd smelled when I first stuck my nose into the cave entrance.

The mask. The coyote cloak. The strong incense inside a dimly lit cave. We were far from the Muiscans and 16th century Colombia, but this was all feeling eerily familiar.

After the preparations were made, Feather stepped into the rope circle at the far end of the row of six and dropped onto her mat. "Okay, everybody," she said, with an impish smile, "pick a launch pad."

Clees said something to her in low tones. "Alright," she replied, in a way that made me think he might have gently rebuked his pixie protege. "Clees and Manec will take it from here," she added. "Toodeloo."

She settled onto her grass mat, covered herself with her blanket from the waist down, and closed her eyes. Manec placed the husk mask over his face and stepped to the center of the room with his incense-filled abalone shell. I was about to take the mat situated farthest from Feather, at the other end, when Clees directed me to one near the middle. I moved, reclined onto my back, and made myself as comfortable as possible on the crude floor covering. Then I drew the blanket up to my chest, pulling the hoodie taut around my head.

Clees positioned Vee within the rope circle immediately to my right. On her right side was Maggie and then Feather. Kyle was situated on the other end, at the spot I had first tried to take, and Rebecca was between us. I looked over at Vee, but her eyes were already closed, the blanket pulled up under her chin. I turned the other way to get Rebecca's attention, maybe words of reassurance, but she was whispering something to Kyle. I realized that I was on my own and that this was going to be *my journey*, come what may. After staring up at the cave ceiling for another minute and giving myself a silent pep talk, I closed my eyes.

My heart was racing, so I took some deep breaths trying to relax, hoping my spinning mind would take the hint and follow these slower respirations. The incense had filled the cavern by then, and while I was growing to like the acrid, resinous scent, I also started to worry that maybe I wouldn't get enough oxygen.

Another minute went by, and I heard Manec speak to Clees, again in that foreign tongue. My eyelids suddenly felt like they were weighted with stones, and I was forced to close them again. I could hear Clees walk past my mat, and I strained to steal a peek through thick smoke and slit lids.

Then Manec began to sing. It was a dreamy, otherworldly sound with all the haunting qualities of a low, slow whale's song. The layered harmonics were beautiful and intoxicating, and as I tried to lift my head to get another look, Manec's soothing voice, together with the thick incense, dropped me deep. I wanted nothing more than to fall asleep, floating on the wavelike fluctuations of his sweet song.

And that's when the earthquake struck.

CHAPTER THIRTY-FIVE

The ground beneath my mat shook violently and Manec's singing was drowned out by the sound of a freight train barreling towards us. I felt rock dust falling from the ceiling onto my closed eyelids and I tried to raise my head, but it was plastered to the mat. My arms were anchored, too, and pinned there as I was, terror began to rip through my chest. The locomotive sound grew louder, and I was certain that the cave was about to collapse from the convulsions inside the mountain and that we were all going to die. I tried to scream for Clees, but whatever sound I made just merged with the cacophony inside the cave.

Suddenly, the shaking subsided and I could hear Manec's song again and wondered why he was singing in the middle of an earthquake. I struggled to release my frozen arms from the heavy gravity, and with great effort went to throw the hood off my head so I could see better as I made my escape. But I was no longer wearing the sweatshirt. When I finally pried my eyes open, I saw that I wasn't in the cave anymore either. The rope circles had disappeared along with the mats and the people occupying them.

Then I noticed Clees sitting to my left.

"The earthquake?" I asked.

"Only in your mind, Metis, the ground trembling beneath your most deeply held beliefs. It's over now."

"What is this? Where are we?"

He didn't answer, just left me to survey a place that made no sense to me at all. We were sitting with our backs against a purple-gray rock face. In front of us was a flat plateau of packed earth, maybe 150-feet across, situated roughly at the midpoint of a massively high mountain. It sat among a range of mountains, as though we'd traveled instantly to the highest peaks of the Himalayas riding the buoyant waves of Manec's song. The surrounding terrain was unlike any I had seen before, the mountains undulating as if they were breathing, even massive crags and underlying bedrock rising and falling with a living pulse.

The light was bright, but there was no sun that I could see, and neither of us was casting a shadow. Nothing was casting a shadow. Despite the altitude, the air was not cold, but must have exactly matched my body temperature, because I felt nothing at all. There was no breeze, no weather to speak of. Perfect calm.

Off to my left was a straight dirt road that traveled downhill from our high vantage point for what could have been hundreds of miles. Yet I could see clearly into the distance, the smallest detail in sharp relief, even at the farthest point along the low horizon. The long road spilled onto the plateau in front of us, then continued to my right, passing directly through a banged up storage container like the ones you see on the back of 18-wheelers or stacked on cargo ships. Navigating the interior of this incongruous, metal expanse appeared to be the only way to get to points farther up the mountain.

"Where are we, Clees?" I asked him again.

"Unbounded alternative to restricted Worldborn unreality," he answered without further explanation.

"Where are the others?"

"Having their own experiences. This one is yours."

I pinched myself to see if I could get back to the cave. Nothing. Then I repeated, out loud, "Wake up, Roger, wake up." Still nothing. If this was a lucid dream, it was the most lucid I'd ever had.

"Is this some kind of super vivid dream?" I asked.

He answered evasively again, without looking over at me. "Gateway dimension between illusory world and real world beyond every limitation of time, space and distance. It's not a physical place, it's another state of mind."

"You mean like the Borderland?"

"More refined. The Waiting Place for wide awake, happy dreamers."

"The waiting place?" I replied. "Like in the Dr. Seuss book? But that's not a good place…"

"… or a final destination," he interrupted, finishing my sentence.

I looked around again, trying to figure out why anyone would dump an ugly, old storage container—with splintered crates, trash, and other detritus spilling out of its open cargo doors—at this elevation in pristine alpine terrain. Then I heard Manec's song again, off in the distance to my left, down the seemingly endless road.

"Go there," Clees said, and the moment he spoke it, I was at the base of the mountain, standing on the shores of an enormous turquoise sea, looking up at the plateau. I could see Clees clearly a hundred or a thousand miles above me, sitting where I had left him, his back against the purple cliff.

"Too strange," I said under my breath, and a faint voice spoke in response. I turned to see who was there, who had answered, but all I heard were the leaves rustling on swaying trees, the screeching and mewing of shorebirds swooping in aerial displays, and the lapping of waves on the sand under my feet.

I walked to the edge of the sea to dip my hand in the water, as the surrounding sounds seemed to merge into one, creating the impression of a voice again… familiar, this time, but still indistinct and indiscernible.

Suddenly, I heard a thunderous rapping sound echo through the mountains and looked up to see Clees standing on the plateau, staring down at me. I wanted to rejoin him but thought it might take me a week to cover the distance.

"Only if you accept the old laws," that strange, otherworldly voice responded to my thought, and through some elastic distortion of time and distance, I was suddenly standing on the plateau next to Clees again.

"Did you do that or did I?" I asked him.

"Yes," he replied.

"How did I move so fast, Clees, what kind of massless space is this?"

It was the third time I'd asked him about our puzzling surroundings, and he hadn't given me a straight answer yet.

"This is a journey without distance to a destination that has never changed on a road that takes no time to travel," he responded obliquely, and I felt frustrated. Then I thought to tell him about the voice.

"Someone spoke to me down there, Clees. I couldn't make it out clearly, but the voice sounded familiar."

"As I've been telling you, Metis, we will be requiring exceptional help on our mission, and who better to fill that role than those you recognize and trust."

"Those I… what do you mean?"

"Ones who were your biggest fans when they occupied a Worldborn body. Less resistance that way, when it's those you knew best—shortcut to getting immediate assistance. We need to act with alacrity now, and there are many poised to help you."

"You mean like guardian angels or something?"

"That term, while invoked often, carries some baggage with it for many Worldborns," he answered, "weighted with quasi-religious associations, or simply too vague, mysterious, and ethereal for useful application. Not many people can relate to a guardian angel or know how to communicate with theirs. It's far easier to connect with intimate relations. Like a 'Guardian Grandpa,' for example, or other kindred spirits, with the emphasis on spirits."

I stopped and stared at him. "Guardian Grandpa? Is my grandfather here, Clees, is that what you're saying?"

"Remember when we saw the couple and her elderly father emerge from the fog bank at the Borderland? Do you recall the light, feathery forms that appeared before them, took on human shapes, embraced them with gossamer arms?"

"Yes, I remember. Tell me, is Geejay here, was that his voice? It sounded so familiar."

"Those helpful beings are called Wide-Awakes. They live in a different dimension of your mind. Wide-Awakes, like your grandfather, are no longer asleep, they don't exist in a body, and don't need to return to the mad, maniacal, and manic merry-go-round of the dream state to learn further lessons. Wide-Awakes are finished with the Worldborn illusion. For them, time is almost over."

"So, he *is* here," I said, tears forming in my eyes, "that *was* Geejay's voice."

"Where else would he be? And now you need to strengthen your connection and communication with him and others to create an unbreakable bond of cooperation on both sides of the veil. That's precisely why you chose to come to the Waiting Place, Metis, to anchor yourself in that process."

"My grandfather's here, I knew it. I knew I would be with him again," I said this smiling, looking around, hoping Geejay's friendly face would twinkle into view before me. "And he's with others, you said, my cosmic cousins or adoring ancestors, whatever you called them?"

"Yes, those you knew and trusted back in the world of linear time and solid space. And because your ancestral dream team retains no trace of worldly limits, their images can be called upon at all times. Whenever you ask, they will answer. The moment you ask, they will rush to meet you. Even at those times when you are too afraid to receive their guidance, their answers will be held for you, awaiting your readiness. You can never call on them in vain."

"So, you're saying that Vee, Justina, Martin Newbold, Mr. Peter Howe, even the ice cream shop guy—we *all* have our own guardian grandpas and long-ago relatives ready to help us, all the time, just ask?"

"Your illusory planet contains nearly eight billion Worldborns, Metis, all lost, lonely, and afraid, all of whom need guidance, direction, and a reassuring presence by their sides. So, yes, all have access to benevolent interveners who can reach into their illusion with infallible signs and inspiring synchronicities intended *just for them*."

"I'll get guidance specific to me? I'll know what to do?"

"Guidance that's matched perfectly to your special function in our pre-arranged plan. If you allow your grandfather, as well as other Wide-Awakes, they will show you clearly what to do, precisely where to go, and specifically what to say to do your part. Some of their messages might seem strange or surprising to you, even unrealistic. Suspend your judgment and follow their timely guidance exactly. *Exactly*, Metis, without deviation. Understood?"

"Yes, Clees, understood… exactly, without deviation."

He smiled, then took my arm and guided me towards the purple-gray cliff face but stopped before we reached it. "You still have some obstacles to overcome, Metis, old distractions piling up, blocking your advance, stopping you. Don't get stuck on the lower rungs of the ladder, move with courage and conviction now, confront the blocks head-on, so we can all climb together to an ageless new age."

I wasn't sure what he meant by obstacles, but he said that last part with such urgency, I had to respond. "I won't get stuck, Clees. I'm climbing with you… and with Geejay."

Then we sat down again with our backs against the wall of stone. I inhaled deeply, trying to imprint all that I had seen and heard there so it would stay with me long after the otherworldly journey was over. I glanced over at the old storage container again, crumbling, and eerie, and decided that the long road didn't pass through it at all.

"Guess it leads to nowhere," I said under my breath.

"To everywhere, actually," Clees responded, and I didn't understand.

We rested silently for another hour—or was it a day, I can't be sure—and I remember a marvelous, quiet calm spreading through me that was so pervasive, I would have gladly remained there for an eon or two.

But that was not to be. Without warning, Clees began to sing Manec's song, his voice clear and irresistible.

"Wow, Clees, you have such an amazing voice," I said, but he didn't respond, just kept singing; music from the minstrel mystic. I was flooded with that same feeling I had inside the cave when Manec started his vocalizing—an overpowering need to fall asleep. I didn't resist; I just let myself sink slowly into Clees' trippy, euphonic sounds and drift off. The last thing I heard was the sound of the heavy doors of the storage container bumping against the metal frame, almost beckoning me.

CHAPTER THIRTY-SIX

It was Feather who shook me back to my body.

"Peek-a-boo," she said, her smiling face twelve inches from mine. "Are you back, city boy, or do you need a few more minutes?"

I sat up slowly with her help and looked around. We were inside the cave. Manec was gone, the other rope circles and mats had been picked up and put away, and the medicine man's pungent incense had largely dissipated from inside the main chamber. The others were gathered near the entrance talking softly, minus Rebecca who was circling the room extinguishing candles along the wall.

"I've seen this before, the dancing eyeballs," Feather said, looking down at me, giggling. "Dad wants to head back to prepare dinner soon, but you can just lie here awhile, Roger; let your brain reboot."

Rebecca came over and knelt next to Feather.

"I was with my Grandpa Joe," I told her. "I heard him, Rebecca, I felt him. His presence was so real."

"I was hoping you'd find each other," she replied, "he'll help you now in every way he can if you will allow him."

"Were you guys on the plateau, too?" I asked, "I didn't see you. It was so beautiful there except for that ugly, old storage container."

They both looked at me warmly, then Rebecca said, "None of us had the same experience you did, Roger. It's an intricate matrix beyond this illusion and personal details vary based on what you need to see."

I nodded and looked around again. "So, what do we do now?"

She waited a beat, then put a hand on my shoulder. "Take some deep breaths, get up slowly, then join us when you feel more on terra firma."

Feather took Rebecca's hand as they stood and walked over to the others. I shook the muddle from my head with difficulty, needed five minutes to get to my feet, then gathered my rope and mat and returned them to the reed baskets. I carried my folded blanket over to Kyle's duffel bag and stuffed it in.

"Looks like you got your money's worth," Kyle said with that unflagging Ferguson enthusiasm.

"My grandfather was on the other side, Kyle. He wants to help me. He was real, I didn't make him up or dream him."

He nodded. "That's beautiful, man, and it's just a preview."

"There's more?"

"Not today, but you'll gain greater clarity now, get more constructive guidance, too. It's coming, Roger, just hang in there. Clees is working with all of us on the fine tuning, all over the world and in every dimension."

He leaned over, grabbed the duffel bag, clapped me once on the shoulder, and called out for everyone to ready their flashlights as we made our way from the main chamber into the passageway. Before I fell in step behind Vee, I looked back, took a deep breath, and tried to inhale the sights, sounds, and scents of that ancient meeting place made of rock and possibilities.

CHAPTER THIRTY-SEVEN

As we walked from the main cave to the stone bowl and the horses, Vee came close and spoke so the others couldn't hear. "You would not believe what just happened to me, Rog. It was like my mother's entire family tree showed up. They were standing next to a big, turquoise blue sea and it was so beautiful. They showed me my whole life, like it was a movie on fast-forward, and they said that they were always by my side, but that now I have some work to do about it. Crazy. How about you?"

I told her that I couldn't make sense of it yet, that the place I went to was totally foreign and inexplicable, but that my grandfather was there, along with others who seemed very focused on my welfare.

She just smiled, grabbed my hand for a half beat, then fell into the single file procession again until we reached the cave entrance. I remember little about the descent from the high hills down to the Ferguson home in the ATV—except that I wasn't holding onto Vee's seat back nearly as hard, and the two hawks were sailing above us, escorting us all the way to the ranch, swooping at times no more than a dozen feet above our heads and drawing delighted hoots in return from Vee.

Once we arrived, we all gathered on the front porch to drink from a tall pitcher of iced sun tea and watch the tourists depart in a cloud of dust and rented vehicles through the fading summer light. After twenty minutes, Kyle came out with a steaming pot of black bean chili that he spooned into large bowls, handing each of us a chunk of homemade bread to go with it. I felt very spaced out as I ate, but I was also incredibly hungry and was deep into my second bowl of the thick, spicy stew before the others had finished their first.

As I was mopping up the last mouthful with a crust of bread, Feather began an animated recounting about retrieving arcane information during her journey from "twin truth holders in a parallel energy field."

Rebecca shared that she traveled back in time to Delphi, faced a tribunal of temple priests, "and secured my freedom with no small amount of grit and determination after two dozen centuries. It was a long-awaited liberation from a seemingly endless imprisonment that will allow me to be of greater help in the present."

Others described highlights from their own teleportation and out of body experiences, but I kept quiet. Then Maggie straightened her back and spoke. "From what I've gathered, this is exactly what Ferguson family members have been doing up at the caves for almost a hundred-fifty years. The same methods used by the Esselen that allowed their entire clan to commune with ancestor guides and decamp from this world in one harmonized leap. I also believe that this is the very gold Roger and Vee wanted to spread throughout South America and send to Europe via the Spaniards. Tell me if I'm wrong, Clees, but this is what your early incubation training was all about in Greece, too. This same process has been maturing and evolving for thousands of years…"

"… and it's finally ready to come out of the caves," Kyle added, finishing his mother's sentence.

"Yay," Feather cried out, clapping from where she sat on a bannister railing. "I've been waiting forever for this." Everyone laughed as the precocious girl vaulted from the railing into her father's arms.

Clees had his eyes closed the whole time, nodding almost imperceptibly as the others spoke, slowly rubbing the center of his forehead above his eyebrows with two fingers. He was sitting on a padded outdoor chair under one of the Ferguson's front windows and, a trick of the light, perhaps, caused by the last rays of the setting sun bouncing off the wavy, pioneer-period windowpanes, but that forehead spot he was gently kneading was shimmering with a brilliant, penetrating light.

After a minute of silence, a pause long enough to get Vee's impatient right leg jiggling, Clees opened his eyes. He spoke in a strange, modulated voice that seemed to match in amplitude both his upper brow pulsations and the beams of western light illuminating the home.

"That's correct, Maggie. The priests of Apollo and the Delphic Oracles used the incubation lairs of Greece to make contact with spirit helpers standing outside the illusion who could point Worldborns back to reality. The buried treasure with which the Zipa and her priest intended to enrich the world was merely the infinite gold concealed within every one of us. The Esselen, too, understood that nothing could threaten their essence—neither Spanish oppression, nor the illusion of mortality—and understanding that, they rendered this world completely undone."

He stood up then, walked over to where Feather was sitting on Kyle's lap, and crouched down in front of the remarkable girl. "No more lairs, no more caves, no more hiding, and no more concealing what we know to be true, Feather. Mount up and get a firm grip on the reins, because it's time to ride for home."

Feather threw her arms around Clees' neck and squeezed hard. He picked her up and moved back to the cushioned chair. She held on for another moment, then dropped onto the armrest with a contented sigh that let us know our day with the marvel-a-minute Ferguson family was over. We left the ranch at 9:30 and by the time the Volvo hit the winding highway, I was feeling drowsy and quickly fell asleep in the back seat next to Vee, who was also nodding off.

When we reached Rebecca's house and she suggested having a late-night cup of tea on the deck, I declined, said my goodnights, and went up to my bedroom. I threw off my clothes and closed my eyes with Clees' words echoing inside my head to act with courage and not get left behind.

CHAPTER THIRTY-EIGHT

The following morning, I woke early again, but not early enough to beat Vee to the kitchen where I could already smell an elaborate breakfast cooking.

I heard voices in the backyard when I went into the bathroom to wash up, peeked out the window and saw Maggie talking to Vee at precisely the same spot at the back fence where her son had been conferring with Clees the day before. Apparently, you had to rise with the sun and the horses to have one of these early morning tête-à-têtes with a Ferguson.

When I went downstairs, Rebecca was cutting a thick, aromatic frittata and portioning it onto five plates. I also smelled a small pot of chai tea brewing and realized that Vee's staple beverage had made its way into Rebecca's awareness and onto her breakfast table. I helped her carry it all out to the porch, thinking how quickly I was falling in love with this all-day, outdoor California living. I set the plates onto a circular wooden folding table that someone had placed at the center of the spiraling deck with five chairs spread out around it.

Rebecca had me ring an old cowbell that was lying on one of the benches to signal meal time, while she brought out a freshly cut bowl of fruit. Vee and Maggie started over from the far end of the yard, just as Clees came through the back gate. The Wailing Garden must have had an early morning contingent of comfort seekers needing his attention.

During breakfast, I became lost in thoughts about the previous day's cave journey, while Vee peppered Maggie with questions about her Scottish lineage and how long she'd been aware of accessible and unceasing help from Ferguson ancestors.

"It came in steps for me, weak and sporadic at first as my fears and mental static blocked out their messages, kept them at a dimensional distance, but then it got stronger and sharper. By the time I had Kyle, I was using my intuition and their reliable guidance to decide for me on just about everything. I put them in charge, and the more I stayed out of the way, the more help I got. Today, the guidance is just as clear as my willingness to listen, as unwaveringly present as my desire to sense and see it. Thickheaded as I am, I finally have more than a little willingness to trust their plan."

It was obvious Maggie had been working with this process for a lifetime, and she had a down-to-earth way of explaining all this supernatural stuff that made it seem more practical to me. She held the floor capably for another five minutes, then as we were finishing up the last bites of the frittata, she shifted the conversation.

"I'm going to take Vee up to Monterey today to see Wadestill, have her fixed up with her own tattoo. Want to join us, Rebecca, girls' day out? We'll return by three or four, no later. I'm due back at the ranch by five."

"Well, I wouldn't want to miss a visit to Wadestill's. Maybe he'll give me a touch-up." She threw the hair off the back of her neck in a coquettish gesture, revealing her inked kila. Then she turned to me. "Wadestill is an old high school mate of Maggie's who also happens to be the best tattoo artist south of San Francisco," she said. "With all the people showing up with an interest in ritual daggers these days, Wadestill has made kila tattoos a bit of a specialty."

"I like your plan," Clees chimed in. "Do your day in Monterey. I was going to suggest an afternoon alone with Metis anyway—some unfinished business from yesterday's cave experience and tying up loose ends from the past two and a half millennia."

He turned to Vee with a half-smile, "Be sure to sit stone still for the tattoo master, Miss Verilee. Don't get Wadestill telling too many of his stories. He likes to gesture with his hands, and if he gets going with gusto, you could end up with a meaningless ink blot poked onto your skin, instead of a meaningful message."

"Thanks for the tip," Vee responded, "and don't think I forgot, Clees. So, whatta you have… shoulder tattoo… ankle bracelet? Come on, let's see it."

It was like he'd been waiting for this question all through breakfast, ready to answer as soon as she asked. He just extended his right hand and sitting in the palm was a handsome gold lighter with an intricate kila etched in metallic relief on its side.

"Or if you prefer," he said, and opened the other hand, "my pen." It was a simple, six-inch stem of silver with the writing end shaped into a three-bladed arrowhead. He clicked it and the ballpoint popped out from of its tip. Maggie started laughing so hard at Clees' unexpected legerdemain, she almost spilled off her chair.

"You have a kila in your fist for every occasion?" Vee asked wide-eyed.

"I'll have what I need when I need it."

"I want to learn how to do that," she said, "make stuff come out of my hands."

"Doesn't take learning, Miss Verilee, takes knowing that everything you see is an illusion, a thought congealed into matter. And, by extension, everything you want to see is also the concretization of thought. See it as you want it, and it is."

"Simple for you to say."

"Simple for you to do," he came back at her, "maybe not easy yet, but simple." And he meant it.

The women took off shortly after in the same 1960's pick-up that Kyle had been driving the day before. Maggie took the wheel with Rebecca and Vee on the bench seat next to her, the three of them packed in tight. Vee had her arm dangling out the passenger side window and waved goodbye. Rebecca leaned over from the middle spot and gave us a half wave, too.

"Get a last look, boys," Vee yelled. "I'll be wearing the mark of the three-edged bolt when I get back and it's going to kick butt."

Clees smiled and I gave her a thumbs up. When they were out of sight, we returned to the kitchen and a pile of dishes, and I wondered why Clees didn't just snap his fingers and wipe the plates clean. Instead, I washed and he dried.

After the dishes were done, I grabbed a travel magazine that Rebecca had left for me, one that featured an article about her Wailing Garden. I slipped out the sliding doors, and settled into a deck chair. The article took up a full page, half of which was covered with a photo of Rebecca standing inside a profuse patch of ferns, leaning against the trunk of the massive eucalyptus tree. Studying the photo and reading the complimentary piece, I could understand why people were drawn to visit from far and wide.

I was riffling through the rest of the magazine when my eyes settled on an ad for an adventure company offering mountain climbing expeditions to the Himalayas. That's a funny coincidence, I thought, but I bet their alpine mountains didn't undulate and breathe, and I'm sure there are no rusty storage containers tainting the views. I then slipped into a reverie about my cave journey just as Clees stepped out onto the deck.

"I think I need to go back to the Waiting Place, Clees, get a better look at that storage container," I said, as he took a seat next to me. "What was it doing there? What's inside?"

"It's no empty tin can, I can assure you of that."

"At the end, when the journey was fading out, I sensed that the metal box was calling out to me, like it wanted me to go in there."

"The Wailing Garden," he said then, looking out past the hammock towards the back fence.

"What about it?" I asked.

"Intuit a spot in the flourishing greenery. Close your eyes, hold your kila to your heart, ask for help. See what happens."

"Now? I should go now?"

"We still have plenty of time, Metis, but there's no time to waste," he replied.

I put the magazine down, got up slowly, looked out towards the Wailing Garden, then back at Clees. "Okay, I'll give it a try," I said, then stepped off the deck, ventured through the backyard feeling a kind of anxious excitement, and entered the gate into Rebecca's inviting thicket.

I had just tucked myself into an Adirondack chair behind a big thistle bush when I spotted Martin, the bookstore owner, walking slowly into the garden from the street side looking for a place to sit. He seemed to be taking the temperature of a number of available spots along the wood-chipped paths, perhaps employing his intuition before settling at the base of the big eucalyptus tree. He glanced in my direction and I inched my head back behind the thistle so as not to distract him. But I also thought seeing Martin like this was no coincidence and decided that I would return to his bookstore on Sunday before leaving Carmel, as I had promised I would. After twenty minutes, he got up and exited the gates, and moments later I heard the engine of an old car wheeze and struggle to turn over. His Subaru, no doubt.

With Martin gone, I felt less self-conscious and, while I didn't know how to go about it, the garden did seem to be assisting me with its unique botanical accelerants. I needed only a few deep breaths with my eyes closed and the kila pendant held loosely in my hand, before a clear vision of the Waiting Place filled my awareness. I knew I was still sitting behind the thistle bush in a quiet corner of Rebecca's garden, but I was also fully aware of standing on the plateau again, the big storage container off to my right.

Immediately, I heard a sound coming from the detritus-filled, corrugated container, a slow, rhythmic hammering of some sort, and I wondered if this was a muted version of the loud rapping I heard during my cave journey, echoing through the mountains. I was strongly drawn to investigate and started moving towards the metal span. When I got a few feet from the darkened entrance, its wide doors spread open, I stopped. The methodical banging was still loud here, but sounded more like an insistent metronome than a hammer. I felt a tickling along my spine as I walked forward, but fear stopped me again when I got under the lip of the entrance.

"Move with courage now," Clees had said, so I girded myself and kept going. The light grew dim as I went deeper inside the littered container, but I was still able to see that many of the unopened boxes and crates were labeled with my name in thick black marker. That was odd. A moment later I noticed something small and shiny farther up ahead, and as I got closer, I realized that this was the object generating the rapping sound. But it wasn't a hammer or a metronome; it was the amplified ticking of a pocket watch.

"You're a noisy thing," I said, and as I reached down to pick it up, it quieted to a whisper the moment it was in my hands. I turned it over a few times, then it registered that I knew this watch. It was mine. Well, not mine originally, but given to me by grandfather when I was about twelve-years-old. He had received it from his father at about the same age.

It was a vintage Longines with a sterling silver case, a simple pearlescent dial, thin sweeping hands, a small square calendar window at the bottom of the face, and an eight-inch, silver braided chain with a circular spring clasp on the end. My earliest memories of it were seeing it in a side-pocket of GeeJay's trousers when I was a kid. It was always there, and he was frequently checking it, but he would cheerfully take it off and let me play with it when I asked. I often pretended that I was a hypnotist, swinging the old watch in front of his face as he feigned being in a trance.

"I forgot all about you, where have you been hiding?" I spoke to the Longines, and I wondered if my grandfather had somehow placed it inside the container for me to find. The watch started vibrating in my hands as its own hands started spinning backwards, the date in the calendar window retreating in unison. Suddenly, everything changed with bright images in full-color being projected from the watch onto the dark, steel walls of the storage container.

At first what I was seeing was familiar—everyday scenes from my current life in New York, engaging with Manon and other colleagues at work, meditating in my Village apartment, and aimlessly and anxiously walking the streets of the city at night. Then the scenes started going further back, to my years growing up in Scotch Plains, Vee and I playing on the backyard swings of my childhood home, the incident in the ice cream parlor when Vee stubbornly rejected the ice cream from the counter man, visits to my grandparents' home in Pennsylvania, and images of GeeJay's factory. I also saw a young Rebecca, gazing at me with great interest and affection as we talked by a river next to the paper mill.

There were other incidents that I'd forgotten, or buried, and then the images picked up speed and flashed more quickly, but also became less immediately familiar. I was able to identify several of the same places and people that I'd seen when Clees did the lightning round procession of my former lives. The reversal of time continued with many of the images triggering not memories, but emotions. Feelings of fear and anger, worry and upset, even a horrible sensation of suffocation in one. Another scene evoked a desire for revenge, in another there was overwhelming sadness and a sense of great futility. In some scenes, I experienced sexual desire, in others, a determination to wield power, and even a wish to hurt others—to take their lives. I particularly noticed the absence of joy in my past history. Where was the laughter, the happiness, the fun?

Abruptly, the past life parade being projected onto the container walls slowed and stopped. I saw someone whose physical appearance was foreign but somehow familiar. I knew this young man—it was the Metis me. And next to him was Empedocles, the Greek philosopher and provocateur, looking just like himself, clad in the same purplish-brown toga that I'd seen him wearing that first night in the mews. This was my Clees, back in Greece, appearing no older or younger, of indeterminate age, frozen in time.

The two of us were in a confrontation of some sort, facing off with an angry mob consisting of about twenty-five men, also toga-clad, clearly our Greek countrymen. Several of the older men carried bound scrolls which they waved like cudgels, while others were armed with sticks, threshing tools, and a few wielding a labrys—the ancient Greek double axe.

They were not happy, these people, that much was clear, but I couldn't make out their words or understand what had gotten them so upset. From time to time, a formidable-looking man with a gray beard wearing a light brown toga and holding a rolled-up scroll, would step up and yell at Empedocles a foot from his face, the index finger of his right hand punctuating the air next to Empedocles' head. This man appeared to have some authority and influence, the others quieting when he spoke and treating him with deference.

My avatar friend simply stood calmly before the man and the mob, sometimes answering quietly with a few brief words, but mostly just listening. At least twice he turned to the Metis me with his usual kind smile, seemingly an attempt to reassure me, but I appeared less sanguine about our predicament than he did, more jittery, ready to spring at those in the crowd who got too close.

Within minutes, the situation escalated as the brown toga man directed the mob to seize Clees, while overwhelming me physically. We were both marched to the grounds of a small amphitheater where the formidable man read from a decree on his scroll to a crowd that had since swelled to include women and children.

As the young Metis stood restrained at one side, Empedocles, who never once struggled against his captors, was taken to a four-foot, stone pillar with a flat top, situated in the middle of the amphitheater. A hulking man holding a sharp-edged labrys approached, as Empedocles was shoved towards the stone column. They were getting ready to behead my mystical mentor and even as I watched from the safety of centuries inside the steel container, I grew agitated.

Several young men in the mob lowered Empedocles' head to the stone monolith as I watched myself struggle against the strong arms restraining me. The executioner held his deadly axe high above his head, preparing to slice the life out of my teacher and friend. Its edge came down fast and hard, but instead of the splatter of blood, there was a shower of sparks. The metal axe bounced violently off the stone surface and flew out of the executioner's hands. Empedocles' body vanished, leaving his toga to tumble harmlessly in a clump of fabric to the ground.

The crowd gasped and surged forward, confusion on their faces.

The brown toga man and the executioner pointlessly kicked the pile of abandoned cloth. The Metis me grew still as he studied the stone pillar wondering where Empedocles' head had rolled. But the bloodthirsty mob did not stay frozen for long. Absent Empedocles, they quickly turned to his protege, their next best option… me. I was dragged to the stone pillar and, unlike Empedocles, fought hard and frantically for my life.

"Don't let them take you, Metis, kick them, get free," I yelled at the horror film being projected before me, pleading with my former self to stay alive, my voice echoing inside the enclosed metal span.

The executioner picked up Empedocles' deserted toga and threw it to one side. I watched as I was pushed over with my head held steady, the double axe lifted again, even higher than before, and this time brought down on a neck that snapped and severed, my head dropping into the sand, rolling sickeningly towards the feet of the cheering crowd. Emaciated dogs rushed over and tried to snatch the dismembered head, but someone spiked it from the ground with a wooden gaff and lifted it above the faces of the satisfied crowd as it dripped red. The throng paraded out of the amphitheater with Metis' detached head on a stick leading the procession, the people's retribution complete, their blood thirst slaked.

I saw the slumped torso of Metis on the ground, and I felt weak, frightened, powerless, and sick to my stomach. Then I remembered the old timepiece, fully opened my hand, and watched it begin to spin again, new images revealed as the projections advanced to the future, towards the present.

I felt lightheaded and anxious and was desperate to get out of the suffocating container. I stumbled past the boxes, and just as I reached the garbage strewn entrance and the light beyond, my eyes opened and I was back in the Wailing Garden, fully present and aware, with no sense of a time warp or need for a dimensional adjustment.

Immediately, I realized that this is what Clees meant by the old storage container leading you everywhere. Everywhere you need to go, everything you need to see… whether you want to or not.

I sat for another ten minutes, brushing my hand over a soft, purple thistle flower, thinking about Metis and Empedocles and the way our lives appeared to have ended in Greece. Where had Clees disappeared to, and where were the others, Calabris and Ismene?

Was that violent death a past life experience that Clees and my grandfather wanted me to see? Did the horror of that slaying remain, the ancient shock traveling with me in my unconscious from one life to the next, keeping me from fully living now? Did that explain my current timidity, fear, and saturnine moods?

My mind was consumed with these questions, and I wondered if there were answers that would ever bring me peace.

CHAPTER THIRTY-NINE

I took my time walking back to Rebecca's, wandering the soft footpaths while appreciating her green sanctuary in an entirely new and personal way. When I finally reentered her yard, Clees was lying on the hammock, watching me closely as I approached.

"Decapitations can really get your attention, can't they?" he said with the flicker of a smile.

"You disappeared. You took off and left me to be beheaded."

"And yet you stand here before me, head affixed, alive and well. Imagine that."

"You could have saved me. If you could make yourself vanish, you could have vanished me."

"Maybe. But you learned more about not losing your head by losing your head. You also discovered something vitally important about what holds you back, what keeps you locked in the past, something you'll need to overcome if you're to remain fully present for the considerable tasks that lie before us."

"What holds me back?"

"Remember what Feather said on the hillock about you acting all bewitched and bewildered? It's a defense you developed after you left your head behind in Greece. You never asked me what became of the jaguar priest in Colombia. Executed, too, right alongside his Zipa and carved into even smaller chunks. Echoes of these seemingly grisly deaths led you in later lives to act as if you knew nothing, retained no knowledge. It has been a way of protecting yourself, of trying to stay safe, but it hasn't worked. So, you can stop now."

"Just like that, I stop?"

"Or not," he shrugged, "but things will go much easier for you if you can bring the emotional release full circle and let go of the past. You'll have to pry up some floorboards, and you'll need help, but you can do it." Then he abruptly changed the subject.

"There's a place nearby that I'd like you to see, Carmel Meadows. It has lovely trails adjacent to the ocean. We can continue our conversation there, but it's too far to walk. We'll need to take Rebecca's car. Can you be out front in five minutes?"

It irked me when he'd pull these conversational 180's just when I felt close to getting some clarity. But I told him that I'd be down in five and ran up to the bedroom to grab my sweatshirt, anticipating a ten degree drop near the ocean. Then I went out to Rebecca's Volvo parked in the driveway. Clees was standing by the car and threw me the keys.

"You've demonstrated your abilities behind the wheel, Metis, you drive, I'll navigate."

Clees guided me through side streets out to the highway, where I made a right turn to head south. We passed an open-air commercial center on our left called The Barnyard and were slowed by heavy traffic as we passed another handsomely landscaped shopping complex east of the highway. While we inched forward, I decided to tell Clees about seeing the Paperback Warrior in The Wailing Garden.

"Yes, I'm aware Martin was there."

"You saw him?"

"And you. I was looking in, but perhaps not in the way you think."

I can't get any privacy from you, you know that?"

"Is it privacy you want?"

He had a point.

"It just sort of feels like you're spying on me all the time."

"Metis, our minds are joined. We're connected, you and me, in powerful ways, ancient ones. Same mind, no private thoughts. So why struggle against it? Left alone, you'll be lost to flounder for many more eons."

I didn't respond, just turned my eyes to the road as traffic began to move again. We proceeded south along the coast, passing a picturesque, well-manicured resort and restaurant complex on our right with sheep grazing next to a cluster of well-restored, 19th century buildings.

"So, Martin goes to the garden because he's trying to locate his blocks, like me?" I asked, resuming the conversation.

"Martin had an eight-year-old son who died in a car crash a decade ago," Clees said. "For a long time, he was filled with rage towards the inebriated motorist who he perceived was at fault in the collision. Then he fell into a heavy darkness."

"His son was killed by a drunk driver?"

"Martin's son, his name was Karl, left his physical body in that incident, yes."

"That's why he goes into The Wailing Garden, to try to get over his anger?"

"And his guilt. You see, Martin was the drunk driver. And in the months that followed, the guilt consumed him, filled him with self-loathing. He had legal troubles at first, then his wife left him, and later depression enveloped him. He believed himself to be an evil father, morally bankrupt, permanently contaminated, ruined forever—an irredeemable mistake."

"Whoa, that's heavy stuff," I said, feeling my stomach lurch. "How does anyone ever feel good again after something like that? How did he ever recover?"

"He buried his feelings of shame and pain at first, completely avoided them. Rebecca told me that you and Vee were marveling at the volume of books he consumed, wondering how Martin could read so many—they were his refuge. He read at a frantic pace to distract himself from his guilt and grief. He was running away, trying to stay one step ahead of the emptiness and despair, evade the stabs of self-hatred, hoping to make some sense of Karl's death by searching for intellectual answers on the pages of books, primarily spiritual science, religion, and philosophy texts. Take this road here, Ribera," he said, pointing.

The right turn for Ribera Road came up fast, and after I made it, Clees indicated that I should go straight through a neighborhood of suburban homes. These were modern by Carmel cottage standards, built in the 1960's, I guessed, many with a covering of small pebbles in their front yards instead of lawns, a low maintenance landscaping option in this part of California.

Clees picked up his thread as we came to a street running parallel to the ocean. "The reading immersion helped Martin for a while, certainly kept him from his worst impulses. But it wasn't until he met Rebecca that he began to look at the event from a different perspective, found another way to repair from the pain he was experiencing."

"She did therapy on him or something?"

"Or something. Martin believed his feelings about the past were his enemies in the present. Rebecca relieved him of that belief. Remember what I told you at the ice cream place—that we can start a new history any time we want, that we are not at the mercy of our old stories? Martin's suffering was happening in the present, not in the past, and could only be corrected in his mind in the present, by changing his thoughts *now* about what happened *then*. With one requirement—a willingness to confront the difficult feelings full on, rather than sidestep them. Once he resolutely engaged with the upset, a trial that included brief but intense corporeal symptoms, Rebecca was able to safely help Martin get beyond his grief by releasing a reservoir of tears and transforming the guilt into forgiveness. In this way, he was no longer reliving the incident in his every waking moment. Understanding this process is the way out of the imprisonment precipitated by 'tragic events' like the one Martin struggled with, rendering them undone and unremembered forever and for all time."

I was skeptical and told him so. "I don't know, Clees, that just sounds like denial, like pretending Karl's death didn't really happen, that Martin wasn't to blame at all, la-di-dah and kumbaya."

He smiled infinitesimally, knowingly. "To Karl's body, something did happen. It was a tragedy on this level, Metis, there's no denying that—but there is so much more to the matrix of meaning around these events than you are aware of, more at play than you can presently grasp. There are no accidents, remember, no random events."

"So, now you're telling me that Karl's death was *not* an accident?"

He paused for a moment to lower the window on the passenger

side and sniff at the ocean air rushing in. "The simple answer is no; it was not an accident. Not ever, with anything. But if you really want to put a knot in your brain, consider that father and son had a pre-arranged agreement and knew what was coming before they stepped into this incarnation, whether fully recalling their covenant or not. They were directors in their own stories, working from a script they had both written to free each other from an endless cycle of mutual misadventures."

"A past-life pact about a gut-wrenching death in a life still to come? Really? And they both agreed to this?"

"Correct. An agreement made for reciprocal release from lifetimes of wrong thinking and misguided actions. As Martin's guilt dissipated, so went Karl's and, ultimately, this process became a deliverance for all Worldborns, a win for everyone. Like Martin and Karl, you are also in charge of all that happens to you here. The world is not happening *to you*, Metis, it's happening *by you*. All power in your hands, all authority over your life assigned to you. You are the dreamer. It is your show."

I felt my mind reeling and took a deep breath. "Oh, man, I am so lost here, Clees. I just don't get it."

"You will, my friend, you will come to understand all of it. For now, just know that there are no mistakes, no blame. All involved in that exchange were innocent. No one did anything to anyone. No Karl as unlucky victim, no Martin as reckless offender. Only benign gifts for everyone being used to maximum advantage now."

The Volvo had slowed to a snail's pace as I struggled to absorb what Clees was saying, and I put more pressure on the gas pedal.

"I should also mention that Martin received an unassailable sign from his departed son assisting him in the final step of the guilt release, a compassionate reminder from Karl of their pre-determined plan, one that sealed Martin's journey of self-forgiveness."

"So, after all that pain and suffering, it was Martin's son, from the other side, who ultimately helped free him, relieved him of responsibility, let the whole drunken death thing slide?" I apparently still sounded unconvinced.

"You doubt it?" Clees said, turning to fix me with his gaze as he closed the passenger-side window. "Were you not in the presence of your grandfather just yesterday, along with other Wide-Awakes unreservedly committed to helping you advance to an unburdened and abiding peace and joy? Why not Karl, then, freeing his father from an unbearable, but unnecessary pain?"

I squirmed in the driver's seat but didn't respond.

"In any case, Martin was making daily visits to Rebecca's garden at her urging during this healing period. When he and I met, he was well along in reframing his son's death, preparing himself for his role in our mission now."

"His role? You mean as bookstore owner?"

"Martin is more than the Paperback Warrior. He is also *The Kila Keeper*. I instructed him on how to embed energetic messages into his masterful metal pieces, like the one resting near your heart right now, to help people stay focused on their own unique place in our rescue mission—the part assigned to them that only they can fulfill. His is no small task, and Martin would never have found this meaningful purpose without the incident with Karl and his own revealing journey through a dark night. A valuable journey it was, filled with profound gifts… lovely and perfect."

A devastating car crash. The death of a child. Crippling guilt. Years of suffering. And Clees called it *lovely and perfect*. I knew then that I had so much more to learn.

He indicated a "Dead End" sign where a couple of cars were parked against bollards under a pine tree with long, heavy branches that drooped over the street. I parked next to the others at the top of a large flight of stairs built from rail ties that descended towards the ocean.

"Carmel Meadows is just down there," he said, stepping out of the Volvo and moving towards the stairs, apparently ending any further discussion about Martin and his son. "You don't need to lock the car here, it's perfectly safe."

I locked it anyway, threw on my sweatshirt, and came around to join him on the steps. Instead of descending all the way to the beach, we left the stairs halfway along, emerging onto a wide, flat mead with hard-packed dirt trails that crisscrossed one another over an area that stretched a half-a-mile in either direction. The well-traveled walking paths were sandwiched between the crashing waves of the Pacific Ocean two-hundred-feet in front of us and multi-million-dollar, beachfront homes on the land side.

Despite the obvious appeal of the spot, I saw only one older couple sitting on a bench a hundred yards or so up the meadow. Clees and I started in the other direction and before we'd taken ten steps, he'd reached his full oratory stride again and he was clearly not starting with the light stuff.

"If you want to have an experience that is beyond any restriction of time and space, Metis, one that reverses, and surpasses, the unhappy and unnatural laws of this dream world, you must start thinking of life as a kind of game. One requiring a heightened level of attention if you want to play. And I know you want to play because you helped rewrite the rules."

"This is beginning to sound familiar," I replied.

"Yes, this will all sound familiar as I've been insistent on this point throughout—the answers all Worldborns are looking for will come when you're paying attention fully. No more sleepwalking through life. Sometimes you'll hear a clue, sometimes you'll smell it, or taste it, or touch it. Your job is to notice. When you stay present for all of them and put more than one synchronistic sign together in succession, then you're on your way. We all are. This is assured."

"On our way to... ?" I trailed off.

"The ultimate goal of the game is to transition forever from this arduous field of play to a dimension of the mind that there are simply no words to describe."

"Try," I urged.

"Beyond this aching world there is a *Fantasia kind of big possibilities place*—I think that is how Miss Verilee once put it, correct? It's what we've been talking about since the day we first met in the mews—

not changing the world or making it a better place, but changing our minds about the world. Then, all together, we can watch the dream world disappear and reimagine our way out, ultimately returning to our real friends, our true family, and our only home."

Clees and I had to step to either side of the path as a big shaggy dog, some sort of retriever mix, bounded past us chasing a pink rubber ball that had soared over our heads into the surrounding meadow grass. I reached out to pet the speedy fellow as he went by, but the dog never saw me. It had only one thing on its mind, getting to that lobbed orb.

"That's total focus right there," Clees said as he stopped to watch the retriever. "The collective awakening would be so much easier if Worldborns had that kind of canine acuity and singular commitment."

A fit young woman wearing a FC Bayern München shirt jogged past carrying a plastic ball launcher. She smiled and said, "Hey there, guys," in accented English as she chased after her four-legged companion. Clees continued to stare at the frisky dog until it had found the ball, grabbed it in its mouth, and dropped it at the feet of its owner, tail wagging furiously, eager to fetch again.

"There is a lot of competition for attention in this world. In fact, the demands on attention right now are enormous, countless things trying to distract and frighten you, seize your awareness, stop you in your tracks… so you never reach that big possibilities place."

"Feather said something at the picnic area yesterday about life being similar to an action-packed video game," I said. "Is that what you mean about playing with life?"

"She and I have spoken about this before, and it's an apt metaphor. These battle-based entertainment games are microcosms of life in this world of murder and attack. Everyone plays at these survival games, every single day. You set out with your weapons, clad in armor, thread your way through constant dangers, try to avoid unseen traps, and live always anxious and on edge, hoping against terrible odds to reach higher and higher levels of accomplishment. But even if you reach your goals, you're never really satisfied and never trust your victories because you know that the next challenge, the next ambush, a new enemy or a more lethal assassin is waiting just around the corner, preparing to render all that you've achieved up till that point meaningless."

"And then you're shot down or blown up or run over by a tank, and you drop dead," I said, "so you reload and start over, hoping the replay will be different."

"Which is exactly like dying in this world and beginning again. Remember what you saw at the Borderland? That's the equivalent of a restart button. The previous game means nothing, you're completely uninjured, fully refreshed—your severed head is intact and reattached," he stared at me hard for emphasis, "then you commence a new game, a new earthly life, with your defensive arsenal restored and your arrows back in their quiver as you make another run at it. But what have you gained?"

"Well, don't you get better at the game each time you come back, theoretically anyway? Because you've gained experience and learned what works and what doesn't?"

"Sounds good in theory, Metis. But what if you don't want to remember those past life lessons because they're too painful? Or you don't know the object of the game to begin with? Even worse, you've been playing by the wrong set of rules all along, chasing after nothing?"

"That would be horrible," I replied.

"And there you have it. What a cruel game it is, no? And the game just goes on and on, endlessly, life after life. Some players, overcome with the futility of it, tap out and don't bother playing anymore; they just give up. Which is why we must reinvent the game without delay, do a complete one-eighty, change the goals, revise the rules, get clear on the purpose. New goals, new game, new and wondrous outcome for all."

The exuberant mutt and the München woman approached, heading back the way they came. This time the dog stopped to sniff Clees and get a belly rub. After a half-minute, the woman said cheerfully to her pup, "*Auf geht's, Oscar,*" as she ran ahead, but the dog didn't budge.

She stopped, looked back and called out again, "*Los, Oscar! Zeit nach Hause zu gehen!*"—a more forceful command, if my dusty German served me correctly. But, still, the dog didn't move. As the woman started to walk back towards us, Clees knelt next to the dog and spoke quietly in perfect German, reassuring the pup, "*Alles gut, alter Freund, geh mit.*" Oscar licked him on the face—Clees apparently tasted good to both dogs and horses—then turned towards his approaching owner.

"He likes you," she said, "he's a rescue and was abused as a puppy, so he doesn't usually warm up to men, especially ones who speak German. You must have a gentle way with animals. Oscar is a great judge of character."

"I spent some time near Munich, maybe he recognized me," Clees replied smiling, referencing her team shirt, I assumed. The woman laughed, waved goodbye to us, and ran on. Oscar looked back a half-dozen times before the two passed from view behind a stand of bay laurel.

"You spent time in Munich?" I asked.

"It was about three-hundred years ago in this dimension of space-time, so I doubt Oscar was around, but memories are long. No one forgets anything, neither dogs nor men."

"So even a beheading from twenty-six-hundred years ago can stick with us, linger in our psyches somewhere, keep us from getting to our *Fantasia* places?"

He didn't look at me, or answer right away, just kept his eyes fixed on a series of large waves crashing into some jagged rocks fifty yards off-shore. But I could see that he was thinking how to reply after planting the seed on this subject back at the house.

"The paralyzing fear and unacknowledged guilt leave impressions on the deep subconscious, influencing thought patterns and self-concepts from one illusory existence to the next, regardless of gender, race, birthplace, or any other life circumstance. So, yes, your decapitation as well as the Muisca mutilation lay obscured in your unconscious, and the fear you connect with their distant memories remain as blocks. Rebecca has been unrelenting with you and Miss Verilee on this point for good reason; bringing the dark of your unconscious past to the conscious light of the present allows for a brand new, clean moment. In the clarity of that light, you will know with certainty what is required of you to fulfill your destiny now."

We walked on in silence for a while looking out towards the Pacific. The day was perfect for sunning and water sports, and on the beach below a cluster of high school kids was throwing frisbees, chasing each other along the shoreline, and flirting inside a circle of surfboards pin-headed into the sand around them. More questions were forming in my head, but Clees seemed transfixed by the teenagers, and I didn't want to interrupt.

"Go ahead, ask," he said, "it's why we came here." I took a long breath and then spoke a question that had been on my mind for weeks.

"How many people like you are on the planet right now? Is it just 'Mystical Clees' whipping around the world enlightening people, or are there lots of you?"

"Your questions are imprecise so my answers might seem incomplete or ambiguous," he began. "First, you assume that I'm on the planet right now, and I don't. Second, you believe that I must travel great distances to communicate with other Worldborns, but I've stated repeatedly that globe-trotting in the traditional sense is unnecessary when one is able is to travel instantly by thought. That was the point of our journey to the outer rims of space."

He slowed his pace, closed his eyes, lifted his nose in the air, inhaled deeply, and then grinned happily. "Can you smell it, Metis, the rich aroma of one of our favorite dishes—dolmades being prepared in the little village of Areopoli in Southern Greece?"

I stared off in the direction his nose was pointing, over the ocean towards the horizon. "Are you being serious? You can smell food cooking thousands of miles away?"

"Or perhaps I'm there now," he replied, his eyes still closed, "having a bite with some old friends."

"So, you can, like, split yourself up… be on the beach in Carmel… over in Greece… anywhere you want to be at the same time?"

"And there's your third imprecise question, whether I can be in two places at once, like the indigo children Rebecca spoke about."

"So, can you?"

"Can *you* be in more than one place in your nighttime dreams, Metis, jump from one vivid scene to the next with no time ticking past? Can you fly without effort over the ocean and above the clouds, feeling light and free? Did you not get a taste of this sitting in Rebecca's garden today, while simultaneously experiencing a self-induced, past life regression at the Waiting Place?" He spun these questions at me without glancing over. "It is *exactly* the same here, just another intricate dreamland. So, can I be in two places at once? *Can't you?*"

He opened his eyes, turned, and started walking again. "Onward, Metis."

I noticed a bit of worry creep in just then, the thought that if Clees was out there helping all these Worldborns everywhere on the planet, and working with spirit guides in other dimensions simultaneously, maybe he wouldn't have any more time for me. As if he was tuning into my anxious thoughts, he stopped and winked, letting me know that all was in perfect order.

"So, I'm aiming for an alternative way to think, or rethink, about everything I see, everything that exists?"

"The dynamic we're fostering will take Worldborns beyond thought, past reason and logic; it tunes out the thinking mind and amplifies the intuitive channel, thereby transcending all illusions. An absolute destiny shift, a conversion that changes everything, will then be set into motion. More Worldborns will master the shift, accelerate it, and show others how to do the same."

He stopped and extended his arm to keep me from stepping on a mole I hadn't noticed that was swim-crawling across the path at our feet. When it disappeared into the scrub growth to our right, he continued walking. And talking.

"So, if people won't be going on cave journeys anymore, what then?"

"Miss Verilee was correct when she concluded that incubation methods taught over millennia are no longer practical. It is not possible to bring thousands of Worldborns to the Ferguson caves, Greek incubation lairs, or other ancient places traditionally used for the practice of 'form to spirit metamorphoses' with its concurrent illuminations. But undeniable progress in the evolution of Worldborn thinking—one that it has taken countless life cycles to reach—means the process *can* finally emerge from the metaphorical caves. The thought shift will be experienced by thousands initially, then by millions, without the elaborate rituals performed by wise men, shamans, mystics, and the oracles of old."

"Okay, so assuming lots of people start divining and sharing all these earth-shattering ideas, what then? What's the plan, how do we know when things are clicking?"

"The clicking, Metis, is clearly audible already," he said, then pointed to the pendant at my chest. "The message of that shibboleth is being communicated to all way-shower communities now. It is spreading, being recognized universally. A crucial network of Worldborns is becoming aware of and sharing more of the consequential synchronicities and discoveries that will precipitate the shift."

"And that will allow us to lift off and elevate out of here?"

"No, not then, not yet. At first will come a series of experiences that defy all rational explanation and end all doubting. When enough Worldborns entirely change their minds, a moment of initial awakening will occur when all will understand that they are dreaming a dream, that everything here is an illusion, and everyone in it is delusional. That understanding is the escape hatch and will usher in a period when Worldborns begin to collectively participate in their unfolding futures. As Rebecca likes to say, 'The best way to predict the future is to create it ourselves.' That will happen.

"While the path is not fully paved beyond that point, a peaceful planetary phase will likely follow as Worldborns share a glimpse of a wholly different world, one whose loveliness will be so intense and inclusive they will begin to forget this place of pain and sorrow. This healed vision will feel miraculous to all, a state of clear awareness punctuated with gentle dreams and echoes of a forgotten home. Intervals of a shorter duration can be expected then, experienced as an unbroken stream of predictable miracles and the disappearance of the universe… as this world is shined away. Then, Metis, then we will vanish into the real world, voluntarily and together, out of time and space, with no effort at all, back to before the beginning of time."

"A period of predictable miracles?" I asked. "A time before time? What does that even look like? What does it mean? I can't imagine it."

And he must have known that I couldn't imagine such a thing, that I would have no concept of how Worldborns could set a future course of miracles into motion, because my last words sat between us, untouched.

We walked in silence for another few minutes as Clees followed a trail that meandered through some tall vegetation, eventually made a U-turn, and circled back to the Volvo.

"Not Verilee's Loop but a good place to walk and talk, don't you think?" he said of the beachside meadows.

I didn't respond, just thought, yet again, that this would be a terrible guy from whom to try and keep a secret.

CHAPTER FORTY

Clees and I returned from the highland meadows at 4:00. We walked around the house to the backyard, where Vee and Rebecca were sitting on the Adirondack chairs sharing a bowl of red grapes and cutting thin slices from a wedge of white cheese. Vee had a big smile on her face as I approached, then stood up and enthusiastically extended her right hand. I reached out to take it, not understanding the formal greeting, then spotted a square patch of thin plastic film on the inside of her wrist and, underneath that, her new tattoo.

"Hey, man, I'm a Sister of the Flaming Kila. On fire and in focus."

The tattoo had a layer of protective ointment over it, in addition to the clear wrap, but it was still easy to make out. Wadestill must have had both steady *and* talented hands because the image was striking. It measured about four inches long and maybe an inch and a half wide. The metal arrowhead itself was rendered in silver tones with deep blue highlights, the tip of the kila pointed towards her palm. Then, using a black, bold typeface, Wadestill had fashioned the word ESTIA into a stylized arrow shaft, giving the unique tattoo a formidable appearance.

But Vee and Wadestill hadn't stopped there—along the sides of the kila appeared licks of reddish-orange flame, conveying both speed, urgency, and intensity. I remembered one of Vee's colored pencil sketches having similar splashes of red flame and realized that she must have used one of her own drawings to guide Wadestill's tattoo needle.

"Like it?" Vee asked me.

"Love it. It's powerful looking," I replied.

"I know, right? Wadestill rocks. You should get one, Rog; seriously, this guy's amazing. Cool dude, too."

Vee moved her arm to give Clees a closer look and he nodded his approval. "Quite impactful, Miss Verilee. It will leave a memorable impression."

Vee was glowing with the praise, her new body art clearly giving her a lot of joy. "Yeah, I really love it. Thanks for taking me up there, Rebecca."

Rebecca smiled, then ended any further discussion about tattoos, suggesting we share an early dinner on the back deck. I remember our last evening together as intimate and familial, with everyone, including Clees, helping to prepare a simple meal in Rebecca's kitchen, a mood of lightness and fun enveloping our foursome.

At one point, Clees demonstrated an astonishing ability to slice and dice at a speed that blurred his knife blade. When Vee asked about this preternatural skill, he responded by chopping a cucumber into sliver thin slices and flicking them onto the backsplash of Rebecca's stove with blinding precision to form a perfect smiley face.

"You could get your own cooking show with cutting skills like that, you know?" Vee said, staring at the cucumber slivers as they dribbled down the vinyl panel.

"I thought we were here to pitch the Cartoon Network; what happened?" he responded, and Vee laughed.

Our food prep went on like that for another half hour, the amusing verbal sparring between Clees and Vee continuing uninterrupted and providing some welcome comic relief that we all seemed to need. During dinner on the deck, Empedocles was in a particularly cheerful mood, playing the "guess which hand" game with each of us, instantly materializing the most fascinating objects in his palms: a canine tooth from an extinct Greek dog breed he called a "Molossus" (" … loyal companions, I had two of them…"), a chunk of ice he chipped from the Beardmore Glacier in Antarctica (" …don't worry, I'll put it back…"), and a fragment from a 1300-year-old Swedish runestone (" …this marked the grave of my friend, Gorm The Benevolent, a man of light and Valhalla…"). Each item had an amazing or amusing story attached to it, told by the most spellbinding raconteur in this world or any other.

After the meal had ended and Clees wrapped up his wondrous sleight-of-hand, my eyes settled for the dozenth time on the spiral pattern of Rebecca's deck.

"How'd you come up with this design?" I asked her.

"I copied it," she responded.

"From a home improvement catalog?"

"From inside the temples at Delphi," came her response, "but the flooring there was constructed of Grecian marble, not wood, and inside the spiral was a honeycomb pattern."

"Honeycomb? Why was that?" Vee asked.

"The combination of hexagonal and spiral shapes created a geometric conduit that aided transport during incubation and heightened personal discoveries and uncoveries," Rebecca said. "Hexagonal geometry carries consciousness down and into the dark—a participant who walked this mandala in preparation for incubation could accelerate his or her transformative descent."

I stood up and stepped heel-to-toe along a short stretch of the hypnotic spiral that wasn't covered by porch furniture. "So why just the swirling pattern, Rebecca, why didn't you add the hexagons, too?"

"Because you'd likely vomit, especially on a full stomach," she answered, and I quickly sat down. "When preparing for an extended incubation journey in the lairs at Delphi, participants would often fast for three days or more beforehand, just to be safe."

"*Down and into the dark*," Vee muttered, repeating Rebecca's words. "That's like the Esselen pictograph man with his face in the ground."

"The mythical cinder biter, correct," Rebecca replied, "making the descent of transcendence."

"No getting off the hook there, then?" Vee asked. "With the dirt dive, I mean."

"The clearing piece is not an afterthought, Miss Verilee, nor incidental," Clees replied, his tone sobering somewhat. "It is an essential step on the journey, vital to our mission."

Rebecca looked over at Clees, letting him know that she would take it from there. She leaned forward, placed a hand on Vee's arm, and when she spoke next, her words came out slow and dreamy—totally lucid and clear, but from a faraway place in her.

"Locked and blocked inside every mind is a distant memory of our real world, but that knowing is faint. What oracles do best, what Ismene excelled at, and what I carried forward into this life, is the ability to safely assist people in clearing the blocks to seeing and receiving." She fixed her meditative gaze on Vee and me and continued. "If left buried beneath the surface, underground and inaccessible, these shadow pieces can keep people stuck for lifetimes, unable to move forward, never fully free."

Rebecca turned her head then towards the gate of The Wailing Garden, faintly visible in the flickering light of the porch candles. "I tried once to take the truth beyond the temple walls, to share what I knew about closing the *quantum loop* with our guides in other dimensions, to point more than just the Greek elite to the escape hatch. It didn't go well... until Calabris arrived. That's when we all found each other. I stopped divining the future under the thumb of temple authorities and started assisting those ready to plumb the depths and cross their own valleys of death and desolation to eventual freedom."

By the time Rebecca was done, all four of us were looking wistfully towards the garden beyond, taking long breaths, lost in our own thoughts. After several minutes, Vee shifted in her chair and turned back to the table. "So, it was Calabris who got you out of the temple, freed you from bondage to the omphalos?"

"The omphalos stone was only a symbol of the oracle's abilities and omniscient vision, Vee. I wasn't chained to it or anything. But leaving the temple was prohibited for Ismene and it was only with Calabris' metaphysical manipulations and, frankly, some very 'matrixey' maneuvers, that I was able to steal away and stay away."

"I'll bet he used his trusty kila to do it, too," Vee said, whacking Clees on the arm. "And you wouldn't even let me play with the thing a little."

Clees smiled, unfazed by Vee's ribbing. "The ritual dagger is known in ancient Buddhist lore as the overcomer of obstacles, the piercer of blocks. So, the relationship between a 'rider of the kila,' like Calabris, and a truth oracle like Ismene makes complete sense. They just acquired their knowings on different sides of the globe and from different aspects of their right thinking. When they came into contact, they recognized each other immediately for who they truly were, and who they could become together."

"The Piercer of Blocks," I said, repeating Clees' words. "That would be a really cool name for a superhero, piercing stuff with his wild and wicked, three-bladed kila, then transporting people instantly beyond this world."

"Wild or wicked, wearisome or welcomed, the excavation work must be done, so don't wait too long to get your hands dirty," Rebecca said, looking from me to Vee, reclining back on her porch chair, and closing her eyes. I thought she'd spoken her last words for the night, but a moment later she shifted her weight and when she opened her eyes again, they had such a longing in them.

"Marty Newbold recited a poem to me once when we were talking about the grief he carried and how to confront it. It was by a Spanish poet, Antonio Machado, and I memorized one stanza.

> *'Last night as I was sleeping, I dreamt—marvelous error!—that*
> *I had a beehive here inside my heart. And the golden bees were*
> *making white combs and sweet honey from my old failures.'*

Do you know what this poem is about?"

"Not honey, I'm guessing?" I replied.

"No, not honey," Rebecca responded. "I believe Machado was writing about waking from this dream and returning to our true selves, to home sweet home—where every error is corrected, no one is a failure, and all are joined with untroubled hearts forever."

CHAPTER FORTY-ONE

After the plates were cleared and cleaned on that last night before we were to leave California, Vee went into The Wailing Garden at around 9:00 and stayed there for a long time. I'm not sure how long because she didn't return before I fell asleep.

The next morning, when I woke early and walked into the kitchen, she was sitting there alone.

"I'm not going back to New York with you today. I've been talking with Rebecca, told her what I was shown during the cave journey and about that cinder biter stuff. I've decided to stay with her in Carmel for a couple more weeks, stop in to see Martin at the bookstore, head down to the Ferguson's again. Feather told me something during our porch dinner that shook me. I have to speak with her about it again, go deeper with Big Sur's budding soothsayer."

"What about Massoud and work?"

"No big deal. I finished up my last job before we came out and I've got nothing to rush back to. Justina is working her ass off on a big case, spending tons of hours at the office, so she won't miss me." She was eating a bowl of cereal at the kitchen counter and swirled the last soggy morsels around in the milk. Then, she added, "Besides, it's time."

"For?"

"To pull the rug back. I have to go for it, Rog, I can't put it off any longer."

I stared at her for a moment, then walked over and kissed her on the forehead. I understood her meaning, and there was nothing more to say, so I smiled reassuringly and turned to leave. Before I did, she tugged on my shirt sleeve, drew me down to her and hugged me hard. I felt her forearms shaking, maybe from the intensity of the embrace, maybe out of fear for what was to come next.

I straightened myself, left the kitchen and went up to my room. I did not expect to be leaving California alone, but I was learning quickly to abandon my expectations. I decided to pack my bag early for the evening flight home, then stroll into town to visit Martin Newbold's bookstore one last time. Nobody was in the house when I went downstairs, and I couldn't see anyone in the backyard either. I didn't look particularly hard because I felt like walking into Carmel alone.

I slipped out the front door, stepped onto Casanova, and followed the same route Rebecca had used to take us into town a couple of days earlier. As I approached Martin's bookshop, I spotted the vintage Mustang with the Vermont plates again, parked on a side street, and thought about why this repeated sighting might be a notable coincidence. As I was turning this over in my mind, I felt for the kila necklace against my chest.

When I entered the store, I saw Martin standing behind a display case showing his jewelry to an older couple whom I vaguely recognized. It took me a few seconds, then I realized it was the same couple who had been sitting on the lone bench at Carmel Meadows the day before when I went walking with Clees. I recognized the pair because the man was wearing the strangest hat, the same one he had on at the beach, one of those black, three-cornered numbers that was last fashionable during the colonial era.

I stared at the couple for a moment, thought it might be rude to interrupt, and didn't want to go through the effort of starting a conversation with strangers. I decided to walk around the store for a while, maybe fool around with those Tibetan singing bowls until Martin was finished. Suddenly, I felt an energy bolt shoot from the middle of my forehead down to my feet and I stopped still. I thought about the kila pieces spread in front of the beach couple, the synchronistic Vermont Mustang outside, and said out loud, "What the heck are you thinking, Steiner? This isn't a coincidence, it's a sign."

So, I turned around and walked directly back to the trio. Martin looked up immediately and greeted me with enthusiasm, as the man and woman, probably both in their late 50's, turned to see who had drawn the bookseller's attention.

When I reached the counter, I said hello to Martin, then addressed the man directly. "Hi, my name's Roger. Roger Steiner. That's a great hat. Must be good in the sun…"

" …or for a revolution," the woman interrupted, nudging the older man, apparently her husband.

"Meet the Glaziers, in town from your neck of the woods," Martin said in his perky way. "They're both professors at Columbia University in New York."

The man removed the cocked hat and held it in one hand as he reached to shake with the other. "Nice to meet you, Roger," he said in a deep, clear voice, one I imagined he used to good effect in Ivy League lecture halls. "Chris and Lily Glazier, fellow east coast travelers."

"Cool, yeah, I live in the city, too, here visiting friends for a long weekend." I was not ready to share more details about my adventures in California. "What do you teach at Columbia?"

"I teach clinical psychology," Lily Glazier said in a charming voice with the hint of a New England accent, "and Chris here is head of the American History department… as well as a wannabe militiaman."

"Well, not exactly that," her husband responded, looking momentarily flustered, but not deterred. "It's a Minuteman hat, true, but I don't wear it with military aspirations. Do you know who the Minutemen were?"

My father had served in the army and was an American history buff, an appreciation that he passed onto me, so I actually did know who they were. "Civilian partisans during the Revolutionary War," I responded, "mostly from Massachusetts, I think. Used unusual tactics and mobilized at a minute's notice, so they were indispensable and well-regarded during the colonial war for independence."

"Exactly right, wow!" Chris responded, clearly impressed. "It's that part about the Minutemen being ready to go into action at a moment's notice that prompted the tricorn actually. Lily and I aren't so much interested in revolution as we are in a radical evolution of the mind, one we both think is unfolding now. The hat here is to help remind me to stay alert and be ready to act in a flash on any unusual signs that might show themselves, in the very tradition of the Minutemen. So, while Lily might dislike the hat, she approves of my intentions. Of course, the tricorn isn't bad for sun protection, either."

Professor Glazier kept talking, mentioning a friend in Columbia's theology department who told them about three-bladed arrowheads, how it related to focus and synchronicities and, ultimately, to a destiny shift. I grabbed Martin's display case for balance and was having a hard time listening, overtaken by this "chance" encounter with the Glaziers, a couple from New York who I'd seen twice in twenty-four hours, who were self-described "spiritual evolutionaries," and who had come all the way to California in search of clues. And I'd almost let this meaningful coincidence, chock-full of messages, get away from me. I promised myself I would never let that happen again.

Lily was rolling her eyes from time to time as her husband continued speaking, but she clearly adored the man and was as fully on board with his stated mission as he was. The Paperback Warrior just stared at the three of us with the delighted look of a mystical matchmaker. After another ten minutes of Martin filling the couple in on the work of David Bohm, and how it was important for everyone to spend time working on their inner blocks to receive more serendipitous messages, the Glaziers and I exchanged contact information and promised to meet up once we were all back in New York.

As they left the bookstore—Lily with a pair of kila earrings, Chris with a brooch-like, three-bladed pin that he immediately attached to his tricorn hat—he turned and mentioned that they were driving down the coast. "We're off to visit some Native American burial sites, a tribe called the Esselen who were supposed to possess arcane knowledge of alternate dimensions." I nodded, tightened my grip on the display case with one hand, and waved farewell with the other.

Martin was smiling knowingly as he directed me up to his office, and as I followed, my mind flashed to the story Clees had shared about Martin and his son. This sweet and generous man in front of me had dealt with so much pain, had fought such a hard battle with crushing guilt, thinking himself an irreversible mistake without remedy. But Clees had assured me that Martin's struggle led to a final triumph of forgiveness and freedom that benefited not just him and his son Karl, but all Worldborns, for all time. Although I didn't understand how any of that worked, I was glad Martin's burden had been largely lifted.

Once in his office, he served me more of his special licorice tea blend and, between sips, I mentioned that we had been down to the Ferguson ranch.

"Do you know them, the Fergusons?" I asked, wondering how much Martin knew about their caves.

"Not well," he responded, "but I've met them all, even the young mother before she died in an awful accident. Interesting family, been on the coast for generations. The little girl is especially intriguing, very dynamic and inquisitive."

"Yes, her name's Feather."

"Feather, right, difficult name to forget. Difficult girl to forget. I was so impressed with her, so fascinated by some of the things she said, I felt she had to have one of my kila pieces. So, I gave her one. I mentioned the other day that I made both a ring and a neck pendant from the unusual chunk of metal that Clees gave me. You got the pendant. It was Feather Ferguson who got the ring."

I hadn't noticed Feather wearing a ring, but I'd been so focused on the girl's many other engaging qualities, I could have missed it. Thoughts of Feather and her magical presence prompted another question for Martin.

"I was wondering if you have any idea how synchronicities and Bohm might be connected?"

"Interesting question," Martin replied, rubbing his chin in concentration. "The concept of synchronicity was advanced in psychology by Carl Jung in the mid-twentieth century. Jung wrote about synchronicities being a sign of alignment and harmony with the cosmos and fates, that sort of thing. He also suggested that these unlikely coincidences might have a greater meaning—that they might be interventions of a deeper order with metaphysical significance, helping us grow and evolve in consciousness."

"Interventions," I said, thinking about my own ancestral interveners, "that's interesting. You don't think there's any reason why Bohm the physicist would have been aware of Jung's psychological work? It wouldn't have influenced his research into quantum theory at all?"

"On the contrary, I think there could be a link," Martin replied. "I need to do more research on this, but Jung was a close collaborator of the European physicist and Nobel laureate Wolfgang Pauli. Together they were exploring whether synchronistic phenomena and observations of the paranormal might have scientific explanations."

"So, Jung, Pauli and Bohm were contemporaries?"

"Correct, and physicists of that era were certainly exchanging quantum ideas, as these were quite new and exciting. Now you have me thinking that interactions between Bohm and Pauli were likely, and that the three of them might have been exploring a controversial concept that was growing in popularity at the time—that quantum theory was the key to finally bringing science, psychology, and spirituality together."

"So, you think that Pauli could have communicated Jung's ideas about meaningful coincidences to Bohm, and Bohm could have incorporated those ideas into his writings?"

"I can't see why not," Martin said, sipping thoughtfully at his tea.

"Okay, but I'm still missing the connection between synchronicities and the blocks that Bohm talked about? Is there one?"

"That's tricky and I'm not sure," he said, reaching into a creaky desk drawer and pulling out a battered notebook held together with several thick rubber bands. "I told you the other day that when I first met Empedocles, we spent quite a lot of time together. Every encounter with him was enlightening, as you might imagine, so I kept a diary of those visits."

He shuffled through the dog-eared notebook, and as he did, I saw densely written notes and scribbles on every page. "Yes, here we go. Empedocles did touch on the synchronicity concept quite a few times actually. He told me that Jung was certainly right about them having deeper meaning, but that he didn't take it far enough, that Jung had stopped short of fully understanding their true significance and value.

"He said that these unlikely coincidences were more than a sign of being in alignment with non-physical realms, they were *messages from* these unseen dimensions. His exact words to me were, 'Synchronicities are brief fissures in the tight latticework of the world's illusion that hint at something much bigger on the other side of the illusion. They speak of miraculous possibilities not born in this dimension. Coincidences that defy explanation confirm that there are benevolent forces and guiding entities speaking to us from a place that transcends this persistent illusion, entities trying to help us by sending messages that will set us free.'"

I got chills as Martin was speaking.

"Wait, there's more," he continued, flipping through the pages. "He told me that we must prepare ourselves to receive these vital messages, 'giving them our supreme attention with every fiber of our being.' This sounds very similar to Bohm's writings."

He stopped to decipher more of his scrawled margin notes, making mumbling sounds as he did. "I don't know how I could have missed this. I can see clearly now the thread connecting Jung, Pauli, and Bohm… as well as Empedocles. I think David Bohm had concluded that our unconscious personal blocks are what interfere with us picking up more of these liberating synchronicities and hidden messages. That's why he was imploring us to excavate them with all we've got, 'with our muscles and bones,' as I shared the other day. Bohm was clearly synthesizing Jung's psycho-spiritual insights with his own emerging breakthroughs in quantum theory. And Empedocles' thinking was millennia ahead of them all."

"So, it really is about pulling the rug back," I said under my breath.

"What's that?" Martin asked.

"Sorry, I was thinking of something I read once about the need to clear out the emotional dust balls from under our inner floorboards, how this can lead to transformational insights."

We both sat in silence for a minute, until I saw the time on a shelf clock behind his head.

"I think I need to be heading off, Martin," I said, as I finished the last mouthful of tea. "I actually have a plane to catch in a few hours."

"Yes, of course," Martin replied, still staring at his worn notebook as if more revelations might spring from its pages if he concentrated hard enough. After another few seconds, he cinched it with the rubber bands and put it back in the drawer. "Well, Roger, this was certainly an illuminating exchange. I'll miss having more of these visits with you and Vee."

"Actually, Vee's going to be sticking around for a while, and she's definitely going to stop in again," I replied. "I'm sure she'd love to hear more about this Bohm-Jung connection if you'd care to share it with her."

"Absolutely, I have some integration to do on this, but I'd be happy to fill Vee in. You opened my eyes today, Roger, thank you."

He came around the desk and gave me a firm hug, one that Feather Ferguson would have applauded, and I left him in his office. As I was bounding down the balcony stairs, and before I was out of earshot, I heard him reopen the creaky drawer where he had dropped his notebook.

CHAPTER FORTY-TWO

I took a meandering route back to Rebecca's house, intentionally veering towards the ocean. I kicked my shoes off at the head of the beach and tucked them under my arm as I crossed the hard-packed sand barefoot, making my way up the coast to Rebecca's cloistered neighborhood. When I finally reached her gate, Clees was sitting on her front stoop with a mischievous smile as I approached.

"I leave you alone for a couple of hours and already you're forming a militia?"

"Spying again?"

He laughed, but with a look of infinite kindness.

"There's no urgency for you to acquire one of those tricorn hats," he said, "but that state of poised alertness the professor talked about, the expectant stillness of the mythical warrior ready to pounce—spot on. I think the Glaziers can become useful allies once you return to that city of yours that never rests."

"Yeah, we already talked about it," I said. "We exchanged phone numbers just as they set off to see some Esselen burial grounds."

"Ah, the Glaziers are wasting no time piecing clues together, impressive. Maybe you should acquire one of the tricorn hats after all, Metis, you'd look good in one."

"Yeah, thanks, but no thanks," I replied. "Anyway, Chris and Lily are definitely on a mission. I'm going to reach out to them as soon as I return to New York, see what more I can learn. And I want them to meet Vee. I had an intuition on my walk back that she and Lily would become fast friends."

Before I could say anything more, Vee stepped out the front door with Rebecca close behind. Vee immediately came over to me.

"You cool?" she asked, as Rebecca took a seat next to Clees on the stoop.

"Not really. Clees just told me I have to wear a weird hat as part of my initiation into the mystics' guild, and I'm not happy about it."

Clees threw his head back and laughed.

"I don't get it, what do you mean?" Vee asked.

"Never mind, stupid joke. Yeah, I'm fine, just a little overwhelmed, I guess. Mixed feelings about leaving. I don't want to miss anything."

"You both have recalibration work to do in the weeks ahead and everything's on schedule," Clees said. "Our work together is complete for now, so, no worries."

I crossed my arms and looked down at my shoes, shuffling in place, and Rebecca must have read something in my body language, because she didn't let it slide.

"Say it, Roger, speak it out loud. This is important," she urged me.

I hesitated but spoke. "I don't know, I still feel like I'm slow on the uptake here, like I'm holding you all back. Everyone I meet seems to be clear on their purpose, barreling ahead, while I'm stumbling along fifty paces behind. It's bumming me out."

"Same," Vee said, looking from Rebecca to Clees. "Why does it seem like Roger and I are the only ones who have no memory of all these shared past lives and ancient pacts? Feather knows that I was this Calabris dude and, Rebecca, you remember that you and I were some sort of super couple. Clees shared an incredibly involved story about me being the Muiscan Zipa with Rog as my jaguar priest, but it's all a blank to me, not even a flicker of recognition. It's not only frustrating for Roger, it's also pissing me off, if I can be completely honest." Vee placed a hand on my shoulder, affirming our bond.

Rebecca shook her head, not disparagingly, but with affection and tenderness. At the same time, Clees started to reel us both in with an absorbing look that had some sort of vibration connected to it. Vee must have felt it, too, because even with just her hand on my shoulder, I could feel her entire body start to quiver.

Suddenly, I couldn't stand up any longer, and Vee and I both sank at the same time to Rebecca's flagstone walkway, settling on our backsides. Then, inexplicably, I started to cry… and I couldn't stop. These weren't whimpers either, but heaving, whole body shuddering sobs. I looked over at Vee and saw that the same thing was happening to her. She seemed to be trying unsuccessfully to brush her tears away, repeatedly failing to stanch the flood of feeling pouring from her eyes.

I looked up to see Clees' face raised to the afternoon sun, his eyes closed, a reflection off the slates creating a shimmering effect around his head. That center spot on his forehead was doing that bright light, pulsating thing again, the same illumined, optical effect as on the Ferguson's porch. Each time I caught my breath and tried to look up at him, I saw only a brilliant glow, then my body would convulse again, and the gushing resumed. Vee was kind of doubled over at first, then she fell to her side in a curled up fetal position, her own waterwheel going full force.

I'm not sure how much time passed, ten minutes, maybe longer. Clees and Rebecca never moved, neither of them rushing inside to grab tissues or anything, and I was glad for it. This bone deep release, this letting go, felt like it had been waiting to happen for a lifetime, maybe several hundred of them, and I didn't want anyone messing with me at that moment. After a few more minutes, my body started to quiet, and the spasms eased. Vee appeared to be in a deep sleep, her body completely spent and silent.

Rebecca left the stoop and moved down to sit next to her, but never touched her. Before Vee opened her eyes, Clees started to speak in a soft voice, his words deeply soothing in a way I had never heard from anyone before, and I wondered how he was doing that, imbuing his words with a palpable sense of serenity. It was an ineffable moment, one that Vee and I would reflect on many times afterward, our words never quite capturing that remarkable feeling.

"My two star pupils," he began, and I looked at him to see if he was being flippant, but he was completely sincere. "Tell me, Metis… if you were standing before a very large class filled with students at every grade level, and there were quite a few stragglers among them, many reluctant students, who would you send to ensure that everyone caught up, no one fell back or was left behind? Would you send other stragglers, assign the job to other reluctant pupils?"

He stopped to let his words sink in, and as he did, Vee stirred. Clees waited as she sat up slowly with Rebecca's help, wiped her nose, started rocking slightly and listening intently.

"I would entrust this important task to two of my most beloved and trusted protégés; two who had excelled at all previous tests and mastered a vast amount of arcane and vital knowledge together. A thoroughly likable pair with natural relatability, who could meet any disinclined students exactly where they were, speak their language in words they would understand, sit beside them as they faced their own inner trials, always embracing these fellow students with kindness, consideration, and patience." He looked at both of us with a gentle smile, as his luminous lion's eyes sparkled. "What do you say to that, then?"

I felt like I was going to start blubbering again if I opened my mouth, then Vee spoke at just above a whisper.

"But what good are we to you, Clees, if we can't remember the lessons we've learned and can't put them to use? I don't want to mess this up."

"Only a short time has passed since I startled Metis in the mews and ushered you through a seam in the cityscape, Miss Verilee. We're just at the beginning."

His mention of those early experiences at the start of the summer put a smile on both our faces.

"Ah, there you go, gold stars for the both of you," he said, extending the classroom metaphor. "Let me assure you that I have picked wisely. I have not chosen in error. I can also assure you that your current forgettings are purposeful… and temporary. Because you do not understand what anything means yet, I will understand it for you until your minds fully realign themselves."

"So, we still have to go around feeling like the dumb clucks in class?" Vee asked.

Clees smiled at her sweetly. "Don't worry, Miss Verilee, you'll be able to remove the dunce caps soon enough."

Vee pulled at the sleeve of her tee shirt and mopped her nose again. The flood of intense feelings that had burst inextinguishably from both of us just minutes earlier had largely flowed on, but Vee was still tearing up and sniffling.

"I've never cried like that before," she said quietly, looking up at Rebecca who put an arm around her, drawing her close. "Never. That was crazy."

"Until you understand what the tears are about, what they're for, it can feel a little crazy, yes," Rebecca said, appearing to well up a bit herself.

"So, what are they for?" I asked.

"What are they for?" Rebecca repeated my question, then started gently stroking Vee's hair before she answered. "The best way to make a desert bloom, Roger, is with lots of life-giving water. In time, if you're patient and diligent, and if the parched soil is drenched again and again in those healing waters, the dry and barren desert becomes a lush and beautiful garden."

Dry deserts. Healing waters. In that moment, I think I had a glimpse of what Rebecca's Wailing Garden was all about and why it meant so much to her.

Vee leaned against Rebecca in an effort to stand on wobbly legs, they spoke in whispers for a moment, then Vee looked down at me and said "Later, Rog," as the two of them walked around the house into the backyard. Clees and I stood, too, staring at each other for another minute without speaking. I suddenly felt so much affection for the man—this mystic with his miraculous messages and aura of total calm—I just wanted to fall into his arms and squeeze him hard. He stepped forward and embraced me before I could move, and I realized that this was the first time I had hugged my new-old friend.

"Just the first that you remember," he said softly into my ear, reading my thoughts as we held each other, an apparent reference to our lives together in Acragas.

I stepped away and thanked him for this journey, for the many lessons in the weeks that came before, and for whatever lie ahead. He responded kindly, without acknowledging or disregarding my gratitude. "This world does not exist, Metis, but the love and beauty here are real."

Another brainteaser, but I didn't care to parse them anymore. I was starting to trust that all of Clees' mysterious musings would eventually make sense to me. I loosened my grip, told him I needed to make some last-minute preparations before my flight, and went up to my room. I sat down on the bed, stared out the window, and had the startling thought that nothing I believed about the world up until that point, nothing that I thought I knew about myself or understood about my life, meant anything. Nothing at all.

CHAPTER FORTY-THREE

I rested on the bed for a half-hour, recorded what had just happened on my iPad, then dozed off briefly. I came down two hours before my flight to find Rebecca idling the car in the driveway ready to take me to the Monterey airport.

Clees wasn't around and Vee didn't come out to say goodbye, although I felt okay about that. Even as she walked off on shaky legs an hour earlier, I sensed she had already started to drop into something thick and private. I knew Vee would be safe. I also knew that California, the Fergusons, and especially Rebecca had something to offer her that she wasn't going to find back in New York. I have never known fully what it was—the support and kindness of a surrogate mother perhaps, a protected place to go dark, to descend and deepen—whatever it was, I had no doubt that she needed it, and that the time was right.

Rebecca and I barely spoke on the drive to the airport, but before I stepped out of her Volvo, she passed me a bag of freshly baked treats to take on the plane. She also handed me a wrapped, shoebox-sized package that she said was a gift from Clees. I took it, hugged her goodbye before getting out of the car, promised to call her in a few days, and walked to the terminal with the gift box tucked under my arm.

I opened the package before I boarded so I could put its contents into my carry-on bag, only to find a pair of those blue, high-top sneakers inside, the ones that Clees was often wearing that I kept admiring. I studied them closely looking for a brand name or label, couldn't find one, and concluded that he hadn't bought them at the local Carmel athletic store.

I decided to stuff my old sneakers into my suitcase and wear Clees' gift back to New York. He must have been studying my shoe size the entire time I was in California, because when I slipped them on, they fit perfectly. After a few minutes, I heard my departure gate being announced and stood to toss the box and its wrapping away. As I did, a small gift card fell to the ground. I opened the envelope and read the message, written in a plain, unadorned print on a square of white cardstock:

> *"Sorry, Metis, I couldn't find barley biscuits or yak butter, and was unable to arrange an upgrade to first class. But I trust you will find these uncommon high-tops to be comfortable travel companions during your upcoming odysseys."*

He signed it, *"Forever, Empedocles (long ee sound at the end)."*

I was smiling as I disposed of the packaging, wondering if by walking in his shoes, I might understand more about the mysteries of the man. Then I tried to imagine what he meant by "upcoming odysseys," completely aware that Empedocles never did anything by accident and including these words held some greater meaning.

While I still had a Wi-Fi signal and before the plane took off, I did an online search for the term "odyssey," remembering that Homer's epic Greek poem by the same name described the travels of the hero Odysseus after the Trojan War. His ten-year wandering of the world took him on a perilous journey to the land of Cyclops, passed the irresistible island of the Sirens, through the seas of a six-headed monster, and eventually brought him home.

I thought about Odysseus and his epic adventures during the entire five-hour flight to New York.

CHAPTER FORTY-FOUR

It was strange to be back in the city alone, without Clees nearby to whisk me away to impossible places or Vee with whom to compare notes and anticipate our next encounter.

I received a text from her the day after I arrived in New York checking on my flight home and telling me she wouldn't be in touch until she returned to the city, maybe in two or three weeks, she wasn't sure. She closed the text with the simple, laden words, "Love you truly," and I sensed that her being close to Rebecca—the former Delphic Oracle—was already triggering tectonic shifts out there on the coast of California.

The following Saturday morning, I was lying on my apartment floor doing stretches on a yoga mat when I heard the building's front door opening and closing repeatedly with that screechy, scraping sound. I stuck my head out of a window facing the street and saw that the landlord had finally hired someone to fix the broken door from raking over the doorsill.

I could only see the top of the man's head and broad shoulders from my ledge, but he had coffee-colored skin and was wearing a bandana under a New York Mets baseball cap. There was a yellow and black, canvas tool bag opened at his feet. He reached into it for a large mallet and some sort of metal bending tool.

I was so happy that the harsh grating noise was finally going to be silenced, I decided to slip on my new sneakers and go down to thank the man. I grabbed my keys, walked out of the apartment, and took the back stairs to the ground floor. As I passed the mailboxes in the lobby, I saw that the big man was packing up his tools, getting ready to leave. He was using his heavy canvas bag to prop the door open.

"Hey, there," I said, as he took a clean rag out of his bag to wipe his hands, "we've been harassed by that grinding sound for months, thanks for finally dealing with it."

He looked up and smiled, and I saw the man's golden eyes dancing against his dark skin, green flecks lightly dotting the edges.

"Glad I could be of service, Metis," he replied. "Your downstairs neighbors will no doubt notice the improvement."

No matter how many times he did this, changed his appearance and took on another identity, it flustered me. I froze in the hallway and stared at him.

"Listen," he said, moving the tool bag out of the way and swinging the door a few times, "not a peep, good as new. But doors, really… so primitive."

I moved closer, looked down mindlessly at the door frame and sill, then stepped outside and joined him on the stoop.

"Does the Super know you're here?" I asked.

"Does it matter?" he answered. "Anyway, I don't think he'd object. Door's fixed and my services are free." He laughed his gentle laugh, closed the glass and metal door one final time until he heard the lock click, then sat down on the top step and motioned for me to join him.

"So, what's next, Clees?" I asked, feeling excited that he was back, and we could commence with more life-altering discoveries and mind-blowing revelations.

"There's plenty you can do on your own to prepare for our impending mission. We also need to wait for Feather, she has an important piece, but she's not yet ready."

"Aha! So, it *is* all about Feather, I knew it," I exclaimed, making light of my previous bouts of jealousy out in California. He smiled at my joke but spoke to some residual feelings he knew lingered beneath.

"We waited for you for some twenty years in Greece, Metis, don't forget. This wait will be considerably shorter. And soon you will understand why there could never be any competition between you and Feather, why that will seem like an utterly absurd notion once you grasp the true nature of your sacred alliance."

"That sounds intriguing."

"Intriguing falls short of what I had in mind, but let's see what unfolds going forward. The part of the story where you are standing closely by her side has yet to be fully written, and some obstacles may emerge to delay you as you pass through the outer rings of fear. But I think nothing is going to stop you this time. My money's on Metis."

"Is there a way for me to know, Clees, while I wait, I mean, if I'm getting closer to some deeper understanding?"

"When this world has nothing left it can scare you with, that would be a reliable indicator," he answered, as he reached down with his index finger to brush the dotted back of a ladybug that had alighted on his workpants. "Being kind to everyone and all things, every day in every way, will go far to dispel your fears and brighten your light. Until then, just do what you do in the world, Metis, aware that you're not fully in it. You have the vision now to see the truth that lies past this vast Worldborn illusion. And, knowing that, you'll never forget to laugh a little at it all."

"So... that's it?" I asked.

He reached back and zipped up the tool bag, then looked at me with a smile and said with flawless pronunciation, "*Vocatus atque non vocatus deus aderit.*"

The abrupt language change caught me off guard, then I responded. "My Latin's gotten a little rusty in the past eight hundred years, Clees, sorry."

He pitched forward with a laugh as the Mets cap nearly toppled from his head. "Allow me to translate for you, then. '*Called or not called, the gods... and guides... are present.*' I added the 'guides' part just for you. Point being, if your adoring ancestors and devoted dream team are always poised and present, ready to respond to you at a moment's notice, why not call on them today and often? Aligning your senses consistently, to receive their guidance constantly, will take you farther, faster than you can imagine."

I stayed silent, thinking about these things he said that I could set my mind to. After a minute, I looked up, waiting for him to share more about our mission together and my role in it, but some part of me knew that there was nothing left to say, at least for now, and he knew it, too.

Without another word, my devoted teacher and forever friend brushed my cheek with his workman's fingers, reached down for his tool bag, and stood up. He descended the front stoop, checked for passing traffic as he reached the curb, strolled across the street with an easy step, and without changing his gait, slipped into the four-inch crack between the Tudor house and Art Deco building and was gone.

Where my sorcerer friend was headed—where we would all be going next—I didn't know. But I was eager to get there, and he said it was assured. And Empedocles always kept his promises.

CHAPTER FORTY-FIVE

Clees was right. No one returns from an experience like the one we had at the Ferguson caves the same person. Every day my mind was leaping past "its previous confinements," as Clees had put it, and the same was true for Vee.

We were both glad for it.

While the heightened intensity of the feelings we had in California had diminished, there was no shortage of opportunities to hone our skills using common sense, and we were getting more proficient at it. Whenever either of us faced a challenge that summer, we trained ourselves to consistently ask for help from our guides and watch for answers in subtle signs and synchronicities, even strange ones. "Ask, listen, then follow the guidance exactly, never adding or subtracting, acting only on what you intuitively feel is right," Rebecca had said to me one afternoon in Carmel while talking in her backyard, echoing what Clees had told me at the Waiting Place. Vee and I were trying to practice this with every question we had, every decision we made, until we were feeling that unmistakable sweet spot of peace that we felt in California with most everything we did.

It was reassuring to have Vee nearby to keep memories of the mystic's lessons alive and create a rough blueprint for how we could use the guidance productively once we received it. We even started to notice that the clues, coincidences, and synchronicities were coming more often and seemed to be connected in useful ways. They kind of built on, enhanced, and complemented one another.

I was also spending a lot less time with my earbuds in since the day Martin mentioned that at his bookstore. A state of Minuteman readiness and warrior-like attention seemed hopelessly out of reach with the random ramblings of countless podcasts filling my head.

One day, earbud-free and eyes up, I was walking through Madison Square Park when I was startled to see Clees' silhouette appear in the mottled bark of a big London plane tree. I immediately wanted to share this strange pareidolia phenomenon with someone, but it wasn't like seeing the Virgin Mary's familiar face burnt into a slice of toast. As far as I knew, no one on the East Coast had ever seen or met Empedocles, except for Vee and me. So, instead of pulling a stranger over to point it out, I snapped a photo of the impression in the bark and immediately texted it to Vee. But no matter how hard I tried to explain the contours of the silhouette to her, she didn't see Clees' face in it.

Then, just two days later, Vee was at a popular barista place in Brooklyn with Justina and had a similar Clees sighting in the steamed milk of the latte she was drinking. When she covertly texted the image to me, I had to agree, it was distinctly the smiling face of Empedocles. Vee joked that she was sipping slowly "to induce extra caffeinated insights," but she didn't sense anything else happening in the coffee shop that was notable, even with all her superb treasure hunting skills on high alert.

In the end, neither of us could intuit any deeper meaning from our face pareidolia experiences but decided that they were not accidents and archived the photos for future reference. Even if they were just cryptic greetings from our favorite Svengali and didn't matter much, Vee and I got a kick out of them, the incidents kept us on our toes and, most importantly, they were fun.

Fun. There you go, Feather… we made it.

Vee stayed in almost daily contact with Rebecca after she returned from Carmel, getting regular and intensive help with her rug pulling from the former oracle. Vee told me that she was spending more time alone to stay focused on the effort, which she described as no easy task. "It's rough when you finally understand that the gun pointed at your head isn't being held by your perceived enemies, it's being held by you."

Vee is so brave.

Rebecca also repeatedly reminded Vee and me to keep our respective kila symbols visible, where they could be easily seen by others on this purposeful quest. From time to time, people would approach one of us, mention the kila pendant around my neck, or notice Vee's spectacular tattoo, and inquire about them. Often, after we'd explain the symbolism of the three-pointed blade, they'd be intrigued, and ask where they might get their own.

One day in late August, I was attending a meeting with some colleagues who had flown in from our Paris office. There was a young woman there, a whip-smart junior account executive named Olivia Bonceur, who was wearing earrings that kept popping out from underneath her shoulder length hair and that I swore looked like mini-kilas. I surreptitiously pulled my pendant out from beneath my shirt and let it dangle more obviously at my chest. At one point, as Olivia was outlining our company's fall project schedule, she glanced over, saw the kila necklace hanging there, and seemed momentarily flustered before continuing her presentation.

After the meeting, she stopped me in the hallway and we had an animated, ten-minute conversation in French about her kila earrings, my amulet, and what it all meant. She told me she'd heard rumors of groups around the world making dimensional jumps to gather arcane information from *"les esprits auxiliaries"*—spirit helpers—and I confirmed that this was essentially true. Before she and her team went off to have lunch with Manon, we exchanged email addresses and phone numbers and I promised to tell her more about what I knew. She was absolutely beaming and gave me a conspiratorial smile as she stepped away. I kept thinking about Olivia Bonceur for the rest of the week.

Things started to heat up even more in September when Rebecca called Vee one Saturday morning and told her it was urgent that we share more about our mission with the Glaziers, informing them about the role of key players, including Empedocles. We had already met with the professors once since we returned to New York, and I was right about Lily and Vee hitting it off like long-lost friends. But Rebecca insisted that we needed to step up our information exchange, adding, "We've learned that the Glaziers are establishing a network among academics at universities worldwide to investigate 'cross-dimensional communication with potential ectoplasm entities,' as they're calling it. They are well-intentioned, but a little off track, and it's pivotal that you redirect them."

We didn't waste any time arranging a dinner at a restaurant near the Columbia campus a week later, and once we shared all we knew, Professor Glazier gleefully slipped his tricorn hat onto Lily's head and swept her up in a tight embrace that was filled with so much joy, the other patrons started clapping.

There were moments during that following, action-packed autumn when I thought my mind powers were approaching a magnitude of mastery and I would try to cast my little kila pendant through the air as Clees had done with Vee on Madison Avenue months earlier. Sometimes the dense chunk of mysterious metal seemed to hover a bit or jump forward a centimeter before gravity overpowered my nascent levitation skills. Mostly, though, I didn't have much luck.

I'll also confess that on one chilly, gray October afternoon, when the sidewalks in front of my building were empty and I could see no one around, a day when I felt mostly confident that I understood the strange physics behind fictitious solidity, I walked up to the four-inch gap between the buildings across the street and tried to step through. Maybe maneuvering past persistent illusions can only happen in close proximity to a fully realized mystic, but it took about a week for the scrapes on my nose and chin to heal.

Later that month, as I walked along the Hudson River a little south of 14th Street, my efforts to pay attention, stay alert, and be aware seemed to reach a portentous juncture. I was thinking about the many ways that Empedocles could manipulate his environment, pulling off simultaneous feats of wonder without so much as raising a pinkie, when I saw a piece of paper skipping in the wind along the promenade and thought to toss it in the trash. I trapped the flapping sheet underfoot and reached down to grab it from the walkway, when I noticed that it was a postcard, an actual postcard, with a photo on the picture side of a bowed bridge in a lovely rural landscape.

I turned it over, but the address side was blank, except for a printed description of the facing image:

The Legend of Brigadoon. This idyllic bridge over the Doon River in the Scottish Highlands is the inspiration for the enchanted Broadway musical Brigadoon—the story of a mythical village invisible to the outside world, except for one special day every hundred years. Plan a visit and experience the joy and magic of this beguiling place.

I read it twice before stepping over to drop it in a trash receptacle, but found myself repeatedly drawn to the photo on the front with that sweet little bridge and decided to slip the postcard into my pants pocket instead. When I got home, just for the heck of it, I did an online search for Brigadoon and discovered that the actual 15th century cobbled bridge featured on the postcard was located in a small village called Alloway, near the western coast of Scotland.

Scotland. The ancestral homeland of the Fergusons. Could that mean anything?

"Experience the joy and magic of this beguiling place," the card read, and it sounded so much like the promising possibilities Rebecca spoke about on her beguiling back deck, my heart began to flutter. But it was the sentence before, the one that mentioned *"a mythical village invisible to the outside world,"* that really got my attention.

I went over to my couch with the postcard in hand, placed it on my lap, closed my eyes, clutched my kila pendant firmly, and quieted my mind with a few deep breaths. Then, out loud, I asked my grandfather, wherever he was, if this bridge in Scotland was significant. And, as ridiculous as this sounds, and I know it sounds ridiculous, from somewhere in my neighborhood, maybe from the funeral home a few blocks over, I heard the slow, evocative wail of bagpipes.

I didn't wait. With a Minuteman's sense of urgency, I jumped up, grabbed my cell phone off the kitchen table and called Vee. She answered on the first ring.

"What?" she said.

"I think I'm supposed to go to Scotland, and I think you're supposed to go with me."

TO BE CONTINUED...

FURTHER READING

I worked on this book for more than a decade, much of that time spent reading the insightful and enlightening words of other writers who have a much better understanding of the ideas I wanted to convey than I ever could. So much of the thinking in this book was shaped by these mind-bending writers and dreamers—people with great courage and an enormous capacity to trust their hearts more than their heads.

I hope that readers with an interest in intuition, synchronicity, non-duality, metaphysics, mysticism, spirituality, quantum theory and other concepts touched on in my story will pick up the books by the authors below—just some of the important writers and thinkers who influenced Empedocles and me.

Richard Bach: If I had the skills to write a shorter book on the same themes that appear here, it would look something like Richard Bach's *Illusions*. I have read and reread this little gem on the unreality of this reality dozens of times, and it has always been a powerful touchstone when I've needed an infusion of hope. All of Bach's books, from *Jonathan Livingston Seagull* to *The Bridge Across Forever,* have inspired my writing and lifted me up when I urgently needed lifting.

David Bohm: *His Wholeness and the Implicate Order* has a lot of the answers, but I'm still learning the language of the questions. What a mind and what a spirit.

Kirsten Buxton: How fun and enlightening is Kirsten's *I Married A Mystic,* which I consumed in one eager gulp, then savored several more times. If you want to know what is needed to hear your inner guidance (don't worry, you have what it takes right now), this book is a compassionate and cooperative companion.

Dr. Larry Dorsey: *One Mind,* a provocative and powerful book, filtered into my mind throughout the writing of this novel.

Robert Greenleaf: A brilliant contribution to the understanding of inspired life purpose, *Servant Leadership* helped me see what real power looks like and what enlightened partnership can achieve.

Pam Grout: The mind-challenging and uplifting ideas in *E-Squared* reminded me (and Feather) that all this nutty stuff is very real and a whole lot of fun.

Carol Howe: Through an amazing sequence of coincidences and synchronicities, I found both Carol and her book, *Never Forget To Laugh,* an intimate biography by this personal friend of ACIM co-scribe Bill Thetford. Beautifully written and revealing, Carol's words left me in awe of this extraordinary man and his incredible story of unfolding enlightenment. It will also explain exactly why, despite what we think we see in the world, we must never forget to laugh.

Joseph Jaworski: My copy of Jaworski's marvelous book on life's possibilities, *Synchronicity,* has more highlighter and sidebar notes than it does clean pages. After a multi-year lull in my understanding of the mystery of meaningful coincidences, this book lit me up again, brought the truth of our extraordinary collective potential to life, and catapulted me to the next level of writing.

Dr. Carl Jung: His seminal work *A Causal Connecting Principle* filled in so many blanks for me. A truly pioneering look into the fissures of our reality.

Peter Kingsley: All of Kingsley's books, including *In The Dark Places* *of Wisdom* and *A Story Waiting To Pierce You,* helped me understand my book's characters and their mysteries in greater depth. But most especially, *Reality,* was the one that blew my mind wide open. Kingsley's ideas influenced almost every word here, and he was the first to introduce me to this book's hero and true historical figure, Empedocles. A jaw-dropping, mind-boggling redefinition of the term "common sense," an idea I wove into my story, was also elucidated by Kingsley. I am indebted to this modern mystic living in our midst.

Paul Levy: In the expansive and impressive *The Quantum Revelation,* Levy made a very complicated subject much easier for me to grasp. It will do the same for you.

Dr. Raymond Moody: *Life After Life* is a classic that changed the world's view on near-death experiences, with astounding anecdotes of people throughout the world who were declared clinically dead and reported on, in vivid detail, their light-filled journeys to the "other side." I struggled with a crippling fear of death for most of my life, and it was Moody's book that gave me an uplifting and positive perspective on a largely unexamined and taboo subject in western cultures. Read it for relief.

Dr. Jon Mundy: A revered member of the "first family" of ACIM, Jon was introduced to the Course in New York City by Helen and Bill in the mid-1970's and is one of our most knowledgeable teachers of this profound spiritual path. A Methodist minister, he brings a deep understanding of traditional Christianity to his eye-opening perspectives on many esoteric spiritual practices. Jon is a teaching treasure, and all of his books, but particularly *Missouri Mystic,* are primers on living the life of an earnest seeker.

Parker Palmer: I am indebted to Palmer for his soul-lifting book *Let Your Life Speak;* a gem that saved my sanity and bolstered my confidence at crucial times during the solitary years of writing this story.

His beautiful exploration of the heart, *A Hidden Wholeness*, runs a close second.

James Redfield: His breakthrough title, *The Celestine Prophecy*, helped me understand that we're not seeing a fraction of what is really happening here, every day, in every encounter.

Gary Renard: *The Disappearance of the Universe* affirmed for me the absolute truth of alternate dimensions, as well as those who populate them, and how wise we would be to listen and learn from them.

Dr. Ken Wapnick: A kind and loving mystic himself, with a delightful sense of humor, I was privileged to call Ken a friend and mentor. He wrote many books related to *A Course In Miracles* and its scribes, but his *Absence From Felicity* is filled with spiritual messages for our time and offers a map to a path that can take you over the rainbow. Many of Ken's dedicated students say that he was the "first graduate" of *A Course In Miracles,* and that was certainly my experience of this generous man.

Dr. Brian Weiss: A respected psychotherapist, Weiss' surprising foray into past lives and alternate dimensions resulted in *Many Lives, Many Masters.* The first of his books, it changed the minds of countless skeptics, including me. So much of my understanding of past life regressions and their power to heal came from an early exposure to Weiss' persuasive and compelling bestseller.

GRATITUDES

While I never met either of them, Dr. Helen Schucman and Dr. Bill Thetford changed my life in ways so profound, I could never fully express my gratitude. Without *A Course In Miracles (ACIM)*, which they brought into the world, I would be lost.

I am equally thankful to my first mentor in the Course, the brilliant, funny and compassionate Ken Wapnick, who edited and helped bring the ACIM books to blessed publication.

And forever hugs to Judith Skutch Whitson, the fourth in this first family of ACIM, who became the publisher of these life-changing texts and devoted all her energies to their preservation.

To this fabulous, fearsome foursome, an enormous thank you for ushering in a miraculous, mind-expanding lesson plan for life.

Along the way, other teachers of *A Course In Miracles* have had an enormous impact and given me a deeper understanding of these principles, particularly Diane Brook Gusic, David Hoffmeister, the age-defying and indefatigable Carol Howe (and her biography of Bill Thetford, *Never Forget To Laugh*), Gerald Jampolsky, Matt McCabe, Joanne Menon, Tam Morgan, Jon Mundy, Nouk Sanchez, and Coreen Watson. If you want to turn your life around in a hurry, find these dedicated, loving ACIM teachers wherever you can—on paper, in person, or online—and put your hopes and happiness, without hesitation, into your hands through theirs.

A big thanks also to Sudie Shipman, a master teacher of *A Course In Miracles*, who was the book's first beta reader and initial line editor, and who gave me the confidence to move forward with it when I was on fragile ground. Sudie used her expertise to ensure the novel's ACIM-congruency and keep it on the rails.

Through a miraculous series of impossible coincidences, I was guided to an agent of great integrity and wisdom, Ivor Whitson. He and his wife, Ronnie—an angel in our midst—became not only passionate supporters of this book in its early stages, but its shepherds. What a blessing to have found them, and an honor to have worked with two people who have given their lives to helping others.

For most of my journey in this life, I have had a guardian angel, an alchemist of love's healing powers named Rosalyn Baumrind. Whenever I would wander off the path into the brambles, which was quite often and for long durations, she would be there upon my return, ready to walk alongside my thorn-torn and broken self again, holding the lantern ahead of me on the long road to home. How, Roz, can I ever thank you?

And, then, there were so many enthusiastic friends, family members, and cherished supporters who kept me upright on the writing journey: Mauro Altamura, John Anka, Carol Armor, Donna Brodie (and everyone who ensures that the Writers Room in NYC remains the safe sanctuary for writers that it is), Vladimir Chronis, Deirdre Coe, Shannon Dailey, Alicia DeArmas (she's "so silly"), Karl Dentino, Tamini Farah, Bill Fitzhugh, Wilder Fitzhugh, Val Fitzhugh, John Florio, Tara Grodjesk, John Guarnescelli, Greg Grimes, Amanda Hale, Zachary Hale, Catherine Hodgkiss (and her belief, love, and encouragemnt at a critical juncture), Glenn Hovemann, Terry Hunt, Wendy Hurcombe, Diana LaGuardia, Alex Lee, Barbara Ishac Lee, Max Lee, Adam Levy, Andrea Martin (the mightiest of Mighty Companions), Sarah Hale Peterson, Becky Prante, Rev. Emmanuelle Rosenthal, Amanda Rubin, Unni Benedicte Salvesen (the fearless Viking with an enormous heart), Gabriele Schwöbel, John Scilipote, Ouisie Shapiro, Helene Silver, Jan Sola, Dianne Stasi, Larry Trepel, Elaine Waldman, Gavin Wilson, and every double-hearted man in my men's group in NYC. That's a lot of names, but there was a lot of love.

And one last expression of immense gratitude to my muse, the indomitable Elfie. Who knew that so much marvelous magic could be infused into an antique, cast-iron door stopper—albeit one with impeccable character and extraordinary good looks?

Thank you all from the deep center of my being. Empedocles—the mystic in the mews—could never have entered my Worldborn heart and mind without you.

ABOUT THE AUTHOR

Allan Ishac worked in New York area advertising as a copywriter and creative director for 25 years. He wrote two regional bestsellers, *New York's 50 Best Places To Find Peace And Quiet* and *New York's 50 Best Places To Take Children*, as well as *The Guide To Odd New York*. He also launched a successful app for locating calm and quiet in New York called TranquiliCity, and created and wrote the Telly Award-winning children's video series, *Hard Hat Harry*.

He has been a student of *A Course In Miracles* since 1986 and is a regular contributor to *Miracles Magazine*. When he's not getting his hands dirty in his terrace garden, Allan is on a bicycle or sharing stories of inspiring synchronicities with other curious and exuberant Worldborns.

Allan lives in New York City—a fantastic, big possibilties place.

**See more about Allan and his idea of fun
at allanishac.com**

www.ingramcontent.com/pod-product-compliance
Lightning Source LLC
Chambersburg PA
CBHW032011310726
48972CB00002B/360